ALL THAT IS
SEEN AND UNSEEN

a novel

DOMINIQUE LAURENT PFAFF

iUniverse, Inc.
Bloomington

All That Is Seen And Unseen

iUniverse books may be ordered through booksellers or by contacting:

iUniverse
1663 Liberty Drive
Bloomington, IN 47403
www.iuniverse.com
1-800-Authors (1-800-288-4677)

ISBN: 978-1-4620-8295-7 (sc)
ISBN: 978-1-4620-8296-4 (ebk)

Printed in the United States of America

iUniverse rev. date: 12/23/2011

PREFACE

The action of this novel takes place almost entirely in the Information Technology department of a community college district. Readers unfamiliar with this arcane corner of the work world may benefit from the following short introduction to its function.

In a higher education organization, the Information Technology (henceforth referred to as IT) department typically maintains (i.e. purchases, installs, monitors and repairs) all the computer equipment scattered around campuses: PCs, servers, printers, network connections . . . It also supports internal email and calendar services, and may help instructors put their course material online (what's called "instructional technology").

Most importantly—at least from the perspective of a software developer, the author's calling for many years—the IT department makes available the software applications (known as "administrative systems") through which many of the institution's functions are performed: creating class schedules, enrolling students, administering financial aid, producing transcripts, paying employees, ordering supplies, keeping track of budgets, and satisfying various bean counters' thirst for statistical data. "Making available" these administrative systems used to entail programming them from scratch for the specific needs of the college: designing the screens/ Web pages into which the data would be entered, figuring out all the logic necessary to properly calculate such things as GPAs and payroll checks, and recording the results in various databases. Nowadays, the tendency is to buy ready-made administrative systems packages (think Quicken on steroids), and to customize them as needed. The pros and cons of these two approaches are discussed in the book.

If it does nothing else, I hope that the above short primer will impress on the reader the importance of IT in the organizational scheme of things. Any system glitch may result in students not being able to register, bills or employees being incorrectly paid, email not reaching its destination. On the other hand, the smoother an IT department operates, the less visible it is to the rest of the institution, with the paradoxical result that it may be under-funded and consequently held in contempt.

Early readers of the novel complained of stumbling on a number of technical words and acronyms. I'll explain below the two whose meaning is useful to an understanding of the narrative. Non-techie readers are advised to view the rest of the jargon as mere local color, as they would treat obscure nautical terms in a high-sea adventure. The important stuff is the human dynamics, which is accessible to all.

A *burster* is a bulky, old-fashioned machine that automatically rips apart pages of continuous computer paper for the purpose of distribution.

FTE (Full-Time Equivalent) refers to a way of converting actual students or employees, who may be full-time or part-time, into numbers that can be added up to measure enrollment or staffing density. Thus one FTE may represent one full-time employee, or two half-time employees, or one three-quarter-time and one quarter-time employee, etc. Contracts with management consulting firms typically stipulate the amount of FTE—as opposed to the number of people—that the consulting firm must provide. But in practice, no one keeps track of the hours worked by consultants, which allows the firm depicted in the book to play musical chairs with their staff in order to fulfill their contract obligations at various sites with fewer bodies than the FTES committed to.

I

EXPOSITORY

"Here we come!" reads the subject line that grabs Jim Wright's attention, sticking out like a slalom flag in the avalanche of instantly recognizable junk mail tumbling down the screen on his laptop: political attacks and charity pleas, bargains on Rolex knockoffs, anti-depressants and virility enhancers, new variants on the Nigerian scam . . . and Jim's favorite, those bits of utter gibberish that seem to spell out the DNA of the virus lurking inside.

You have to hand it to humans: it didn't take them long to master this new pattern recognition trick—the most sophisticated spam filters can't get near it—and then to fit it into their competitive habits. Jim imagines millions of people are this very instant engaged in the same game of email triage as he is: middle finger poised over the delete key to better fire away at the unwanted mail as soon as it rolls into view, the object being to wreak such carnage that by the time Outlook posts its count of new messages, there will be no more than a dozen left on the page . . . But Jim himself is reduced to praying for at least two: one for business, one for pleasure—or what passes for either these days. Except that Norton Antivirus has just kicked in, putting his keyboard and mouse out of commission for the time being. He hasn't felt up to the chore of downloading the latest upgrade. The cobbler's children are always the worst shod, aren't they? He might as well get himself another cup of coffee while he tries to identify the sender of the intriguing message from its email address: 3dmina@gmail.com.

Mina Hussein, who else could it be? Her first name is not that common. But what has happened to her Pequeno address? Has she quit too, another casualty of the grand experiment in "change" that he set in motion three years ago? His last post, it turned out. He is wise enough not to see his illness as divine retribution. God, he figures, has bigger fish to fry. Still, he feels an itch of something like remorse as he watches the cream dissolve into the darkness of the coffee. He puts the cup down and walks over to the kitchen doorway to use the jamb as a scratching post. Moral itch . . . Hodgkin's itch . . . there may be a connection after all . . .

Mina at least doesn't seem to bear grudges. In the last two years, she has kept up a fairly steady email patter of positive thinking and office gossip. She hasn't minded his frequent lack of response. Of all the team, it's Grace he is uneasy about, when he has time to worry about anything other than himself. For months after he left, she cced him on all the frantic memos she dispatched to various managers, including his apparently hapless Hartbridge successors. He's saved the entire correspondence in his Pequeno folder, he is not sure why. By then he was pretty much out of the picture, although she may not have known this—let's be frank, nobody wanted her to know. He did try to buck her up whenever he could, and she did sound like she was taking charge. Then all of a sudden she was gone. Not a peep from her ever since. All he knows he's learned from Mina.

Anyone with their head screwed on halfway tight would know what to make of it: all the relationship amounted to in the end was mere professional give-and-take, precariously balanced between the shallow gratitude of the apprentice and the inflated vanity of the mentor. But Jim, whose head is famous for being solidly attached to his shoulders, would like to believe there was more to it than that. And if that's true, there must be another explanation for her prolonged silence, one that he suspects may not reflect well on his own conduct.

He's done all the scratching he can bear at this point, and plods back to the couch, pretty much the only piece of furniture left in the living room, aside from the wireless router on the window sill, and a couple of athletic trophies on the mantelpiece. His daughter Cindy has staked her turf on one of the cushions with a piece of knitting, gaudy and shapeless, probably a baby blanket for some church bazaar. The stitches slant every which way; it even looks like she's dropped some of them. Jim doubts these irregularities are part of the pattern, but it's the thought that counts, he tells himself. On the other cushion, the Milky Way is spinning on his laptop. It makes him nauseous. He should also update his screensaver, instead of feeling sorry for himself.

The hourglass has disappeared, and Jim proceeds with his email triage while his imagination tries to parse Mina's subject line. HERE where? WE who? COME in what sense? By the time he is done, his prayer has been answered: there are indeed two messages left, the one from Mina, and one from Fritz, marked high priority as always, a tic which no longer has any effect on the recipient. He clicks on Mina's line, and the following message pops up:

From: 3dmina@gmail.com
Date:Monday, March 31, 2008
To: Jim.Wright@hartbridge.com
Subject: Here we come!

Dear Jim,

How are things in North Carolina? Any sign of spring yet? Did you get your bone marrow transplant? Is Fritz still running you ragged?

Here in California we're having a drought. It hasn't rained in over a month. Thank God for irrigation! The IT department is still pretty much in a state of chaos, but I keep my nose to the ground, or is it the grindstone? Well, both, actually, according to Google.

Anyway, that's not why I am writing. Are you sitting down? OK, get this:

Grace and I are coming to visit you!!! You didn't think you could get away from us that easily, did you?

I don't know if I mentioned that Grace has been volunteering for OFA. That's Obama for America, in case you don't know (and you have to promise you won't get into a political argument with her ☺). Well, she was just offered a job as field organizer, whatever that is, and she is being transferred to Raleigh to prepare for the primary. She was going to drive across the country anyway, and I had some time off I needed to take, so we decided to make a vacation of it. Pretty awesome, don't you think? I have never been east of the Sierras, so I am looking forward to it in a major way!!! Tarik has agreed to take care of Steven all by himself (with a little help from Abuela, as we live right across the street from my parents again . . .)

We're leaving tomorrow bright and early. We should swing by Greensboro in four or five days, so don't go anywhere ☺. I'll keep you posted with my BlackBerry.

Mina

P.S. I am bringing some baklava . . .

Jim is flabbergasted. His two girls—all right, women—coming for a visit is exactly the scenario his parsing had conjured, but then it had the charm of a fantasy. The imminent reality of it hits him in quite a different way. To tell the truth, he is scared. Scared of the effect that his present situation—not just his illness, but also the hollowed-out house, and perhaps even his daughter's presence—will have on their image of him. The last thing he needs is to see those two look at him with pity instead of admiration. And more precisely scared of the confrontation with Grace. What if he still feels the same about her, while, as reason and evidence suggest, she has moved decidedly on? What if in that forthright way of hers, she undertakes to tell him why she hasn't written, and it turns out to have been all his fault?

He could of course nix their plan, claim that he is quarantined in the hospital, gone away on a family visit, any number of excuses would do. But that would affront his sense of hospitality. It's clear that Mina at least has concocted this trip for the specific purpose of seeing him. He can't slam the door in her face.

Trying to distract himself from his apprehensions, he scans Mina's prose a second time, and is struck by the sure tact that runs under its chirpy surface. By taking responsibility for the visit, she is relieving the other two from having to explain to themselves or to each other what it means, what the stakes are, what they want to accomplish. A simple courtesy detour on the part of two ex-colleagues, what could seem more innocent, even to a wife, since he has never mentioned Joleen's defection?

To give Mina her due, this email is all of a piece with the way he remembers her: cagey at first, convivial once she was put at ease, down-to-earth, diplomatic, non-judgmental. It occurs to him that she was in fact more comfortable to be around than Grace, though—naturally?—he never paid her half the attention. But he is very fond of her for all that. In any case, he can rely on her to keep the reunion light-hearted, to smooth over whatever pain or awkwardness may surface.

The down side is that he won't get any private time with Grace—he is amazed that he could wish for it, given the circumstances, but there it is. And Grace's hunger for meaningful conversation won't be satisfied either, though that's probably for the best. Even at the peak of health, he could never keep up with her on that terrain.

He rolls his head around until he hears a crack of vertebrae. He runs a hand through his hair, along his beard. Still a little thin, and completely gray now, a trip to the barber would help. And a new pair of jeans, while he is downtown. All his clothes float on him, making him look like what he is: a spent man, looking to the end. He decides he can manage that much effort.

He clicks on the reply button, and starts writing a response:

Dear Mina and Grace,

Your friendship means a lot to me.

I am looking forward to seeing you on the fourth or fifth. I'll be home both days.

Too formal. That's the way he always writes, but here it sounds like he is trying to reassert a manager's distance. He thinks for a minute, then resumes typing:

And don't dip into the baklava on the way over here. I
intend to finally keep my promise to fix you a real southern
meal.

Best,

Jim

He clicks on the send button. The die is cast, he tells himself.
And for good measure he adds: Insh Allah. Still he feels restless. He
gets up, remembers his coffee, which is probably cold by now. He
goes back to the kitchen and sticks the cup into the microwave. As
he watches it twirl in slow motion on that desultory stage, he gets the
idea of tracking Grace and Mina's journey on Google Maps. It will
keep him busy in the next few days.

II

COCKY

March 2005. For Information Technology consultants, it was the best of times. The post 9/11 recession was over, and George W. Bush had been re-elected to the satisfaction of the business community at large. The trillions of dollars that had evaporated when the dot-com bubble burst had somehow re-materialized—although not necessarily in the same hands. Awakened from the pipe dream of a "new economy", most investors had flocked back to the safest of time-honored assets: real estate. But there was still plenty of cash looking for a more adventurous life. If the Internet had not turned out to be the ultimate cornucopia, it had not gone away either. Any company that wanted to increase its market share—and what company would not—was obliged to keep its technology infrastructure up to date in order to assert its Web presence. Coincidentally, the Y2K crisis had achieved at least one thing: it had solidified the feelings of distrust that executives had always entertained toward their IT staff.

For several years in the late nineties, CEOs had been led to worry that their planes would fall out of the sky on January 1, 2000, that compound interest on their deposits would be incorrectly calculated, that security systems would fail in their buildings, and that many lawsuits would ensue. They had been forced to hire armies of contractors at top prices to fix software that their own programmers could not or would not touch—in many cases because the programmers had hired themselves out as contractors to other companies with millennium pains. When Y2K went off not with a bang but a whimper, when even African countries with no IT budget to speak of failed to experience any significant business disruption, nothing was easier than to conclude you had been snookered.

It was around that time that technophobic executives learned to throw around terms like "legacy systems", "core competencies" and "process re-engineering". The legacy systems were the computer contraptions that had given them heartburn. The core competencies were those parts of the business that they did understand, the parts that generated obvious revenues—in other words, sales. And process re-engineering meant the replacement of those hated legacy systems, a task they were hell-bent on making someone else responsible for, if for no other reason than the dismantling of their own technology departments would nicely pad profits in the short term.

Enter the age of IT management consulting firms: companies varying in size from the mom-and-pop operation to the IBM type behemoth, many financed by venture capital, whose charge was to recommend, plan and optionally supervise information technology projects, but very rarely to actually execute them—a distinction the people who hired them often failed to grasp.

On a sunny late morning in March 2005, Jim Wright found himself at the wheel of a rented Ford Taurus, driving on Highway 99 toward El Pequeno, a town of 80,000 located between Stockton and Merced in the California Central Valley, where, as a member of the Hartbridge Consulting Senior IT Executive Team, he was to conduct a two-month "technology assessment" gig for the local community college district. The make of the car is mentioned here because it's relevant to the story—not for product placement purposes. Every car rented by the firm's travel coordinator on behalf of consultants below the vice-president level was a Ford Taurus, a policy as integral to Hartbridge's business model as the technical jargon that littered its Web site. The Taurus was an American car, an important touch in those patriotic days. It was conservative, sizeable but not ostentatious, suggesting experience, solidity and success without drawing attention to the consultant's expenses that would be charged to the client. It was a bit of a gas guzzler, but crude oil stood at forty dollars a barrel . . . and mileage was also charged to the client.

It was Jim's first foray into the Central Valley, but, preoccupied with his coming assignment, he paid scant attention to the landscape whizzing by him. Flat plowed fields, bare orchards, squat corrugated metal barns, the occasional water tower, silo or processing plant, bathed in a vaguely dirty light. Not exactly the kind of view that made you feel like stopping on the hard shoulder to take a picture. In the midst of that agricultural desert, new housing developments spread outward like grease stains, fancy gabled roofs elbowing each other over cinder block perimeter walls, fast food wrappers entangled in the weeds at their base. On the other side of the freeway from each of these frontier settlements, but inaccessible on foot, cookie cutter shopping malls invited the new homeowners to stuff the trunks of their cars with additional purchases. Jim wondered idly where they all worked. If he had started on his drive only three hours earlier, he would have quickly figured out that most of them commuted all the way to the Bay Area.

In the previous two years, he had spent a fair amount of time in California on engagements similar to the present one: in the Bay Area and Los Angeles, at top-tier universities with typically bloated and backward IT departments. Because of Hartbridge founder Fritz Applefield's previous career as a marketer of administrative software packages for colleges, the higher education market was the firm's niche.

Prior to the founding of Hartbridge, Fritz and Jim had crossed paths professionally on various occasions, notably at King Saud University in Riyadh. In May of 2001, Jim had been forced to return to the US to deal with his son Robert's arrest on drug charges. By the time he was free to re-up, 9/11 had occurred, and Saudi Arabia no longer seemed like the place to be. When Fritz called a year later to offer him a job, Jim felt so grateful, and so little in a position to judge others' entanglements with the law, that he blocked out a piece of information he had picked up on the IT grapevine: Fritz Applefield had just come out of prison after an eighteen-month stint for securities fraud.

As far as Jim could tell, and Fritz had found merit in his analysis, the problem with top-tier universities was their sense of superiority. From presidents on down to administrative assistants, the org charts were crammed with Ph.Ds, often obtained at the same institutions, and people who have incurred six-figure debts over ten years of impractical studies are inclined to attach a near mystical importance to those three letters that have cost them so dearly. On top of that, doctors or not, even those employees stuck in bureaucratic jobs felt entitled to bask in the reflected light of Nobel Prizes conferred on their academic colleagues. Typically, the top brass called in management consultants only when a gun was put to their heads by the legislature, a board of governors or the media, usually in the name of cost containment. You could demonstrate that their hardware was ten years out of date, that their network technicians did not have the skills necessary to debug a firewall, that their business processes required eighty-seven steps where three should have sufficed. But you could not shake their complacency. Your report would be duly provided to whomever had asked for it, and that was as far as it went. A few prestigious references were useful to build the firm's resume, but as Fritz saw it, short assignments were no way to turn a profit in the long term.

Lately, Fritz had decided to focus Hartbridge's marketing efforts on community colleges. First of all, a sense of superiority was much less likely to be an issue there. On the contrary, community college executives, though generally Ph.D endowed, tended to have an inferiority complex, which made them all the more eager to acquire state of the art equipment. And secondly, Fritz had discovered some little-known consequences of the bond funding mechanism that community colleges, particularly in California, had to rely on for capital improvements, given the populace's unwillingness to be straightforwardly taxed. When college districts submitted a bond measure to the voters, they asked for as much money as they could, aware that the opportunity might not present itself again for a long time. They also typically built in some prohibition against the funds being used for salary expenses, since the general opinion on public service employees was that there were too many of them, and they were overpaid. Once the bond measure had passed, the college found that it did not have the personnel required to execute the many projects on its wish list in a timely fashion. Bottlenecks developed in facilities management, purchasing, receiving, information technology. A year before the bonds' expiration, a good portion of the moneys would remain unspent. At that point there would be a scramble to throw cash at anyone willing to spend it without adding to the staff's workload. Luckily, there were no prohibitions against bond funds being used on consultants.

Thanks to the Internet, it was easy, from your office in Florida, to find out which community colleges had bond issues due to expire in the near future. The next step was to meet the chancellor or president at some educational conference, tell them you had heard of their success in steering their institution into the twenty-first century, and offer them a seat on your Executive Advisory Board. If they accepted, and they often did, the only cost to Hartbridge was an all-expenses-paid trip to Orlando for the executive's family twice a year. In exchange, you got a foot in the door—and it was all legal.

This was the background of Jim's drive on Highway 99. Under the guise of technology assessment, his actual mission was to land a three-year IT management contract for Hartbridge.

Following the instructions of his GPS, Jim took the first El Pequeno exit. The District Office was located at the edge of the city—not that he had been able to discern any trace of a downtown from the elevation of the off-ramp—on the Pequeno Community College campus. The district also included another campus fifty miles away in the Sierra foothills. Jim pulled over in one of the visitor parking spaces, stowed his laptop in the trunk, and locked the car. The building in front of him was spanking new and pleasant-looking in a California-turn-of-the-twenty-first-century mold: two stories of stucco in several ocher shades, blue-tinted windows shaded by solar panels in lieu of awnings, an arch or two. Clearly not a cash-starved place. He had half an hour to kill before his first appointment, and decided to limber up after his long journey by taking a stroll towards the Data Center, which the map in his pocket placed at the other end of the campus, between a "beef pasture" and a "dairy unit". This in itself was a good sign: the IT people were far removed from the seats of power.

It was now lunch time, but you wouldn't have known it from the sparseness of the student population, not surprising after all in this rural area. Little knots of kids ambling down walkways, lounging under the trees. Boys with skate boards under their arms, girls pushing baby carriages. A lot of Hispanics, few Blacks. Jim didn't see as many tattoos and piercings as he had feared, and was pleased to notice several hand-printed posters advertising bible classes. The grounds, though short of stately, were well-maintained, and the classroom buildings as inviting as schools can ever be. Even with the occasional intrusion of a thumping bass line from a passing car, the campus seemed blanketed in comfortable placidity. The whole setup reminded Jim of home, down to the smell of burnt meat saturating the air.

Halfway to the Data Center, a city street bisected the campus. Some kind of commotion was going on there. Jim looked over the heads of the rubberneckers. A chunky woman in white jeans had plunked herself down in the middle of the pavement and was playing traffic cop to allow a gaggle of Canada geese to cross at their leisure. The geese were milking the scene for all its worth, stopping every few steps, craning their necks to stare tauntingly at the drivers, then making a pretense of waddling on, only to stop again, gloating over the growing line of stalled cars like hosts congratulating themselves on the success of their party. He was in California after all, land of the righteous clueless. Didn't those people know that geese can fly? All it would have taken to get them to skedaddle was a slow steady creep of bumper against rump. Meanwhile, the woman had probably acquired her extra poundage on the cafeteria's hamburgers. Jim flashed on a long ago hunting expedition in the Saudi desert, dead birds lined up in the shade of the jeep. It may not have been pretty, but it was more honest.

The Data Center turned out to be inaccessible from the campus. The blue diagonal line running in front of it on the map that Jim had taken for a road was in fact an irrigation canal, beyond which, additionally protected by a chain link fence, a one-story prefab building covered in pale-green asbestos siding baked in the midday sun, its small windows barred with chicken-wire. Obviously, the cash lavished on the rest of the campus in the last few years had not flown this way.

Jim ambled back to the District's headquarters to meet with the Vice-Chancellor for Business Services, a certain Bob Johnson, who had oversight on the IT Department, and had therefore been tasked with easing the outsider's insertion into its potentially hostile microcosm—though, naturally, not a word would be said on the issue. Bob turned out to be a pinkish, friendly man with a slightly clammy grip, who seemed not to have fully settled into his executive position (no decorations on the walls of his corner office, and several manually highlighted computer printouts overlapping each other on his highly varnished desk), confessed his ignorance in technological matters but expressed his belief in progress and welcomed the consultant's input.

The two pieces of concrete information that Jim gleaned from the meeting were that Bob played golf and that Dr. Akecheta—that was the Chancellor, appointed a year before, and eager to put his stamp on the District, according to Fritz—had expressed a desire for a "dashboard" that he could consult daily even when on the road to keep tabs on the affairs of the District. Dr. Akecheta had not specified what kind of data should be displayed on the dashboard. When prodded on this point by Bob, he had stated that he paid consultants to figure this kind of thing out.

After a quick lunch at a nearby taqueria, for which Jim paid the tab (it would be charged back to the District a month later), Bob drove him around the campus to the Data Center to introduce him to the IT staff. From the front, the place looked a little more presentable, but not by much. On the street side, the chain link fence gave way to a white wrought-iron fence and an open sliding gate. A couple of dusty crape myrtle trees made do for landscaping in the nearly empty parking lot, and a dark green metal awning cantilevered over slanted tubing shaded a rough wooden porch around the entrance. Jim had to suppress a laugh: that awning alone, reeking at it did of the long-gone nineteen seventies, was enough to have killed the department's hi-tech image in the eyes of the new chancellor.

On closer inspection, the parking lot turned out to be less deserted than it looked at first. At one end of it, an East Indian fella in his late twenties was pacing back and forth on the asphalt while talking on his cell phone, and at the other end, an Asian of a similar age was sitting in his SUV with the door open, smoking. Together, those two made up a fairly good sample of the modern IT work force. But disconnected from each other and from their surroundings as they seemed, their presence did nothing to update the scene.

As they walked in, the busty blonde at the reception desk was talking on the phone in a hushed but business-like voice, her entire posture radiating "do not disturb" warnings. Taking the hint, the visitors stood dumbly at attention for several minutes, during which time Jim managed to pick up the words "staging" and "refi" out of her murmur, concluding that the conversation was not in fact work related. At last, seeming to become aware of their presence, the receptionist rang off with theatrical flair and switched to a chirpy deferential mode to address Bob. Her name was Tiffany Hernandez. Jim took note of the blazing circle of diamonds on her left ring finger.

When asked to let Stanley Gruff—Pequeno's Chief Information Officer—know of their arrival, Tiffany informed them that Mr. Gruff had unfortunately called in sick that day, adding plaintively that she wished she had been told about the present appointment. She would have been able to call Bob to cancel it and spare him the unnecessary drive over. As it was—and she turned her monitor toward him so he could see she was blameless in the matter—the meeting did not even appear on Stanley's Outlook calendar. Jim good-naturedly defended the CIO, arguing for the right of sick people to forget about work. Inwardly, he was pretty sure that the sudden sickness was bogus, that Stanley was simply playing possum. It was the kind of reaction that activated Jim's best fighting instincts. But he could wait. In the meantime, he welcomed the opportunity to meet the staff without their boss hovering in the background. He proposed to Bob that they continue with their visit. Bob agreed.

Her ingratiating smile now encompassing Jim as well as the Vice-Chancellor, Tiffany buzzed them past the inner security door, her hand already poised on the phone receiver. They were standing in a corridor that ran the length of the building, leading on the right to the CIO's office and up a ramp to the elevated floor of the computer room, and on the left, through a warren of shoulder-high cubicles, to symmetrical rows of offices at the end of which the side of a battered stove peeped in a sunlit doorway. Across from the entrance, the corridor bulged out into a sort of foyer, delimited on the far side by a low parapet beyond which, on a platform raised to the same level as the computer room, a military-green metal desk of the same vintage as the building supported an up-to-date pair of monitors. Above them, the top of a dark head could be seen. Whoever sat there had the best view of the goings-on around the place. Jim immediately asked to be introduced.

He remembers that his first impression, after he ascended her platform and could see more of her, was of a conservative South Asian matron: a bun of hair tightly wound at the nape, gold-rimmed glasses surmounted by a deep frown, a hunched body swaddled in a purple salwar kameez. Then, becoming aware of the visitors, the woman straightened up, and Jim had to revise his judgment: she was young, no more than thirty, with a round innocent face, a resolute chin and nimble hands, the left one adorned with a wedding band. Behind the glare of her glasses, her eyes swept from Bob to the newcomer with a sly curiosity that confirmed Jim in his hunch that she would be a useful person to know. He stepped forward to shake her hand. She extended hers with a certain reserve. That was Mina.

Jim glanced at the family portrait on her desk, presumably her husband and little boy, and at the tattered cloth binders on her shelves suggesting that even the system documentation dated from the seventies. Other than that her quarters were understandably bare, since she didn't have any wall space to speak of, a window to the computer room being cut into the back wall, and her front wall being only a parapet.

She seemed to have heard nothing about his assignment, so he explained it to her in the terms he always used with the rank and file: he was here to support the department by making an inventory of their needs, needs that were not always appreciated by upper management—as the saying goes, no one is a prophet in their own land. He fully expected that his final report would result in additional resources and better recognition for the team.

He asked her about her position. She answered that she was in charge of batch scheduling, and he mentioned that he had been a scheduler in Saudi Arabia at one time. Not surprisingly, that seemed to please her. But as spontaneous as this bit of personal disclosure appeared even to him, it did not spring entirely from a natural desire to establish a rapport with someone whose cooperation he was going to need. At each of his contract sites, Jim made a point of dropping various stories into the ears of selected staff. Later, he would be able to start building a picture of the department's group dynamics from the way the information circulated—or not.

He concluded by expressing his hope that she would be able to help answer some of the questions he would have in the coming weeks. She said she would try. He also referred her to Hartbridge's Web site for more information on the firm, confident that she—and whomever else she talked to—would be reassured by its expressed devotion to a **"unique IT co-source contract model** that replaced staff termination and offshore outsourcing with a blend of highly experienced Hartbridge management and talented local employees."

While he talked with Mina, Jim had picked up a few sounds arising from the block of cubicles: the steady clicking of a keyboard, a slurping of coffee, a candy bar being unwrapped, but not a scrap of conversation. As they now walked through it, he noticed that the Asian guy he had seen smoking in the parking lot was now back at his desk. The window open on his screen seemed to be a Java program, suggesting that the IT department had access to some modern technology. Cubicle workers being at the bottom of the pecking order, it did not occur to Bob to introduce them to Jim, and Jim, who knew better than to ignore anyone, let the oversight slide for the time being.

Many of the offices were dark, their doors locked. Bob explained that there had been a number of retirements in the last few years. Given the lack of tech talent in the Central Valley, and the low salaries offered by the college district, most of the positions had remained unfilled.

In one of the offices that were occupied, Jim was surprised to recognize the woman who had played goose traffic cop on campus. Her desk, set against the left wall, was of the same military shade as Mina's, but she was sitting on a blue ergonomic ball, and both her wrists were wrapped in braces. Among the finger paintings plastered on her walls (children) hung a plastic lei (party animal?), several Dilbert cartoons (cynical outlook?), a couple of conference badges (proud of her few business trips). A bowl encrusted with dried-up oatmeal (new year's diet resolutions still in effect?) sat on the top of a messy pile of papers. Her monitors were angled in such a way that a passerby could not see the screens, a fairly reliable indication that she spent a portion of her work day not actually working.

She turned her face toward the door and eyed Jim noncommittally. He stepped forward, offering his hand. For a second she seemed at a loss what to do with it, then stood up awkwardly, rolling the blue ball backward, and knocking the bowl of oatmeal off her desk while she tried to regain her balance. She let out a self-deprecating sigh, picked up the bowl from the floor, put it back on the desk, and finally shook hands with Jim while Bob went through the introductory speech again. Up close, the goose cop struck Jim as remarkably colorless: sallow complexion, lank sandy hair, light gray eyes fringed by transparent lashes, washed-out clothes. Her name, ironically, was Ruby. But having already seen her in action, Jim was spared the mistake of assuming a mousy personality to match her drab appearance. And now, as she faced the consultant, that very appearance underwent a transformation. Suddenly she had a hand on her hip, her chin was up, her eyes were flashing darkly, her body curves made themselves be noticed. "So, you're here to tell us how to run our business?" she said in a voice of mock aggression. She was flirting. Jim peeked at her hands. No wedding ring. He lowered the wattage of his own charm ever so slightly.

Next door to Ruby was a boomer with a shaved head and a Taras Bulba mustache, the Yul Brynner rakishness somewhat compromised by a sizeable paunch. He had solved the monitor privacy problem by setting his desk in the middle of the room and sitting behind it to face the door, which additionally enabled him to monitor hallway traffic. His wall decoration was dominated by a map of Italy and assorted touristy snapshots. Jim also noticed a thermometer, a white board with a calligraphed to-do list fading from age, and an exact replica of the lei in Ruby's office.

His name was Elmore Wollstone. There was something self-important in his demeanor that incited Jim to twit him by asking: "Like Elmer Fudd?" "No, like Elmore Leonard," Elmore replied, "so be vewy vewy caweful how you pwonounce my name." He smirked amicably, pleased with his own wit. All the same, Jim registered a hint of ice in his eyes and a downward curl to the corners of his mouth that did not promise unfailing friendliness.

Elmore did not express any surprise as the purpose of Jim's visit was explained to him, but Jim got the distinct impression that he had been as ignorant of it as his colleagues, that he just liked to appear in the know. When asked about his role, Elmore stated that he was the analyst in charge of the financial systems, and went on to pontificate about being the only one left of the old team and doing his best to drill the new generation in the importance of standards. "If you want to understand our applications", he concluded, "come see me. I have worked on all the systems, so I am the best qualified to give you an overview". "I appreciate your offer," Jim replied, "I'll be sure to make use of it."

The last open office was occupied by Grace. Grace Kirchner. The funny thing, for someone whose powers of observation were always sharpened by new situations, is that he completely failed to intuit at first what she would end up meaning to him. What he saw that day was a geeky girl in Goth trappings: a mass of spiky black hair highlighted in scarlet, a white neck with a question mark tattooed on it, a wrinkled black skirt unevenly hemmed, a flash of shapely legs (yes, he did realize right away that they were shapely) weighed down by black rolled-down socks and clunky black shoes. Her back was turned, and her one monitor displayed a mainframe screen. An iPod lay next to her on the desk, and her head was bobbing to some inaudible rhythm. Her walls were decorated with flowcharts, phone lists, cheat-sheets of EBCDIC to ASCII to Unicode conversions, but nothing to show that she had a life outside the office.

"Wow, so cool!" she suddenly exclaimed, "I got it."

The next thing Jim knew she had jumped out of her seat and into his arms. The impact got her out of her trance. She raised her face to him and reddened, a bashful reaction that Jim wouldn't have credited from a Goth.

"Oh, sorry, she said, I didn't see you. I was going to show a colleague something. Did I hurt you?"

Thank goodness, she didn't have any nose ring or tongue stud, and only one pair of earrings, although there was enough hardware in those to stretch her earlobes permanently. Her blue eyes were enormous, a pair of robin's eggs bulging out of their thick nests of mascara.

"Not a bit," Jim replied. "Saved us from having to tap you on the shoulder to get your attention."

"You want to talk to me?" She asked doubtfully. It was by now clear that Stanley Gruff had failed to inform any of the staff of his coming. Another round of introduction was effected, to which her answer was: "Well, OK, welcome!" You could almost hear the implied "whatever". All the same her handshake was warm and firm (no wedding ring), and she answered his subsequent questions about her job quite readily.

On the way out, Jim made a point of taking a detour through the cubicle farm to shake hands with the few workers who were at their desks at the moment. As expected, he found them a pretty uncommunicative lot, but not predisposed against him as far as he could tell.

They stopped by Tiffany's desk again to enquire about the office that Stanley Gruff was supposed to make available for the consultant, but Tiffany claimed total ignorance on that subject too. Jim played cool about this new contretemps. If Stanley was dumb enough to show his hand this early in the game, it was no reason for Jim to follow suit.

At the end of the afternoon, after a tour of the campus, Bob dropped him back at the District's parking lot, and he drove on to the corporate apartment he was to occupy for the duration of his gig. But the work day was far from over for him. As soon as he had found where to plug in his laptop and how to access the wireless network, he downloaded the Pequeno IT staff list and copy-pasted it into a new spreadsheet, to which he started adding rows and columns. Over the next two months, he would regularly update this document. But he kept a separate copy of his initial draft as a way to test the accuracy of his first impressions. This is what the spreadsheet looked like that night:

Name	Title	Code name	Characteristics	Follow-up
Stanley Gruff	Cio		recalcitrant	
	Operations Director		retired	
	Applications Director		retired	
	Instructional Technology Director?			
	Network Services Director?			
Tiffany Hernandez	Administrative Assistant	Busty Blonde	Side job in real estate. Disloyal	Ask for salary and budget data
Mina Hussein	Production Control Specialist	Paki Fox	Too smart for job	How long at pequeno? Check spread of item about scheduling in SA.
Ray Gomes	Computer Operator		Night shift	
Ruby Mcconnell	Senior Network Coordinator	Mother Goose	Angling for worker's comp	Supervisory duties?
Josh Kim	Network Coordinator		Out on campus	How are outside assignments tracked?
Sandra Rappini	Network Coordinator		Out on campus	Ditto
Erin Brown	Network Coordinator		absent	
Alex Vanourian	Network Coordinator	Rainman	autistic	

Elmore Wollstone	Programmer/ Analyst IV (financial system)	Fuddy-Duddy	baby boomer. Rests on his laurels	Ask for application documentation. relationship to Ruby?
Grace Kirchner	Programmer/ Analyst IV (student system)	Geek Goth	Millennial not gen x	Why only one monitor?
Michelle Williams	Programmer/ Analyst IV		on maternity leave	Personnel system?
Wei Ng	Programmer/ Analyst III	Malborough Man	friends with GG	Java programming?
Rajiv Gupta	Programmer/ Analyst III		Not a joiner	
Sandip Krishnamurti	Programmer/ Analyst III	Blackberry	busy social life	Gay?
	Pc Support Technicians?			
	Systems Programmers?			
	Web Designers?			

During his nightly briefing with Fritz, Jim waxed cautiously optimistic about the probability of success at Pequeno. The management structure was decimated, the staff seemed atomized and demoralized, and core applications still resided on a mainframe. Out of modesty, he didn't mention one of the main reasons for his confidence: the way all the various personalities he had met that day had warmed up to him in short order. But of course, Fritz had counted on that very effect.

Inwardly, Jim was more than cautiously optimistic. It seemed to him that parlaying an investigative gig into a long-term management contract at this godforsaken place was going to be a piece of cake. He couldn't have been more wrong.

III

CHARMED

A text message, sent 04/01/2008, 10:17 PM:
smwhr btw kingman n flagstaff . . . TOY . . . mina n grace

Jim maps the portion of I-40 between Kingman and Flagstaff, clicks on Satellite View. He sees a flap of wrinkled beige skin, mottled with black spidery lesions. He tries to overlay the picture with a memory of his beloved Arabian desert, but the feeling is not there. Perhaps it's a question of altitude. He tries to find a point that has a street view attached. All he gets is a wide swath of asphalt under a bursting sun. What he would really like to do is to sneak the little yellow man onto the backseat of the girls' car. Too bad the technology won't allow it yet. Anyway he would need a microphone attached to the camera. Even then, he doubts he would hear what he wants to know, no matter what good friends Grace and Mina may have become in the last two years.

"Are you OK? Would you like some tea? We can stop around Seligman if you're tired . . ."

"I am fine. Driving long distance is a blast. Flagstaff or bust. A cup of tea would be nice, though . . ."

"All right. Here you go. Hey, I was thinking, do you remember your first impression of Jim?"

"How about yours?"

"You first."

Mina throws her mind back to the spring of 2005. It was just after they bought the house on Oakdale, a two-story, three-bedroom, 2,000 square foot brand new home on a tenth of an acre lot, with a two-car garage, a master suite with walk-in closets and a Jacuzzi in its own bathroom, gables in the nursery, a fireplace and cathedral windows in the living room. The American Dream come true. But what had really sold Mina was the kitchen: a center island with a second sink, granite counters so shiny they seemed designed to release a cooking jinni, and a profusion of cabinets with those carousels that would make storage a breeze. No more standing on a chair to retrieve a salad bowl, no more clattering of pots and pans as you tried to fish out the one at the bottom of the pile, no more running out to your parents' house to borrow some detergent because only the smallest size containers fit under the sink. The beauty of these new housing developments, aside from their architectural finesse, was that it hardly took any imagination to see yourself living happily there. Mina fixing dinner for a group of friends while Tarik clicked away on his computer in the study. Tarik and Mina in front of a roaring fire, or relaxing in the Jacuzzi. And in future years, Steven riding his bicycle within the safe confines of the cul-de-sac. To summon these images of bliss, you only had to visualize the new trees grown to their full sidewalk-shading size, and the complete strangers in the houses next door turned into friends. What you were not supposed to think about was the possibility of one of you losing their job just about the time when the balloon payment on the adjustable rate mortgage came due. But Mina did think about it.

So it was with some trepidation that she greeted the rumor that the chancellor had hired some consulting firm to look over the IT department. Ruby, as usual, was the one circulating the gossip, but as she had heard it from Tiffany, who had access to Stanley's email, it was probably true. The first person Ruby had talked to was Elmore, who had recounted some horror stories about the time, twenty years before, when the IT department had been taken over by a bunch of consultants, how they had systematically pumped the IT staff for technical information, and then, when they had squeezed them dry, had tried to lay them off. The staff had fought back by joining the union. The consultants had been foiled. All the same, Ruby pledged, if the new set of interlopers expected to get anything out of her, they had another think coming. What they may not realize was that she had trained herself long ago in the art of talking without saying anything. Come to think of it, she was glad now that she had never found the time to complete the LAN diagram that Stanley had asked for. It was the kind of thing you did not want to see fall into the wrong hands. She suggested that Mina might want to move her documentation out of sight. She was going to advise all the programmers to do the same.

Mina thanked Ruby for the news, but did not commit to any course of action. Generally, she shied away from being identified with any clique. And although she was careful not to show it, she found Ruby somewhat annoying. Nevertheless, she was worried enough to shoot an email inquiry to Bob Johnson, with whom she was on friendly terms, as he often came to the data center to pick up his own computer reports. In his reply, Bob assured her that the consultant (singular) would be there for two months only, and that his purview would be limited to assessing the department's needs. He also gave her two important pieces of information: the name of the company, and the consultant's arrival date.

Armed with this knowledge, Mina pursued her investigation with a visit to Hartbridge's Web site. When she came to the phrase "staff termination and offshore outsourcing", her heart skipped a beat. She could see that the context meant to disparage it as an outmoded practice. Nevertheless, the mere fact of its being spelled out in black and white confirmed the possibility of the scenario outlined by Elmore. It wasn't only the steady income she was afraid of losing, but the 100% medical coverage for her family. There were not many jobs nowadays that offered such generous benefits.

She was too wedded to her persona as exotic outsider to think about making common cause with the rest of the staff, but she felt spurred to devise her own counter-strategy. She left the scheduling folders on her shelf, but put her list of operational passwords under lock and key. And for good measure, she decided to greet the consultant in full salwar kameez regalia. Nothing in her experience served so well to keep others at a distance. It would also be a subtle warning that any personnel action against her might lead to a racial discrimination complaint.

As a Chicana, Mina did not in theory need to appropriate her husband's ethnicity to qualify as protected minority. But due to her name, her Pequeno coworkers had originally assumed that she was some kind of Arab. She had never disabused them, at first because a

Hispanic heritage was hardly exotic in the Central Valley, and since 9/11, as a token of solidarity with Muslims.

Reluctant as she generally was to pollute the sanctity of home with work problems, Mina did talk to Tarik about the consultant's impending visit. Tarik, an engineering consultant himself (except he did the actual engineering work, as opposed to telling other people how they were doing it wrong), pooh-poohed her fears, making fun of what he called her paranoid tendencies. And it's true that he has more reasons to mistrust his fellow human beings than she does. But he does not fully appreciate her own ethnic handicap. He has not grown up as a smart Mexican girl in the Valley, getting straight As in Math in high school, only to be advised by your oh, so very nice counselor against calculus in favor of keyboarding. OK, maybe that story is just an excuse. What's undeniable is that in March 2005, it was the news of the consultant's arrival that triggered Mina's paranoia. Soon, it would break out on the home front as well. A period she refers to inwardly as her "twilight zone" . . . She prefers not to think about it.

"You know, it's funny, but before I met Jim I was really paranoid about the whole consultant thing . . ."

"Because of Elmore's mob rousing tales?"

"I thought Ruby did the mob rousing."

"Right. He told the tales, she did the rousing."

"Anyway, I don't know if you remember, but I was so freaked out about it that the day he was scheduled to arrive, I decided to wear my salwar kameez . . ."

"How did you know when he was scheduled to arrive? *I* didn't know."

"Oh, Bob Johnson had mentioned it in passing . . . So when I heard the buzzer, I peeked over my monitors. I saw Bob chatting with another guy. Taller even than Bob, but BIG. Big hair, big shoulders, big butt."

"Yeah . . ."

"And dressed to a tee, oh my! The way his suit hung, not a crease in the armpits, you could tell it had been custom-made, in a fabric you wanted to run your hands over. That's how I figured out who he was."

"Typical management consultant look . . . That's what I thought too."

"Or politician. But the hair is what got me the most. I thought, how do those guys manage to have so much hair? And how come it stays in place no matter what? Do they use hairspray? Do they wear barbed-wire weaves underneath?"

"And that's all you saw?"

"No, the really weird thing is that when he came over to shake my hand, I changed my mind about him on the spot. I don't know how to explain it. There was something about him, an "aura", like my sister would say, confident . . . considerate . . . modest . . . funny . . . Not at all the arrogant son of a bitch I expected. And when he got a load of me in my salwar kameez, he didn't seem put off at all. I got the feeling, how can I say it, that he *saw* me. Not my ethnicity, gender, or job title. *Me.* Do you know what I mean?"

"I sure do."

"After that I could never think of him as the enemy. And he didn't turn out to be, did he?"

No response from Grace.

"But how about you? What was your first reaction?"

"Look, there's a gas station up ahead," Grace says. "We'd better fill up while we can."

The gas tank has been filled. Grace has replaced Mina at the wheel. One more hour to Flagstaff, after which the plan is to stop at a rest area and crash for a few hours. This first day of their journey has gone well, although they started late because little Steven, Mina's son, threw a tantrum when he figured out that his mother wasn't just leaving for work. Mina's mother swept the poor little guy into her arms and started rocking him, which only increased his sobbing. It was Tarik who managed to calm him down by standing him on the sidewalk, crouching at his eye level, and talking to him seriously.

"Mommy is going to see a sick friend," he said. "You remember when you had the measles and Mommy stayed home to take care of you?"

Steven nodded yes reluctantly, pointing to a measles scar on his upper lip with a chubby finger.

"Well, Mommy has to take care of her friend now. You understand, right?"

Steven gazed at his father through his tears, and nodded again.

"So, we have to be brave and let her go. You and I can take care of each other for a week, can't we?"

At that point Tarik straightened up. The boy wiped his face with his fists, and took his father's hand manfully. Fifteen minutes later Mina and Grace were on the road.

"What a bit of expert parenting that was on Tarik's part!" Grace remarked, reflexively eager to point out any husband's sterling qualities, as if it was her duty to prop up other people's marriages, though she does not believe in it for herself.

"I know. Isn't he something?" Mina agreed, glancing wistfully at the adhesive family portrait she had just stuck on the dashboard of Grace's car. Grace concluded with relief that everything was all right between those two.

Mina seems to have fallen asleep. The only sound in the car is the soft clicking of the rosary hanging from the rear view mirror, another one of Mina's decorative touches. The silence feels luxurious to Grace. She isn't used to the type of bright small talk that comes naturally to the other woman. The only topics they have discussed at length so far are Steven's pre-school accomplishments and the presidential campaign. It turns out that Mina voted for Hillary Clinton in the primary. She doesn't think that a man of color has any chance of winning the presidency and that even if he did, he would be assassinated before inauguration. Besides, though she was impressed by his speech on race, she does not trust a rookie like Obama with the most important job in the world. Grace figures she has three more days to change her mind.

Strangely enough, they have not spent any time reminiscing about their Pequeno experience, which is basically the only thing they have in common. Perhaps they both sense that they have different perspectives on it. But now Grace has recklessly opened the floodgates with her question about Mina's first impressions of Jim. So what were hers, and why would she rather not share them?

She remembers it was the day she finally figured out why every month or so, one enrollment count out of thousands failed to get updated when a student added or dropped a class. As a work-around for this inexplicable bug, a batch program was run every night to recompute all enrollment counts for the current term, but this was a kludge, and Grace had long been determined to find a real solution. The most thrilling aspect of her discovery that day was that the bug had been left in the registration module by the legendary VLP, whose initials were all over the student system. VLP had been a crack programmer, and even if her language had only been COBOL, Grace could appreciate the elegant simplicity and symmetry of her code. Unfortunately, VLP had retired a couple of years before, so Grace could not give her the good news. But Wei would get a kick out of it. Grace took out her earbuds, made for the door, bumped into something, and found herself enveloped in male pheromones. But when she looked up, she was confronted with an old guy—fifty at least. Gray hair, thick glasses, a round nose, the rest of his face covered with a moustache and a beard, a bulky torso. Santa Claus—in a very expensive business suit, the pants held up by appropriately santaclausian red suspenders. (But how could she have noticed the suspenders then, as he didn't take off his jacket?)

It occurred to her that this might be one of the IT consultants Ruby had warned her about. She hadn't paid much attention at the time, first because she found Ruby's frequent irruptions into her office an unwelcome distraction, but more importantly because in the two years she had worked at Pequeno, she had come to be proud of its computer applications: students were able to apply, register and get their transcripts online; business officers could keep track of hourly encumbrances in real time; the data extracts required quarterly by the State Chancellor's MIS office were always filed on time and accepted with barely an edit; there were workflows for purchase orders, employee leave and hiring requests; and Wei and Grace were putting the final touches on a Web application that would allow instructors to turn their grades in from their vacation homes in Hawaii or France. Let the consultants poke around, she had thought. Maybe the IT department would finally get the kudos it deserved.

Mina hasn't mentioned the Southern accent. But that's what struck Grace immediately when he opened his mouth. Grace had never before met a real live Southerner. She was too young to have seen "Gone with the Wind". She had never heard the term "a Southern Gentleman", had never argued whether it applied more to Ashley Wilkes or Rhett Butler. To her a Southern accent evoked dopey country music and racial discrimination—it did not invite her to take the personage standing a foot from her any more seriously than his quaint appearance warranted.

Still, running into someone—literally—is an embarrassing way to make their acquaintance. She even suspected that she had stubbed his toes. But he didn't show any sign of being hurt or offended. His first reflex upon being hit had been to put out his arms to steady her. And then he had humorously brushed off her apologies. Pretty smooth stuff. She looked up at him again. Behind the thick glasses, his green eyes were twinkling.

Bob introduced them to each other. Jim said a few irreproachable words about his objectives as a consultant, words that Grace didn't really listen to, assuming she was being treated to a well-rehearsed spiel, sincere and homey as it sounded. Then he started asking questions about her position, skillset, projects and wishes. She was soon thoroughly impressed by his technical knowledge, his understanding of issues, and most of all by his positive attitude, which nicely contrasted with Stanley's pessimism. Meanwhile she was aware of the way his gaze held her, full of a warm curiosity that was very flattering. What did Mina say . . . that she felt he really saw her. That's exactly it. On how many people did Jim have this effect, Grace wonders, and how much was the warm curiosity heartfelt, how much a cynical ploy? One thing she concluded from the first few minutes of conversation with him was that Jim was no dummy. She was right about that.

IV

STRATEGIC

Fritz Applefield's strategic mantra regarding technology assessment gigs consisted of three bullet points:

- Make friends
- Make a quick showing
- Make opportunities

Unlike the "best-practice methodologies" and "work products" advertised on Hartbridge Consulting's Web site, this list of objectives was not copyrighted, or even stored anywhere in the firm's private knowledge base, but it was no less etched in Jim's memory.

Making friends

To fully appreciate the difficulties attendant to this particular objective, it is necessary to keep in mind another list: the set of means that were not available to achieve it. Also unwritten, but familiar to all management consultants, were a number of prohibitions, failure to comply with any of which constituted a firing offence:

- No conversations on popular culture
- No expression of political or religious opinions
- No flaunting of wealth or status
- No sharing of Hartbridge's trade secrets
- And the one that summed up the others:
- No fraternizing with the client's staff

Making friends under such constraints was something of a challenge, but one Jim was well equipped for. Although at the time he never stopped to wonder why Fritz had come looking for him when he started his new company, it was probably not for his technical and managerial skills alone. The fact was that Jim was fairly loaded with that elusive asset that goes by the name of charisma. And Fritz knew his own deficiency in that area.

Within the first couple of weeks, Jim managed to score golf dates with Bob Johnson, Vice-Chancellor of Business Services, and with the Director of Admissions and Records, an energetic, shoot-from-the-hip kind of guy by the name of Roger Wilkins. Each time, by the ninth tee, Jim had fairly sized up his man. Bob was steady, modest, methodical, devoted to the welfare of the district. Once he was convinced that a particular course of action would reduce costs and/or enhance services, he would probably offer his unflinching support. On the other hand, Roger, intent as he seemed on projecting the image of a maverick, Jim suspected of being a herd animal. For instance, he had no sooner registered Jim's southern accent that he started peppering his speech with "y'all's" and "yes, Sir's". He would be easy to win over, until a more powerful individual disagreed. But won over he must be: directors of admissions typically had veto powers on new administrative systems.

Most of the time during those first two weeks Jim spent out on campus and at the district office, informally interviewing students, instructors, counselors, deans, executives and the occasional administrative employee. The goal of the exercise was to elicit negative comments that could be used to make a case against the IT department's current technology infrastructure or management. The process rarely failed. But beyond the instrumental aspect of these interviews, Jim simply enjoyed talking to people. He, who had spent his childhood literally hiding in the woods, had come to relish the prospect of addressing perfect strangers, of enticing them to open up to him, of making them like him. He knew he was very good at it, without deeming it necessary to probe the nature of his talent—never look a gift horse in the mouth was how he saw it. He only felt grateful for the mixture of circumstances and experience that had brought it to its present near infallibility. The only thing that remained from his original shyness was a terror of public speaking.

From his encounters with a client's staff, Jim wasn't content to accumulate friends and information; what he was after, if only for his own intellectual pleasure, were the patterns of thought and behavior, the currents of influence and power that underlay punctual interactions. To him, an organization was as exciting an object of scrutiny as a painting by an old master, which, subjected to x-rays, reveals another painting behind, or two, or three. All that is seen and unseen . . . It was all part of the big picture.

This time the interviews yielded mediocre results: the marketing director (though not the students) complained about the registration system being taken offline every night from midnight to six AM; students resented the library's restrictions on downloads; deans criticized the switch from Eudora to Outlook; some instructors had trouble putting their course content online; a couple of executives expressed a wish for easier access to district data. As for the counselors—at least those Jim had been able to talk to, all baby boomers who should have retired years ago—they were outright hostile to the computers into which they were forced to record their contacts with students, per state requirements. They had signed on to their career as social workers, not bean counters, they argued. In several of their offices, Jim noticed unplugged monitors stashed in corners, keyboards wedged between piles of catalogs. Curiously, the administrative staff seemed happy with their applications, although they were still mostly presented on green (i.e. mainframe) screens.

Meanwhile, Jim was not making much progress in IT. After a couple of days, during which Stanley Gruff continued to play possum, an office was made available to him, a tiny room, at the very end of the corridor, previously used as a junk closet, the green metal desk that occupied most of it threatened on all sides by rickety metal shelves stacked with discarded PC parts. As passive aggressive behaviors go, it was not very subtle. Still, Jim held his peace.

Stanley finally showed up the next Monday. The first thing Jim noticed upon entering the reception area was that Tiffany was not whispering on the phone or surfing real estate Web sites, but typing some document with the Pequeno letterhead. The door to Stanley's office was open, an oblong of sunlight on the carpet in the hallway indicating that the blinds had been pulled up. Jim poked his head in, and saw a man on all fours fiddling with the network connection on the far wall.

"Beg your pardon," Jim said. "I was looking for Stanley Gruff."

"You're talking to him," the man answered without turning around. He pulled the cable out, inspected it at length, shoved it back in, wiggled it a little more, and finally stood up, face red from the exertion. "And you are . . . ?"

"Jim Wright, from Hartbridge Consulting. I was sorry to hear that you've been sick. Are you feeling better?"

"I'm all right," Stanley said. He brushed dust off his hands and extended one to Jim.

"Nice to meet you. Thank you for freeing an office for me."

"No problem."

Stanley Gruff turned out to be a twitchy little guy, skinny but somehow soft, with thinning hair, a poker face and shrewd black eyes. He was wearing a mint green polyester shirt with short sleeves, navy polyester pants, a tie that clashed with the shirt, and cheap loafers. Jim couldn't help feeling sorry for the guy, whose career he had no trouble imagining on the spot: the working class background, the misspent youth, the accidental discovery that he was smart, the computer skills learned on the job, the entirely meritocratic ascension to middle management, and then the stall, because he had neither the political savvy nor the fashion sense to be appreciated by the executive class. Which would had been Jim's story, in fact, but for Joleen's taste for high living. Without the pressure of her spending habits, Jim would never have been prompted to seek job opportunities in the Gulf States. He would not been free to remake himself into a leader, far from all the social markers that kept him down at home. He would not have benefited from Waheed's civilizing influence.

Strange, he reflects, not for the first time—his eyes meanwhile following the I-40 route on Google Maps—how often a curse turns into a blessing. What's new is this: he is no longer sure that it's all right to deliberately inflict curses on others in the belief that they may be blessings in disguise.

"Do you have a few minutes to talk?" Jim asked, as Stanley started moving toward the door.

"Not now, I am afraid. I am due to a meeting at the district. But check my schedule with Tiffany. I'm sure she'll be able to squeeze you in sometime today."

Things did not improve when Jim and Stanley were finally able to sit down together. Jim started with a few neutral questions about hardware, software, teams, vacant positions. Stanley did not volunteer any information beyond what each question demanded. Jim apologized for taking Stanley's time over such basic stuff, which he had unfortunately not been able to find on the IT Web site. Stanley retorted that no one outside the IT department was interested in these kinds of technical details, and besides, as Jim could see, his staff was so thin that they could barely keep the proverbial wheels turning, let alone find time for public relations. Jim couldn't help suggesting that perhaps more attention to public relations would have prevented his own visit. After all, if the chancellor had been happy about the IT department's performance, he would not have called in consultants. Stanley replied that the chancellor was new, and perhaps not that well informed. Realizing that he had let himself get nettled, Jim offered an olive branch:

"Why don't you help me better inform him, then?" he proposed.

"Even at the risk of causing Hartbridge to miss out on a big fat contract?"

"Even at that risk. While I work *at* Pequeno, I work *for* Pequeno."

Jim had injected the classic formula with such a dose of sincerity that for a moment, he himself believed it. But Stanley didn't make much effort to hide the fact that he didn't.

The one advantage to Jim's cramped office—one that Stanley may not have envisioned—was that to reach it, he had to go through the entire building, thus getting many opportunities to practice "management by walking around", a technique that had very undeservedly fallen out of fashion, in Jim's opinion, one that was not in any case part of Stanley's leadership repertoire, as evidenced by the relaxed way most of the staff went about their work—when they were working at all.

Busty Blonde—AKA Tiffany—spent most of the time at her desk negotiating with building contractors and mortgage brokers. Inspired by a new reality TV show, she and her husband were apparently making a go at something called house flipping. Where they got the capital for it, given her clerical wages, Jim could not imagine. The one time Jim asked her to Xerox some document, she got off the phone just long enough to show him the instruction sheet pasted above the copier.

Sandip Krishnamurti turned out to deserve his code name of BlackBerry. When he wasn't out in the parking lot calling friends, he seemed to be emailing them in some Indian language.

Fuddy-duddy Elmore liked to organize lunch-time cultural slide shows (the one Jim ran into concerned the Sistine Chapel) using his personal laptop and the department's projector. These events took place in the lunch/conference room, were attended by many district and campus employees, and ran well into the afternoon. Judging from the number of times that Jim saw Elmore bent over his laptop instead of the district provided desktop, the planning process itself occurred during the work day. Later, Jim was told that the slide shows were the last remnant of a previously bustling social scene that had included birthday cakes, Halloween costume contests and parking lot picnics. Indeed, rummaging through the dusty detritus crammed on the conference room shelves, Jim had one night unearthed a photo album documenting a quarter century of such festivities, in the days when Pequeno was "a family", as his informant claimed. On several of the pictures, which from the look of them dated back to the seventies and eighties, Jim recognized a slimmer and hairier Elmore mugging for the camera. He had a moment of revulsion toward the place for its having been allowed to purr along comfortably for decades while the rest of the work world kept getting torn apart and rebuilt on different models, and toward Fuddy-duddy for the lifetime of avoiding challenges upon which the man had apparently built his self-importance. Well, Jim was there to change all that.

Except for Rainman, the "network coordinators"—who were in fact mere PC support technicians, responsibility for the network architecture, as well as instructional technology, having been delegated to a separate department a couple of years before—were usually marked "out on campus" on the reception's bulletin board. The lack of help desk ticketing software made it impossible to know what clients the support technicians were actually supporting, or what problems they were solving.

As to Mother Goose, her monitors being turned away from the door, it was hard to tell what she did all day, but in any case it did not seem to include the duties Jim would have expected from a senior PC technician: mentoring her junior colleagues or attending to servers.

The others: Mina the Paki Fox, Grace the Geek Goth, Malborough man Wei, and the programmer named Rajiv, for whom Jim had not yet found a nickname, pretty much kept their nose to the grindstone. Only Grace and Wei, and occasionally Sandip and Rajiv, gave any evidence of working together. The programmer/analyst in charge of the Personnel and Payroll systems was out on extended maternity leave. The only computer operator worked the night shift. The mainframe systems programming position had been outsourced to a private firm after the incumbent's retirement. The applications director and operations director positions were vacant. A pretty dispiriting climate. Jim found himself itching to roll up his sleeves.

Getting information out of anyone in the department was like pulling teeth. They did not understand his questions, or were rushing out for an appointment, or agreed to pull some documentation together, but never found the time. If he sat down for a break in the lunch room, any employee present would quickly pack up their snacks and leave. Jim suspected that Stanley was at the bottom of this resistance, since it had started after the CIO's return from sick leave. But he had no evidence to back up his hunch. One of the downsides of email was that it allowed intrigues to be conducted entirely underground. It wasn't until the Hartbridge contract became a near certainty that his suspicions were proved right. Busty Blonde inadvertently—or not—forwarded an old message from Stanley to all the staff, where he enjoined them to cooperate with the new consultant, but only to the extent that it did not interfere with their work. "Remember," the message concluded, "that your first priority is to keep the systems running." Jim could have strangled the bastard. But, after all, he was only being strategic, no more no less than Jim. No point getting hot under the collar. By that time, a solution to the Gruff problem had been found anyway.

Both because he was in no hurry to get back to his anonymous condo, and because he wanted to have the freedom to snoop around,

Jim tended to stay at the office after hours, when he could count on having pretty much the run of the place. Only Paki Fox, Geek Goth and Marlborough Man ever worked overtime, Paki Fox to verify that the nightly jobs were properly scheduled, Geek Goth and Marlborough Man completely absorbed in their coding, and oblivious to his presence, although Geek Goth's office was next to his. As for Stanley, he promptly left every day at five to commute back to his ranch somewhere in the Sierra foothills.

One night Jim decided to take an inventory of the equipment in the computer room. He had to ask Mina to unlock the door, which she did somewhat reluctantly, accompanying him inside as if he was likely to make off with one of the servers. They started chatting about tape drives, bursters and printers. Jim recounted some of the mishaps that had made him sweat bullets in his operator days. Mina giggled the whole way, as he had hoped. Pretty soon she was showing him her system for pulling scratch tapes, the folders where she filed copies of report distribution sheets, a Microsoft Access database she was in the process of creating to keep track of maintenance contracts. "Shouldn't Tiffany be doing that?" Jim asked. Mina couldn't help rolling her eyes. "I know what you mean," Jim said. From that day they were buddies. Thanks to her, Jim obtained many tidbits of social gossip on the other members of the team: that Elmore had to keep working to pay for his son's Stanford tuition, that Tiffany hoped to be able to make house flipping a full-time career, that Ruby had four kids and sang in Karaoke bars. Wei's wife was pregnant, Sandra was pursuing a Cisco certification, Rajiv had recently got his green card. But Mina never volunteered any comment on her colleagues' professional skills or work habits. And the Saudi Arabia trial balloon never came back to him until after he unleashed it on Elmore.

Making a quick showing

A quick showing was a small but high-visibility project that would demonstrate Hartbridge's capacities to executives and board members while the idea of a three-year contract was floated to them. One idea Jim had jotted down under that heading was the "dashboard" desired by the chancellor. And this is where he first ran into the necessity of depending on the good will of the client's staff for the actual execution of projects that would later figure as the consulting firm's accomplishments.

Hartbridge had several licenses for one of the tools that are used for creating dashboards: customized Web sites that provide interactive views of a business' key performance indicators in the form of charts and graphs, the goal being to give the user, typically a manager, the sensation of driving a sports car—hence the tool's name. What Hartbridge lacked was any knowledge of the data that would need to be queried to animate the dashboard, or the staff to develop it.

One evening, hearing that the keyboard clicking next door had given way to a banging of drawers and rattling of coat hangers, Jim bounded out of his chair and made for Geek Goth's office. In the month or so that they had been neighbors, Jim had learned a few things about Grace Kirchner. She was not only conscientious, but enthusiastic about her work. She seemed to have a good overview of the district's database, enjoyed learning challenges, and wasn't overly deferential to constituted authorities. A not unusual combination of traits in a Millennial, and one that could prove helpful to Jim.

As he entered her doorway, she was in the process of donning a black leather jacket bristling with buckles and zippers. A backpack and bicycle helmet sat on her desk.

"Are you leaving?" Jim asked. It was a dumb question. Given the general attitude of the staff toward him, he expected her to answer: "What does it look like, Bozo?" Instead, what she said was:

"I was planning to. Why? You have a better idea?" On anyone else's part, he would have taken the response as a come-on. But there was nothing flirtatious in her tone or manner. She just seemed casual, curious, and oddly well-disposed toward him.

"I need your help with something. Do you have a few minutes?"

"Sure."

"May I sit down?

"Go ahead."

Jim parked himself on one of the two guest chairs in her office, tilting it back against the wall and crossing his legs ankle over knee, this demonstration that he was in no hurry intended to incite in her a like disposition. It worked. She took off her jacket without a fuss, rotated her chair to face him, grabbed a legal pad and a pen, and sat down expectantly. She was wearing some kind of athletic black Mary Janes, black leggings under a short flouncy black skirt, several layers of tops—one of them not black, he was glad to see. The hem of her leggings on one side had rolled up. Over the next hour, he would find his eyes returning again and again to this small kink. Forcing his eyes up, he looked at her face, and blocking out the sooty eyelids and harsh lipstick, noticed that she had a dimple on her left cheek. She could have been his daughter.

Jim explained his dashboard idea. Grace didn't seem thrilled about the prospect of catering to the CEO's needs—"whims" is the word she actually used. But having just completed a project, she confessed that she was looking for something to do, and when she heard that the work would be done in WebFocus, a tool with which she was familiar from her previous job, her interest perked up.

They set about brainstorming for data that the dashboard could display.

"Enrollment figures, to start with. By term, campus . . ."

"Department, time of day, campus-based vs. online . . ."

"And all permutations of these dimensions . . ."

"Goes without saying. By the way, I need to mention that all this data is already available on the intranet, although not in graphic form."

"And not on the same page as the chancellor's calendar, I'll bet."

"Too true."

"Come on. Give the man a break. He has other things to do than hunt all over the place for important data."

"There's something called a bookmark."

"But it's not the same as having it all in the same window."

"And what will the chancellor do, when he sees that enrollments in Cattle Science are down today?"

"Pay for happy cow ads on the cable channels, of course."

She laughed.

"If I didn't know you better, I would suspect that you are fearful of change," he twitted her reflexively, fear of change having by that time become the consecrated explanation for any staff resistance to management plans, and any hint that an employee might suffer from that weakness usually resulting in their falling in line without delay.

She laughed again, this time dismissively.

"For one thing, you don't know me at all. And for another, change is my middle name. So there."

"Sorry. I didn't mean to hurt your feelings."

"Chill, as we say in my set, I was just ragging you. Don't worry, I'll work on your project. When is it due?"

"In a month or so."

"OK. I'll show you a prototype next Friday. Will that do?"

"You're a trooper. Oh! And you will get credit for this. But . . ."

"Don't mention it to Stanley?"

He winked in response, glad that he didn't have to put into words his fear of the snag they would likely hit were the CIO to hear that one of his employees was working on a project assigned by the consultant

A couple of weeks later, the dashboard was ready to demo. Jim managed to wrangle a half-hour meeting with the chancellor, his first one, in fact, Dr. Akecheta having until then dealt exclusively with Hartbridge's CEO. And as he needed Grace to conduct the test, (it wouldn't hurt either to show the chancellor that the consulting firm had already managed to enlist staff cooperation), he felt obliged to inform Stanley of the coming appointment.

"Go ahead," Stanley said, fixing on Jim an amused look, "I have complete faith in Grace." Very sporting, Jim thought, or does he know something I don't?

But no, he really meant it. Grace came through with flying colors.

On the day of the appointment, they drove to the district office in Jim's car.

"Wow," Grace commented, "you could fit a family of six in here . . . and the dog. Ever think of downsizing?"

"Company policy," Jim answered. "And I need the trunk for my golf clubs."

"Ah . . ."

They had to wait outside Dr. Akecheta's office for close to an hour. When he finally let them in, his apologies were so profuse that you were led to doubt their sincerity. The Chancellor was a short, rotund man, with a jowly face under a sheared afro, his complexion as dark as his three-piece suit. His arms, held out as if he was trying to occupy more space, ended in tiny hands. There was no a hint of humor in his heavy-lidded eyes.

Jim and Grace quickly set up the laptop and started the demo. Things were going swimmingly, when suddenly, as Grace drilled down from one pie chart into another, all the captions disappeared. The shapes and colors were still gorgeous, but you couldn't tell what you were looking at. It was like watching a movie with the mute on. She tried another report. Same problem. Another one. Ditto. There was obviously a bug in that particular version of WebFocus, which was still in .1 release. Grace glanced at Jim in alarm. He winked back his confidence in her crisis management skills. Sure enough, she got the idea of clicking on the weather tab, which linked to an external application unmarred by the Webfocus bug. Dr. Akecheta went on nodding self-importantly. A few minutes later, having received the chancellor's congratulations for a job well done, they were back in the car. As soon as they had pulled out of the parking lot, Grace started laughing hysterically, banging her head over the dashboard, her hair bouncing around like a frolicking Pekingese.

"My God, he didn't notice anything. We could have shown him data from General Motors and he would have been just as pleased."

"Simmer down, will you, the commotion is distracting me from driving. And please fasten your seat belt!" Jim grumbled. Inwardly, he was guffawing too.

Making opportunities

There were basically three types of projects that could justify a three-year IT management consulting contract at a community college: a district-wide network overhaul, an instructional technology plan, and an administrative systems migration. Unfortunately, the first two were out of the question. Jim had been made to understand that the Director of Network Services and Distance Education, a man by the name of Peter Santelli, who reported to the Vice-Chancellor of Academic Services instead of Bob Johnson, as Stanley did, was protected by the Academic Senate and teachers' union, and as such, he and his department were untouchable. Hartbridge was going to have to make a case for an administrative systems migration project.

According to Fritz, the chancellor was already on board. First of all, he liked to see his picture on the Executive Advisory Board tab of the Hartbridge Web site. Second, his kids—a second marriage, this time to an irreproachably African American attorney—loved Disney World, and Hartbridge's headquarters were conveniently located in Orlando. And third, he was determined to make the Pequeno Community College District a "premier" institution of higher learning, to sharpen its "competitive edge", to "steer it into the twenty-first century". Half of his work life being spent traveling, he had read enough airline magazines to know what was wrong with "legacy" application systems: they were hosted on "obsolete mainframes", they were poorly documented, lacked "integration", and were too dependent on a few developers' specialized skills and knowledge. Frankly, Fritz doubted that Dr. Akecheta could have picked the District's mainframe out of a lineup of Linux servers (and in fact, the modern mainframe at Pequeno was capable of running the Linux operating system), or knew the meaning of the term integration, or had any idea of the programming skills required to maintain non-legacy applications. But that was neither here nor there.

It was too bad large budgetary decisions were not left to Dr. Akecheta's judgment. They had to be ratified by the Board of Trustees. At the first Board meeting that Jim attended, he became painfully aware of the politics that would weigh on their decision.

Board meetings took place in a large room built specifically for the purpose in the District Office building. The room was equipped with WiFi internet access, a huge plasma screen as well as a ceiling recessed projector and projection screen combo, and several high-definition PTZ cameras. The walls were painted a soothing lilac and decorated with large, high-resolution photographs of Central Valley agricultural landscapes: almond trees in bloom, cows in rolling pastures, mist over plowed fields. The table at which board members sat was made of the same blond wood as the kitchen cabinets in Jim's corporate apartment, and backed by leather-upholstered armchairs. The seats reserved for the public, on the other hand, were interlocking molded plastic chairs guaranteed to make your butt sore after ten minutes. On the right side of the room, a set of sliding glass doors opened onto the campus lawn to accommodate the overflow of spectators on the rare occasions when some agenda item attracted public attention. Jim was surprised to find that this was one of those times.

He noticed that a sizeable proportion of the spectators wore oversized purple tee shirts with yellow lettering on top of their street clothes. Bob, who was sitting next to him, explained that they were members of SEIU, the union that represented classified employees. Among them, Jim recognized Ruby, flanked by two kids who must be her children. It was the first clue he had that the IT staff was unionized.

The meeting was delayed by the chancellor's late arrival. In the meantime, the video conferencing system was set up to allow the remote participation of one of the board members currently deployed in Iraq. It was, what, seven in the morning there. Talk about dedicated service. Finally things got underway.

Jim had tuned out during the approval of the minutes. Suddenly he became aware that his company's name was being mentioned. Some grizzled firebrand in Hawaiian shirt and Birkenstocks was pounding the podium, demanding to know why the Hartbridge technology assessment contract, which was over $50,000, had not gone out for public bid, per state law, why, Silicon Valley being so close, a Florida firm had been selected, and why the Faculty Senate had not been consulted on this questionable expense, in violation of shared governance. His speech was greeted with resounding applause from the SEIU ranks, and with assenting nods from a couple of Board members, who, it later transpired, had connections with local IT consulting firms.

It was bad. If so many factions within the district's power structure already begrudged a mere $60,000, two-month gig, how were they going to react to a $600,000 a year, three-year contract? Jim had a long phone discussion with Fritz that night. Together, they explored strategies for bringing various opponents to Hartbridge's side. None of them seemed feasible within the required time frame. In the end, it was Fritz who hit upon the only practical solution: Stanley Gruff would have to go. Faced with the prospect of an IT department entirely bereft of managers, and fearing the computer disasters that must ensue, for which they would be made accountable, the Board would have no choice but to rely on the IT management consulting firm already "on the ground". Jim expressed some ambivalence toward this course of action. "Don't worry," Fritz said, "I'll take care of it myself."

Jim was ambivalent. The more he delved into the affairs of the IT department, the more he was forced to acknowledge that they were in better shape than at first appeared. After all, no one he talked to could remember any instance of the kind of major snafu that plagued newly installed software packages: a crash of the registration system on the first day of class, a couple of decimal points off on payroll checks. The district's applications seemed to be able to keep up with changes in federal and state regulations. And according to Grace, the student, personnel and financial systems did in fact talk to each other, in other words were integrated. Also according to Grace, Stanley had played a major role in bringing about this mysterious efficacy. He was an excellent project manager, a shrewd analyst, and Pequeno's first Web master. All in all, it seemed counterproductive to jettison such assets, which might come handy when Hartbridge found itself confronted with actual work.

A seemingly innocuous incident rallied Jim to Fritz's solution. One morning, coming back from a campus visit, he found a cluster of men hanging around Grace's door: Bob Johnson, Roger Wilkins, and another guy who turned out to be the main campus' Business Officer. Three good old boys, slaphappy with each other, but obviously vying for Grace's good graces—the Magi kneeling in front of Baby Jesus. The girl herself sat with her chair turned toward the door, her black mane flaming out, her elbows resting on the edge on her desk, her milky legs at sixes and sevens, her blue eyes goggling with fond indulgence, pretty much the way she looked at Jim whenever he came into her office. It was not the first time Jim saw her entertaining these visitors, but usually they came singly, begging for a new report or a change to an algorithm. And although she always started by scolding them for believing that "all it took was to push a button", she usually yielded to their entreaties.

As Jim good-humouredly joined the three Magi, he felt a headache coming on, a sign that he was in fact in a foul mood. Looking for the cause of his irritation, he found it in the amount of programming work that seemed to get done around the IT department following mere verbal agreements, without the benefit of service requests, prioritization committees, Gantt Charts or Quality Assurance team.

It was the way Jim himself had liked to work before he became a manager—with minimal bureaucratic interference. But he had learned that it had significant drawbacks: without a paper trail, the IT department could not demonstrate its productivity. And users, spared from having to write business requirements or wait months for their projects' completion, were allowed to continue thinking that their requests were indeed just a matter of pushing a button. He didn't blame Grace for being ignorant of those liabilities, she was just a kid out of college, but Stanley should have known better. The "employee empowerment" philosophy the CIO had claimed to espouse was mere sloth. However talented he may otherwise be, as a leader he was dragging the department down. Hartbridge would have to do without him.

At this point in his recollections, a new train of thought detaches itself from Jim's mind and assumes a distinct presence, with its own unsought and unexpected take on things. In this obtrusive entity, though a stranger to him for many years, Jim recognizes his conscience. "Isn't it possible," it suggests, "that your foul mood had an element of jealousy about it? That you longed to replace Stanley Gruff as the person Grace looked up to? That you wanted to have the means for keeping the three Magis at a distance? That you agreed to let Stanley go partly as a way to get rid of rivals?" Jim rejects his conscience's theories out of hand. For one thing, they suppose a psychological complexity that's not credible in a simple guy like him. And for another, throughout his career, he has made a point of never letting personal feelings interfere in the discharge of his professional duties, at least not since that time, nineteen years ago at King Faisal Hospital, when he narrowly escaped losing his mind, his job and possibly his life.

In any case, he wasn't the only one the Magi's visit put in a foul mood. A little while after they left, and Jim was back in his office, he heard Fuddy-duddy complain to Grace about the noise they had made, demanding that she better control her guests in the future. For all the Renaissance man gloss and Taras Bulba bravado, he was the kind of fella who dumped on a woman rather than confronting other males. It was good to know.

The bird clock in the kitchen is playing a mourning dove's call. Jim tunes into his present surroundings. It's 9:00 PM, and Cindy is due back from her nursing courses at UNCG. He drags himself to the kitchen, assembles a little scatter graph of pills on the counter, downs them one by one in anticipation of Cindy's daily question: "Did you take your medicine, Daddy?" It's not so much that she doesn't trust him to take care of himself, he suspects, as an indirect way to express her love. God knows, she didn't learn emotional fluency from him. But she is a good girl, even if it took him until now to see it. His being stuck at home has had some benefits. He was able to coax her into going back to college. It took a lot of time—of which he has plenty—and patience, which he has had to learn, to convince her that she was not an idiot. But now she is thriving—and already a good nurse to her father. Curses and blessings . . .

He washes a couple of dishes in the sink, takes some soup and rolls out of the freezer, sweeps a few crumbs off the floor. Exhausted, he goes back to the couch and his laptop, where he finds an email from Grace:

From: grace.kirchner@barackobama.com
Date:Wednesday, April 2, 2008
To: Jim.Wright@hartbridge.com
Subject: Another day, another 800 miles

Dear Jim,

Made today's target! We are now ensconced in a scuzzy motel on the outskirts of Weatherford, Oklahoma. Don't worry, Mina has inspected every nook and cranny for bedbugs. She is now taking a well deserved shower. We had a grueling day: nothing but country music on the radio. You would have been in seventh heaven. Tomorrow we are aiming for Nashville (more country music . . .) Wish us luck.

Grace

V

EXEMPLARY

"Heard anything from Stanley lately?" Grace asks.

The bedside lamps have been turned off, but as in every motel in Grace's experience, the drapes don't close properly, and a ray of street light falls on Mina, who, it turns out, is busy arranging her jacket for maximum coverage over the thin blankets. The heater is as loud as a jet engine, but it's all roar and no action, as Jim might have said.

"Nothing since his usual Christmas email letter. Didn't you get it?"

"No, I don't think I ever gave him my current email address. So, what is he up to?"

"He is doing great. His wife has retired too, so they're both working full-time on their organic farm. The kids are helping out, after all. They're doing the farmers markets, they have a CSA. And of course, Stanley is in charge of the Web site. You should check it out. I never knew vegetables could look so artistic."

"Well, I am glad it all worked out in the end. I was kind of worried when he decided to retire all of a sudden three years ago."

"Me too. It was weird, because the week before he had mentioned that he was planning to replace the burster as soon as the new fiscal year rolled around. I thought he might have found out he had cancer or something. But obviously that wasn't the case."

"Didn't it ever occur to you that Hartbridge might have had something to do with his leaving?"

Mina turns on her side to face Grace, who looks nowhere near falling asleep, her head propped up on her hands over the scrunched-up pillow, her raised knees tapping against each other in a restless way, her eyes fixed on the ceiling as if all she wants to know about life is written up there.

"Hey, I'm the one who is supposed to be paranoid, remember?" Mina says. "Anyway, at that time, Hartbridge was Jim. He would never have done something like that."

"So why do you think Stanley retired just two weeks before the first Hartbridge contract expired? Just a coincidence?"

"Not exactly, no, but you don't have to imagine some underhanded maneuver on Jim's part."

"I am not necessarily talking about Jim. But there was always somebody behind him."

"Fritz the Kat . . ."

"Exactly. And you wouldn't put underhanded maneuvers past him, would you?"

"Definitely not. But my point is that there is a simpler explanation."

"Like . . ."

"Like Stanley never got over being turned down for the vice-chancellor job. The last year he was there, he was just going through the motions. On top of that, he probably felt insulted that the chancellor had sicced some consultant on him. And it must have burned him that Jim was so much more energetic. He probably went to his financial adviser, found out that he could live quite comfortably on his pension and investments, and figured, the hell with Pequeno. I would have done the same. And I'll tell you something else that proves Hartbridge did not get him fired. Somebody, I don't remember who, but someone trustworthy, told me that Hartbridge offered him a job as soon as they knew he was quitting."

"How interesting! They offered me a job when I quit too."

"Did they? I never knew that. But they didn't get you fired, did they?"

"Not technically. But I've always wondered whether all the headaches I endured after Jim left were not deliberately inflicted by them."

"You mean they were trying to force you to resign? Because you were not going along with their games?"

"Yes."

"But why would they offer you a job in their company then?"

"Probably to conciliate me, so that if I ever filed a lawsuit for wrongful termination, they wouldn't be named in it. I am sure they knew that I wouldn't take them up on their offer."

"Sounds pretty sneaky . . . But in any case Jim was gone by then, so it couldn't have been his fault."

"You're right, it couldn't have been his fault . . ." Grace concedes, inwardly limiting the concession to her own case, for she is far from sure of Jim's innocence in the matter of Stanley's retirement. In fact, later events proved that their beloved boss had no compunctions about sacking people without cause when it served his company's interests. However, Mina knows nothing about that part of the story, and Grace would not dream of enlightening her.

For all her best intentions, Grace's attempt to clear Jim's character is not quite successful. Mina picks up the note of mental reservation in her voice and becomes uneasy. The detour to see Jim was her idea, and she wonders if in her eagerness, she didn't force Grace to revisit a past she would rather have forgotten. She spends some time adjusting her jacket, which slipped down when she turned on her side, and resumes:

"You're not having second thoughts about visiting Jim, are you? Are you scared to see him sick?"

"A little . . ."

"Don't be. If you need strength, you'll find it. Anyway, he is going to pull through, you'll see, like he did the first time. Don't you remember how he used to stomp down the corridor with his thumbs hooked up in his suspenders, making the walls vibrate, and he would holler . . ."

"Howdy, y'all, it's hot out there. Looks like a fine day to get some work done inside!"

"Exactly. That man is not going to give up the ghost. So let's have faith, that's how we can help him, now."

"You're right, as always."

"Not always, but often enough, as I tell Tarik. And now let's get some sleep, shall we?"

And with this Mina turns towards the wall, fusses with the covers one more time, and becomes stone still. But Grace lies awake for a long time afterward.

She remembers the corridor at Pequeno. A gloomy tunnel, its bare walls still stained yellow from the ancient days when, unbelievably, smoking was allowed in offices, the op-art pattern of the carpet optimistically designed to hide dirt—an effective ploy, as it turned out, since you got so dizzy at first glance that you averted your eyes from it forever after. Most of the doors on each side locked, those that were not offering glimpses of unfriendly faces, the faces of people Grace did not really wish to know. And pervading all this, a quiet so dense that it seemed to press against your rib cage, to paralyze your brain cells. Abandon all hope, ye who enter here. This was how Grace had felt every morning when she got to work for her first two years at the district.

Her bike locked, her hair shaken free from her helmet, she would still feel fit and rosy from her ride, already working on a neat piece of code in her head. As soon as she opened the door, however, her mood would plummet. She would tiptoe through Tiffany's security airlock to punch herself in, hoping not to get scolded for some error in her paperwork. By Wei and Rajiv's usually still empty cubicles. And then head down, breath held, eyes squeezed shut, until she turned on her computer and everything was all right again. But suddenly, without the benefit of new paint or carpeting or colleagues, the corridor became bright and cheery. This was the first change Jim made when he was appointed interim CIO by the Board of Trustees. He infused the place with his energy.

After the pleasant surprise of their first encounter, Grace had more or less put the new consultant out of her mind. For one she was busy, and for another Stanley had made clear that the consultant's mission was none of the staff's responsibility. But as Jim occupied the office next to hers, she had been forced to notice that if nothing else he was a hard worker—a quality that always compelled her respect. Without ever trying, she had come to identify his car—always the same gold behemoth, how did he manage this feat of rental consistency?—from the fact that it was often the only vehicle in the parking lot when she arrived in the morning, and always the last one when she left. And while he was in the office, he didn't waste any time on the posturing and backslapping she would have expected from his type. Mostly he seemed intent on getting a clear and objective picture of the department's portfolio—an unexceptionable goal, after all. Yet from the reactions of her coworkers to his inquiries, you would have thought he was trying to pry state secrets out of them.

Time and time again, she found herself lending an ear to his frustrating exchanges with them. It seemed there were as many ways to blow him off as there were distinct personalities in the department. Wei and Rajiv suddenly lost all command of the English language. Sandip, Josh, Erin and Sandra exhibited the manic distraction of staff under too much work pressure. Tiffany politely insisted that all questions to her be put in writing. Ruby flirted shamelessly in between aggressive professions of ignorance. Elmore went off on endless anecdotal tangents that invariably showed him in a flattering light without providing any useful information. And Mina was shyer than ever.

Through all their rebuffs, Jim remained courteous, patient, even funny, but inwardly he was bound to be disheartened. On top of that, since his company was located in Florida, he must be far from friends and family, of whom however not a single sign could be discerned: no pictures on his desk, no phone call after hours. The poor guy must feel lonely.

So it was essentially out of a sense of fairness and empathy that she encouraged his overtures: a friendly smile when they ran into each other in the corridor, a few observations on the Central Valley climate around the water cooler, a longer set of questions about the student system, smoothly cast from her doorway one evening. Still, she was quite a bit surprised the first time he actually sat in her office, and even more that he should ask for her help on one of his projects. When he explained that it consisted in creating a dashboard for the chancellor, her initial reaction was to be irritated at the political nature of his priorities. Hard worker he may be, but not above brown-nosing. As she had nothing to lose by being frank with him, she let him know how she felt. He surprised her again by not taking offense at her criticism. On the contrary he looked as if he was stimulated by it. She instantly relaxed in the belief that she could be herself with him. This sense of freedom would remain at the core of her relationship with him—but probably not of his with her.

As soon as they started brainstorming the dashboard, she made another discovery: he was a kick as a work partner. Smart, creative, not afraid of a laugh. Plus he had a ton of experience, and the sang-froid that came from it. Without his calm presence, she would have lost it during the demo to the chancellor when all the graphs turned caption-less. And he gave her credit for her work in front of Akecheta and in front of Stanley, as he had promised.

Now that she thinks about it, it was amazingly gracious on Stanley's part to congratulate her for a project executed at a consultant's behest. In fact, she sees now that it was wrong for her to bypass his permission, even if the project did not interfere with her other duties, and even if she usually made her own assignments. By working for Jim, she was unwittingly undermining her official boss. Jim himself must have understood this. Perhaps this is what he intended.

She remembers being disturbed by a cryptic glint in Stanley's eyes as he shook her hand over the dashboard success. Wistfulness or schadenfreude? Had he already given up on his managerial prerogatives, or did he foresee that Grace would become the consultant's fool?

She was not really shocked to hear of Stanley's imminent retirement a few days later. As Mina just put it, for the last year he had merely been going through the motions. She felt sad for him, aware that men his age often took retirement as a harbinger of death, but relieved at the thought that the guerilla warfare he had enlisted the staff into waging against Jim would come to an end, that Jim would at last be able to get things done. Sure enough, Jim was soon named as Stanley's replacement.

The only drawback to the new management structure, as far as she was concerned, was that Jim would want to move to Stanley's old office at the other end of the building. She would miss having him as a neighbor. Oddly, though, he declined that privilege, and after getting Tiffany to open all the locked doors, he settled on the office across from his old closet, so that he now sat kitty corner from Grace.

The room Jim selected was a little smaller than Stanley's office, but otherwise similarly laid out, the building having been designed in more democratic days when managers did not feel they had to assert their status by having windows on two sides. And its furnishings were not much shabbier. Like the old-school manager he was, Stanley had made do with the same equipment as his staff: green metal desk, green metal shelves and cabinets. On his desk, aside from the usual family snapshots, neat piles of bulging manila folders, and an in-and-out basket that was never used, Tiffany preferring to let Stanley extract his own mail from the rubber band-bound batch delivered every morning, the most prominent object had been a hardware repair toolbox. In retrospect, Grace wonders whether his very frugality and handiness may not have ruined his chances of being promoted to a vice-chancellor position.

Several explanations for Jim's choice of office circulated at the time. Tiffany claimed that Jim was allergic to the fumes of the copier that stood just outside Stanley's office. Ruby gave him credit for respecting Stanley's memory. Elmore suspected that Stanley's office was reserved for Hartbridge's president, a man by the name of Fritz Applefield, who would shortly arrive on the scene, according to him. Much later, Jim would explain to Grace how his walking back and forth the length of the building allowed him to keep an eye on the staff. "Management-by-walking-around, the eggheads call it," he concluded with one if his winks. "A fancy way of saying when the cat's away, the mice are gonna play."

The second change Jim made was to institute regular staff meetings. Grace was delighted. At her previous job with a small venture company in Berkeley, taskforces would form themselves as needed around each project. They would meet to kick around ideas, develop project plans, divvy up tasks, check on progress, celebrate accomplishments. Everyone was young, smart, and considered work a major occasion for fun. Software development would naturally segue into nerf ball games, happy hour drinks, sometimes even clubbing. It was a blast while it lasted. On the other hand, the company had gone bankrupt, had even failed to meet its last payroll. When she had seen the ad for the Pequeno job on Craigslist, Grace had jumped at the chance of a steady paycheck for as long as she wanted it. Besides, at that point, she was only too glad to leave Berkeley, where she was having boy trouble.

When she arrived in the conference room for the first staff meeting, Jim was already there, his jacket off, his shirt sleeves rolled up, his red suspenders blazing. He had seated himself at the end of the conference table, unlike Stanley, who, at the three or four meetings he had convened in the last two years, would always pick one of the side chairs—a gesture of humility that unfortunately did not result in the staff taking more initiative. Jim, clearly, had no problem with being in charge.

"Where is everybody?" he asked in his booming, genial voice, after checking the wall clock, and seeing that the room was still half-empty.

"Well, Tiffany has to watch the door, Mina is running some urgent jobs, Sandra is out on campus," Elmore volunteered. "And Alex is uncomfortable in meetings."

"Tell you what. Ruby, can you call Sandra on her cell phone, tell her to get her butt over here unless she is fixing the Chancellor's machine? I'll go fetch the others. Visitors and reports can wait for half an hour."

Elmore cleared his throat. "I think you should know that Alex has a condition that makes it very difficult for him to be in a room full of people," he enunciated in a supercilious whisper. His chest was puffed up, his eyes had that cold, pointed look he got when his authority was challenged. He reminded Grace of a rooster fighting for his harem.

"I'm sure Alex can tell me if that's the case, but we ain't a scary bunch, are we?" Jim answered without lowering his voice. A few minutes later the entire team was assembled around the table. Other than Grace, the only person to have brought writing material was Jim. He looked the group over, a gleam of satisfaction mingled with curiosity in his keen green eyes. It was nice to see such confidence.

"OK, I've asked you in here," he started, grabbing the table in both hands. The table rocked from end to end. "Holy smoke!" he interrupted himself, "This table is wobbly! We gotta get it fixed." From then on, this would be the way he started each meeting, though he never did anything to get the table fixed. When Grace finally asked him what he meant by this weird opening, he claimed it was a trick designed to overcome his natural shyness. Grace did not believe him.

He had convened the meeting to explain that he would be serving as interim CIO until a permanent one could be hired, that this may take a while, and that in the meantime he expected the IT department to accomplish great things. He wanted to start by asking for the team's input on what they saw as the department's most urgent needs.

The staff squirmed on their seats. They were all wearing their official rank and file masks: backs hunched, eyes lowered, mouths primly closed, a conspiracy of respectful resistance. Even Elmore was quiet, having lost his first cock fight.

"Don't y'all talk at the same time!" Jim joked. Still no one opened their mouths.

"There must be one little thing somebody can think of," he persisted. "Just blurt it out. We're among friends."

It was Mina who finally came to his aid. When she raised a bangle-adorned arm, it seemed at first that she only wanted to re-twist her hair knot, but as Jim followed her movement with his eyes, it took on a more decisive aspect. For a few seconds Mina merely sat with her hand in the air, during which time Jim's gaze settled on her face with a soft-focus benevolence perfectly calibrated to melt her shyness. Soon, she was lowering her arm and opening her mouth.

"I would like to have some help in the computer room," she piped up in her tiny voice. "It's not so much that I have too much to do, but I am afraid what would happen if I got sick. I mean, Ruby is trained to operate all the mainframe equipment, but that's not her job."

"So, Ruby, you're trained as a computer operator?" Jim asked brightly, turning the full force of his charm on her. "I was a computer operator at one time . . ."

"In Saudi Arabia, right? Hey, maybe *you* can fill in for Mina when she's out sick." Ruby laughed, flipping a strand of limp hair to underscore the playfulness of her answer. She was flirting, but she was also letting him know that she did not consider computer operations a part of her current job description.

"You bet I could," Jim answered without missing a beat. "OK, then, first item: op-er-a-tion-al re-dun-dan-cy," he said, making a show of writing it down on his legal pad.

After Mina had broken the ice, other members of the staff came up with improvement ideas. Sandra made a case for better backup tools for the Windows servers. Sandip talked about hiring a quality assurance person. Wei needed a Mac to test Web applications on that platform, so he could return his wife's machine to her. Elmore argued for team building activities such as staff lunches. Tiffany clamored for new office furniture. Even Alex had an idea for recycling PCs. As to Grace, she suggested making financial data available on the Intranet the way student and personnel data already were. In hindsight, she sees what a mistake that was: she had stepped on Elmore's turf.

Jim took down all the requests, and assigned each requestor the task of finding out what it would take to make them happen. There would be another meeting in two weeks, at which point they would all report their findings. He asked that the reports be put in writing so they could be shared. He himself would shortly email the action items from the current meeting. As he told Grace later, he was modeling desirable behavior, another tenet of management philosophy that he preferred to call "Monkey see, monkey do".

And for a while, it worked. At the next meeting, everyone came equipped with a legal pad or laptop, if not necessarily with a completed assignment. Within a month, the IT department had acquired two Macs for application testing and faculty support, a plan to backup all the Windows servers had been drawn up, new desks and chairs for everyone were on order, two work-study students had been recruited to help Mina, and a staff lunch had been scheduled. A miracle of productivity. And a new perspective for Grace on some of her colleagues.

Tiffany, for instance, had run with the furniture assignment, combing online catalogs, cajoling vendors into promising major discounts, polling the staff on their preferences. She had got the three required bids, obtained the Vice-Chancellor's OK to charge the purchase against Measure F bond funds, pushed the purchase order through accounting—no mean feat in itself—all in record time. Even her personality seemed to have changed: instead of irritated glances and huffy responses, she greeted administrative requests from staff—especially Jim—with helpful alacrity. It made you believe in people's ability to change.

But it was Mina who surprised Grace the most. Until then, they had had minimal dealings with each other. Mina did her job so well that it was invisible. And anyway, her job was not that highly skilled, as far as Grace knew. She had not yet come to see, as she does now, that there is little correlation between the actual demands of a job and its rate of pay. So she was thoroughly impressed with Mina's presentation on the "redundancy" problem.

As Mina explained, hiring another mainframe operator was more or less impossible at that point. For one the hiring process took too long, and for another, it seemed there were no mainframe operators left to hire in the US. But the financial aid office at the campus was always looking for work-study placements, and there were plenty of students who would jump at the chance of getting their foot in the IT door, no matter how unglamorous the actual position. Mina would take care of training them, and if they turned out well, they could be hired as temporary employees, and then made permanent. Jim himself thought it was a great idea.

The staff lunch on the other hand was a little disappointing. Elmore made a valiant effort to revive bits of Pequeno folklore, but Ruby being the only employee old enough to remember any of it, it failed to inspire a new congeniality. And Jim, preoccupied by something that day, did not help much.

Grace had feared that as Jim was now her boss, their occasional chats at the end of the day would cease, that their relationship would be more constrained. But the chats continued, if anything more relaxed now that they had a future. There was always business to discuss, but other topics cropped up here and there: politics (Grace gathered that Jim was a Republican), religion (he was a Christian . . .), music (Country of course . . .), movies (Ocean's Eleven and The Bourne Supremacy), his family in North Carolina (a wife and two grown kids that he didn't see very often). On the face of it, a complete hillbilly. So how come they got along so well? It was an unfathomable mystery.

She no longer saw him as a Santa Claus type. After all, he was no older than her own father would have been if he were alive. As to his girth, he would certainly have benefited from losing thirty pounds or so, but the weight was well distributed—not an ounce of flab on that man. In any case, he was so unselfconscious about his appearance—and so well dressed—that he could pass for handsome. But the most salient trait of his physical persona was his signature aftershave, a potent blend of musk and roses that remained suspended in the air for hours after he left. He had obviously never heard of scent sensitivity. Oddly, Grace found that she rather enjoyed that retro smell. It must have been some sort of behavioral conditioning: whenever she became aware of the aftershave, some form of stimulation was sure to follow. Come to think of it, the aftershave was probably the key to the corridor's makeover.

In spite of their differences, she had come to like him very much. And he seemed to like her well enough too, or he wouldn't have spent so much time in her office shooting the breeze. For an alpha male, he was remarkably tolerant of her inclination to speak her mind in front of him: to question his objectives, to challenge his plans, to criticize his carbon footprint. Is it just that he never took her seriously?

Underneath the sass, Grace did take Jim seriously. It was a real joy working for someone who not only knew what he was doing, but did not hesitate to take action, someone who faced every day with hope and courage. That was all real, she is still sure. He has taught her so much, including a lot that she is going to use in her new job. What would he think if he knew it will serve the cause of getting a Democrat elected President? Not that she intends to tell him. No political discussion, Mina has ordered.

Suddenly, she is overcome by compassion. This beautiful man, yes, beautiful, no matter what else may be true, what is left of him? How can he stand the idleness, the powerlessness? How does he face the prospect of complete annihilation? And how can Grace and Mina help, since, as Mina has reminded her, this is their mission? If you need strength, you will find it. Grace hopes that's true.

Hartbridge had proposed a three-year contract. But because of fierce opposition from the unions and some members of the Board, the uproar having made headlines all the way to the Sacramento Bee, a one-year, two-full-time-equivalent contract was enacted instead. One FTE was reserved for the Chief Information Officer position—that was Jim—the other was supposed to be allocated in rotation to various experts, "per District priorities and decisions". In fact, from the start, the priorities and decisions were entirely left to Hartbridge.

A few weeks after the signature of the contract, the first Hartbridge "expert" arrived. He was so unmemorable that Grace can't recall his name or appearance. In her memory, he figures only as So-and-So.

His charge was to conduct a "gap analysis" of Pequeno's administrative software suite, in other words determine the differences between what the student, personnel and financial systems did, and what the users wanted them to do. He showed Grace a list of questions several hundred pages long. Many of the questions turned out to be irrelevant for a community college, and many others plain incomprehensible. It was the first of the boiler-plate "proprietary" documents from Hartbridge that Grace encountered. The expert was planning to distribute the questionnaire to various user groups for their input. All he needed from Grace, he said, was a list of the main student users. She gave him the names of all her customers, but warned him that they may balk at completing the questionnaire. He brushed her off as if her opinions were of no consequence.

That evening, Grace walked over to Jim's office. It was the first time she sought him out. Until then, he had been the one doing the visiting. She found him hunched over his Hartbridge laptop. His necktie was loose, his shirt was wrinkled, his hair slightly disheveled. He looked weary, in fact a little deflated. Grace was surprised. As far as she could tell, everything was going gangbusters in the IT department. For the first time, she felt a hint of concern for his health.

He raised his eyes from the keyboard.

"Graaace . . ." he drawled, in an ambiguous tone in which you could read either irritation or relief.

"Are you in a bad mood?" she blurted out. "I can come back later . . ."

"Today or tomorrow, you're gonna let me have it either way," he grumbled. "So, shoot."

"You sure?"

"Go ahead."

"I'd like to talk about this gap analysis document."

"What about it?" he snapped.

This was not very encouraging.

"And sit down. You're giving me a sore neck."

Grace pulled up a chair and sat on the edge of it across his desk. Jim leaned back, rolled his neck, cracked his knuckles, put his feet up on the desk.

"Better?" she asked.

"Much better."

Grace forged ahead. She told him she didn't think that the gap analysis document was appropriate for Pequeno. She feared that users would not know how to complete it on their own, and would end up bringing it to her. She was trying to be tactful, but she must have conveyed her doubts about the expert's qualifications for the task, because the first thing out of Jim's mouth was an apology for him.

"Give So-and-So a chance," he said. "He is new on the job."

A new expert. Now there was an oxymoron. If Jim had not been so uncharacteristically down, she would have voiced her sarcasm. As it was, she swallowed it.

"Anyway," Jim continued, "the point of the exercise is not to get a complete list of desired functionalities. The point is to get our customers to start taking ownership of their systems. After all, they're the ones who should be responsible for program specifications. By spoon-feeding them, you have made it too easy for them to know nothing and do nothing. The result is that the IT department gets no respect for all its great work. We're gonna change that."

What he said made sense. All the same, as Grace had predicted, within a month all her users would trickle back to her office, begging her to complete the questionnaire for them. She didn't have the heart—or the authority—to say no. She spent many hours compiling answers, and turned the completed spreadsheet over to So-and So. Soon afterwards he was replaced by another "specialist", and the document was never heard of again.

But that evening, Grace was simply glad to see that Jim looked more relaxed after winning the argument.

"OK, I'll let you get back to work," she said, standing up.

"I'm too tired to get back to work," he answered somewhat languidly. "But what else is there to do around here?"

He seemed to be fishing for an entertainment idea.

"Go for a walk?" she proposed.

"In this heat? It's like an oven out there." It must have been July, by then.

"It's not that bad. It's nearly seven o'clock. And there is a shaded walk along the canal just behind the data center. It's very nice at this time of day."

"How do you get to it? This place is surrounded by a barbed-wire fence."

"There is a security gate in the fence. Would you like me to show you?"

"You got a deal," he answered, jumping out of his chair.

And so they took their first walk along the canal . . .

This will not do. If she continues on this trip down memory lane, she is never going to fall asleep. Time to switch to her alphabet game, a variation on counting sheep that she finds more effective. Tonight, let the category be . . . adjectives describing positive human attributes:

Astute . . . brave . . . courteous . . . daring . . . effective . . . funny . . . garrulous . . . honorable . . . intelligent . . . just . . . kind . . . levelheaded . . . mature . . . natty . . . optimistic . . . philosophical . . . quick . . . resourceful . . . shrewd . . . tenacious . . .

She is out.

VI

ENTHUSIASTIC

"No way we're going to make Nashville tonight . . ." sighs Grace.

"It's OK. I warned Jim it might take us five days."

"But I emailed him last night that we were aiming for Nashville today."

"So, we'll email him again . . . He said he would be home both Friday and Saturday."

"But what about your flight back?"

"Not till Sunday afternoon. It's an hour and a half from Greensboro to Raleigh, so we can even stay in Greensboro on Saturday night. That'll give us plenty of time to visit, even have that Southern meal that Jim has talked about. And your job doesn't start until Monday, right? So, we're good."

"OK, let me revise our itinerary," says Grace, fishing her BlackBerry out of her backpack.

They are three hours behind schedule, and it's pretty much all Grace's fault, a fact Mina has kindly refrained from pointing out. Unlike Grace, Mina was not trained to say what she thinks. Lately, Grace has started to appreciate the merits of verbal reserve. She has figured out that "respect, empower, include", the Obama campaign motto, sometimes requires keeping your mouth shut, even if you already have all the answers. It feels hypocritical, at times, and even a little disrespectful, to listen gravely while people go off on tangents or hear themselves speak. But there is something else nestled in that patience, aside from its strategic usefulness: a kind of peace, a recognition that she does not have to bear the entire burden of the conversation. On the other hand, you can take the strong, silent attitude a little too far, as Mina herself recognizes in the case of her "twilight zone" period.

The day started badly and went from there. First, they overslept, the alarm on Grace's BlackBerry having failed to go off. It seems that Grace had set the timer, but forgotten to activate the alarm. Not wanting to appear paranoid, Mina had not set the alarm on her own BlackBerry. "Well, at least we got a good night's sleep!" Mina commented, stretching her arms overhead as Grace frantically jumped out of bed.

Their bags packed, they made their way downstairs, where they had been promised a continental breakfast. What they found instead of a dining room was a corner of the lobby set with one rickety folding table, four rickety folding chairs, and a rolling cart laden with a coffee thermos, an empty jug of orange juice, an near empty carton of milk, two types of sugary, artificially flavored cereals, and a couple of donuts leaking Rorschach blots of grease on their cardboard box. There was also a big bowl of the usual tiny packets of "grape jam", which, there being no bread, must have been provided for the sole purpose of smearing on table and chairs. Some brave soul had obviously risen to the challenge, as every surface was sticky. On top of that there was no tea. Grace now understood why the night before, the receptionist had oddly touted the breakfast fare at a nearby coffee shop as an alternative to the motel's offerings. Mina would have made do with a cup of black coffee and a donut, but Grace could not stomach the idea. So they had to drive to the coffee shop, where the fare was indeed as good as advertised, with the unfortunate consequence that it was crowded, and it took them half an hour to get served.

Then Grace realized that they were out of fresh fruit. Mina suggested Walmart, whose red, white and blue sign towered over the skyline a few blocks away. Grace recoiled in horror. Mina remarked that even Walmart these days offered organic produce, but that wasn't the point, according to Grace. The point was the Walton family making billions on the back of their workers, who were paid so little that they were encouraged by management to apply for food stamps, and were prevented from joining a union. Unlike the health food mania, which seemed mere neurosis to Mina, the class warfare argument resonated with her. Her own father started as a bracero and was later involved with United Farm Workers. In any case, they lost another hour finding a politically correct grocery store. But now, a whole bag of incomparable organic California Navel oranges is sitting on the back seat of the car. And it turns out that Grace's insistence on organic food is not strictly a privileged middleclass obsession. Mina has just learned how, for instance, hormones fed to cows to increase milk production result in udder infections which then have to be treated with antibiotics, which end up in the milk, which contributes to the growth of antibiotics resistant bacteria, not to mention misery for the cows. Breasts filled with pus. Yuk! She has made a mental note to buy organic milk for Steven from now on, no matter how much more it costs.

"OK, how about this? We stop around Memphis tonight. It's six hours from Memphis to Knoxville, and five hours from Knoxville to Greensboro. So tomorrow, we can visit Memphis, and the day after, we can drive through the Smoky Mountains in daylight, and get to Greensboro in time for an early dinner. This way we will work in a little tourism, for your first time east of the Sierras. So far the landscape has been pretty much a non-event, don't you think? Although, to be fair, we drove through the few picturesque parts in the dark."

"I agree, not much to look at since we left California. But you know, I don't mind. It's the drive I love, the feeling of distance, of freedom. And night time driving is the best, especially in the desert, don't you think? Complete darkness, the headlights seeming to make the road ahead spring into existence out of nothing, like a miniature creation. After a while, all my usual worries fly out the window like . . . like dollar bills escaping from the bank robber's bag . . ."

"Nice image," says Grace, reminded of all the cash that must have flown out of Mina and Tarik's hands in the last few years, all for nothing, apparently, since they no longer live in the big house she was so proud of. Mina seems to be at peace with her altered circumstances. How interesting. A lesson for America? For if Jason is right, the economic situation is about to get much worse. According to Jason, who, as a rising star in Barack's economic team should know what he is talking about, so many financial institutions are sitting on paper derived from bad mortgages that the recent Bear Stearns debacle is soon going to look like a picnic.

"And now," Mina declares, "I call the Jim Wright's fan club meeting to order. What's your favorite memory?"

"Of Jim?" Grace asks with some reluctance.

"I mean," Mina corrects herself, suddenly aware that her question may have sounded too personal, "of the good times we had when Jim was our boss. We did have good times as a team then, didn't we?"

"Yes, we did. One thing for sure, he knew how to motivate people."

"I know! He was a real leader, that's what I liked best about him."

"So, what's *your* favorite memory of Jim's leadership?" Grace enquires, once more throwing Mina's questions back to her, an evasion Mina fails to notice, eager as she is to rekindle her friend's enthusiasm toward their ex-boss with a well-chosen story.

"That time when the burster broke down, I think."

"That's a good one."

"Mind you, it was bound to happen. The last time the repairman came to fix it before that, he told me it was so old he could no longer find parts for it."

"Stanley was going to get a new one, right?"

"But then Stanley quit, and I didn't want to bother Jim. He had so much on his plate as it was."

"And of course, the burster decided to quit too on the day we were scheduled to print the student registration cards for the fall term."

"So there I was. Ten thousands cards printed . . ."

"Twenty-five thousands, actually, since we sent them to any student that had registered within the last five terms."

"You're right. I forgot. Anyway, there I was with four boxes of registration cards to separate before five o'clock, and no machine to do it. I was in a panic. Plus, I was afraid it was my fault that the burster wasn't working, that I had set it up wrong for that kind of paper . . ."

"You mean cardboard, the thick, slick kind used for wedding invitations. Guaranteed to give you paper cuts."

"And the perforated lines around the cards were not much help either, as I found out. I mean, it would have taken a Sumo wrestler to compete with that two-ton machine, not a person with no upper-body strength, like me, no matter how much I swim. But I was so afraid of calling attention to my mistake that I started tearing the cards by hand anyway. Of course, after a while I realized I was never going to get the job done by myself, so I asked Hui and Lin to help."

"Even with three people, there's no way you could have managed it."

"We must have been at it for half an hour when Jim waltzes into the computer room by chance, and he sees the mess: boxes of uncut cards, cards lying half-torn on the burster, piles of cards on the table and cards scattered on the floor, and the three of us with hair falling into our eyes, sweat dripping from our faces, arms covered with ink, trying to tear the frigging cards apart. And he says . . ."

"Doggone it! It's like the old plantation in here. What's wrong with the burster?"

"That's right. How did you know? You were at the other end of building at that point."

"Are you kidding? Lin and Hui told that story for months afterwards."

"Ah, of course . . . So he rolls up his sleeves, and he tries to fix the burster himself. After fifteen minutes of fiddling with it, and shredding a bunch of registration cards in the process, he sees that it's useless, which at least made me feel like I wasn't a total idiot. So he goes out to my platform, and he hollers . . ."

"All hands on deck over here. We got a problem that calls for teamwork."

"And let me tell you, with that forceful voice of his, he didn't have to say it twice. Wei and Sandra and Rajiv popped out of their cubicles right away, and then you showed up, with Elmore at your heels. Even Ruby got off her butt, I couldn't believe it."

"Yeah, but all she did was to plant herself at the door with her arms crossed on her chest, offering moral support, she said, since her carpel tunnel prevented her from helping us any other way. As if . . . Anyway, it was Elmore, I think, who figured how to fold several pages back and forth until they were easy to separate . . ."

"Pretty soon, remember, we had a little assembly line going: Jim, Elmore and Wei were folding and tearing out chunks of pages, I was distributing them to you and Sandra and Hui so you could separate individual cards, and Lin was bundling them with rubber bands. In the end we finished the job by four thirty, and we were all pretty jazzed."

"That's when Jim invited us for drinks at the Dark Room café for the first time . . ."

"And Sandip asked to come, even though he hadn't done anything, and Jim said sure, he was such a nice guy . . ."

"All in the name of team building . . . He was ever the optimist . . ."

"So were you," Mina remarks a little sharply.

"So I was," Grace sighs in response.

"In the end, everybody came along except Alex. We had a ball, didn't we? Rajiv, Sandip, Josh and Wei played darts, remember, and Ruby sang along a Michael Jackson tune on the Karaoke box. We were all a little tipsy, I think."

"Except Jim. Even after two drinks, you could see the wheels in his brain spinning. It was that night that he proposed to offload the whole student registration card process to a printing company. As a matter of fact, I had already thought of it, but I was afraid you would not like the idea of outsourcing one of your tasks. But all you said was 'Go ahead, make my day'. You, quoting Clint Eastwood. It was unreal. You must have been more than a little tipsy."

"So you said you would look into it . . ."

"And when I talked to Roger, he was all for it. The next week, we met with a representative from a printing company that had done several mailings for us in the past, and taking all the factors into account, we found that the printing company could produce the registration cards on nice colored stock with graphics and mail them for less money than we had spent doing the job ourselves. It was one case when outsourcing was the right solution: it cost less, and did not put anybody out of a job."

"By the way, we are still using the job you wrote to create a disk file instead of printing the cards. Until the migration is complete . . . I bet it's going to take another five years. The way I see it, my job is secure. Anyway, I am taking a class in Oracle DBA next Fall."

VII

EFFECTIVE

In retrospect, it seems to Jim that the burster incident was the high point of his Pequeno stint. Just an old-fashioned four-alarm fire, but the team had come together to put it out, and then a long-term technological solution had been devised, written and implemented in record time. And he had been in the thick of it, getting his hands dirty as in his days as data center manager—a real manager, he wants to say. The days before "leadership", "vision" and "strategic thinking" became the fig leaves regularly thrown over boondoggles or complete inaction. Before politics became the name of the game. At heart, he realizes, he was always an engineer type. "Build a better mouse trap" business executives used to be advised. Jim spent much of his life building better mouse traps, only to end up stranded in the hall of mirrors of the "post-industrial world", a world where everyone is a middleman between two other middlemen, and all that is produced is "information". It is true that he hadn't come by this insight when he accepted Fritz's offer, but even if he had, he would still have taken the job, because he needed the money. This is how pacts with the devil are made.

He recalls the summer of 2005, the heat strangely muggy for a place that without irrigation would have been a desert, and even so he was aware of a spring in his step every day when he entered the insufficiently air-conditioned data center.

It was a pleasure to see Mina take in hand the two little Asian girls sent by the Financial Aid Office, and Tiffany make time in her busy real estate schedule to get acquainted with the help desk ticketing system. At the very least, the IT department was finally going to be able to account for the time spent supporting PC users. But Jim was also hoping to use the new software to keep track of programming service requests. "Metrics," as Grace was fond of repeating whenever Jim broached the subject of accountability. It was a word she had learnt from him. At their first staff meeting, she had written it in capital letters, and then built a doodle of overlapping geometrical shapes around it on the whole page of her legal pad. He had not taken it as a putdown. As no one else had brought any writing material that day, he hadn't been able to see what they got out of the meeting.

Further down the hall, budget graphs popped up on Rajiv's screen. He was building the financial data web site under Elmore's guidance, which forced him to get out of his cubicle and practice his English. As to Elmore, he was clearly relishing his adviser role. Jim had noticed how patient and understanding Fuddy-duddy could be with people who knew less than he did.

Originally, Ruby had claimed the server backup project for herself, but after a couple of weeks, arguing that she could not find enough dedicated time to make headway in it, she had delegated it to Sandra. And Sandra, in a show of honesty that Jim appreciated, confessed that she was in over her head. In one of their nightly conference, Jim asked Fritz to recall the "systems migration specialist", a useless bozo parachuted on the scene as the contract-stipulated second FTE because nobody else was available at the time, and whom Grace has seen through in ten minutes. What Jim needed instead was a Windows backup expert. He had to stretch the truth a bit to get Fritz's attention, claiming that Pequeno's internal auditor, who reported directly to the Chancellor, had put a high priority on the project—as indeed he would have if he knew that mission critical servers were not currently being backed up. Miraculously, the next week, a new guy showed up, and his skills lived up to his resume.

His name was Rick, and he not only knew what to do, but he was good as explaining it. He took Ruby, Sandra and Alex under his wing, and within a month, backup software had been purchased and installed, and the five enterprise Windows servers were being automatically backed up daily. A restore process had even been tested and documented. It would turn out to be the last time Jim got his way with Fritz.

Meanwhile, every cubicle and office had been fitted with new furniture. The new desks were the L shape modular kind that are mounted against walls, with the keyboard tray set in the corner, so it became impossible for the staff to orient their monitors in such a way that no passerby could see their display. Jim was thus able to discover that what generally occupied Ruby was playing Solitaire. As the weeks went by, though, between the server tasks entrusted to her by Rick, and the PC support calls automatically assigned to her by the ticketing system, she found less and less time for computer games. Another advantage of the furniture makeover was that Mother Goose had been forced to dispose of the piles of stained papers and food incrusted dishes that had previously littered every surface in her office. Ruby expressed pride in her new environment and talked of a new beginning.

And of course there was Grace. You could throw any amount of work at her, and she would gobble it up like candy, then come back to ask for more. What boss wouldn't be thrilled? The flip side of her efficiency was her brutal honesty. But Jim didn't mind, in fact he enjoyed the challenge. Smart as she was, Grace lacked the wisdom that comes with experience. Every objection she raised to his way of doing things he saw as an opportunity to induct her into the more esoteric aspects of the IT business. She invariably grasped the point of his lessons. Mentoring her was very gratifying, and to a certain extent, it helped keep him honest. In one of their early conversations, she had brought out the issue of his having to serve two masters. He had responded with the stock argument that while he worked at Pequeno he worked for Pequeno. And whereas Stanley had refused to believe it, Grace had obviously wanted to. It was that trust that would later incite him to look for alternatives to the standard contract-sustaining projects mapped in Hartbridge's knowledge base.

"The truth," whispers his conscience, "is that dealing with Grace wasn't much of a challenge for you. Let's face it, she wasn't the first enthusiastic female to put her talents at your disposal. By summer, you knew you had your pet subordinate wrapped around your little finger. As to keeping you honest . . ."

But Jim objects to his conscience's harsh way of putting things. It seems to enjoy hacking away at the tendrils of feeling that inevitably weave themselves around professional relationships, and then it calls "truth" the decimated landscape. If things had been as simple as that, he argues, would I now be torturing myself trying to understand? Anyway, the pet subordinate turned out not to be altogether defenseless.

The first time Jim and Grace spent any time together outside of the office, it was at her suggestion. She had come into his office to slam the systems migration bozo. As was often the case, he had to fight the urge to laugh and tell her she had hit the nail on the head. And then, out of the blue, she told him about the trail that ran along the irrigation canal in the back of the data center, claiming that it was cool under the trees at that time of day. She seemed to be fishing for an invitation. He thought, what the heck, I could use the exercise.

He knew her well enough by then not to construe her offer as a seduction attempt. She was part of that new generation whose interactions with the other sex were remarkably free of erotic undertones. Jim often saw her peers on campus, mixed groups of young people joshing and arguing amicably as if the last thought on their mind was to score a date. It was refreshing. His own thoughts may not be as casual, but his actions were fully under his control.

As soon as they came out of the shade of the building, the heat fell on them like a ton of bricks. But by then, she was already holding the gate in the barbed wire fence open for him. She explained that she came in that way every day after riding her bike along the trail.

"Where are those trees you promised?" he asked.

"Oh! Just a couple hundred yards from here," she answered with a vague gesture of the arm, intimating that walking a couple hundred yards in that furnace was no big deal. A second later, though, she was wrenching herself out of her flimsy shirt and tying it around her hips. Underneath, she wore one of those camisoles with the bra built-in, pulled over a short cotton skirt with irregular pleats. Her legs were bare, her feet shod in clunky sandals. Perhaps as a concession to the weather, there was barely a touch of black in her outfit. The scarlet strands had washed out of her hair, replaced by dark auburn highlights that looked natural.

Grace walked ahead of Jim, turning back encouragingly every few steps. He found himself observing her with the curiosity of a zoologist faced with a new animal species. The first thing that struck him was that little Grace was in fact rather tall for a woman. Perhaps out of self-consciousness, she walked slightly hunched over, her head ahead of her body, her arms flailing, her legs swinging about with a sort of double-jointed gawkiness. For an athletic girl, her skin was surprisingly un-tanned. She must be as diligent with the sunblock as she was with her work assignments. And there was very little evidence of the muscles you would have expected to see on a bicyclist. Underneath a smooth layer of creamy flesh, Jim could discern the points of her shoulder blades, the miniature dunes of her vertebrae. Beads of sweat formed at her nape, were funneled down her question mark tattoo by the line of fine sunlit hairs that traced her spine, trickled lazily down her back, and disappeared into the yawning canyon of her camisole. He was transfixed.

"You know, we're out of the campus grounds now," she said, shaking him out of his contemplation. "You could take your shirt off. Nobody will care."

"It's OK," he answered, "I can see the trees now." He felt a little silly, but he could not face the idea of appearing in public in undershirt, dress pants and wingtips.

At the edge of the trees, Grace waited for Jim to catch up with her, and they went on side by side in the dappled shade. It was indeed much cooler now. A breeze was stirring the fronds, birds were waking up from their naps and issuing tentative tweets. There was a scent of cut grass in the air. The water in the canal flowed strong and silent. Jim inhaled, felt the buzzing circuitry of his purposeful mind seize up, then shift into idle mode.

"So, how long did you work in Saudi Arabia?"

"Off and on, fifteen years."

"Get out of here! Fifteen years?" she repeated, her blue eyes goggling with undisguised horror.

He guessed at the pictures she must have of the place: women shrouded from head to toe, walking five steps behind their men, forbidden to drive, ineligible to vote. How was he going to explain to her the magic it held for him? How, in fact, did he explain it to himself? Mentioning the hunting expeditions in the desert, the thrill of driving recklessly on empty roads, the distant sightings of primitive Bedouin encampments, the way all business stopped at the call of the Muezzin, or the intense sense of freedom he had found away from his marriage, none of this was going to pass muster with Grace.

She would be equally unimpressed with the financial advantages of working as an expat in the Gulf States: the big salaries, the tax exemptions, the free trips all over the world, the luxury of compound accommodations, a lifestyle he would never have had a chance to experience back home. So he found himself talking of Waheed.

"It's not that bad," he protested. "When you work there, you don't have many dealings with the locals. And given that most forms of entertainment are prohibited, you cultivate human relationships. In Saudi Arabia, I made friends, one of them the best friend I ever had. Waheed, a Palestinian from Lebanon who worked with me for a while at the IBM franchise in Riyadh. We used to get together after work and sit for hours at the terrace of a coffee shop, sipping tea and talking about everything. It wasn't like here, where conversations between guys don't stray too far from business, football and mortgages. We talked about love, we talked about literature, music, world affairs. It's pretty ironic, but whatever I know of Western Culture I owe to a so-called Arab. He lent me books, tapes, CDs, DVDs. Cervantes, Dostoevsky, E.M. Forster, John Kennedy Toole . . . Rear Window and Diva, Bach and Shostakovich . . ."

"Bach and Shostakovich? I thought you were strictly a Country Music kind of guy."

"Not strictly."

She burst out laughing, and then turned toward him, scrutinizing his face as if his features might reveal the tell-tale marks of an appreciation for classical music. He guessed that she managed to find them among the facial hair, that she was busy redrawing his picture on her mental sketch pad.

"Hey, I too have CDs I could lend you. Ever heard of Modest Mouse?"

"Modest Mouse?"

"My favorite Indie Rock group. Just kidding!"

"Why kidding? I might like it for all you know."

"For all I know you're the King of Norway. But I'm learning . . . And where is Waheed now? Have you stayed in touch?"

"He is back in Beirut right now, but he may come to San Francisco this fall."

"Then you've got to convince him to make a detour to see the world famous town of El Pequeno. It's culturally very sophisticated, as you know. We have Mexican food, we have Karaoke bars, we even have a movie multiplex."

"I suspect he'll take a pass."

"You're right. I would too."

She was just babbling, but Jim had taken note of her indirect offer to replace Waheed as a friend by lending him some CDs. He was touched, actually.

They walked all the way to a little kiddie park with a sand box and a jungle gym, where stocky Hispanic women chatted on benches while their tots built ephemeral forts or made themselves dizzy on the carrousel. Jim and Grace sat for a little while, not talking much, and then slowly turned back toward the data center while the sun set without fanfare. They went back in to grab their things and waited for each other under the awning.

"Alright, then," said Grace, adjusting her bike helmet.

"Alright, then," answered Jim, fingering his car keys. He held out his hand, and she shook it heartily.

Again, his conscience insists on being heard. "And what did *you* learn about Grace's personal life," it asks, "during the year when you saw her daily? When did *you* show an interest in her for herself, as opposed to how she could serve your objectives?"

There must have been a dispatching mix-up in Heaven. Jim's own conscience would know better than to make these kinds of accusations. It would remember that consultants are utterly constrained as to the amount of personal interest they can express toward a client's staff. And besides, where Jim comes from, asking personal questions is just not done. But in fact Jim did learn many things about Grace: that she earned both a B.A. and B.S. at some private college in Oregon, that she had only one job before the one at Pequeno, but Pequeno hired her as a Programmer/Analyst IV anyway because that was the only way they could pay her enough, that her father died when she was nineteen, that she liked Shostakovich's Preludes and Fugues and loved all of Bach. And he did care about her as a person. To his errant conscience, he submits the evidence of two separate occasions when he acted as a Good Samaritan to Grace.

It was some time after their first walk, but before Hurricane Katrina. Mina had left early to take her child to the doctor, and Jim had gone into the computer room to make sure the work-study trainees had properly mounted the tape cartridges for the nightly mainframe backup. When he came out, he had a sudden feeling that something was out of order. He looked around, and noticed that Grace was inside the security airlock with a man. She was leaning against the inner door, her hair mashed against the glass, her shoulders hunched, her hands knotted together behind her back. She looked as if she wished to be somewhere else altogether. The man, on the other hand, a dark young fella with the kind of face you see in soap operas, was slouching at ease within kissing range, ogling her with a contrite look so patently false that he would after all have flunked a Days of Our Lives audition. Protected from detection by the relative obscurity of Mina's area, Jim was just standing there, unsure what to do, when the guy reached out a hand toward Grace. Jim saw her flinch. In one leap, he was at the door.

"Ah! Grace. There you are," he cried out good-naturedly, loud enough to be heard through the glass by both of them.

Grace turned around. Jim opened the door and motioned her inside.

"The meeting is about to start, you know. And you, young man, will have to leave. This is a secure facility."

"Sorry," the guy said in an unconvinced tone, casually retreating toward the outer door. "I thought this was after hours." Then resuming his hang-dog look to address Grace: "Call me, OK, I am still at the old number. I'll be back there tonight."

Jim waited at the door till the guy left the building. When he turned around, Grace was right behind him. She was shivering.

"Thank you," she said. "An old boyfriend. I don't know how he tracked me down."

"Probably by googling you. Your name is on the IT staff list on the Pequeno Web site, remember?"

"Ah! Of course. I shouldn't have gone into the airlock, but he was ringing the bell incessantly. Didn't you hear it?"

"No, it's much too loud in the computer room to hear the bell. Anyway, I don't think you should ride your bike home today. He might follow you. I assume you don't want him to know where you live, right?"

"No!" she cried out in horror. Must have been *some* kind of boyfriend . . .

"Tell you what. Give me half an hour to wrap things up here, and then I'll drive you home."

"What about my bike?"

"It'll fit in the trunk of my car, I think. See the advantages of a gas guzzler?"

She rolled her eyes fondly, no longer afraid.

They left twenty minutes later. Jim was able to fit her bike in the trunk by removing the front wheel. Before driving off, he surveyed the parking lot and the adjacent street for any sign of the guy, and continued to check his rear view mirror throughout the trip to make sure they weren't being followed. They weren't.

Grace directed him to a modest residential district between the campus and what passed for a downtown in El Pequeno, a neighborhood of tidy clapboard bungalows impaled on American flags and dwarfed by huge sycamores. Grace lived in a cottage at the back of a larger house. Jim parked the car, lifted the bike out of the trunk and carried it through the side yard to her porch, where she re-assembled it, thanked him again and said goodbye. Jim ended the day in a downtown bar, drinking Scotch and watching reruns of Lance Armstrong winning the Tour de France while musing on a mystery: how a gawky, over-educated girl totally devoid of feminine wiles could have more admirers than a Southern Belle. The truth was, as pleased as he was with the progress he was making at work, he was getting lonely.

Another day around the same period, Grace was attempting to demonstrate to Jim that Pequeno's legacy student, personnel and financial applications were in fact integrated. Jim had dragged one of the guest chairs next to hers and straddled it, his elbows leaning against the chair back within an inch of her shoulders. She was logged on to the test system, and was showing him how assigning an hourly instructor to a class was automatically reflected in the instructors' payroll record and in the department's budget. She kept having to switch back and forth between several screens, which was a pain in the ass.

"Why don't you have two monitors like everyone else in the department?" he asked, faintly irritated.

"Everyone else has two monitors? I wasn't aware of it," she answered sheepishly.

"Yes, they do. Do me a favor, request a second monitor. We don't get any points with our customers by skimping on computer equipment."

"Oh, I don't know. I don't want to make waves. I'm sure the network people will get around to me when they have the time." She seemed uncharacteristically tentative.

"I have been here for nearly five months," Jim said. "I think it's time they made the time."

At that very moment, from the corner of his eye, Jim became aware that Ruby stood in the doorway. She had a hand on her hip, and was flipping her hair.

"Sorry to interrupt," she sang out. There was a sarcastic note in her voice. "My son got into a fight at school this morning. I've got to go talk to the principal—again. You know how it is with kids. Always . . ."

"Go ahead," Jim interrupted. Then, turning toward her: "And before you leave, would you make a note to set up a second monitor for Grace? It'll save me a world of aggravation, if nothing else."

"You the boss," Ruby replied coyly. But then, as she started moving away from the doorway, she added: "That is if there are any spare monitors left . . ."

"If there aren't, please have Tiffany order one. I'll sign for it."

"Okey dokey," came her breezy answer. She was already at the other end of the corridor.

Having recalled these two good deeds, Jim is waiting for his conscience to give a round of applause, but hears nothing. He is not going to get off that easily, he suspects.

A few days after Jim asked Ruby to set up a second monitor in Grace's office, he got a call from a certain Charlie Weissman, who introduced himself as the Business Representative for SEIU local

2545, the union that represented Pequeno's classified employees. Weissman requested an informal meeting "to introduce himself and air some staff concerns". Jim knew better than to reveal any anxiety by inquiring into the nature of these concerns right then and there. Instead, he proposed to meet over lunch at a taqueria not far from campus, his treat. The rep accepted.

In his entire career as a manager, Jim had never dealt with unions. They were certainly not part of the landscape in Saudi Arabia, but even in the US, IT personnel was rarely unionized. With his libertarian leanings, Jim was not inclined to look upon unions with a great deal of sympathy. On top of that, he was pretty sure Charlie Weissman was a Jew. His name, for one, but also his nasal New York accent. Jim had spent enough time in the Middle East to come to see Israel in a different light from that offered by American media: not the poor little country trying to survive in the midst of fanatical enemies, but a colonial power intent on getting rid of the natives by any means necessary. Waheed's own parents had been forced to flee their home and orchards. Fifty years later, while Jewish families despoiled in the Holocaust were able to recover their Swiss bank accounts and Impressionist paintings, Waheed's only inheritance was still the house key. And in Jim's experience, American Jews were rabid Zionists to a man.

He was therefore relieved, the next day, to feel an instant liking for the fella who bounded toward his table with his hand already extended, his open face lighting up the darkness of the restaurant, his casual attire: jeans, running shoes, and a plain tee-shirt, a further invitation to informality. In fact, because of his tightly curled hair of an indeterminate color, gray-blue eyes, narrow face and hooked nose, Charlie Weissman reminded him of Waheed. But even if he hadn't, Jim would have been prepared to give him a hearing. As much as he objected on general terms to certain opinions or character traits, he rarely wasted time actively disliking individuals. Like God, he thought he could find some use for everyone.

He got up and they shook hands.

"Have you ordered? Do we need menus?"

"No. Here's one. Please sit down."

Weissman jittered into his seat like a man on fire, took the menu, slapped it back on the table without looking at it.

"Thank you for agreeing to meet me on such short notice. This is not an official meeting, in fact, I'd like to keep it off the record, if it's OK with you."

"By all means. So, what can I do for you?" asked Jim, relaxing at the sheer sight of Weissman's nervous energy.

"First, I want to say that I've heard of lot of good things about you."

"You have? What kind of things, if that's not being too nosy?"

"Hmm . . . that you are a people person . . . that you are getting things done . . ."

"That'll do it. I appreciate the feedback. Any more and I would start blushing. So now that we've poured the honey, what kind of fly are we aiming to catch?"

Weissman laughed. He was quick on the uptake, for a union bureaucrat.

"Well, there are some concerns among the IT staff about an external consultant being put in a manager's position . . ."

"Go on."

"You see, strictly speaking, this kind of situation is prohibited by the union contract. I don't know if you are aware of it, but twenty some years ago, the IT function at Pequeno was contracted out. The staff was given a choice between being hired by the consulting company or getting laid off. Either way, they would lose all their benefits. And let's add that the consulting company had not endeared itself to the workers with its blitzkrieg tactics. This is when SEIU was called to the rescue. We've made sure ever since to include in every contract a provision against consultants managing classified staff."

"Well, now, you got me stumped. Did you talk to the Chancellor about this?"

"We will. But first, I thought we should give you a heads up, see if you would be amenable to a compromise. You may find it hard to believe, but the union does care about the welfare of the district at large."

"While you're working *at* Pequeno, you're working *for* Pequeno?"

Weissman laughed again.

"That's *your* playbook, isn't it? I wouldn't put it quite like that, but in any case *I* am sincere about it."

"So am I, I ask you to believe."

"I trust that you are. And this is why I am talking to you. You see, the union is quite aware that it's practically impossible to recruit qualified IT managers to come work at Pequeno for the salaries we can afford. From everything I hear, you seem to be highly qualified. We don't want to jeopardize the work of the IT department by making your life difficult. What we would like to see is for one of the department's vacant managerial positions to be filled internally, at least on an interim basis. This would give you cover and make the staff more comfortable. It would also solve another problem: Board policies prohibit external consultants from authorizing any expenditure. I know that to get things done, you need to be able to make small purchases without having to get the Vice-Chancellor's signature every time. If there is an internal manager on site, he/she can sign off on purchasing requests. How does it sound?"

"It sounds OK to me. I must say I am surprised, pleasantly surprised, not only by your candor, but by the union's willingness to cooperate with Hartbridge, especially given your past experience with consultants."

"Actually, it is with you personally that we are willing to cooperate."

"I am all the more honored. I am not sure I have the power to instigate the kind of hiring action you recommend, but I will look into it and let you know what I find . . . off the record, of course."

"Of course."

They shook hands, and Weissman was rising from his chair when the waitress showed up at their table. He had obviously forgotten about the meal. He sat back down with an embarrassed look, picked up the menu, opened it, slammed it shut again before he had time to read any of its offerings, and ordered randomly:

"Vegetarian burrito. Extra guacamole. No sour cream. Tap water."

They had a good time over lunch, leaving business aside, and instead talking about Lance Armstrong and Tiger Woods, world affairs and human nature. Charlie turned out to be a thoroughly disillusioned Zionist. He promised to take Jim fishing one of these days and Jim said he was counting on it. They were at the coffee stage when Charlie's cell phone rang. He apologized and picked up the call. A few seconds later he was leaping out of his chair, dropping the paper napkin to the floor in his haste. He caught himself short, seemed to remember something.

"Just one more detail," he said self-consciously. "The union contract also prohibits all Pequeno managers from handling equipment." He saw Jim's puzzled expression and added. "This is to prevent them from running the shop while the workers are on strike."

"Good thing I am not a *Pequeno* manager, then," Jim replied with a wink. "I like to keep up my operational skills, in case I get demoted to the rank and file."

Charlie made an open-hand gesture of apology, said his goodbyes and was gone.

It wasn't until he was back at his condo that night that Jim had time to think about the implications of his meeting with the union rep. The Mexican food had not agreed with him, and he was gulping down Peptobismol straight from the bottle, all the while looking at himself in the bathroom mirror with a jaundiced eye and telling himself for the hundredth time that he should cut down on the business lunches and start exercising, when he figured out that Mother Goose must be the "concerned staff" who had ratted on him. All the evidence fit:

- She had been wearing the union colors at the first board meeting he attended.
- She had declined to help with the bursting of the registration cards, and was probably happy to project her guilt feelings onto the boss for his own willingness to put his hands to the dough.
- She had resented his order to get Grace a second monitor, and was trying to forestall any further meddling on his part by having it brought to his attention that he wasn't authorized to make purchases for the district.

But underneath all that logic, he sensed a deeper current: Ruby must be jealous of the attention he was giving Grace. He remembered how physically close he had been to Grace when Ruby appeared at the door a few days before, how he had failed at first to acknowledge Ruby's presence, how sarcastic her "Sorry to interrupt" had sounded, how flirtatious Mother Goose was generally toward him—an attitude that seemed to swing perpetually between the ingratiating and the defiant. Ah! Of course, she was a classic passive-aggressive, one of the most difficult type of employee to motivate. He resolved to be more careful with his body language in the future, but he didn't have any illusion that it would make much of a difference.

He then turned his mind to the puzzle of filling one of the vacant IT management positions internally. Assuming the Chancellor went for it, and the hiring was left to Jim, what would he do? His first instinct was to promote Mina to the position of Operations Manager. She had quite a bit of experience, she was very conscientious, and lately she had demonstrated supervisory potential in her handling of the work-study students. On the other hand, the entire Operations unit, in terms of permanent employees, consisted of Mina herself and the night operator, who did not seem to need any supervision. Jim also guessed that Mina, with her low salary and self-effacing manner, would not look like management material in Dr. Akecheta's eyes.

Excluding the phantom Michelle Williams, still on maternity leave due to birthing complications, there were three other employees in "senior" positions in the IT department: Elmore, Ruby and Grace. Ruby, Jim excluded right away: she had shown no interest in or ability for supervision, except to pawn off work onto the other members of her team. More importantly from Hartbridge's point of view, she was untrustworthy.

Elmore seemed at first glance a better candidate: he had the most seniority, and he was popular throughout the district because of his little cultural events, which also gave him an aura of intellectual polish that might win the Chancellor to his cause. But Jim recoiled from the idea of making Fuddy-Duddy a manager. For one thing, Jim had hardly developed any relationship with the man, and after five months, still could not tie any work product to his name. For this, Jim blamed himself. At the first staff meeting, he had promised regular one-on-one sessions with each member of the team to review their progress and be apprised of their issues. But what with one thing and another, he had not followed through on his promise. To be honest, as time-honored as one-on-one check-ups may be,

Jim found them mostly painful. He preferred the indirect approach to assessing employee productivity. He realized, though, that the indirect approach had failed with Fuddy-Duddy. In any case, when it came to leadership, it had not escaped Jim's notice that Elmore's style consisted mainly of patronizing those of his colleagues who were willing to be patronized, and bullying those that weren't. Definitely not the kind of manager Jim wanted.

So that left Grace. From the point of view of work output, she deserved a promotion. She was the most self-motivated of the team, she took initiative, she exhibited vision, she was a team player, she had the fearlessness of a born leader. And Jim had no doubt of her loyalty to him. There were also six people on the programming team, so appointing her as Applications Director would make some organizational sense. On the down side, she was very young, fairly new to the district, and her naïve honesty might turn out to be a political liability. More subtly, Jim was bothered by her reluctance to ask the network folks for a second monitor. Did she know something Jim didn't, or was she lacking native authority? And then he had other scruples that he couldn't quite put a finger on, but that summarized themselves in his mind under the heading of throwing his pet lamb to the wolves. Well, if they were going to make a go of it, she was going to need a lot of coaching. This was a task Jim looked forward to.

When briefed on the situation, Fritz showed himself categorically in favor of Grace. Work ethic, leadership qualities, or even popularity were of no concern to him. All that counted was a willingness to work for the Hartbridge team. Somehow, Jim must have let slip more about his friendship with Grace than he was aware of, since Fritz seemed so convinced of her suitability. What he actually said, and Jim blushes now to remember it, was:

"Come on, Man, it's a no-brainer! I bet your little Goth is dying to spread her legs for you! Tell you what: you manage to get her to our side, and I'll make an exception to the no-fraternizing rule."

Fritz's habit of pumping him for the tiniest bits of office gossip had often irritated Jim. It seemed so old-womanish. Now Jim realized that office gossip was integral to Hartbridge's business model. He couldn't at the time afford to be disgusted. But from then on he became more guarded in his conversations with his boss.

In the end, there was no contest. The Chancellor made clear that he would not approve the hiring of any manager lacking a higher degree. As it turned out, only Grace was a college graduate. Even Elmore, though he had flitted from major to major at a variety of colleges, had dropped out before completing his B.A. Grace it would be.

No wonder Jim's conscience has punched out. It's lunch time. But Jim is not hungry. He will force himself to down some cereal, and then he will get ready for his barber's appointment. This will be the first time in weeks he gets out of the house on his own, an act of great courage, if truth be told. The last time he drove to a medical appointment, he found himself on a section of freeway he did not recognize, and none of the signs made any sense to him. His mind froze, his hands started to shake. He thought the cancer had got to his brain. He made himself visualize the billions of neurons that must still be functioning in there, and marshaled them to the task of finding his way by sheer strength of will. And after a few seconds that felt like a century, the trick worked. As it turned out, his brain is intact . . . for now.

There is a gushing sound coming from the kitchen. Has he left a faucet turned on? No, it's rain pouring from a downspout onto the back patio. Not a great day for an outing. He comes back to the living room, pulls the drapes apart, another first since the latest round of chemo. It's lucky the drapes did not agree with Joleen's new decorating scheme, or the living room would be curtain-less. She took the very rocks from the rock garden. Fact is, this place is not fit for guests. He thinks there may be an old coffee table in the garage. He will look into it tomorrow.

He gazes out the window. The new neighbors across the road have decorated their front yard with a plaster bird bath crowned, appropriately for today, with a couple of cherubs smooching under an umbrella. Two crows have parked themselves head to tail on the rim of the bird bath, seeming to mock the cherubs' lovey-doveyness. But behind the fountain, a dogwood tree is showering pink blossoms among the rain drops. It'll have to do as a good omen.

VIII

PEDAGOGIC

"Looks like we'll have fair weather tonight and tomorrow morning in Memphis," Grace announces, wrenching herself away from her BlackBerry after realizing that they have just entered a dead zone.

"No flood, no tornado?" asks Mina, pushing her glasses up on her nose. Her eyes are watering from staring at the road. She wishes she was driving her own Subaru Forester instead of Grace's rattling old Toyota Corolla with its manual transmission and tendency to blow across the road at the first gust of wind.

"No flood, no tornado in sight. On the other hand, it's raining in Greensboro . . . Want another cookie?"

"No, thanks, got to watch my weight," says Mina, patting her waist self-deprecatingly.

"Your weight looks fine to me . . . So what do you say we camp out tonight? I found a state park just on the other side of the Mississippi, not far from the Memphis Botanical Garden. It's even got showers."

"Isn't it going to be cold in a tent?"

"Not any colder than in that motel in Weatherford. Besides, the sleeping bags I brought are rated for—25 degrees Fahrenheit. You'll be as snug as a bug in a rug. And the tent takes about thirty seconds to set up, even in the dark. I've done it a bunch of times. It's no problem."

"Don't we have to make reservations?"

"Not according to their Web site. But I am going to call them as soon as I get some bars. We don't want to get off I-40 and wander down a surface road for twenty minutes only to find that the campground is closed. As Jim would say . . ."

"Measure twice, cut once," they both say at the same time, and giggle. It was one of Jim's most frequently repeated mottos, technocratic imperatives couched in the language of folk wisdom, a big part of their ex-boss's charm—and effectiveness as a teacher. Those mini-parables have stuck, though they don't sound quite as authoritative without the Southern accent.

"You know," Mina continues, "I don't think I ever told you how sorry I am that I did not support you when you got promoted to Applications Manager."

"But you did, remember, that time at the church . . ."

"Santa Magdalena."

"Right. Besides, I understand. You didn't know me that well at the time. Plus, you were preoccupied with your own stuff . . . You didn't see what was going on."

"Preoccupied is a nice way of putting it. What you mean is completely bonkers. But I can't get off that easily. The thing is, I kinda knew what was going on. I saw Ruby going around the office stirring people up. I heard some of the nasty whispers. I didn't take part in any of it, but I didn't defend you either. The atmosphere around the office was so horrible that all I wanted was not to be sucked into it. And to be completely honest, I think maybe I resented you a little bit too."

"Why?"

"Because *I* would have liked to be promoted, isn't it obvious?"

"But you know why it didn't happen, right? That ass Akecheta couldn't abide the thought of non-college graduates attending his frigging managers' meetings."

"I know. Jim explained the whole thing to me. And it's my problem if I dropped out of college when I gave birth to Steven. But sometimes people don't think rationally."

"Tell me about it."

"Also, you know how you sometimes get so absorbed in your own thoughts that you don't even see people? It took me a long time to figure out you weren't just stuck up."

"Well, I am afraid that sometimes I *am* a little stuck up . . ."

"But not with me. I think it was when we worked on outsourcing the registration cards that I started to change my mind about you."

"But that was before I got promoted, no?"

"I know, I know. Sometimes I am slow."

"And what could you have done against Elmore anyway?"

"You keep talking about Elmore. Why? I didn't see him going around the office, parking his big butt on everybody's desk and making scandalized faces."

"But you weren't always there. You often went to the swimming pool at lunch time . . ."

"Still do."

"Good for you. And I used to bike home for lunch. But when you happened to be around at lunch time, didn't you notice how he always sat at the end of the lunchroom table as if he was holding court? And how, when you entered the room, the conversation often seemed to change topic?"

"Maybe . . ."

"Frankly, because of his rooster complex, I have always seen him as the department's covert ringleader. He didn't have to go around to people's offices to stir things up. He had Ruby do that for him. Poor Ruby, always looking for friends, always disappointed."

"Until Myrtle arrived."

"Until Ruby became Myrtle's patsy, I believe. And even that didn't last."

"Boy, you've become pretty cynical, in your old age."

"No, just more aware of politics."

"Well, I guess we'll never know for sure what happened," sighs Mina, quite willing to let sleeping dogs lie.

"I guess we'll never know for sure. Life is full of mysteries," Grace concludes with a shrug for Mina's benefit, although those same dogs are barking quite loudly in her head. And then, looking at her watch: "Hey, it's time I took the wheel. Why don't you take the next off ramp so we can switch side? There seems to be some kind of town ahead. Maybe the reception will be good enough to call the state park."

A few minutes later, the call has been made, and Grace is in the driver's seat. Mina is looking for something to listen to on Grace's iPod, as the Toyota is so old that it's not equipped with a CD player, and all the radio stations are playing Country Music or preaching the Gospel of Prosperity, which would make Jesus turn over in his grave, if he had not fortunately risen from it. Left to her own thoughts, Grace reverts to the time leading to her promotion to the Pequeno managerial ranks.

One morning around mid-August 2005, she got a call from Jim. He had never phoned her before, and his voice sounded so small and tense in the receiver that she imagined he must be stuck somewhere on the road. A car accident?

"Where are you?" she cried out.

"In my office. Can you come over for a minute?"

"Sure."

This was strange, and the strangeness increased when Jim asked her to shut the door behind her. She had never talked to him with the door closed before. She felt paralyzed by a confusing mixture of excitement and foreboding. He told her to sit down, fiddled with a paper clip, and said, a little brusquely:

"I'll come right down to it. What would you think of being promoted to the position of Applications Manager?"

She was so astounded that all she could answer was: "Why?"

"Because you deserve it, for one. You are the most productive member of the programming team, you have demonstrated vision, initiative and leadership potential. I think it's time you got rewarded for your good work." He was looking at her intently, but there was something mechanical about his praise.

"You said: 'for one,'" she couldn't help remarking. "What's the other reason?"

Unexpectedly, his face brightened, the twinkle returned in his eyes. He leaned back in his chair and stuck his thumbs in his suspenders.

"You ain't gonna let me get away with anything, are you? OK, there is another reason. Not that I didn't mean what I said about your qualifications. But you know that, right?" His stare became searching and warm at the same time. For a second, she was reminded of Zach. She shooed the thought away. Jim was much more mature and unaffected.

"I think so."

"The fact is we've hit a snag with the union. There is apparently a clause in the contract that mandates the presence of an internal manager in every department. So I thought of you."

"I am flattered," she started automatically. What she really felt was panic, which she was going to have to try and put it into words in a hurry, before he took her silence for consent. "But I don't think it would work."

"Why not?" he asked, rocking in his chair and stroking his beard. His calm interest in her reasons gave her the courage to go on.

"First I don't have seniority, and seniority is important to the folks here. Then I am not sure I would be good at bossing people around. I don't understand them well enough."

"Ah, but seniority doesn't hold a candle to a title, take it from me. And authority can be learned. I learned it. At heart, I am a pretty shy person . . ." His voice trailed off. His eyes had a faraway look. All of a sudden, his shyness seemed plausible to Grace. The realization caused her a prick of pain, disappointment immediately overlaid by compassion.

"I remember you saying that once, but I couldn't believe it," she said, trying to sound more skeptical than she felt, for his sake if not her hers.

"I'm not joking," he insisted, straightening in his chair and picking up the paper clip again. "Just wait till you see me speak in public and you'll see what I mean."

"Really?"

"Yeah, and I'll need you to buck me up then." The paper clip broke in his hands. With a casual flip of the wrist, he tossed the pieces into the trashcan five feet away, seemed pleased with his marksmanship. Grace felt subtly relieved by this show of dexterity, and the satisfaction it gave him.

"I'll do whatever I can," she said in a tone of mock subservience, underneath which she already sensed a real surrender.

"I'm counting on it. In the meantime, I can show you the ropes of management. I think together we will accomplish great things, and have fun too." He paused, his face lit up with confidence. Fun and accomplishments. No doubt about it, he knew what chords to strike with her.

"So, what do you say?"

"I'm not sure."

"Why don't you sleep on it? I can wait till tomorrow for your answer. But I hope you'll say yes."

And of course, she did. In truth, the proposed promotion did not particularly appeal to her as a career move. When Grace thought at all about the future, she vaguely saw herself involved in something politically relevant, not stuck forever in geekdom, even—or especially not—as a manager. In her mind, IT work was a lark, like waitressing for other people her age. Mostly, and she was aware of this at the time, she went along Jim's plan so as not to lose his esteem.

He was so happy about her acceptance that he gave her a hug, the first ever. She felt as if they had reached a new level of trust in their relationship.

"Don't worry. You won't be alone," he promised. "I'll be right with you every step of the way." And so he was, for a short while.

It was going to take a month or so for the paperwork to go through. In the interim, Grace was to keep the news of her upcoming promotion to herself. But Jim dropped by her office more or less every day, and she felt more emboldened to visit his. He suggested she start getting acquainted with the various units of the IT department to look for possible efficiencies. He asked her to put together a list of the programming projects currently on her team's plate, warning her that her new functions were going to take a bite out of her own programming time, and that she was going to have to learn to delegate. "Delegate to whom?" Grace asked. "Wei is the only person on the staff who is familiar with the student system." "What about Elmore?" Jim answered. "He told me that he's been around long enough to have an overview of the entire application portfolio." This was news to Grace. Ever since she had started at Pequeno, Elmore had systematically dumped any student related programming request onto her desk, pleading ignorance on all subjects other than finances. "And I get the feeling that Elmore is not overly busy," Jim concluded with a wink. Grace laughed. She could see his point.

He told her of his plan to use the help desk ticketing system to keep track of all service requests. He also wanted to develop a Web form that users would have to complete as a first step in getting any programming done. "In any well-run shop," he explained, "there is either a recharge system or an external committee whose function is to triage incoming requests. This avoids leaving it to IT staff to do their own prioritization. As a rule, we don't want to have to say no to our customers. They already mistrust us, because they don't understand what we do. Brushing them off only adds to their prejudices. It's going to take some time before we can set up any formal prioritization process, but in the meantime, we can make the customers do a bit of triage themselves by forcing them to detail their requests in writing. Often, that's all it takes to give them second thoughts about the relative importance of their pet project."

"I know what you mean," Grace exclaimed. "I have noticed how every time I email some people to ask them to do something, I get an email back from them asking for more information."

"Yep, sloth is the mother of invention. Make people work for what they want, that's the idea."

"Except that often, the email thread gets so long that it seems it would have been quicker for them to do what I asked in the first place."

"Human beings are funny that way, aren't they? They will spend a lot of energy procrastinating."

"But you're not like that, I'm not like that."

"Don't be so sure. I am quite capable of procrastination . . ."

"About what?"

He was in her office at that moment, sitting cross-legged on one of her guest chairs, his right arm resting on the top of the other chair, his left hand wrapped around his ankle. Between his bunched-up sock and perfectly creased pant leg, an inch of skin was showing, dense and ruddy and matted with dark hairs. He gazed abstractedly at the wall behind her. Suddenly he seemed to shake himself up.

"My expense sheet, for instance . . ." he said with a wicked grin, turning his eyes back to Grace. For some reason, she felt that he had at first meant to talk about something else. After he left, she searched the wall for clues about his thought processes, but couldn't find anything of interest among the job lists and data diagrams. As for his claim that he procrastinated on his expense sheets, it was no fault at all, as far as Grace was concerned. Any time he spent on Hartbridge business was time stolen from Pequeno . . . and from her?

Jim's optimism was contagious. Grace found herself looking at the impending change in her functions with hope and determination. She started to get out of her office more, dropping by Mina's desk to look at the day's schedule, taking note of the supplies that got delivered, asking Tiffany to show her the ticketing system, learning to locate the various pieces of equipment in the computer room, chatting with Elmore about his current work. She quickly became convinced that she would be able to master all the technical aspects of her new job without too much difficulty. She even started having some ideas for improvements.

The social aspects of management were a little more daunting, but she made a conscious effort to be milder, friendlier, more conventionally feminine. She even got a professional haircut. If Jim could conquer his shyness, she could conquer her own gnarly individuality—at least temporarily.

But over the mentoring and self-improvement anecdotes, what best captures the essence of that pregnant period is a vignette Grace dug up last week, as she prepared for the trip to North Carolina by rereading her journal. In an entry dated August 26, 2005, in between rants about the Bush administration's malfeasance, and descriptions of chance encounters on her daily bike rides—a desultory attempt at painting some charm over her Central Valley exile, as she sees now—was the following sentence:

"Running into Jim in the corridor today, I felt such a surge of joy and recognition passing between us that we might as well have thrown our arms around each other and danced a jig."

Curiously, it is the first reference to Jim in her journal. But the discovery did not overly surprise her. She has often observed that the important events in her life, and the twists and turns of her emotions in response, are rarely reflected in her writings. Is it because it's impossible to know what's important until much later? Is it because she is embarrassed by her own feelings? As well she should, if the hopelessly naïve enthusiasm of her jig dancing metaphor is any guide. Looking back, she can see how her hope of a glorious partnership with Jim blinded her to the dangerous situation he put her in by asking her to pry into the affairs of the various IT units before she was entitled to it by her position. From her colleagues' point of view, she must have looked like an obnoxious teacher's pet and busybody, her every innocent question serving to warn them that she would be a meddlesome manager if they let it happen, unlike Stanley—and come to think of it unlike Jim, who mostly left the staff alone for all his showy activism. Wittingly or unwittingly (and given the length of his experience, the former is more likely than the latter), he was setting her up as the bad cop to his good cop. No amount of mild femininity was going to atone for that role.

On August 29, 2005, Grace came in to the office in a state of intense worry. For several days, the media had issued dire warnings about a major hurricane heading toward Louisiana and Mississippi. In particular there were concerns regarding New Orleans' levees, on which maintenance had been delayed for many years while the US focused its resources on demolishing other countries' infrastructure. The day before, New Orleans Mayor Ray Nagin had ordered the mandatory evacuation of the city, but had provided no means for the third of the population without transportation to obey his order. Early that morning, hurricane Katrina made landfall in Louisiana, and by the time Grace left for work, there was talk of water rising on both sides of the Industrial Canal. It was in moments like these that she regretted not believing in the power of prayers.

As she turned on her computer, Mina came to report a production problem that needed immediate attention. Grace got so completely absorbed in this puzzle that she barely noticed the strange noises coming out of the long empty office next door. At some point, Jim appeared in her doorway. He must have noticed her knitted forehead and shaking hands.

"What's the problem?" he asked in his genial voice, although he looked a little nervous too.

"Something went wrong with the attendance run last night. I have never touched that system before, and I can't figure out where the bug is." She was so anxious she had trouble getting the words out. It was one time when she didn't feel gratified by Jim's attention. All she wanted was for him to go away so she could get back to her frantic investigation. But he didn't move.

"I can't see why you're so flustered," he said. "Are you unsure of your problem solving skills?"

"Not really," she had to admit.

"Then don't act as if you are. If you want people to look up to you, you've got to show you're in control. Don't ever let them see you sweat."

"Easy for you to say," she protested. She meant as a man, as a manager, as a laid-back Southerner, as his unique self. But he did not ask for clarifications.

"Look," he said instead, bringing his hands up and holding them about ten inches apart with the fingers gently curved, as if cupping the head of a child. For a big bear of a man, he had very well-turned, expressive hands that often seemed to be saying something softer than his words. "You're gonna figure it out. That's a given. So, chill, as you would say. When you're done, come join the staff meeting."

Amazingly, Jim's speech did calm her, allowing her to concentrate on the problem at hand in a more logical fashion. Once she had time to think about it, she felt grateful for his advice, and even more for his overlooking her bad mood, for staying at her side while she tried to shoo him away. It was in moments like these that he showed how attuned he was to her. Twenty minutes later, having applied a patch to the attendance job and emailed Mina that she could rerun it, she made her way to the conference room, where the staff meeting was just starting.

Jim was seating in his usual spot at the head of the table, going through his rocking ritual just as Grace entered the room. Every member of the staff was present, except Erin, who had called in sick, and Josh, who was on vacation. Even Mina's work-study helpers had been included, both of them timidly perched on spare chairs lined against the wall as if ready to bolt at the first argument. While Grace made a quick survey of her colleagues' writing materials, finding that the legal pads now outnumbered the laptops three to one, she was struck by a general look of expectancy in the room, and discovered that Rick, the Hartbridge Windows expert, whom she had not seen in a week or two, was missing. In his place sat a woman with champagne-colored hair and a burgundy suit whose cunning darts did not quite succeed in smoothing out a lumpy body.

Grace walked around the table to her usual seat, which happened to be straight across from the unknown woman, facilitating a closer observation. She appeared to be in her fifties. She had a sagging face, sad droopy eyes and a vague mouth forced within artificial borders by a lip liner that matched the color of her suit. Her hair had been ironed into a limp bob, her pink silk blouse was tied with a bow. To complete the impression that nothing in her appearance was left up to chance, she wore pearl earrings, a pearl necklace and a pearl ring above her wedding ring on a exquisitely manicured finger. The mixture of control and defeat that she exuded somehow reminded Grace of the prep school headmistress who, after many years of abuse, had shot her cruel lover dead. A movie based on her was about to be released, so the actual story had been retrieved from its mediatic mothballs. Annette Bening seemed completely wrong for the role.

Jim introduced the woman as "Myrtle Gatewick, one of Hartbridge's crack consultants with a broad range of IT skills and a special emphasis on communication." She was going to replace Rick, whose job with the Windows servers was more or less done. Her immediate assignment was to review the architecture of the district's Web site, but she would also have a look at the department's processes and documentation, and be on hand to assist Jim in any other project where her experience could be of use. He asked her to say a few words about herself, but she demurred, claiming that Jim had said quite enough. "However," she added, scanning the faces around the table with moist eyes, "I want to say that I am looking forward to get to know each and every one of you."

In your dreams, Grace retorted inwardly. She had taken an instant dislike to Myrtle. She was also furious at Jim for springing this woman on the department unannounced, after dangling before her eyes a future where she, Grace, would be his partner. And he may have intuited her state of mind, because he took the time at that point to turn toward her and ask if she had fixed the attendance bug.

"Yes, of course," she answered somewhat impatiently.

"See what I told you . . ." he concluded with a wink. Grace was mollified.

"As a matter of fact," Ruby intervened in her most grating tone, "the Windows Server project is not complete. We haven't implemented failover."

"That's why I said the project was 'more or less' done," Jim replied with another wink. At this rate, Grace thought, he was going to get sore eyelids before the end of the meeting.

"So, you meant less rather than more," Ruby insisted, flipping her hair in her characteristic gesture of sexually charged belligerence.

"Is the glass half-full or half-empty? Anyway, hold your horses, Ruby. Rick will be back in a bit. In the meantime, Myrtle will be glad to help you with the new server configuration, right, Myrtle?"

"Be glad to," said Myrtle, patting Ruby on the arm soothingly. Ruby was appeased.

"So," Jim resumed, rubbing his hands together with the relish of someone sitting down to a sumptuous dinner, "does anyone have an issue they want to talk about?"

"Well," Mina piped up, "I am worried about the burster."

"Again? What reports do we still burst, now that we've outsourced the registration cards?"

"Attendance and grade rosters. I was able to burst the Fall attendance rosters, but I don't know what's going to happen when we try to do the grade rosters. And the optical reader is on its last legs."

"Didn't you guys just complete a Web application for instructors to turn in their rosters?" asked Jim, pointing to Grace and Wei with his chin.

Grace looked inquiringly at Wei, who as usual, nodded to signify that he was yielding the floor to her. The problem with Wei was that he didn't trust his English.

"Yes, and Roger has agreed to release the new application this fall, but the deans of instruction at both campuses insist on our continuing to print paper rosters for teachers who don't know how to use computers."

"What the heck! This is the twenty-first century. Any teacher who doesn't know how to use computers should retire, plain and simple."

"Is this what you are going to tell the deans?" Elmore asked in his suavest tone. Elmore was the team's main customer relations proponent. What was interesting was how often, in Elmore's sphere of responsibility, customer relations turned out to preclude any change to the status quo.

"I have a good mind to," Jim replied. "But there's probably a more diplomatic way of getting what we want. Does your application have a print function?"

"Yes, of course."

"Are you going to ask the deans to print the rosters themselves?" Elmore suggested, his voice practically dripping with honey. This poisoned socratic civility had become his standard method for opposing Jim since he had had to renounce straightforward male aggression in the face of his boss's superior brawn.

"Not exactly. Anybody got a better idea?"

Grace was thinking hard. Make them work for what they want, Jim had advised. As a student of anthropology, she was also curious to see if the ancient tactic of shaming, so frowned upon in current child-rearing circles, could be revived in a work environment.

"How about this?" she ventured. "First, we schedule a number of training sessions for the instructors. We make sure the deans attend. Once they've seen how easy it is, we ask them to provide a list of the teachers who will need paper rosters, explaining that the IT staff will have to print the rosters manually, as we have decided to buy new laptops for the faculty instead of replacing our failing burster and optical reader."

Jim laughed out loud.

"Now we're grinding corn! Well done, Grace. That's a pretty slick piece of thinking. Do y'all see it?"

"Well, technically, faculty laptops come out of a different fund than mainframe equipment," Ruby interjected.

"But the customers don't have to know that," Jim answered with a third wink. Grace, understanding at last what he was trying to do, forbore any in petto sarcasm.

It was now Sandip's turn to voice objections.

"I don't like the idea of releasing an application without having it subjected to a formal quality assurance process," he said with a click of the tongue and an Indian head wag.

Grace couldn't help rolling her eyes—she hoped discreetly. It wasn't the first time she noticed Sandip's reluctance to see other people's applications go into production, perhaps because he produced so little himself.

"Are you volunteering to act as QA team?" Jim asked, imperceptibly motioning to Grace to keep quiet.

"No!" Sandip cried out, plainly horrified at the idea. "But this is something I feel strongly about." Another click of the tongue, another Indian head wag.

"OK, then, seeing as we don't have a QA team, we'll have to trust that Grace and Wei have done their due diligence in testing the application."

"Yes," Wei assented, "we test on all browsers. And Admissions staff, they do beta testing."

"Very good. Tiffany, can you schedule a meeting with Roger, Grace, Wei and myself to go over the release protocol as soon as possible?"

"Sure. But it might be better if Grace scheduled the meeting, as she talks to Roger every day."

"But I am asking *you* to do it," Jim replied.

It was the first time Grace heard him getting huffy. And with Tiffany, of all people. She immediately suspected that it was a strategic mistake. She glanced around the room to see what effect if any his mini-outburst had had on the rest of the staff. Mina, Wei and Rajiv seemed a little shaken. Ruby's face had shut down in revolt. Sandip's eyes were drilling into his laptop, either because he was trying to detach himself from the scene, or because he was absorbed in something else altogether. But Elmore blinked sensuously, like a cat contemplating a still quivering mouse. As to Tiffany, although her color was a little heightened, she sat with her back erect, her chin up, her crown of blond curls undisturbed, the Queen of the Data Center.

It was Myrtle who took responsibility for bringing the meeting back on track.

"Anything else any member of the team wants to share?" she asked in a motherly voice.

"New Orleans is under water!" Sandip shrieked. At that, everyone jumped up out of their seat to crowd around Sandip's laptop, and the meeting broke up.

When Grace returned to her desk later that morning after conferring with Mina on the attendance run, she understood the reason for the noises she had heard earlier in the office next door: the new consultant had been quartered there. Myrtle was standing stock still in the middle of the room, her shoulders slumped, her square heels digging into the carpet, looking, with her flat butt and non-existent waist, as if she was impersonating a Stonehenge monolith for a game of charades, while Ruby busily connected her laptop to a brand new printer, her diligence causing Grace to remember that her own second monitor had not yet been delivered. Without moving a muscle, Myrtle tracked Grace's progress across the doorway. Her gaze had nothing motherly about it. Grace comforted herself with the thought that her office was closer to Jim's than the Hartbridge interloper's.

The following Wednesday, Jim was scheduled to leave in the early afternoon to fly back to North Carolina for the Labor Day holiday. The Hartbridge contract provided for bi-weekly three-day weekends so that consultants could return to their faraway homes, with all travel expenses recharged to the District. But Jim had not gone home for a month and a half, often working through the weekend, so he was now tacking five extra days to his vacation, trying to make up for lost time with his kids before they completely forgot him, as he jokingly explained to Grace. She was sorry to see him go. His presence had become a daily fix of positivity in her work life. He taught her stuff, he made her laugh, he trusted her. But she was becoming conscious of being attached to him in a more personal way. As a human specimen, so different from her and yet to strangely sympathetic, he fascinated her. In many ways, she found him admirable, and in others, touching. For all the obvious asymmetry in their relationship, which should have assigned to him the role of protector, she often experienced a pang of weightiness on her side, as if *she* was responsible for him. Last but probably not least, she had started to realize that he was in fact quite sexy.

As the IT staff, joined by Bob Johnson and Roger Wilkins, gathered around the security door to bid him goodbye, Jim became emotional. He joked and held men's arms as he shook their hands energetically, but when it came to Mina, he bent over and buried her in a hug. Soon he was hugging all the women—making sure to include the little pat on the back meant to dispel any sexual apprehension—while Roger loudly complained of gender bias. Grace, who, arriving late, was watching the scene from the corridor, instinctively ducked back into her office. A second later, she was crushed in his arms, flooded with his cologne-drenched pheromones. And then he was gone. There had been no pat on the back. He had found some pretext to come looking for her, she realized, and understood that she had hid in her office with precisely that object in mind.

If Grace had feared that she was going to feel forlorn in Jim's absence, she had not imagined the extent to which it would alter the group's dynamics.

On Thursday morning, Elmore brought a 32 inch TV with an old-fashioned rabbit-ear antenna to the office, setting it up with Sandip's help at Jim's end of the conference table and tuning it to CNN so the staff could watch the unfolding New Orleans catastrophe in full-size communion. From that point on, very little work got done. Somebody would wander into the lunch room, ostensibly to get a cup of coffee or microwave some popcorn, get mesmerized by the sights of devastation, make some loud remark that would attract a colleague or two, and pretty soon the entire staff was gathered around the screen.

"Oh my God! There's a bloated body floating down the street."

"Look! A car up in a tree!"

"They say a bunch of elderly patients got drowned in a nursing home!"

"Imagine. People stranded on roofs for four days with only the clothes on their backs!"

"25,000 refugees held prisoners at the Superdome!"

"No food at the Convention Center, and all the toilets overflowing!"

To Grace, it was unbearable, the abandonment of an entire community to a Third World fate, in this, the richest country on the planet. What she saw on the victims' faces, apart from the fear, the thirst, the hunger, the desperation, was a long-standing sense of humiliation finally made complete by the callous incompetence of the authorities. By Wednesday, she had stopped watching TV, and only kept up with the tragedy through the New York Times online. And although her colleagues paid lip service to an indignation similar to hers, it seemed tinted in some of them by a ghoulish enjoyment.

But it was their reaction to the wild reports of lawlessness that drove her around the bend: snipers shooting at FEMA helicopters, babies raped in the Superdome, bodies of slain refugees piling up in the Convention Center. While studying the first Gulf War at school, she had heard about the rumor of Kuwaiti preemies ripped from their incubators by mad Iraqi soldiers, a story much trumpeted at the time, which later turned out to have been fabricated by the Kuwaiti authorities for propaganda purposes. The New Orleans horror tales had the same flavor, although the propaganda machine was harder to locate in this case. But her colleagues bought every bit of scandal, as if they were glad to be confirmed in their worst imaginings of black socio-pathology, or perhaps as if the bad behavior of the victims could somehow atone for the national dereliction in giving them succor. Upon further investigation, the Katrina rumors would prove to have had no more basis in fact than those of the Gulf War. But at the time, in the absence of evidence either way, all Grace could do was to get angry.

As she walked into the conference room at some point, the TV screen was showing a few young men wading through waist-high water, carrying cardboard boxes on their head. This was the looting that had finally motivated a mass mobilization of the National Guard. Tongues were clucking around the table.

"To think," she cried out while striding up to the sink to fill her cup with water before hurrying back out, "that with billions in property damage, not to mention the tens of thousands of human beings in mortal danger, stopping the theft of a few soggy loaves of bread and pairs of jeans is the top priority!"

All eyes turned towards her. She had never before voiced her political opinions in front of her colleagues, and she felt a cold wave of disapproval wash over her as she retreated.

"Well, you're entitled to your opinion," she heard Elmore say composedly.

"What's up with her?" asked Sandip.

"Must be that time of the month," Ruby replied.

"You know," Tiffany commented, "there are going to be great flipping opportunities in New Orleans as soon as they fix the levees. I wish it wasn't so far away."

"Don't ever let them see you sweat," Jim had warned. From that perspective, Grace had just blown it in a major way. But she rebelled at the idea of even passively condoning meanness and bigotry. The truth was the truth and clamored to be told. Besides, Jim himself had recently shown signs of temper.

On Friday, the boss being out of sight, everyone left early in honor of the holiday. Myrtle had been mostly invisible for the last three days. She had been interviewing various District officials, according to Roger, who was one of the interviewees, and although Grace could not see the point of this frantic socializing, she was glad to be left alone at the office.

But by the middle of the next week, with Jim still on vacation, Grace started to notice a marked change of attitude toward her on the part of her colleagues. Suddenly, Tiffany could not make the time to create a Heat account for her, Ruby wanted to know what business she had in the computer room, and Elmore called her questions about the financial system "nosy". Sandra, Erin, and Sandip made a point of being engrossed in their cell phone displays when they passed her in the corridor, and even Mina seemed ill at ease when Grace stopped by her desk to go over some tricky part of the schedule. Only Wei, Rajiv and Alex kept their usual manner, and in the case of Alex, it didn't mean much, since he was more or less autistic anyway. Grace wondered whether her Katrina outburst could be the cause of this new hostility, but rejected the notion as far-fetched.

Meanwhile, Myrtle was making headway in her stated project to get to know each and everyone of the staff. She seemed to spend a great deal of time in the lunchroom preparing elaborate salads with ingredients she brought to work in an insulated tote bag. Pretty soon, while ostensibly washing and chopping, she was exchanging dieting tips with Elmore, children's pictures with Ruby, and specs for the latest electronic gadgets with the others. As for Tiffany, she had apparently piqued Myrtle's interest in the real estate opportunities in El Pequeno. Passing the lunchroom on her way to the bathroom, Grace caught snatches of the Queen's promotional speech:

" . . . hottest housing market in the country. Prices in the Valley have doubled since 2002, and they're still rising. So, why rent, when you can buy a nice place with no down payment and a very low interest rate? Even if you end up not staying here, you can resell in a year and make a lot of money. Basically, you can't lose, that's the beauty of real estate investments. Come by my desk when you get a chance, I'll show you some properties that my husband is renovating . . ."

In the background, Myrtle could be heard punctuating each sentence with "really?", "fascinating" and "I'll do that".

In short, sad sack as she may look, Myrtle was revealing herself to be a consummate wheedler. And even when she wasn't interacting, she listened. Several times, Grace spotted her doing her Stonehenge impersonation around the network printers located in the cubicle area, which was highly suspicious since she had been provided with her own printer. On one of those instances, Grace heard Ruby's combative voice rise over the cubicle partitions:

" . . . a good mind to tell him that I find his cursing offensive. And I don't appreciate his invading my personal space either. If he wants to . . ." At that point, the door bell rang, and as it was Roger, Grace went over to greet him, missing the rest of Ruby's tirade. But she guessed that Ruby was talking to Sandra or Erin about Jim's occasional mild oaths and his one-time hug. She was flabbergasted. Until then, she had had a sense that Ruby would be only too glad to be hugged by Jim. Nor was this new recruit to the language police above punctuating her own sentences with Shits and Fucks. Grace briefly considered putting Jim on his guard, but decided not to, as it might have sunk Ruby in his opinion. One thing you didn't do was rat on your colleagues to their supervisor, except of course in cases of gross dereliction of duty where whistle-blowing was required. Anyway, Myrtle had heard the tirade. Let her rat to Jim if she wished.

Thus puzzled, frightened and lonely, Grace hunkered down in her office to await Jim's return.

IX

EVIL

There's nothing worth listening to on Grace's iPod, as far as Mina is concerned. The songs are either too wordy or lacking words altogether, and none of them have the kind of tight beat you might want to dance to. But Grace being lost in thought, Mina keeps the earbuds on so as not to disturb her. By and by she starts thinking as well, her consciousness, like her fellow traveler's, drifting back toward the end of August 2005. However it's not the Pequeno drama that claims her attention. Of course, she likes Grace, and always considered Jim a great guy. Since he got sick she has even come to see her former boss as a friend, so she feels bound to do whatever she can to comfort him, which right now consists of reuniting him with his ex-protégé. But she has always steered clear of office politics, has refrained from bringing work home. Tarik barely knows the names of her colleagues, and she had to brief him at length before Grace showed up on their doorstep so he would treat her with appropriate warmth. No, what Mina turns over in her mind is her twilight zone, the period during which, as she put it to Grace a while ago, she went completely bonkers.

It all started, she imagines herself telling the talk show hostess . . . Wait, where should she start? How about the day, May 30, 2005 to be exact, when she found a complete stranger in her living room? Or before that, with the fateful paperback novel she bought at Walmart? With 9/11? Or all the way back to that insidious counselor who tried to discourage her from taking calculus, or even to earlier schoolyard taunts? To be honest, she knows that she only needs to go back to the time when they moved into the house on Oakdale.

Once her father's pickup truck had disappeared behind a bend in the cul-de-sac, and Tarik and Mina, their arms still around each other, re-entered the house and closed the front door behind them, they were struck by how empty their new home felt. The cramped cottage they had rented from Mina's parents had always been overflowing with stuff. But all of it could have fit in their new living room, and indeed had while they were unloading. Now that the beds and dressers and clothes and linens had been carried upstairs, the dishes and pans stowed away in the kitchen cabinets, Tarik's still packed computer equipment shoved into the study, and the couch, armchairs, coffee table and entertainment center spread as far apart as possible from each other in the living room, it still looked like a deserted basketball court. She foresaw that even once Steven's toys had been dug out of their wicker chest and systematically flung to every corner of the floor by the toddler, as would surely happen the very next day, they would amount to no more that a scattered flotilla on that varnished ocean.

Vertical surfaces were just as unforgiving: in spite of the cathedral window and fireplace and open plan kitchen, there was a huge amount of empty wall space all around, silently daring the new homeowners to assert some taste and personality. That night, as she made a last round of the ground floor, locking doors and turning off lights, the purr of central air conditioning muffling the echo of her footsteps, Mina wondered if she was up to the challenge.

When it came to home decor, Mina didn't know what she liked, only what she was moving away from: paper flower garlands around the windows, nichos sheltering the Virgin of Guadalupe and Korean War medals, posters of Cesar Chavez with an Eagle coming out of his head and shirt stripes turning into ploughed furrows, Christmas lights in the shape of jalapenos hung year round, painted tire planters and plastic covers over the upholstery. Far from her to criticize her parents' sensibility, nor was she unaware that in some artistic circles Chicano kitsch was all the rage, but the new house demanded different aesthetic choices—more mainstream, and, let's say it, more middleclass. It wasn't a question of one-upping the new neighbors. More deeply steeped in Catholicism than she knew, Mina had never made a religion of Darwinian competition. But on the other hand, she didn't want to be laughed at behind her back.

The problem was that after paying for the various costs associated with home buying, and with a mortgage that consumed more than half of their combined income, Tarik and Mina had very little money to devote to home decoration for the foreseeable future. They were going to have to make do with posters after all, albeit not of the political or religious variety, and they must be properly framed.

They looked for framed posters at the local Home Depot, but the selection there was anemic, in numbers as well as subjects and color schemes: gray flowers, brownish pears, black ruins, the kind of pictures that are bought wholesale by motel operators. "How about something abstract?," Tarik suggested, and Mina agreed, immediately seeing it as a solution to her status anxiety, since no one dares laugh at abstract art.

Having grown up in California in the wake of Prop 13, a voter initiative intended to lighten the tax burden on property owners, which ended up decimating all but the most "basic" of school programs in poorer districts, Mina had never taken any Art Appreciation course, while Tarik, who had attended a good high school in Pakistan, had only paid attention to the scientific subjects that would be his ticket out. The couple would have been as babes in the woods trying to find some abstract pictures for their walls, were it not for Google, the most democratic educational institution ever devised, putting as it does mankind's entire cultural heritage at your fingertips, and even guiding your choice with tactful hints.

Mina pursued her research at work, in between glances at the mainframe console and trips to the computer room to mount tapes. One thing she liked about her job, apart from the fact that she had been able to put Tarik and Steven on her medical plan, was that it consisted of a fixed number of tasks. Once these were done, she didn't have to feel guilty about attending to her personal affairs. Measured against such advantages, the lousy pay and lack of respect were of little importance.

It took her only a few hours to order a couple of abstract posters that not only she wouldn't be ashamed to display in her home, but that in fact attracted her: one by an artist named Wassily Kandinsky, the other by a certain Mark Rothko. Funnily enough, once the pictures were hung, they irresistibly turned representational, the Kandinsky suggesting a sombrero parade viewed from a balcony, and the Rothko reminding her of the back wall of a bodega, on which successive generations of graffiti have been rolled over with paint remnants in various shades of red. Looking at them made Mina smile. You could take the girl out of the barrio, but you couldn't take the barrio out of the girl, she realized, and somehow felt comforted. But she kept her whimsical interpretations to herself.

Why did she not share them with her husband, the talk show hostess might ask? It's not as if she was afraid of appearing ridiculous to him. When they first met, they had spent a whole afternoon lying on the campus lawn, making a game of discerning faces in the clouds above them. It was one of those rare spring days in the Valley when in between storms, the clouds take actual shapes. The grass had been damp, but they had pretended not to notice, slowly, excruciatingly, working their way to a kiss. Tarik claimed he had fallen in love with her imagination. Indeed, throughout their courtship, she helped him see flaking-paint speedboats racing along her parents' porch rail and creation scenes worthy of the Sistine Chapel in the water stains on his bedroom ceiling.

It was to remain their deal: he provided the seriousness, the goal-oriented striving, and she the liveliness, the prattle, the fancy. So why did she stop honoring her side of the contract?

The usual reasons, she would have to say: life, growing older, a baby. And on his side, a demanding job that often made him unapproachable. Not to mention the subtle effects of anti-Muslim sentiments after 9/11, although Tarik himself never reported being the object of discrimination, and although he was only a nominal Muslim. In retrospect, Mina sees that he started retreating into his shell much before they decided to buy a house. She also sees how, as long as they lived in the old house, it was easy to pretend not to notice. At the old house, liveliness had automatically been provided by the busy traffic of family and friends: the borrowing and returning of kitchen utensils, the gifts of squash and tomatoes, the baby-sitting exchanges, beer on the porch with her father, giggly conversations in the bedroom with her sister Anna, and all the improvised dinners, aside from the official fiestas. Sometimes Tarik kept working, many times he was sucked into the social maelstrom. He had not seemed to object, even though this was not his family, his culture. After a couple of drinks, his lustrous hair falling on his forehead, his soulful eyes lit with cheer, he might even join in a birthday song or argue about soccer teams with her father. Later, in their bedroom, Mina would round off the festivities by gently satirizing the dinner guests and passing on any bit of gossip she had heard.

Of course, none of this would qualify as "communicating", that bafflingly deep type of conversation deemed essential to the survival of a couple by all the relationship experts in women's magazines. But on one hand, Mina had in front of her eyes on a daily basis the example of a couple—her parents—whose survival did not seem to depend on communication, and on the other hand, what's the point of communicating when the deepest stuff on your mind is a bunch of worries?

"Rekindling the romance" is another marriage-saving strategy recommended by the relationship experts. However, Mina never had to remind Tarik to buy flowers on Valentine's day, and he would have been totally unmanned by black garter belts. As for the effectiveness of the candle-lit dinner, it relies either on great play-acting—which neither of them was any good at—or on communication, bringing us back to square one.

One marriage-saving idea that often presents itself to a struggling couple without any help from relationship experts is a home improvement project—an attempt to fix the relationship from the outside in, so to speak. And what with the general real estate frenzy at the time, when it seemed that you could not only live like princes, but actually make money from borrowing, the idea presented itself to Tarik and Mina in full force. It was Tiffany who put the idea of buying a home into Mina's mind. And when Mina brought the subject up to Tarik, he was immediately on board. It was time for them to strike out on their own, out of the family cocoon. Time for Mina to have a decent kitchen, and Tarik a study where he could work late at night without waking the boy. Time to fully embrace the American Dream, like everyone else.

The family cocoon. An interesting choice of words on Tarik's part, the talk show hostess might remark. Aside from crowded living conditions and the social stigma of renting, what were they escaping? For herself, Mina is not sure. Perhaps the feeling of living in a fish bowl, the down side of all the mutual aid in the old neighborhood being that everyone was into everyone else's business. If you came home late one night, if you were seen talking to a male colleague at the supermarket, the news made the rounds of the entire block.

Perhaps the sense of having never really grown up, what with a mother who would walk into your home with a duster in hand and attack the nooks and crannies you had missed while summarizing the plot of the latest telenovela, and with a father who insisted on checking the oil in your car. For Tarik, she is even more at a loss. His only complaint ever was that Grandma spoilt Steven.

In any case, for a while, the home buying project did rekindle their relationship. After a couple of meetings, though, they declined Tiffany's services. For one thing, Mina did not feel comfortable involving a colleague in her personal life. For another, the houses that Tiffany had to offer were rehabs, the type put on the market after the body of an old lady is found half-eaten in it by her fifty cats, or after a meth lab bust. Mina knew that however pristine the new sheetrock and sanded floors may look, she would forever smell cat piss and decomposed flesh, see the AK 47 lying on the kitchen counter and fists punched through walls. And finally, Tiffany's real estate transactions were a little too complex, involving as they did something called cash back at closing: the buyer agreed to get a loan for a house appraised by a friend of Tiffany's at a jacked-up price, and Tiffany returned the difference in cash to the buyer, who could then use it to pay debts or further improve the property. Tarik could not see what was in it for the seller—he never bought Tiffany's claim that she was doing this out of friendship—but he did grasp that the bank making the loan came out the loser. In Tarik's opinion, it was never a good idea to try and cheat the big guys.

In the end, Tarik and Mina made use of a legitimate real estate agent, a legitimate mortgage broker, a legitimate appraiser, a legitimate inspector, and bought a brand new house in a brand new development at the edge of town, a twenty-five minutes drive from their old cottage. All the legitimate professionals confirmed that real estate was the best possible investment, that the new house was a great deal in the current market, and that the new owners would be able to refinance under even better terms within two years. Mina's parents reacted to the news with understated resignation. If they had not themselves quite achieved the American Dream, they could not begrudge it to their daughter, however abhorrent the idea of incurring a huge debt seemed to them. Plus the kids were not moving far. Steven would still be within baby-sitting range. And finally, the vacated cottage could now be rented for a few more pennies to some of the many Mexican immigrants who were converging on the Central Valley because of the construction boom.

Once settled in the new house, and after completing a few more purchases on credit to make the living room less echoey, Tarik and Mina started drifting apart again, and this time, Mina was fully aware of it. They had wanted more room to breathe. What they got was more room to clean, more room to light, more room to cool, more room to feel lonely. When the first electric bill came, they had their first argument about money. Tarik wanted to turn the air conditioning off. After all, they had lived without it at the old house. Yes, but the old house was shaded by trees on all sides, and Steven, like Mina, was very sensitive to heat and smog. Well, there had been no air conditioning and no trees around the house when Tarik grew up in smoggy Karachi, and Steven was his son too. In the end, they compromised by setting the thermostat at eighty degrees, but the next electric bill was still astounding.

Mina had looked forward to having a real garden, instead of a concrete patio surrounded by potted geraniums. She now realized that the dirt in her new backyard, packed to a cement texture during construction, would require mechanical digging and much amendment, which of course, they could not afford. Nonetheless, she attacked a narrow area along the back fence to plant some drought-tolerant trumpet vine that would hide the as yet undeveloped wilderness of weeds and building debris beyond. But without the chatty interruptions of passing neighbors, and keeping in mind the two thousand square feet of floor that needed vacuuming later in the day, it turned out to be dispiriting work. With her father's help, she did manage to plant a couple of vines, which soon died for lack of watering. And where was Tarik all that time? In his study working on his computer, trying to make the money she was spending, he claimed. Thank God the front yard had been landscaped by the developers and equipped with automatic sprinklers.

Whenever her family came to visit, she now felt a duty to entertain them, given that they had driven half an hour to get there. On their side, they seemed to be ill at ease in their Sunday best, afraid to scuff the floors with their shoes, waiting for their hosts to tell them where to sit, unsure that a tamale casserole was the right thing to bring.

Her own parents, whom she had known for twenty-nine years, were behaving like strangers. She wanted to shake them, to shout: "It's me, Mina, your daughter. This is not Church." But of course, she didn't. Instead, she tried to break the ice with music, but even Carlos Santana sounded puny in the solemn space. She tried barbecues on the backyard deck, but a pitiless sun drove everyone back inside. She tried to engage in gossip, with little success: gossip, like humor, does not travel well. And then she started resenting Tarik for his lack of cooperation in her entertainment efforts. Oh! He was still prompt at greeting guests at the door, and never failed to stack the dishwasher at the end of the evening, but in between, pretexting a business phone call to make, he might get up from the table and disappear in his study for hours. When he re-emerged, his soulful eyes often had a sullen cast to them. Once, he even left the house, and she didn't realize he had been gone until she heard his keys clunk on the vestibule credenza upon his return. This frankly scared her. In such a large house, it was too easy to lose track of your partner's movements, to feel that you were both spinning out of orbit in different directions. Yet, again, she said nothing, afraid that a remark on her part might lead to an argument.

Isolated from her family, estranged from her husband, her energy sapped by a lack of money to carry out any project she might dream up, Mina took refuge in reading. Every time she went to the supermarket, she would add a book or two to her grocery cart, mostly romances and the occasional thriller—she wasn't up to any slice of real life. She couldn't have expected that among the escapist literature she deliberately sought, one book would speak directly to her concerns. Considering the pain and suffering that resulted, you could call it a case of shelving malpractice. Companies have been sued for less.

She does not remember the title or author, but it was the story of a American woman—more successful than Mina, of course, but that only made it worse—married to a Middle Eastern man, who comes home one day to find that her husband has flown back to his country with their two kids, and has no intention of bringing them back. After 9/11, he has come to hate the US, and does not want his children to grow up in its corrupted culture. For the rest of the book, the successful woman fights to get her kids back, and she does, eventually, at great expense and after a lot of dangerous adventures, having discovered that the legal system is pretty useless in such cases.

It was not the first time Mina heard about parental abduction. Along with head lice, bullying and pedophilia, it was one of the bugaboos of modern childhood regularly brought up by the media. But usually, when parents abducted their kids, it was during the custody battle attendant to a divorce. What was different in this case was that there had been no divorce, not even an argument, so the successful woman had no clue about the impending flight. Horror of horrors, the husband had even made sweet love to her the night before. How could you trust any human being after such an experience? More to the point, how could Mina be sure that it would never happen to her?

Enter Samir—last name unknown. On Monday, May 30, 2005, Mina came home from work to find a bundle of sheets on the floor of the living room. She was perplexed. Had her mother come unannounced to see Steven, decided to strip the beds while she was there, and dropped her burden on the way to the washer because of some emergency? "Mom?" she called out anxiously. There was no response. Mina lay her keys on the credenza and strode toward the bundle. Suddenly she noticed that it had feet. It was a man in a white kurta and pajamas, engaged in Muslim prayer. His butt was skinny, and the soles of his feet were gray and calloused. He did not stir to acknowledge her presence. She walked straight to Tarik's study. He wasn't there. She went all over the house looking for him. At last she heard him close the front door. She rushed back downstairs to meet him. He had a guilty look on his face.

"Ah! Mina," he said with false cheer.

The praying man straightened up. He was in his twenties, dark and starved-looking, with thick hair and a sparse beard and mustache. He wore a green crocheted beanie on his head, and stared at Tarik as if he was the Prophet himself.

"Mina, this is my cousin Samir. He has just arrived from Pakistan. Samir, this is my wife Mina."

The man did not move. Out of sheer polite instinct, her mind already boiling with anger, Mina advanced toward him to shake his hand or give him a hug, whichever he preferred. He stepped back, looking down at the ground while mumbling a nearly inaudible "hello". Mina felt herself flushing to the roots of her hair.

"Tarik," she said firmly, "can I see you in the bedroom?"

"In a minute," Tarik answered, "let me put these groceries into the fridge."

He took his time, but finally he made his way up the stairs. She motioned him to close the door behind him.

"What the fuck is going on?" she heard herself say.

He was shocked. He had never heard her swear before. But he was smart enough not to remark on it.

"I am so sorry to spring this on you," he said, "but I didn't have time to warn you. Samir called me from the airport. His sponsor never showed up. I could not leave him there. After all, he is family."

There were so many things wrong with his explanation that she didn't know where to start tearing it apart. She seized on the least relevant detail.

"Which airport?"

"San Francisco."

"You mean to say that you made the trip all the way to San Francisco and back, and you could not find the time to call me?"

"I forgot to take my cell phone."

"And before leaving the house?"

"I was in a hurry. Samir sounded terrified. Anyway, it wouldn't have made any difference. I couldn't say no, don't you see? You would have done the same."

He had her there. Family was sacred. And Tarik had always been willing to aid and shelter any member of hers.

"But at least if you had called me I wouldn't have had a near heart attack when I found him crouching in my living room."

"I said I am sorry. What else do you want me to say?"

"You could tell me how come I never heard of this cousin of yours."

"He is a distant relation. He lived in Lahore, so I hardly ever met him."

"And how did he know our phone number?"

"My parents gave it to him. Anyway, this is just for a few days, until he manages to get hold of his sponsor. And he won't be too much of a burden in this house, since we have an empty bedroom."

He had her again. But for the first time, she consciously wished that they had never moved.

Tarik had promised that the cousin would not be a burden. And it is true that he did not occupy much physical space. Scrawny as he was, and only a few inches taller than Mina, she was pretty sure she could have wrestled him to the ground. All the same, he quickly managed to take over the entire house.

The first thing that happened was that wine disappeared from the dinner table, and a Tupperware of chile verde brought by her mother had to be re-frozen. Then the living room became unusable for entertainment purposes because the cousin kept flopping down to pray in the middle it, his bedroom being for some reason an inadequate environment for worship. Tarik claimed that Muslims prayed five times a day, but that seemed very much of an understatement as far as Mina could see.

Other than praying, the cousin spent his time lolling about on the couch, watching soccer on the Hispanic channels or playing video games. He did not help with any of the housekeeping chores, not even to wash his own clothes, which as far as Mina could tell, were limited to three sets of kurtas and pajamas. At least, his lack of possessions meant that he was in no position to make much of a mess. But right after he moved in, Mina started to notice a faint sulfuric smell pervading the house. It wasn't that he was dirty. From the soapy rings he left every day in Steven's bathtub, Mina could tell that he bathed regularly. It wasn't anything he ate, as he was content to eat the vegetables that Mina served—he stayed away from the meat, because it wasn't Halal. The smell wasn't any stronger in his bedroom, although that didn't mean much, as he hardly spent any time there. He didn't shave, so the culprit couldn't have been some weird aftershave. All the same, mysteriously, he was slowly stinking up the place. When discreetly probed on the subject, Tarik claimed he couldn't smell anything. But from his exasperated look, Mina suspected that he suspected her of suspecting Samir.

Samir's one contribution to the household was to play with Steven. This however failed to endear him to his hostess, as the play seemed designed to pull the boy away from her. She would be reading to her son, and Samir would distract him by building a tower of blocks. Or she would be cooking, Steven hanging on to one of her legs, and

Samir would materialize in the kitchen, crouch two yards away and hold out his hands, beckoning for the boy to join him instead. She felt all the more threatened by this behavior that she could not object to it rationally. On top of that, even though he spoke some English, he conducted all his conversations with Tarik in Urdu—to Mina, he barely said a word. Tarik, who at first made a point of sticking to English, soon reverted back to his mother tongue. It was as if her entire family was being taken away from her.

Meanwhile, Samir didn't seem to be making much effort to contact his sponsor, except that on the first Friday, Tarik drove him all the way to Lodi where he had supposedly been promised a job in a fruit packing plant. To Mina's consternation, they were both back in the evening. The job had apparently fallen through.

It was in this tense context that the Lodi terror case broke out. Mina missed the first reports, but by the time she came home the next Monday evening, it was all over the local news. When she entered the living room, Tarik and Samir were both glued to the TV set, and Steven, propped up on Samir's bony lap, was crying unheeded. What struck Mina was the haunted look on Samir's face, and the angry tones in Tarik's voice. She retrieved the boy from Samir's clutch, and dandling him in her arms, asked what the fuss was about.

"Oh! Nothing much," Tarik replied sarcastically. "Just the beginning of another anti-Muslim witch hunt."

"Where? Why?"

"In Lodi, that hot bed of terrorist activities, of all places."

Mina's heart stopped. Wasn't Lodi Samir's original destination? Her mind a whirl with questions about this extraordinary coincidence, she found it hard to concentrate on Tarik's explanations. Nothing much was known at that point anyway, except that a truck driver of Pakistani descent and his son had been arrested on charges of being members of an Al Qaeda cell planning terrorist attacks in the area.

"Imagine how desperate Al Qaeda must be, to be targeting a town where the tallest building must be three stories high," Tarik continued. "On the other hand, what a gift to Bush & Co, just at the time when they are trying to get the Patriot Act renewed. The whole thing is so obviously a farce, and the media is so happy to go along.

You see, while they're covering one story, they're creating another one. I expect that in the next few days, we'll be hearing reports that dozens of Muslims in the Valley have been beaten up by excited mobs. It makes me sick."

Mina had never seen her husband so riled up. She made the mistake of trying to reassure him.

"But if those two men haven't done anything wrong," she said, "I'm sure they'll be released."

"You and I must be living in different countries," he sniped, and zapped the TV off, thereby closing the topic.

In the next few days, Mina followed the story on the Web from her office. When she learned that one of the two alleged terrorists had just returned from Pakistan, arriving in San Francisco on the day before Tarik picked Samir up at the same airport, and that moreover the same man had just started working in a fruit packing plant when he was arrested, the coincidences became very hard to swallow. Wasn't it possible that Samir had been part of the same cell, that he had somehow been tipped off to the dragnet, that he had hid in the airport for a night and then called Tarik to his rescue? This would explain why he had kept to the house ever since, why he looked so scared, why he spoke so little. As to the trip to Lodi, he could have attempted to get in touch with the cell leader, only to find that things were too hot there. After all, Tarik himself had confessed that he hardly knew the guy. And it didn't take long, in these days of the War on Terror, for young Muslim men to turn into fanatics. But when she tried to communicate her suspicions to her husband, he grew outraged again, and this time directly at her.

"Are you going to turn against us too?" he hissed. They were in bed, and Steven was asleep in the next room, otherwise Mina felt that he would have shouted. "I would have thought that you, of all people, would have a better understanding of racist scapegoating." With that comment, he turned his back to her.

And so weeks of anguish and silent discord passed. Samir stayed on, supposedly waiting for the hysteria to cool off before joining his mysterious sponsor in Lodi. In July, the London bombings added another layer to the clouds of suspicion surrounding men of Pakistani origin. Tarik reacted by growing a beard. In early August, Abuela bought the recently released DVD of Aladdin for Steven.

After watching it for a few minutes, with Samir providing a snide sounding running commentary in Urdu, Tarik yanked it from the DVD player, causing Steven to throw a temper tantrum, which triggered a frightening nose bleed—the first of many, as it would turn out. When, later that night, Mina asked Tarik what he could object to in a Disney cartoon, he claimed that it was ethnocentric and vulgar. Ethnocentric, a story that takes place in Persia? Disney, vulgar? Mina was flabbergasted. For once, though, she pursued the topic. She really wanted to understand how her husband felt, but he couldn't, or wouldn't, explain.

In mid-August, she found one of Tarik's own kurtas in the laundry hamper. He only wore kurtas on festive occasions that involved other Pakistani acquaintances, when she would also don the salwar kameez at other times used as employment insurance. She took the shirt out of the hamper and brought it to his study, her eyebrows raised in surprise. This is how she learned that he had been attending the Friday services at the local mosque with Samir. They had even taken Steven along instead of dropping him off at the day care center. Until then Mina had not even known that there was a mosque in El Pequeno.

A week later, as she was vacuuming her husband's study, Mina, more or less accidentally, knocked a pile of papers off his desk. Among them was a statement for a savings account she knew nothing about. This was the straw that broke the camel's back.

It was useless to bury her head in the sand. Something was going on, and if Tarik was keeping it from her, it could only mean harm. The next day at work, she retrieved an online article on international parental abductions she had idly bookmarked after reading the prophetic Walmart novel. It provided a list of signs to look for to determine if your spouse is preparing to abduct your child:

- Secret bank account: check
- Visit from member of abductor's family: check
- Grooming child to accept separation from you: check
- Change of jobs: not that she could tell, as Tarik worked as a contractor, developing safety systems for oil refineries. But as such he had several employers, and one of them, for all she knew, might be in Pakistan.

- Application for passport or visa for child: she hadn't found any evidence of that, but that didn't mean it hadn't happened.

Her heart racing, she started a new Google search on parental kidnapping, this time narrowing it to Pakistan. It didn't take her long to find what she was looking for: Pakistan did not have an extradition treaty with the US, and was not a signatory to the Hague Convention on International Child Abduction. In other words, if Tarik spirited Steven back to his home country, she would have no legal recourse. Nor could she afford a mercenary to kidnap the boy back, as the successful woman had done. As for her husband's family, she was sure they would be all too happy to shelter both abductor and abductee. In the seven years that Mina had known him, Tarik had gone back to Pakistan twice, but she had never met his parents. The first time was before their marriage so it was understandable that he went without her. The second time, he flew back abruptly after learning that his father had been hospitalized with a heart attack, so again, there was a good excuse for leaving her behind. When he talked to them on the phone, which was rare, he took care of the reciprocal greetings because of the language barrier. But Mina had always suspected that Tarik's parents did not approve of his marrying a non-Muslim, and that it was the reason why he had never taken her to Karachi. As a consequence she didn't even know where they lived in that huge city, much less expect to succeed in enlisting the help of a member of his extended family, as the successful woman had done.

Pursuing a second line of inquiry, Mina then did a search on terrorist psychology, and although its results were much less definitive, she did find several articles stating that no consistent terrorist profile has been identified, that terrorists are made, not born, that becoming a terrorist is the end result of a process that starts with a gradual dissociation from social and emotional ties. This jibed with the biographical sketches of terrorists she had read over the years: intelligent, well-educated young men from good families, whose parents could not believe their ears when they were told their son had driven a plane into a building or detonated a bomb strapped to their body. And wasn't Tarik an intelligent, well-educated young man from a good family? Hadn't he become gradually dissociated from his social and emotional ties? Wasn't he ripe to be recruited by

Samir? . . . Or worse, was it possible that he had married Mina just to get his student visa changed into a green card, and had bid his time in a sleeper cell while plotting some spectacular act of terrorism? No, that was taking the paranoia too far. No matter that the latter scenario had actually happened, she refused to give it a hearing.

She stared at the screen, on the verge of throwing up. Until now she had loved Google as a friend and teacher. Suddenly she saw it as sinister fortune teller, letting her pick the cards that would spell her doom. And there was no other authority she could consult. No talk show hostess, not the FBI, because that would be treason, not her family, who all loved Tarik, and of course, not Tarik himself. You do not ask your husband whether he is a terrorist and/or a child abductor.

This is how, at the beginning of September 2005, while the residents of New Orleans contemplated the devastation of their lives wrought by Hurricane Katrina, and Grace endured her coworkers' guerilla warfare, Mina found herself shut off in her own private hell.

X

PROMOTIONAL

As much as Grace has tried to impress her camping expertise on Mina, she feels a little apprehensive as they drive around the deserted campground on the outskirts of Memphis, looking for a spot to pitch their tent. Although the night is clear, a ground level mist is wrapped around the tree trunks in a way that reminds her of any number of slasher movies. She finally selects a site partly hidden from the loop road by a curtain of bushes, but close to the rangers' booth and just far enough from the washhouse to be out of hearing range of flushing toilets. Thankfully, they have barely anchored the rain flap when another car drives up to a nearby site, a rented minivan loaded with two young German couples, who wave hello and quickly proceed to unload the car with stereotypical efficiency. Grace walks to the washhouse to take a quick shower. By the time she comes back, the Germans have not only set up camp but cooked dinner, and are sitting at the picnic table eating, drinking, and listening to Satie's Gymnopedies played at low volume. The ideal camping neighbors.

Reassured as well by the transformation of the campground from wilderness outpost to mini-village, Mina in turn ventures to the washhouse to clean up and call Tarik and Steven, while Grace shoots a quick email to Jim:

Dear Jim,

Sorry, sorry, sorry, only made it to Memphis tonight. All my fault for being picky with my food, as you remember. But along I40, looking for anything to eat that doesn't come out of a factory is like shopping for query software that's

both user-friendly and versatile. I am soooooo looking
forward to a home-cooked Southern meal (but don't put
yourself out on our account, OK? One more Wendy's
burger won't kill me). At least, we are now on your side of
the Mississippi. Couldn't quite see it in the dark, just a big
void under our wheels, but symbolically, it was awesome.
Anyway, our new ETA is Saturday around four o'clock.
Let us know if that still works for you, and what we should
bring other than the baklava.

Much love.

There. It's sent. Grace wonders whether Jim is still up, whether
he is right now reading her loving sign-off, whether that comforts
him in any way. She'd better not go there. Better to muse on the
unimaginable past when people were not yet safely tethered to the
Internet while camping out in the woods, how impractical it must
have been, how daunting, how lonely. To think of her own father,
who used to portage in the wilds of Ontario. There was real courage.
OK, better not go there either.

It's really amazing how this trip, in spite of the exhilaration of
driving, in spite of Mina's cheerful chattiness, and in spite of the bright
future of political activism that awaits her in Raleigh, is stirring so
much angst. For once again she finds herself reverting to memories
of the Pequeno Community College District. And this time she's
reaching the most problematic period of her relationship with Jim,
the part she wishes she could thrash around with him honestly, if
such a conversation were ever possible.

How do you think I felt, she would like to ask him, when I found
your door closed on the morning when you came back from your
Labor Day vacation? And when I could not talk to you for an entire
week? When you welcomed a parade of my colleagues, but did not
have time for me? When every evening found you closeted with the
Myrtle character, who suddenly seemed to have become your best
friend? When the few times I passed you in the hall, you frowned
at me as if I was your most troublesome employee? Meanwhile, and
you could not be unaware of it, I seemed to have become the office
pariah. People were whispering all over the office, shutting up as

soon as I approached. I couldn't get any help from anybody except Wei. Even Roger, always eager to tell me about his work problems, let me know by changing the subject that he did not want to hear mine. And to think that I had so looked forward to your return! Between the disaster in New Orleans and the nastiness at work, I had had a pretty rough week in your absence, believe me. The main thing that had kept me going was the certitude that *you* liked me.

Over the weekend I drove to Berkeley to see some friends from my previous job. We went to Jupiter to have a beer and hear some jazz. I was afraid we would run into Zach, but my friends assured me that they hadn't seen him there for a long time. Zach is the ex-boyfriend you rescued me from once, remember? And I want to thank you again for it. You must have scared him plenty, because he has never bothered me since. Anyway, my friends and I had a great time. The music was interesting, the beer excellent, the conversation as comfortable as the old jacket that I was in fact wearing, this being summer in Berkeley, and the stage being set on the back patio. Even the cold felt good, compared to the Central Valley furnace. The upshot was that I realized how isolated my life was in El Pequeno, and how I was depending too much on my job for satisfaction. My friends were all encouraging me to move back to Berkeley. They said they would be on the lookout for a job for me, that I shouldn't wait too long, because my skills were getting outdated in that hole—sorry, that's the way they saw it. And all through their arguments, valid as I acknowledged them to be, I knew I wouldn't budge, because of my loyalty to you. Yes, loyalty. I may have realized by then that I was attracted to you, but I was not in love with you, not then, not ever. We were just too different in age, experience, outlook for that feeling to emerge. So the attraction was just frosting on the cake of a very rewarding work relationship. I may have miscalculated a bit on that score, but in all honesty, that's the way I felt at that time.

When I saw your gold Ford Taurus in the parking lot that Monday morning, I heaved a sigh of relief. You had come back. Your plane had not fallen from the sky. You had not been dispatched to another Hartbridge site without warning, like Rick. You would be there to brighten my work day, to teach me management skills, to protect me from my snarling coworkers.

But when I got to the end of the corridor, I saw that your door was closed. I felt as if I had been slapped in the face. You very rarely closed your office door, and never this early in the morning, before the schmooze sessions with Pequeno executives, and the interviews of complete strangers you occasionally conducted for reasons unknown to me then. An hour later, I heard Myrtle plod down the corridor on her way back to her desk, and figured she was the person who had been claiming your attention. I had trouble getting my mind back to the program I was working on. By the time I walked past your office on my way to the lunchroom to make some tea, your door was open, but you were gone. For reassurance, I had to make do with the sight of your garment bag draped over a chair, and the unmistakable scent of your aftershave.

All day long, I waited for you to stop by my office, to park yourself uninvited on one of my spare chairs, showing by that gesture how confident you were that I was glad to see you. I waited for you to tell me about your vacation and your new ideas, while the twinkle in your eyes and the ease of your arms on the chair backs demonstrated that you were glad to see me too. You never came. And at the end of the day, Myrtle stationed herself in your office again.

The next day, I started noticing that while I couldn't get a hold of you, other staff had no trouble doing so. And they were not just stopping by to say hello. They were marching down the corridor with that pinched look of self-righteousness that I have come to recognize as characteristic of people about to commit an act of deliberate meanness. They would enter your office in the straightforward manner of people who have an appointment, and then push the door shut behind them with a flourish exuding a nearly sensuous enjoyment. Given the hard time they had been giving me in your absence, it wasn't rocket science to figure out that the meetings had something to do with me. And as my political opinions, obnoxious as they may have seemed to them, would not have warranted a coordinated attack, I had to conclude that the cause of their indignation was my coming appointment as Applications Manager, which must have been leaked to them somehow. My colleagues were coming to you to try and stop it, and you were giving them a hearing, you, who had come up with the idea in the first place, and who had more or less forced my hand by cleverly alternating the blandishments and calls for help. Oh yes, I was onto your charming tactics, even as I fell for them.

I personally witnessed Tiffany, Elmore and Ruby's incursions into your office. But several other "private" appointments had been blocked out on your calendar that week. I wondered who else might have spoken against me. Could Sandra, Erin, or Josh have been recruited by Ruby? Did Sandy follow Elmore's lead? I feared that even Mina might have been pulled into the conspiracy. The only people I was sure of were Wei, Rajiv and Alex, and the only reason I was sure of them was that their various handicaps removed them from the reach of cliques.

And then, to add insult to injury, I had to listen to Myrtle's friendly advice. Myrtle, whom I didn't know from Adam, and who had not inspired my trust by cozying up to my detractors, delegated by you to teach me the finer points of office politics! Hello? From the way she insinuated herself into my office without a word on Friday, and then closed my door behind her with the same unctuous relish as the three backstabbers, I sensed right away that there was some treachery afoot. But I was so startled by her audacity that before I had recovered enough to tell her I was busy right then, she had sat down, folded her hands in her lap confidentially, and pinned on me a scowl of managerial superiority underlaid with such personal spite that I half expected her to start addressing me as "My Pretty". I found myself scrambling to reconcile her new witch-like persona with the image of her as long-suffering clod that I had foolishly entertained, and in the interval, she launched into one of the most absurd speeches I had ever heard.

She claimed that you had asked her to talk to me, "woman to woman". By itself, the appeal to gender solidarity would have been enough to turn me off. I mean, what did I have in common with that sneaky matron? And then she told me that my appointment was going to be announced at the next staff meeting, but that I should refrain from publicly reacting in any way, not even—or especially not—to thank Jim. (Like, pretend I am not there? How would that look like?)

"You see," she explained, "your colleagues are upset about your promotion. They feel that there is some favoritism involved in it. To be honest," (the liar's favorite preface . . .), "I can see how your behavior contributes to their impression. At the last staff meeting, I observed how often you nodded in agreement at what Jim was saying." (I see, how silly of me not to look bored.) "And I am afraid Jim is also responsible. He compliments you too much, seeks your input too often." (I understand now why Stanley avoided meetings like the plague. Why bother if they are such emotional minefields?) "Be assured that I have brought this to his attention. Now, of course, what you do outside the office is your own business." (Did I hear that she suspects us of having an affair?) But in the office it's important to maintain a professional distance at all times."

It was like being sucked into a Kafka novel. I could positively feel myself turning into a cockroach, my eyes popping out like antennae, the rest of me withering inside a hardening shell. But in a way, Myrtle's little homily succeeded: I maintained the proper professional distance by not telling her to go fly a kite, thanking her instead for "sharing her concerns". I had already decided to disregard everything she said. It was perhaps the first time I so consciously dismissed a person, the first time I did not try to see their point or communicate mine. I found it dangerously exhilarating, and had to promise myself that I wouldn't make a habit of it.

Before I left for the weekend, I further observed the professional conventions by doing what everybody else had apparently done: I brought up the Outlook calendar and scheduled an appointment with you for the next Monday afternoon.

At this point in her imaginary tirade, Grace distinctly hears another voice in her head, casual, unassuming, winsome, and recognizes it as Jim's, although it has shifted from a bass to a baritone, and the Southern accent has paled. "As I feared you would," it says, and Grace understands that he is responding to her last sentence, that he has listened all along. She can't see him, but she senses a slight displacement of air in front of her face, like the flight of a moth. It is his famous wink.

"So that's why it took you the whole weekend to accept my meeting request. Let me tell you that if you hadn't, I would have tended my resignation on Monday morning," she retorts.

"I was afraid of that too."

"So, what do you have to say for yourself?"

"In general?"

"No, in particular, about what was going on with you that horrible week."

"Could you be a little more precise? I have a hard time figuring out what you want to know." It sounds like his usual ploy of buttering her up by asking for help, but given that this conversation is predicated on complete honesty, she has to accept that perhaps he does need some pointers.

"OK, to start with: why did you snub me at the very time when I needed your support most? Didn't it occur to you that I would think you were siding with the people who were plotting against me, and feel very hurt?

"Well, I suspected you were unhappy, but I couldn't afford to do anything about it. Can't you see that by appearing aloof, I was trying to protect you?"

"Protect *me*?"

"OK, and myself too. But you most of all. Believe me, your colleagues had made me acutely aware of my indiscretion in showing you a marked preference. They had also convinced me that they were fully capable of making your life hell if they wanted to. And here is the nub of it: I could not stop them, because, according to the union contract, I did not have a manager's powers over them, and they knew it."

"So you thought that if you acted cold to me, they would treat me better, even though I was still getting promoted?"

"Doesn't seem to make much sense in retrospect, I admit. The thing is, I felt like I had been caught with my pants down. It seemed everybody but me, even Myrtle, who had been there only a few days, had noticed that I liked you more than I perhaps should have. And it seemed there must be something about you that I had overlooked, some reason why you were so unpopular with your peers."

"So, you *were* cold to me. I knew it. I remember feeling somehow defiled in your eyes, like a Victorian bride whose groom expresses doubts about her virginity on the wedding night."

"I guess there is some truth to your image. The uproar had made me doubt myself, so naturally, I started doubting you too. If I had been a fool, didn't it follow that you may have fooled me? It occurred to me that your friendship for me might have been a mere ploy to advance your career, that you may not be the person I thought I knew. In any case, it looked like my tapping you for a management position had been a major goof. It wasn't a thought I enjoyed, as you can imagine."

"So why didn't you revoke the appointment?"

"It was too late for that. The appointment had been approved by the Chancellor. I couldn't tell him I had changed my mind without looking like an idiot. Plus, my effectiveness would have been compromised. A manager who lets his subordinates dictate his decisions is pretty much finished."

"I don't hear any concern for me in all of that."

"Oh! It was there. I just didn't know what to do about it."

"So you waited for me to clear things up . . ."

"As I knew you would . . ."

"If I were the person you thought you knew."

"You got it!"

"You know, the more I live, the more I think those feminists were onto something."

There are many more questions Grace would like to ask Jim about the week of their estrangement, questions about what went on during his interviews with her colleagues, and more pointedly about Myrtle's role in the conflict, a role which to this day remains a mystery to her. Could the Master Wheedler, under the guise of "getting to know each and everyone" of them, have actually encouraged the staff to voice their complaints to Jim? Was she herself opposed to the appointment? And if so was she acting on Hartbridge's behalf or pursuing her own agenda? Was she, then and later, Jim's ally or his enemy? But for now her mind is getting as foggy as the woods outside the tent, her thoughts scattering away like moths when they get too close to a fire. One second everything seems so important, the next nothing is. When Mina comes back from the washhouse, she finds her friend curled up in her sleeping bag, her hand still wrapped around her BlackBerry.

Dream or daydream, what is remarkable about Grace's imaginary conversation with Jim is that his answers are pretty much those he would give her in real life—if complete honesty could ever be achieved in that realm. What should we make of this? Would we be willing to accept that a spiritual connection between separated human beings may in fact exist? Or would we need to find a more rational explanation?

In real life, of course, the week of estrangement between Jim and Grace was not resolved through such satisfyingly forthright communication, but through the usual muddle of comforting words on one side and eagerness to forgive on the other. The gash was closed, the wound scarred over. But some grace and innocence were lost on both sides. The friendship, though it endured, veered off in a subtly different direction. And once it was severed by force, all the unresolved suspicions would creep back to poison its meaning.

As she waited for the fateful Monday afternoon meeting, Grace fought off mounting self-doubts. Could there be more to her colleagues' sudden hatred than resentment at the teacher's pet, as Myrtle had claimed, or indignation about the rules of seniority not being followed, a reaction she herself had warned Jim about? Was there something about her that had annoyed them all along? Her edgy clothes, her brusqueness, her lack of conviviality? Truthfully, she had not cared very much about most of the people in the Pequeno IT department, and, as she thought of her current job as a mere parenthesis, she had not made much of an effort to accommodate herself to her environment. But didn't her very aloofness justify her colleagues in arguing that she would be a poor manager? Did she even want the position? She had to admit that she didn't, not really, other than as a learning opportunity, a useful line on her resume . . . and the promise of a closer relationship with Jim. She had to admit that her main concern was Jim, which was why his betrayal hurt so much.

Imbued as she was with a belief in the power of spontaneity, she did not rehearse what she would say to him at the crucial meeting. All the same, as she walked from her office to Jim's that afternoon, her heart started pounding. It was with an intense sense of relief that she found his door open, though the joyful feeling was immediately succeeded by an awful intuition that his chair would be empty. He seemed determined enough to sever all bonds between them that she could imagine him resorting to the final humiliation of standing her up. When she saw him sitting at his desk, she nearly turned around to flee, so shocked she was to find her prediction disproved. By staying at his post, he had already won half the battle.

As for Jim, his head retracted into his shoulders, his gaze fixed on his laptop, his fingers digging into the keyboard as if his life depended on the memo he had been wrestling with ineffectually for the last fifteen minutes, he was attempting to project the image of the boss as cranky bear. Inwardly, he was bracing himself for a confrontation with a young woman he was pretty sure of having wronged, and whom he knew to be fearless. And yet, along with the guilt and apprehension, he was conscious of a delicious feeling of adventure. The neat thing about interacting with Grace was that he could always count on being surprised by her: her repartee, her point of view, the ever varying mix of admiration, affection and challenge with which she responded to him. It was true that as his conscience put it, she wasn't the first enthusiastic female to put her talents as his disposal. But he had never quite experienced the sense she gave him of a real personal connection, beyond the usual professional—and occasionally flirtatious—utilitarian connivance. With Aisha, of course, it had been pure passion, nothing professional about it. In any case, Grace entertained him. He was willing to withstand a good deal of friction to keep the entertainment coming.

Marshalling her resolve, Grace walked in, took three steps toward the desk, turned around, walked back to the door, stopped. Jim, who had caught her movements in his peripheral vision, feared for a second that she was going to leave. Instead, she put both hands flat on the door and slammed it shut with such force that the noise must have traveled the length of the building.

"There," she said, catching her breath, "just making sure everyone knows I am talking to you."

Jim frowned, his sense of decorum disturbed by the bang of the door and the barely contained hysteria in her voice. He looked at her more carefully, and noticed that she was shaking. Was she going to turn violent? That would be more friction than he was prepared to withstand—at least in the work place.

"Please sit down," he commanded in a low tone, returning his gaze to the keyboard to give her time to compose herself.

"No, thank you. I prefer to stand."

"Whatever makes you comfortable," he conceded gently. There was a silence. When he raised his eyes again, he saw that hers were pooling with tears, the watery medium intensifying their blueness.

He was petrified. This was the last thing he would have expected from his geek Goth, his IT Amazon, with her relentless logic and black belt in sarcasm.

"Don't cry," he pleaded lamely, "I can't stand to see a woman cry."

"Well, deal with it," she answered with a chop of her chin that settled his untidy fears like a paperweight, "because I am not going to make myself not feel what I am feeling so you can avoid feeling anything at all."

The sheer length of her rejoinder forced her to take another deep breath. She thought about what had just come out of her mouth, and although it was a little convoluted, or because it was, she was rather pleased with it. Her face relaxed. Her pooling tears, which had a second ago threatened to overflow the dam of her lower lids, were somehow re-absorbed, leaving her eyes particularly shiny. She was now able to look at Jim, who also looked at her with a sheepish version of his wonted geniality. At that moment, they both knew that the crisis was over. But of course, she wasn't going to let it go at that, and that was just fine with Jim. He was in no hurry to see her leave.

"So, tell me why you're upset," he started, gamely handing her the ball.

"I just don't see how we can work together if I no longer have your trust."

"What makes you think you don't?"

"Come on, you know what I mean. I haven't had a civil word from you for a week, while you receive in pomp all the people who object to my promotion."

"You've noticed them trooping into my office, eh? Looks like we kicked up a hornet's nest, doesn't it?" he asked, leaning back in his chair and sticking his thumbs into his suspenders. His eyes were twinkling, his whole body language clearly expressing that he had not taken her detractors seriously. She finally accepted his invitation to sit down.

"Who were they, apart from Elmore, Tiffany and Ruby?" she asked, curious about her colleagues, now that her main question about Jim had been answered.

"You don't want to know."

"OK, I understand, secrets of the confessional and like that. But at least tell me how many."

"A couple more."

"*A couple more?*"

"It's not important."

"And what did they have to say?"

"Petty, stupid stuff. They're just jealous. Don't you worry about them."

"How could I not worry, if I am going to have to supervise them?" she asked, standing up again to give vent to her anxiety. "Remember how I tried to warn you. I think we should reconsider." She paced across the room a couple of times, stopped again in front of him, searched his face. Nothing changed in his relaxed stance.

"Naw, it's going to be all right. Just give them a couple of weeks to adjust," he said with a casual sweep of the hand, as if knocking off a row of tin soldiers from a shelf.

"You sure? What if they're right? What if my personality is not compatible with a manager's role? You haven't told me what they said about me, so I don't know what I could do differently, but maybe there are some things I need to change?"

"You don't need to change a thing. You're fine the way you are." There was a mixture of sternness and warmth about Jim's demeanor at that moment that felt outright paternal to Grace. So she did what a daughter would do: she trusted him to know better than she did. It was the effect Jim had sought, but in the emotional contagion of the moment, he had also meant to convey a less role-defined affection for her, a meaning which she obviously failed to pick up, as she did not sit down again.

The meeting ended soon after, with Grace apologizing for taking Jim's time, and Jim answering "not at all". She left his office feeling a little encouraged, and he tried to focus on his memo, the consciousness of the conjuring trick he had just performed weighing on his mind. For until he saw the tears in her eyes, he had not been certain that she was fine the way she was. Nor was he sure, even now, that everything would be all right with her colleagues. The more experience he acquired at managing people, the less confident he became at predicting their behavior. There were just too many variables in the human psyche. Often, these days, his very poise seemed to him a willful delusion. It would keep him aloft as long as he did not look down, but it might not perform the same miracle on Grace. Innocent, impetuous, straightforward Grace, who expected all the truth and nothing but the truth from everyone, and particularly from him—the very thing he could not give her.

As planned, at the next staff meeting, Jim announced Grace's promotion to the title of Applications Manager, effective immediately. From the look of sullen dismay she saw on her colleagues' faces when she entered the room, Grace guessed that they had already been informed of the failure of their plot. Contrary to Myrtle's instructions, she had decided to make a short speech in response to the announcement. It wasn't just a matter of defying the matronly snake, but of showing the others that she wouldn't slink into her new role as if it was something to be ashamed of—the wad of bills slipped into the decolletage of a whore. She does not remember what she said, only that it was pretty innocuous stuff, gratitude for Jim's trust and hope for the future, yada yada yada. What she does remember is the sickening silence that greeted the speech's conclusion, and the covert nonplussed glance that passed between Jim and Myrtle. That tenth of a second moment is the one she has never forgiven him. And then, as the meeting was breaking up, and everybody was running back to their desk, Elmore surprised the hell out of Grace by offering his congratulations. He did it from the corner of his mouth, to be sure, but she was thankful to him all the same for this small act of decency. Later, she would come to see it as one of the signs that he had in fact been the plot's instigator, but had at last been seized by remorse. Now she wonders if he, like the others, had not in fact been manipulated by Myrtle.

XI

PATERNAL

On Friday morning, when Jim finds Grace's message in his inbox—tagged with a characteristically apt subject line of "Delayed!"—he is much relieved. The fact is that the promised visit has up to now seemed so dreamlike to him that he hasn't even mentioned it to Cindy. But here she is, standing in the living room doorway, pulling on the sleeves of a sweater she has thrown over her pajamas, one bare foot scratching the other, her head tilted to the side in that tentative way of hers, her mouth slightly gaping, her black eyes depthless. It was the color of those eyes that first made him doubt whether she was really his daughter. As she grew up other traits of hers increased his suspicions: her slow-moving gracelessness, her lack of drive, her precocious, wayward sexuality. From his intermittent perspective as an ex-pat father, it seems that she only stopped sucking her thumb when she started making out with boys.

How ironic that she is the one who has stuck by him through his sickness, whereas Robert, green-eyed, quick, charming Robert, now on parole thanks to the expensive lawyer his father spent all his savings on, doesn't even bother to call. He has conveniently bought the convenient tale of psychological abuse woven by his mother to justify her escape. It's true that Joleen can be pretty convincing when she decides to be—though most of the time she finds it more amusing not to be convincing at all. Poor Cindy. Between a self-centered, unreliable mother, a father who was probably too demanding when he wasn't absent, and a more gifted baby brother she had never asked for, is it any wonder that she grew up to be tentative?

"Hello, Daddy," Cindy says, her voice at its breathiest in the morning, before her sinuses have had time to drain. "Have you taken your medicines? Would you like me to make some breakfast?"

"Hello, Sweetheart," Jim astounds himself by answering. He has not used this term of endearment on his daughter since she was five years old. She is astounded too. She stops scratching her foot, steadies herself with one hand on the door frame. Fleetingly, her black eyes seem to melt, losing some of their opacity. It is the change of a moment, quickly overlaid with her normal blank expression, which Jim suddenly intuits may be just a cautionary stance. Poor Cindy. "I'll cook breakfast," he continues. "I feel up to it today. And talking about cooking, we're gonna have some guests for dinner tomorrow."

"Really?" she asks, incredulous, but willing to suspend disbelief.

"Yep. Just got an email from two of my ex-employees in California, the place I worked at when you came to join me for the river rafting trip, remember?"

"Sure. That was my best vacation ever!" she claims with such unusual emphasis that she dislodges some mucus in her throat and suffers a coughing fit.

"Well, they are traveling to Raleigh, and they are going to stop by tomorrow afternoon. Their names are Mina and Grace. Grace is just about your age, as a matter of fact, and Mina is a couple years older. Both very nice girls. I think you'll like them. Now, I've gone and promised I would fix them a Southern meal. So, I'm gonna need your help."

"Sure . . . if you'll tell me what to do," she answers hesitantly. Suddenly, she slaps her forehead. "Oh, no, I forgot to tell you. The oven does not work."

"Since when?"

"Since last time you were in the hospital. It completely slipped my mind. I'm so sorry."

It is the kind of absent-minded inertia in the face of practical problems that would have earned Cindy a stern lecture from her father in the past. A lecture that she would have cowered under, and that would have passed right over her head. In the last two years, Jim has given up on stern lectures. Not just because he has been too tired for them, but also because he has discovered qualities in Cindy that make up for her lack of pragmatic efficacy—her devotion to him, for instance.

"Alright, then, let's figure out some menu we can do on the stove top," he decides, recapturing some of the unflappable determination he used to deploy as a matter of course in his IT manager days.

And now it's Cindy's turn to demonstrate some resourcefulness. "You know," she muses, "I think there may be a crockpot in the garage . . ."

"Well, let's go see," he says, rubbing his hands together as energetically as in the old days. "But first put some shoes on."

"So, that's why you got your hair cut yesterday," he hears Cindy remark airily as she fumbles her feet into a pair of flip-flops. An apparent non-sequitur, but right on target. Never underestimate the acuteness of women.

Without further ado they slip out the back door in their jammies like kids on an adventure. The cool morning air brushes against the hair on Jim's chest, and he finds himself savoring the sensation, that is until the garage door opens, revealing the most god-awful mess. They start digging through it, promising each other that they will thoroughly clean it up—if, when. At the end of a half-hour, they had excavated the following loot:

- The crockpot, still in its original box, never opened. Wedding gift from his mother, he believes. He asks how Cindy knew about it. She says she used to look at it when she hung out in the garage as a little girl. She thought crockpot meant a crazy kind of utensil, which explained why her mother didn't want to use it. "You hung out in the garage as a little girl?" he asks. This is the first he hears of this childhood habit of hers, and he does not like the thoughts it evokes in his mind. Yes, she says, she liked the quiet. It was a good place to daydream in when it rained.
- A Moroccan coffee table, consisting of a round brass tray, tarnished, not unpleasantly, to a dark brown, over a foldable carved wooden base, very dusty. Bought at the souk in Riyadh in the first flush of his love affair with the Orient. Originally set up in the foyer because that was the only place with room for it, Joleen having embarked on a major home decorating

spree after he left for Saudi Arabia. By the time he came back the next time, the coffee table had disappeared from view.

- A Kilim rug from Turkey. Also bought at the Riyadh souk, this time with Waheed's expert help. Displayed in the living room for a short while, then apparently rolled up around some unidentified object that Joleen has since pulled out, leaving the bits of cut string hanging down. Fortunately, the rolled-up rug lay on top of an old washer, and is not much stained.
- A wrought iron floor lamp found at a garage sale at the beginning of their marriage. Not elegant by any means, but serviceable. Just needs a couple of bulbs.

They spend the morning cleaning and arranging the retrieved furniture, then looking for crockpot recipes online. They finally settle on pulled pork, rounding up the menu with coleslaw and mashed sweet potatoes. Rolls and dessert (key lime pie), mindful of Grace's distaste for industrial food, they will get from a local bakery that touts natural ingredients. And if he can summon the energy, Jim will make hushpuppies, his mother's recipe.

By eleven, Jim is bushed. He had planned to go shopping with Cindy, but, waving the exhaustive list of ingredients she has slaved over in her slow round hand, she convinces him to take a nap instead, so he can conserve his energy for tomorrow. She is in the kitchen, bolting a peanut butter and jelly sandwich before leaving, when he realizes that he never fixed the breakfast he had promised. It's alright for him, he is so rarely hungry, but not for Cindy, who has the appetite of youth. He is not going to tell her that she should have spoken up, because she would hear it as a criticism, but he wishes she would learn to stand up for herself. On the other hand, would she be such a good nurse—or a good Christian—if she did? At this point in his reflections, inspiration strikes.

"I'm sorry," he blurts out, a little hoarsely, so unusual are those words in his mouth. "I completely forgot about breakfast."

"I did too," Cindy answers, the pitch of her voice rising as if she was herself surprised. "I had so much fun."

As her car pulls out of the driveway, he looks around the living room, pleased with the cheerful look achieved by the salvaged objects. They give the room a kind of gypsy bachelor aura, not a bad image to project considering where he is at.

He wakes up drenched in sweat, the comforter twisted tight around his legs. His body feels like an inert mass, divorced from him, and harboring hostile intentions. The bedroom is as quiet and dim as death. One day—sooner or later—he is not going to wake up at all. At moments like this, he has an intimate understanding of what it means. He does not push the thought away, because it is a thought, after all. Right now, all the creatures of his mind seem as precious to him as earthly creatures are to God.

Cindy's best vacation ever? What he remembers of the river rafting trip: her eyes black with fright, her lips blue with cold, her knuckles white over the raft handle, her mouth agape, which must have caused her to swallow a good deal of water, her tossing and turning on the air mattress at night, her sandals too dressy, her unconscious flirtation with one of the guides. Did he really look at her so pitilessly? Did he miss all the signs of the enjoyment she claims to have felt? Or did she reconstruct her memories to fit her gratitude for the rare adventure offered by her dad? The worst of it is that the adventure had not been meant for her, but for Grace.

It had been a trying Labor Day vacation. Jim had come home to find that Joleen had stacked up eighteen thousand dollars worth of new debt on her credit cards, in spite of all his previous sermons. This time, instead of bothering to manufacture some cockamamie justification, she just turned up the sound on the TV. As a last resort, he dug up her wallet and cut all her credit cards in half, tossing the pieces on the sofa next to her. When she realized what he had done, her imperviousness turned to fury. She was in the process of scratching his eyes out when Cindy walked on the scene. Joleen stopped her assault in mid-flight, not out of consideration for their daughter, he is sure, but because the spectacle of her uncontrollable rage did not fit the carefree image she liked to project. Cindy slinked off to her room shamefacedly. Without another word, Joleen packed a bag and left the house. She did not come back the whole weekend.

Left to his own devices, Jim mowed the lawn, unclogged a sink drain, played some golf, watched the aftermath of Hurricane Katrina on the boob tube, thinking dark thoughts about Bush Junior, whose incompetence was bound to hobble the Republican party for decades. All that time, Cindy kept to her room. As to Robert, he was serving his sentence in Leavenworth, and Jim did not intend to travel to Kansas to visit him this time. On Labor Day he called Fritz, vaguely complaining of restlessness. Fritz's solution was to dispatch him to one of the Hartbridge's sites in Southern California that was short of an FTE. Jim left the house that same night without saying goodbye to Cindy, who was working the evening shift at a coffee shop on the edge of town. He spent the rest of the week working in San Diego, and flew directly back from there to San Francisco.

At the Pequeno site, he found himself thrown into another snake pit. In his absence, Myrtle Gatewick, Fritz's newest recruit, a woman who had drifted into IT management from an academic career, and seemed to have no particular technical expertise, had lost no time in establishing herself while undermining him: she had wined and dined two board members without his say-so, and whipped up the staff into outspoken rebellion against his appointment of Grace as Applications Manager. About the former, she stated, truthfully, as it turned out, to have followed Fritz's instructions. About the latter, she claimed that she had merely done her due diligence in probing the department's group dynamics, an easier task for a woman to take on. She further argued that the conflicts she had brought to light were to be seen as a trump card for Hartbridge. They would be a check on the new internal manager's power, and an insurance against the entire department ganging up on the consultants, as not infrequently happened. Objectively, she was right, Jim had to admit. She concluded her homily by cautioning Jim against any appearance of favoritism towards Grace, which might cause the Union to intervene. That last bit, fortunately, was revealed to be sheer bluff. As Charlie Weissman explained, the Union had no say on hiring decisions.

Jim would have liked to set Myrtle straight about who was boss right then and there. The problem was that although, from the Pequeno District's point of view, he was the official CIO, within the Hartbridge structure, Myrtle was his peer, taking her orders directly from Fritz. And Fritz pooh-poohed the potential for conflict in the chain of command.

Between the discovery that the staff he had not so long ago congratulated himself on bringing together was in fact reveling in mean-spirited intrigues, the not-so-subtle challenge to his authority presented by his new associate, and the shamed consciousness of his own failings, Jim felt fairly besieged. To top it all, the one person whose support he could count on was the very person he had to stay away from. In fact, he was no longer sure he could count on Grace. The contagion of wickedness was such as to tarnish his very reliance on her. If that was part of Myrtle's plan, it was brilliant.

He will always be thankful to Grace for initiating their reconciliation. Her very bluntness—although there was a second there when he feared she was going to pull a Joleen on him—and the emotion that her unshed tears had betrayed, were enough to set all his fears about her to rest. In turn, he managed to restore her trust and courage. By the time she left his office that Monday, they understood each other again.

But still, he no longer felt free to stop by her office during the day, and after work, when she tended to wander into his, Myrtle was now occupying her seat—liaising, as she called it. Boring him silly with gossip and half-baked ideas, in Jim's translation. The one bit of silver lining to his gathering cloud was that Myrtle had a sister in Livermore. For economy's sake, all the Hartbridge consultants assigned to a site were normally billeted in one corporate apartment. The Pequeno contract calling for two FTEs, Jim's was a two bedroom condo. He had not minded rooming for a couple of weeks with the migration bozo, and actually enjoyed Rick's company, but the prospect of sharing lodgings with a woman who would as soon use the kitchen knives to stab you in the back as to chop celery had limited appeal. Not to mention the grim thought of her queen-sized pantyhose hanging over the shower rail. But thanks to the Livermore sister, Jim was spared that awful fate. Every day, Myrtle did the one hour commute each way between Livermore and El Pequeno. Jim suspected that after a few weeks, her after-work liaising zeal would abate, allowing Grace to resume her evening visits. And every other weekend, Myrtle would have to fly back to Cleveland to keep an eye on her husband and kids. As the last cheap flights to Cleveland from San Francisco, Oakland or Sacramento were in the early afternoon, (he knew because he had checked the online schedules), he could count on being Myrtle-free one Friday afternoon out of two. It was something to look forward to. Of course, he would time his own travels not to coincide with hers.

In the meantime, there was the ordeal of the staff meeting where Grace's appointment would be announced to go through. On her own initiative, Myrtle had advised Grace to keep her mouth shut during the meeting so as not to inflame the staff's resentment. Jim had refrained from disagreeing with this strategy, but he wasn't overly surprised when the fearless girl decided against it. She made a modest but game little speech, resolutely disregarding her colleagues' hostility. Of course, Myrtle sensed that a gauntlet had been thrown in her face. The murderous glance she darted in Jim's direction was a revelation to him: her weakness was her self-importance. He frowned back, keeping his cards close to his vest. Inwardly, he was cheering Grace.

Grace, wherever you are between Memphis and Knoxville, did you hear this? The one moment you never forgave Jim, that nonplussed glance he and Myrtle exchanged at your promotion meeting, did not mean what you thought. Isn't it regrettable that of all the actions you called him on in that brutally honest manner of yours during the year you worked for him, this one never came up? On the other hand, even if you had asked about it, you might not have obtained the satisfactory explanation mentioned above, because that would have required Jim to badmouth one of his Hartbridge associates, a thing his sense of professional ethics forbade him to do—even as he suspected that Myrtle was not stopped by any such scruple.

In the next few days, Jim spent his leisure time at the condo reviewing his Pequeno staff spreadsheet. Of the five people who has spoken out against Grace's appointment, he felt he could disregard two: Josh and Erin, who basically had no dealings with any of the programming staff, and who, in consequence, had had little to say on their own account, only claiming a general sense among the staff that the appointment wasn't "fair", must have been put to it by Mother Goose—the one time so far that Jim had seen her exert her "senior" authority.

Mother Goose herself was not hard to figure out: her motivation was pure female jealousy. But now that she had complained to Myrtle about Jim's one attempt to include her in the circle of his affection, that strategy for bringing her around was barred. He didn't flatter himself that it could ever have worked anyway. Passive-aggressive employees are not looking for inclusion, but for reasons to maintain their grievances so they don't have to confront the challenge of actually performing. Jim's only hope, as far as Ruby was concerned, was that she would soon manage to parlay her bad back and carpal tunnel into long term disability. This would kill two birds with one stone: it would get rid of her negativity, and provide a justification for hiring a contractor to fill her position. One of the ways Hartbridge made money was by recruiting outside contractors to do work that fell outside the scope of the firm's contract—in other words pretty much anything other than management services. The outside contractors were paid by the client, and Hartbridge collected a percentage of the fees. Lately, Fritz had started nagging Jim about his failure so far to tap into this source of profit.

Elmore was also a fairly straightforward case. Grace, by her energy, efficiency and lack of deference, had from the start threatened the supremacy he had built over decades of staying put while more talented colleagues left for one reason or another. Within a couple of years, Grace had mastered systems and protocols over which Fuddy-duddy claimed the title of guru, and put his life-long accomplishments to shame by successfully completing a long list of projects. It was in front of her office that managers lined up for help now. That an official supervisor's role should be piled on top of all the soft power she had already accumulated—and in particular that he should then be supervised by her—was a revolution he could not allow without a fight. He did not, however, have any management ambitions for himself: he was too old to want the long hours and constant aggravations, as he had frankly acknowledged to Jim. His main object was to defend the status quo—in the name of the department's morale, of course.

To Jim's utter surprise the ambitious one turned out to be Tiffany. It appeared that Busty Blonde, who had shown no great talent or dedication even as a receptionist, thought herself quite capable of leading a technical team, on the strength of her data entry into the help desk ticketing system, and of her experience in bossing building contractors around while moonlighting for her husband's business. He had to hand it to her for sheer chutzpah. If he wasn't mistaken in his interpretation of the way she displayed her generous cleavage over his desk as she made her sales pitch, she was even prepared to sweeten the deal with a little quid pro quo. Luckily, it turned out that

Busty Blonde did not possess a college degree. Jim was able to take shelter behind the Chancellor's prejudices, thus spared the awkward task of explaining that *he* did not think she met the minimum qualifications for the job, a chore normally handled by HR—or not at all. In these litigious days, the standard procedure is simply to refrain from acknowledging receipt of unwanted resumes.

Jim wondered how big the anti-Grace cabal really was, aside from its five spokespersons, and to what extent Myrtle had been instrumental in bringing them together. He was pretty sure he did not have to worry about Alex, Rajiv and Wei because of their marginal position in the group. These three people fairly represented the back bone of the IT work force these days: Eastern Europeans and Asians with excellent skills and exemplary work ethic who would never be considered for leadership roles because of their poor English. This was very convenient for the new generation of Americans, who, as a rule (with exceptions, such as Grace and Mina) felt entitled to power but had no patience for technical learning. And perhaps it was convenient for the foreigners too: barred from entertaining any overweening ambitions, they were able to lead relatively privileged lives while being spared the turmoil of office politics.

What was interesting about Mina, Jim realized, was that although she was American born, she seemed to have managed to tag herself as one of those innocuous foreigners. He did not blame her for it. There were days when Jim himself wished he had remained a computer operator. And in the present situation, her very isolation nearly guaranteed that she had taken no part in the conspiracy. He resolved to make more of an effort to know her, for her sake and for Grace's as well as for his.

Ray Gomes, the computer operator, who, aside from working the graveyard shift, seemed on good terms with both Grace and Mina, Jim similarly eliminated from his list of suspects. As to Sandra, she had occasionally revealed her exasperation with Ruby's sloth, and may in fact covet the "senior" slot, so she was unlikely to follow Mother Goose's lead. This left Sandip, another foreigner, but whose command of the English language was superior to that of most Americans, and who had a good deal of sloth to cover up for, as well as a certain latent cattiness not incompatible with conspiracies. Jim would have to reserve judgment on him.

The computer room was the best place to talk with Mina, out of sight and out of hearing of Tiffany and the other cubicle residents. Taking advantage of the next opportunity when he knew she would be there decollating the reports printed during the previous night's batch run, Jim wandered in. He asked her about her Labor Day weekend. She said she hadn't done anything special. She asked him about his vacation. He said he had played some golf.

Having by then made sure that no one else was in the computer room, he segued into Grace's appointment. Mina was quick to assure him that she thought Grace deserved it. Jim wondered why Mina had not congratulated her. She said she had been afraid of sticking her neck out. "You, afraid?" he asked. "Afraid so," she replied. They both laughed. He wanted her to know that as far as he was concerned, she deserved to be promoted too, that in fact she was practically acting as Operations Manager already, but it was Pequeno's policy to require all new managers to be college graduates. According to her resume on file in Personnel, she had not graduated. Was that true? "Afraid so," she repeated. They laughed again. Did she have any plan to go back to college? As soon as her little boy went to pre-school. How long was it going to take her to graduate? Three or four years from now, Jim would be gone by then. Well, he hoped not, but in the meantime, he was going to see if he could at least get her a raise. She was very grateful for this mark of recognition. At that point his attention was drawn to the boxes and boxes of paper that he had been helping Mina lug as they talked. They agreed to bring up the subject of paper consumption with Grace in her new role as Applications Manager. His hand already on the door, he was about to leave when it occurred to him to make a confession:

"You know, *I* never graduated from college," he said in a conspiratorial tone.

"Seriously?" Mina whispered back.

"Yep. In those days, there was such a need for IT technicians that you would get hired after taking just a couple of courses. And then, how far up you went depended on what you showed yourself capable of, not on a bit of paper. But those days are gone."

"Especially since Dr. Akecheta took over," Mina remarked.

"So, we'd better not let him know. About my lack of a degree, I mean."

"My lips are sealed."

And they proved to be. That bit of information never came back to Jim. He had confirmed that he could trust her.

Grace had been settling into her new position for a week or so when Jim received the email announcing the second annual Hartbridge Western Region Retreat, which would this time take the shape of a two-day rafting trip down the South Fork of the American River. All twenty or so Hartbridge associates working on sites west of the Mississippi were expected to attend this team building exercise, regardless of their other engagements. Expenses would be paid by the company. One thing could be said about Fritz: he knew how to gild his employees' slavery.

It was Fritz in fact who suggested that Jim invite Grace on the trip—although, considering that he had already bought her ticket, it might be more accurate to state that he ordered Jim to conscript her. Fritz was intimately acquainted with the hullabaloo that had surrounded the new Applications Manager's appointment—what Jim hadn't told him, he was sure to have learned from Myrtle. But as the crisis had not involved any of the Pequeno higher management, he had not been worried about it. On the contrary, like Myrtle, he saw it as an opportunity to detach Grace from her rank-and-file cohorts and align her with Hartbridge's objectives. The river rafting trip would show her who her real friends were and cement the partnership. Plus it would give Jim a chance to see her in a wet tee shirt, perhaps to grab her when she went overboard, perhaps to sing Kumbaya to her around the campfire, who knew. In any case, Jim would be in a position to decide whether the game was worth the candle. It was no use for Jim to assert that there was no game. Fritz loved his little lecherous scenarios.

The rafting trip was scheduled for the first weekend in October, but, as he was still ostensibly quarantined from Grace, Jim did not get an opportunity to mention it to her until just a week before. Of course, he could have invited her via email, but he felt more confident in his powers of persuasion face to face. Plus, he wanted to see her reaction. Would she be flattered to find herself inducted into the Hartbridge team? Would she be thrilled by the proposed adventure? And as an aside, would she welcome—or not—the perspective of a physical rapprochement with her boss? Truth was that for all his demurrals to Fritz, and apart from his sincere wish to show her a good time as compensation for the grief she had recently endured, and on top of his honest desire to interact with her in a more leisurely setting, Jim was indeed interested in seeing Grace with fewer clothes on. That was what abstinence was doing to him: it was turning him into an old lecher—like Fritz, though Fritz wasn't known for abstaining from anything. Jim was determined no to act on his lust, but he wouldn't mind getting a better view of what he was renouncing, and confirming that she was lusting a little bit for him too.

At the end of a scheduled meeting with Grace and Mina, during which they had started tackling the paper consumption issue, Jim asked Grace to stay for a few minutes. Probably fearing a new development in the cabal against her, Grace remained standing, her arms crossed on her chest, her blue eyes a little frosty. This unpropitious beginning made Jim so nervous that he stood up in turn and walked over to his bookshelf, pretending to look for some paper. Not finding what he was not looking for, he turned half-way back toward her, as if still absorbed by his unsuccessful search.

"Where was I? Oh, yes. I wanted to let you know that Hartbridge is organizing a river rafting trip on the American river next weekend."

"Sounds cool. Are you going?"

"Yes, of course." He paused, fixed his eyes on her. "And you're invited."

"Wow! I love river rafting. Which fork?"

"Fork?"

"I mean which fork of the American River?"

Jim had a sneaking suspicion that she was stalling.

"South Fork. Two days with overnight camping. All the food is provided."

"The deluxe package. Hartbridge must be rolling in the dough."

And now sarcasm. Things were definitely not going his way. Unaccountably, he felt all his powers of persuasion deserting him.

"So, what do you say?" he asked a little brusquely, unable to bear the suspense.

"Thank you very much for the offer. It would be nice to spend time with you away from the office . . . although not so much with Myrtle, I have to say. I assume she is going?"

"Yeah, but there'll be twenty other people. She'll be lost in the crowd."

Tell her I'll stick Myrtle on another raft, tell her I'll break Myrtle's leg before the trip, he was thinking, made mute by a growing sense of futility. He guessed that she had a bigger "but" in reserve.

"Anyway . . ."

Ah, here it was coming.

"I don't think it would be a good idea for me to be seen hobnobbing with Hartbridge personnel. It would look as if I had been bought off."

Of course, she was right. Jim was stung by a sense of shame. Shame that the conflict of interest as she would see it had escaped him. Shame to find that he had been thinking with his dick, against all his expectations of himself. And shame that his personal attractions had not been enough to override her scruples. For all he knew, she was not at all eager to see him in shorts.

"But your colleagues don't have to know," he mumbled in a last-ditch effort that only increased his self-disgust.

"Oh, they would know, you can bet on it."

She was referring to Myrtle, of course. Never underestimate the acuteness of women.

"You have a point," he conceded. "But I wish you could see your way around it. Will you sleep on it?"

"There's no need," she said resolutely. "I can't go. I am sorry."

"Don't be sorry. I respect your integrity. Maybe another time."

She looked as dejected as he felt, and this put balm on his wounds. He held his hand out.

"Shake on it?" he asked.

"Of course," she answered heartily.

Her hand met his. A second later they were locked in a hug—holding on to each other for dear life as the ship sunk underneath their feet, was how it felt to him. Then, without a word or a look, Grace detached herself from him and fled his office.

Examining his recollections, Jim wonders whether he could really have felt shame over such a small setback as his failure to enlist a subordinate in a pleasure outing. Isn't "shame" too strong a word for the unpleasant feeling he did experience? Wouldn't "embarrassment" be more apt? And why would he have felt as if he was on a sinking ship while he hugged Grace? The ship sailed on for quite a few more months after that. Perhaps, like his daughter, he is reconstructing his memories in the light of his present feelings, which in his case are far from serene. On the other hand, the shame and foreboding may have been there all along, though he refrained from dwelling on them at the time.

What is certain is that he could not bring himself to tell the truth to Fritz about Grace's refusal, for her sake as well as for his, he is still inclined to believe. It wouldn't have done to let Fritz know that the new Applications Manager was not really on Hartbridge's team. So he invented some family emergency, trusting that Myrtle was in no position to worm any other explanation out of Grace. It then occurred to him to ask Fritz if Cindy could take Grace's place on the trip, and Fritz, in one of the many acts of friendship that to this day prevent Jim from judging him too harshly, said yes.

Jim has to hand it to Cindy. For once, she responded to a proposal of his with great decisiveness and efficiency. Within a couple of days, she wrestled time off from work, made the flight reservations, arranged a ride to the airport, borrowed a sleeping bag and a backpack from some friend. And whatever her terror of the rapids, she did not complain during the whole trip. But instead of feeling proud of her, Jim fears that he spent quite a bit of time imagining that Grace would have been a better partner: more agile, more intrepid, more self-reliant, wittier. He sees now that on one level, Grace held for him the role of the daughter he would have liked to have. It is a good thing that she wasn't, given that he also lusted after her. And it is likely that if he had not unconsciously compared the two young women, he wouldn't have thought of substituting one for the other on a vacation which turned out to be the beginning of his rapprochement with Cindy. Curses and blessings, indeed. But still, poor Cindy. Jim regrets the inadequacy of his love for her as she was growing up. Even now, it is still a fostered thing. He can only focus on doing his duty as a father, and hope that his feelings will catch up with it in due time. For love, that most mysterious gift, cannot be commanded.

XII

CHEESY

When did Grace first come to the conclusion that she had only been meant to be a puppet manager? The first instance of the expression in her journal is in an entry dated December 16, 2005, a full three months after her appointment. Even then, it is used in quotes, in the middle of a paragraph where she seems to blame herself for having had the thought, putting it down to "self-importance"—which just happened to be a cardinal sin in Jim's view.

And yet, didn't Jim admit right from the start that she would never have been promoted were it not for the union rule that required an internal manager in every department? Didn't he fail to specify the scope of her new authority, either to the group during the initial announcement, or to herself later on? Didn't he in fact undermine that very authority immediately through his unsupportive attitude during her acceptance speech? Was she so much in thrall to his charm, his savoir faire, his paternal aura to be blind for months to the reality that she was a mere pawn in someone else's game? Whose game, that is the question.

In spite of their reconciliation, something did in fact die for her during her promotion ordeal: her wholehearted trust, a conviction of their common purpose. But as she was deeply attached to the idea of her attachment to her boss, other feelings rose to the surface to fill the gap. She became more forgiving, more self-critical . . . and more sensitive to his sex appeal.

It was with much regret that she had refused to take part in the Hartbridge river rafting retreat. She would have loved to observe Jim in the great outdoors, without the protection of business suit or managerial prerogatives, to find out how brave, masterful, even-tempered he showed himself then, not to mention whether his sex appeal would survive a wet tee shirt. (Hmmm . . . so it seems that at that point already, Grace was quite willing to entertain the idea that her idol had feet of clay.) But she was a little disconcerted that Jim would even propose such an outing, after weeks of keeping her at arms' length supposedly to allay her colleagues' jealousy—given his assurance that he still liked her, this was the way she tried to account for his continued aloofness. Until recently she was inclined to attribute this momentary lapse in judgment on his part to his attraction to her, an explanation that both flattered her (the attraction) and disappointed her (the lapse in judgment). It now occurs to her that Fritz, rather than Jim, may have originated the idea. After all, Fritz was the one who paid for the trip. And since Fritz's motivations can be assumed to have been pure—pure business, of course—Grace wonders what business objective, from Hartbridge's point of view, her participation in the retreat would have achieved. Divide and conquer, by further alienating her from her colleagues? That seems too petty a tactic for a CEO to engage in. Buying her off? Although her refusal had been motivated by her wish to guard against that very perception, she still can't believe that any businessman would count on buying someone off for the mere price of a weekend outing. And what would Jim's acquiescence to either scheme make him, if not a snake of the most slithering variety?

She revisits her own motives for declining Jim's invitation. She is still amazed at the presence of mind that steered her around that particular shoal even as Jim played his siren song. She is proud to have spontaneously grasped an important tenet of business ethics: do not accept gifts from outside vendors. After all, it seems that many people with more experience and influence than her, such as doctors, researchers and politicians, haven't quite got it. But she also suspects that there was a more personal aspect to her refusal: a revenge for Jim's neglect, a way of letting him know that he wasn't the only one with the power to withhold. It is probably a subliminal sense of her own perversity that moved her to hug him so affectionately afterwards—that and a wish for a crumb of the sexual thrill she was renouncing.

In any case, Jim reacted in quite a gentlemanly fashion to being balked, that time as well as others. Even in her short career, Grace has dealt with bosses who would not have been such good sports, who would in fact have retaliated one way or another. It's something to keep in mind.

As it turned out, another outing opportunity presented itself a couple of weeks later: it was now Dr Akecheta's turn to play the retreat card. Like the Hartbridge retreat, the Pequeno Community College District Management Retreat was mandatory; like the Hartbridge retreat, it was scheduled for a weekend; and like the Hartbridge retreat it was announced so late that several people were forced to scrap their entertainment plans, per chance losing money on non-refundable tickets. Yet very few people dared to grumble about any of this. In the corporate world, it is understood that in exchange for inflated salaries, liberal perks and stock options, managers must consider themselves on call 24/7. Dr. Akecheta, who prided himself in having brought (what he understood of) corporate culture to the Pequeno Community College District, deemed it becoming to similarly encroach on his managers' leisure time, although the District's revenues, raised as they were from California taxpayers, were only sufficient to provide for *his* "premier" salary and *his* "second-to-none" perks—but unfortunately no stock options.

For the same economic reasons, the Pequeno retreat was only going to be a semi-lavish affair. It would take place at a luxurious lodge on the edge of Yosemite National Park, one of those grand resorts built in the days of pre-code Hollywood which, following the money, tacked on convention facilities in the eighties, and now offer, on top of gourmet meals and spa services, meeting room rentals, audio-visual packages, and sport-oriented team building activities such as kayaking, mountaineering and horseback riding. But, although the Chancellor, three Vice Chancellors and two College Presidents (and their spouses, if applicable) would stay overnight to enjoy the antique décor and massage therapy—a detail Grace learned from Roger Wilkins—the rest of the managers would have to drive two hours each way on Saturday to attend. As to the team building activities, they would be limited to those that can be conducted indoors with flip boards and marker pens.

The above bit of snark is in fact retrospective. At the time of the announcement, Grace, still trying to adapt to her new role, took the upcoming retreat in stride. On the plus side, she would after all get to spend some time with Jim outside of a work environment, since he had proposed to carpool with Admissions Director Roger Wilkins, Risk Manager Harriet Jellineck and Grace herself. And the best part was that Myrtle would not be of the party. Since she was not a Pequeno manager, she had not been invited.

But first, there was some homework to complete. All the managers had to prepare for the retreat by reading a motivational book entitled *Who Moved My Cheese?*, which would be discussed at one of the sessions. When the book was finally handed out two days before the event, Grave heaved a sigh of relief: it consisted of only ninety-four pages of 24 point text interspersed with black and white illustrations. What it looked like was a fairy tale written for first-graders: one clause sentences, one sentence paragraphs, words of no more than two syllables. The last page even concluded with an un-capitalized "the end". From the point of view of the effort required to read it, it was a piece of cake—or cheese, rather.

But it was a fairy tale, not a genre adapted to deal with the complexities of management, in Grace's untutored opinion. Even as a fairy tale, it was deficient. The protagonists, consisting of two mice and two undefined "little people" (instead of dwarves, elves, or gnomes) were sketchily drawn—actually not drawn at all, in a graphic sense, since all the illustrations represented the same piece of cheese. The entire plot—a quest for cheese—took place in a maze, a claustrophobic setting unrelieved by any picturesque touches (no dripping walls, no sleeping monster) the only place descriptors being references to numbered "stations", a topography reminiscent of the unemployment office. But self-contained at the tale's setting seemed to be, there were occasional mentions of visits by the protagonists' friends, inviting questions as to how the visitors found their way to the maze-dwellers, and why the maze-dwellers themselves did not think of escaping the maze altogether, instead of running around in it in their search for food. But it was the motivation for the quest that Grace found the most confusing. From the evidence, it seemed that the mice and the little people were limited to a cheese-only diet. So when their cheese disappeared from its usual "station", they must have been threatened with actual starvation. But even the one character who remained so afraid of change that he never ventured beyond the original station did not die. Were these characters not subject to mortality? Was the story about survival or about greed?

There were deeper problems with the book's underlying moral. The reader was encouraged to be alert to imminent changes, but dissuaded from "overanalyzing" their origin. It was suggested that the tale's protagonists were responsible for the disappearance of the cheese from its normal spot (it seemed they had eaten it all little by little—it couldn't have been that someone else stole it), but the questions of who put the cheese there in the first place, why that same entity (earthly or divine?) decided to deliver the next supply somewhere else, or who actually *made* the cheese were never answered. The protagonists, little bureaucratic creatures who did not themselves grow or manufacture or transport anything, were left to their individual rat races—helping each other out when not inconvenient, to be sure, but certainly not banding together to demand accountability from the maze master.

In short, *Who Moved My Cheese?* seemed to be the perfect booklet for business executives to distribute to clueless employees on the eve of a stock-boosting round of layoffs. Puzzled as to why it should be made required reading for Pequeno managers, who were mostly well informed and mostly protected by tenure, (even Grace had retreat rights to her former position), she googled it. She found that it had been on the New York Times bestseller list for five years after its publication in 1998. The majority of the reviews were glowing, although she did find some criticisms that echoed hers. She was curious to see how her colleagues would respond. For her part, if she was put on the spot, she wondered whether she should opt for a full-blown literary critique of the book or merely ask the kind of innocent comprehension questions that would occur to a six-year-old. In the end, she decided to let the retreat's ambience dictate her strategy. (Her unvarnished opinion about *Who Moved My Cheese?* was that it was an insult to her intelligence and a waste of management training time. But, as straightforward as she was reputed to be, she never imagined that she could simply state it. Satire is not just more fun to dish out than straightforward judgments, it also serves as a shield for them—albeit a very ineffective one, since people who don't get a joke are the most liable to conclude the joke is on them.)

It was a beautiful Saturday morning, blue and brisk, with scarlet leaves piling up on the dewy lawns, when Grace met the other carpoolers in the District parking lot. The sun was just rising over the distant Sierras, casting rosy tints on stucco walls and on Jim's bare arms. Following the Chancellor's prescription for "business casual" attire, he had exchanged his usual tailored suit for pleated, cuffed khakis and a café-au-lait short-sleeved polo shirt with the top button open, offering a peek at a dense mat of graying chest hair. Grace was reminded of the time, in kindergarten, when she ran into her teacher at the supermarket, and hid behind her mother because the teacher wore shorts and a tank top. Even now, there was something shocking at first about seeing an authority figure in any state of undress. It seemed to make them too vulnerable. But as Jim looked as self-assured as ever, and as his relative state of undress did not reveal any deformity, Grace quickly got over her uneasiness. (No, the bulky dress shirts had not concealed unsightly rolls of fat. And on the other hand, his arms turned out to be as finely shaped as his hands. He could have made a few bucks sitting as a live model in one of the figure drawing classes on campus. The students would have had a wonderful time delineating and shading those smooth flexor and extensor curves and dainty insertion points.)

Harriet Jellineck, who had the pale, meek face of a Flemish Virgin, but was reputed to be a work horse and a no-nonsense stickler for safety, had opted for the same khaki-pants-and-beige-knitted-top look as Jim, a coincidence that Roger was satirizing as Grace joined the group. For his part, Roger wore a white, un-tucked band-collar shirt over black slacks and sock-less loafers. As to Grace herself, all her outfits belonging to the "business casual" category, as far as she was concerned, she had assembled her usual combination of layered tops and flouncy skirt (this one a slightly longer than usual black and gray chiffon creation with pin tucks and a tulle ruffle, finished only the previous night, due to the exacting nature of pin tucks, but well worth the trouble: it danced around her legs of its own accord.) The ensemble was completed by a short denim jacket and a pair of silver ballet flats, only omitting the leggings required for bike riding—that day, to save time on the early commute, she had driven to work.

Inspired no doubt by Jim's example on the eve of the Labor Day weekend, Roger made a big show of welcoming Grace with a hug, which gave Jim permission to follow suit. To even things out, Grace put her arms around Harriet, who, after a moment's confusion, returned the hug willingly. Perhaps, Grace hoped, the entire management group would switch from handshakes to embraces as a form of greeting. It would contribute to team building, and allow Jim and Grace to freely indulge their fondness for embracing each other.

The two-hour drive didn't seem long in the present company. Roger, who had long legs, requisitioned the front passenger seat. Grace sat behind Jim, with Harriet on her right. This sitting arrangement could easily have led to separate men-in-front, women-in-back conversations, a type of older generation sociability Grace detested. Fortunately, Roger always sought the largest possible audience for his clownish skits on national politics, Pequeno folklore, his kids' antics and personal foibles. Pretty soon he had the whole car in stitches, including Harriet. Grace noticed, though, that Roger was reining in the political satire, probably because he was aware of Jim's Republican loyalties, and that his tales of Pequeno folklore were free of his usual digs at the Chancellor's grandiosity. He must have already been aware of a trait of Dr. Akecheta's leadership that Grace would only learn of much later: his reliance on a network of spies to assess the loyalty of his subalterns. In light of Roger's ascension to the rank of associate vice-chancellor soon after, it is in fact possible that he was one of the spies. But he did recount several stories that showed Grace in a flattering light, calling on Jim to concur in admiration. It seemed to Grace that Roger's encomiums had more to do with Jim than with her, that he was using Jim's partiality to her as a male bonding gambit. It was all very interesting.

The landscape along the way was well known to Grace, as she used El Pequeno's proximity to Yosemite to lure her Berkeley friends on backpacking adventures. Here and there, she pointed its features to Jim: the slow progression from flat fields and shady orchards to colorful vineyards and bleak pastures, the scattered live oaks among the rolling brown hills, the first pines and redwoods, the distant peaks, some of them still snow-capped. She had to lean forward to be heard above the ambient din, which allowed her to inhale his flowery aftershave, sometimes to feel his hair brush against her cheek. It was all very nice.

Alas, all good things come to an end. Suddenly, they had driven through the lodge's gate, and the lodge itself stood before them, a monumental version of an alpine chalet, bristling with gables and laced with half-timber, on a background of rocks and evergreens, and even a small waterfall. Through a lobby showcasing coffered ceilings, oriental carpets and river rock fireplaces worthy of Julia Morgan, and down a maze of less lofty corridors—this particular labyrinth was provided with a Ariadne's thread of posted arrows, but somewhere in it Grace lost sight of Jim—into a cavernous and windowless conference room full of people Grace didn't know, their nervous banter insufficient to counteract the chilly atmosphere. It was all a bit scary.

She had to give the Chancellor some credit for knowing how to squeeze premier service out of his administrative staff. For once, her last name had been spelled correctly on both the registration sheet and her laminated name tag. Her conference packet was a cornucopia of goodies: a glossy three-ring binder containing a set of handouts separated by color-coded tabs, a notepad and a thick metal pen, both embossed with the Pequeno logo, an extra-large tee-shirt also bearing the Pequeno colors, a lunch menu, various brochures from the lodge, a Pequeno lapel pin, several energy bars and other artificially flavored candies, all these items carefully stuffed into a sturdy Pequeno tote bag with a side pocket for your cell phone. The whole thing must have weighed ten pounds and cost as much in parts and labor as the registration fees for a five-unit semester course. And Grace had no use for any of it, with the possible exception of the handouts. Just another re-gift or recycle conundrum.

Following the crowd, Grace made her way to the back of the room, where a damask covered table was laden with the most gargantuan "continental" breakfast she had ever seen: croissants, Danish pastries, piles of ham, natural yogurts in many flavors, grapes, quartered pineapples, deviled eggs, four types of coffee, eight types of tea bags, three types of juice in imitation crystal carafes, on and on and on. There was enough food there to pay for Mina's monthly salary.

Bob Johnson, who was to emcee the conference, came to the podium to ask the attendees to take their seats, as the Chancellor was scheduled to make the introductory remarks. Everyone rushed forward, competing for seats in the last few rows, as in grade school. Grace found herself in the middle of the second row, with plenty of empty seats on both sides. As she was arranging conference materials and breakfast fare on the narrow table in front of her, also covered in damask and lined up with more crystal looking carafes, she sensed a large, warm, fragrant presence on her right. It was Jim, sitting down next to her. "Hey," she said. "Hey," he said.

The Chancellor was late. After a quarter of an hour of deferential silence, people started chatting in hushed tones, and then to call each other across the room, and finally to get up and mill around the breakfast table. It is at this point that the Chancellor made his entrance, from a unmarked side door, and accompanied by a bodyguard complete with shades and ear set—Dr. Akecheta's latest acquisition in an apparent bid to compete with the President of the University of California system. The Lodi case had demonstrated that the Central Valley was not exempt from terrorist threats, from which every executive, even from the least consequential community college district, owed it to himself to be protected at all times.

There was a scramble as managers tried to slink back to their places before the Chancellor's eyes fell on them. Shins were barked, coffee was spilled on freshly laundered shirts, muffled curses were heard. Dr. Akecheta looked on the commotion with grim enjoyment. Grace noticed that his concept of "business casual" was a three-piece suit, and felt sorry for the managers who had shown up in jeans. Finally, he cleared his throat and intoned his speech. His voice, deep but monotone, sounded like the rumblings of a distant thunderstorm. He obviously didn't put much stock in his own powers of oratory, suggesting that he had quieter means of persuasion at his disposal.

After an introduction dotted with his favorite buzzwords (premier, second-to-none, twenty-first-century, excellence . . .), the Chancellor got down to brass tacks, which was his expectations for the management team. And these expectations all flowed down from one principle: everyone must bend to the Chancellor's will at all times, both "in action and in spirit". So much for shared governance. Grace started to understand why the Academic Senate and teachers' union were so unhappy about him. He wasn't just a conceited prig, but a tyrant.

The Chancellor's speech was followed by a presentation on Labor/Management relations by the HR director, in which Grace found some useful information on the role of unions in disciplining matters. Until then, her only contact with the Pequeno Classified union had been through the dues that appeared on her paycheck stub. Now she was a manager. She would no longer be subjected to union dues. On the other hand, she would no longer have any advocate in the event of arbitrary upper-management dealings. The more she thought about it, the less sure she was of having made a good bargain.

In the middle of the HR presentation, Dr. Akecheta was tapped on the shoulder by his bodyguard. A few words were whispered in his ear, at the end of which he rose and left the room by the same side door he had used for his entrance, the grave look on his face suggesting that a bomb had been discovered in the potted palms, or that the President of the United States had requested his immediate input on educational reform. As the bodyguard closed the door after them, his business suit and dour demeanor struck Grace as so much like the Chancellor's that the two of them could have been twins.

As soon as the Chancellor was gone, the atmosphere in the room seemed to warm up. Several hands went up to ask questions about the presentation, and Roger made a joke or two. There was a short coffee break, after which Jim was scheduled to speak about the functions of the IT department. It was a subject he knew like the back of his hand, and his presentation was limited to fifteen minutes, yet Grace saw him blanch visibly as he approached the mike. When he started to speak, his voice was strangled, his eyes remained stuck to his notes. He was truly shy after all, who would have thought? Remembering his plea that she should "buck him up" when he had to speak in public, Grace racked her brain for something to say that would put him at ease, but it was Roger who unfroze him with another joke. After that Jim was fairly fluent, but still strangely lacking in his usual charisma. Whether the audience was moved to compassion by his wooden performance, or whether they did not notice it, so imbued they were with his confident image, they applauded him thunderously afterward. "See what I told you?" Jim muttered to Grace as he came back to his seat. "You did fine," she whispered back. She had to stop herself from patting him on the arm.

It was now Grace's turn to take the podium, her assigned topic being Identity Management. Bob introduced her as the youngest manager in the District, eliciting another round of applause. She smiled at the welcoming crowd, conscious of the pleasing way her skirt swished as she moved to adjust the mike. Thanks to her high school debating days, *she* had no fear of speaking in public. She went over the procedures managers should use to request access to various applications for their staff. In passing, she expressed a wish that HR personnel would promptly notify IT of terminated employees so that their accounts could be disabled. She was hoping to force the issue by bringing it up in public, and the HR director agreed that this procedure was desirable "in theory", making the practice conditional on the usual bugaboo: his staff's workload. She concluded by proposing an integrated ID management system, which, by synchronizing the Windows AD directory and the mainframe home-grown security database, would greatly simplify the granting, revoking and auditing of computer logon privileges. Her presentation was received very warmly, causing her to remember by contrast the hostility of her coworkers, and to think that perhaps her place was in the management ranks after all.

The morning activities concluded with a team building exercise, led by the same Organizational Behavior consultant who had recommended *Who Moved My Cheese?* She was an angular middle-aged woman with old eyes and a young manner, bedecked in primary colors and costume jewelry, her unceasing, overly bright smile conveying the impression of an eager cheese-getter who would never find her way to the big dairy counter. Grace wondered how much she charged for her services, and whether a day-long workshop on resume writing and job interviewing for recent graduates of Pequeno's trade programs might not have been a better use of Pequeno's training dollars.

The team building exercise was designed to be an ice-breaker. It involved people walking around in circles, clapping their hands and shouting nonsense syllables according to some beat dictated by the circle leader. Grace, who couldn't even understand the rules, was eliminated right away, quickly followed by Roger, who made a point of disrupting the rhythm. But what was Grace's surprise to find Jim, like a deceptively agile dancing bear, holding on till the end of the game, and being declared the winner in his circle, a victory he accepted with all the aw-shuck modesty of a quarterback. He had never mentioned playing any sport other than golf, but obviously there was a back story to this feat of coordination.

As lunch was in the process of being wheeled into the conference room, there was no time for the debriefing session planned by the bright consultant, but one lesson of the exercise was clear to Grace: different people were good at different things, and you could not always predict who would be good at what. It wasn't particularly deep or controversial, but it was useful to see it demonstrated in practice. That and the fact that being forced to play ridiculous games did in fact help break the ice. The manager's group was much more relaxed and interactive afterward. How relaxed and interactive they would have been if the Chancellor had taken part in the game was probably a moot point: Dr. Akecheta, Grace felt certain, would never allow himself to be touched by ridicule.

Lunch was another orgy, but by then, Grace had given up trying to add up the retreat's costs. After lunch, with the Chancellor still mercifully AWOL, the bright consultant led a discussion of *Who Moved My Cheese?* In Akecheta's absence, Grace expected some of the comments to be sardonic or at least skeptical. She was wrong. Manager after manager stood up to praise the book. The HR director, a man who piled up the paperwork sent to his office into a barricade against intruders—which his secretary would periodically have to excavate in answer to the plea of some desperate manager whose hiring efforts were stalled—recognized himself in Sniff, the rat who is alert to change. Roger identified with Scurry, the rat who, rather than overanalyzing first causes, scrambles in all directions until he finds new cheese. Many people acknowledged their affinity with Haw, the little person who is afraid of change, but finally learns to go with the flow. Grace was about to nudge Jim and whisper some remark about the seamless blend of religious testimonial and sales pitch that characterized many of these interventions, when Jim himself stood up and joined the Haw camp.

He told the group how money difficulties following the birth of his second child had forced him to take a job in Saudi Arabia, although he had never set foot abroad before, and considered North Carolina the center of the world. He confessed how disoriented he had felt at first, and how he had been blown over to discover that people at the other end of the world were not only recognizably human, but also convinced of the supremacy of their own culture. To illustrate—somewhat incongruously—his enlightenment, he recalled the time when, visiting some Sheik's palace, he saw workmen trying to fit an oversized wood door into a stone frame by chipping away at the stone sill instead of sawing the door to size, a much easier task, as any American handyman would have figured out. But when he mentioned the incident to his friend Waheed, he learned that there was a logic to the Arab workmen's procedure: in a country where there are no trees, wood is a much more precious commodity than stone, and therefore planing it down was unthinkable. Jim concluded by attributing his professional success, as well as a much more rounded world view, to his sojourn abroad.

But the intervention that topped them all was that of the District Comptroller, Constanza Marques, an ogre of a woman who was never satisfied with the work the IT department did for her, who was known for regularly reducing her underlings to tears, and who, following her own mysterious policies, constantly shuffled money between budgets in such complex and unexpected ways that not even the best query tools could keep track. There were rumors that some of the money ended up in her own account. In her few dealings with the woman, Grace had been appalled by the combination of cunning, ferocity and obtuseness with which she deflected any reasonable argument and thus got her way. She had been glad that, because of her focus on the student applications, she didn't have to deal with her very much. Now, of course, as Applications Manager, Grace was going to have to deal with everyone. So it was with a keen interest that she saw Constanza raise her hand. To what conversion would she testify? How would she sell herself on the change market? The remarkable thing was that she did neither. Oblivious to protocol, Constanza did not bother to stand up when she was given permission to speak. Instead, ensconced in her chair like an unmovable rock, but in a voice sharp enough to puncture all the hopeful balloons sent up by her colleagues, she flatly declared that she had seen her cheese moved many times in her career, and had finally resolved she was never going to let it happen again.

Her statement was all the more daring that, apparently owing her job to the previous chancellor's friendship, she was thought to be out of favor with Akecheta—and as she had been hired as a classified manager, she had no tenure protection or retreat rights. Either she was mad, or she had some card up her sleeve that Grace would have loved to take a peek at. In any case, her brave speech had gone so much against the grain that it was greeted with a collective gasp, followed by a few chuckles, one of them from Grace. "A toast to our proud Hem!" Roger joked to break the spell, Hem being the little person who refused to change. "You can call me whatever you want," Constanza answered with stony good nature. That day, Constanza earned Grace's respect.

No one felt up to the challenge of following Constanza's act. Grace herself kept mum. Next to the obvious sincerity of the change enthusiasts, Jim foremost among them, and the equal earnestness of the one rebel, her own satirical games suddenly appeared not only beside the point, but outright snide and snotty. And it was true, of course, that change was inevitable, that adaptability was a quality to be nurtured, etc. Seeing other people take to heart the book's lessons had forced Grace to acknowledge that there may be a certain wisdom in their perspective, and consequently to feel more humble herself. By "people", she mostly meant Jim, of course. And she may have been too quick to discount the sincere feelings and valid worldview that underlay her own sarcastic bent: a sense of indignation at social injustice. However, occasional bouts of humility are good for the soul.

After the *Who Moved My Cheese?* confessions, the bright consultant quickly went through some handouts on negative attitudes managers should avoid. Among the dictums illustrating those, there were two of Jim's favorites: "When the cat's away, the mice will play" and "Don't let them see you sweat". Jim didn't seem to notice this potential rebuke to his management philosophy, and Grace forbore to bring it to his attention.

Then there was a presentation on program review during which Grace nearly fell asleep, and then another team building exercise, this one on "diversity". Eight poster boards were taped to the walls around the room, each inscribed with a different diversity category:

Race
Gender
Socio-economic class
Sexual orientation
Immigration status

Ability/disability status
Religion
Age

The game participants were grouped in the center of the room. The bright consultant would read a statement that could be completed by any of the posted categories. Each participant was to select the category that best fit their individual experience, and express their choice by positioning themselves in front of the corresponding board. The diversity statements went as follows:

1. *The part of my identity that I am most aware of on a daily basis is...*

Most women rallied around the Gender poster, most men in front of the Age poster. Of the two black managers, one selected Age and the other Race. No one selected Socio-economic class, Sexual Orientation or Immigration Status. Roger did a spastic number in front of the Ability/disability Status poster.

2. *The part of my identity that I am the least aware of on a daily basis is...*

Most people walked to the Race or Socio-economic Class posters. No one selected Sexual Orientation, Immigration Status or Ability/disability Status. Roger vamped in front of the Gender poster.

3. *The part of my identity that was most emphasized in my family growing up was...*

Many people assembled around the Religion poster. No one selected Sexual Orientation, Immigration Status or Ability/disability Status. Roger did a Bertie Wooster impersonation in front of the Socio-economic Class poster.

4. *The part of my identity that I would like to explore further is...*

A few people walked to the Race or Religion posters, the others stayed put. Roger played drag-queen in front of the Sexual-Orientation poster.

5. *The part of my identity that that serves as my primary compass at work is . . .*

A couple of Genders, a couple of Age. Roger kneeled in front of the Religion poster.

6. *The part of my identity that garners me the most privilege is . . .*

No one moved, except Roger, who used the consultant's pointer as a cane in front of the Age poster.

7. *The part of my identity that I believe is the most misunderstood by others is . . .*

One of the assistant deans, a recent immigrant from Ukraine, strode back to her table, grabbed a piece of paper, wrote "Nationality" on it, and held it in front of her. Following her example, Harriet Jellineck made up her own sign, which read "Mother". After that, pandemonium broke out, as each person decided to create their own category of victimized diversity: "left-handed", "overweight", "allergic", "opera buff", "nerd", "Marxist", "older son", "twin", "genius", "pore speler" were some of the categories Grace remembers. As far as she was concerned they were all valid.

8. *The part of my identity that I feel is difficult to discuss with others who identify differently is . . .*

They never got to that last question, since, Deus ex machina like, the Chancellor re-appeared to make his concluding remarks, extinguishing the general hilarity. Grace, depleted by the day-long effort to rein in her individuality, and never fond of Sesame Street types of games, had sat out the entire exercise, and so had Jim, for some unknown reason.

Dr. Akecheta droned solemn platitudes for a while. He would probably have droned on until *his* dinner time, if the lodge's personnel had not pointedly started to move furniture around. At last, the retreat was over. When the attendees emerged into the open air, the sun was setting behind the mountains. They had come a long way to this beautiful setting only to be shut up in a room without a view. Whether the team spirit that had sprouted between them and the few bits of knowledge they had acquired would help their future performance as managers was very much open to question. But it was a question that was not asked, as far as Grace could tell from the few desultory comments that floated around her in the lodge's parking lot. Most managers, it seemed, were content to bask in the consideration vouchsafed on them by the retreat, and in the memory of the few fun moments they had shared. Replete with food, and clutching their bags of goodies, they turned their minds to what was left of their weekend.

Roger insisted on driving on the way back. And as one of the deans needed a ride back, and as he, an ex-basketball player, was six foot seven, Jim offered him the front passenger seat, taking the middle back seat so he could "sit between two pretty women", as he boasted. It was the most flirtatious comment Grace had ever heard him utter, but of course, it was for Roger's benefit. Older men were weird.

Grace was very glad to be sitting next to Jim. For one thing, his well-padded bulk provided useful ballast as Roger raced down the mountain's hairpin curves. But they had interacted so little during the day, and his behavior had surprised her in so many ways, for better and for worse, that she felt as if the thread of connivance between them had been severed. So it was a comfort to be physically close to him, to test whether that bond still held. Sure enough, after a few minutes of fidgeting, Jim relaxed into the pressure of arm against arm and thigh against thigh, and the heat of his body deliciously diffused through hers, speaking in a clear language all its own. The chiffon skirt melted away, her fears and doubts and snarkiness subsided. She found herself at peace, convinced there was nothing in the world she wanted beyond this sense of sensual torpor. Perhaps, like Constanza, she was a disciple of Hem: she had got her cheese, and could imagine holing up at this particular station forever.

By the time they got back to the District parking lot, it was fully dark. Beyond the reach of halogen lamps and security cameras, myriads of stars winked in the forbidding sky. There was a hushed round of hugs, and Jim waited till Harriet and Grace had started their cars before driving off in his.

Frustrated by the paucity of actual management advice provided by the retreat, and intrigued by the bright consultant's seeming disavowal of some of Jim's methods, Grace resolved to undertake an independent study of management science. As there wasn't much in-depth material on the Web either, she got her friend Everett, who was a Berkeley alumna, to check out a couple of textbooks from the business library. She fetched them the next weekend and ran through them in a couple of weeks. She didn't find them that useful either. It looked like the multitude of empirical studies in Organizational Behavior that had been conducted over the last hundred years either did not reach the level of statistical significance in their conclusions, or were contradicted by other studies. It looked like management fads came and went, unsupported by evidence, and subject to ideological shifts that merely reflected the evolution of the American economy. Most devastatingly, it looked like the nice, humanistic theories espoused by the bright consultant, according to which treating employees well resulted in better performance, had been proven wrong: over the long term, no significant correlation had been found between job satisfaction and job performance. (Of course, this very disillusion was the perfect theoretical basis for the practical ruthlessness of modern executives. But it rang true to Grace all the same. She had seen with her own eyes how Stanley's laissez-faire benevolence—or for that matter Jim's energetic role modeling—had had so little impact on the productivity of a Ruby or Tiffany.) What was Grace to do? Two tidbits gleaned from one of the textbooks further discouraged her: one stated that high achievers may not make good managers because they don't always get along with other people; the other, that *effective* managers spent the least amount of time networking, and the most on communication and human resources management, but that *successful* managers spent the most time networking, and the least on the other tasks. If Grace had to choose, she would opt for effectiveness over success, but the dilemma was dire.

She made a list of her new duties as she understood them. Some were spelled out in a brochure sent by the HR department, but clearly showing Akecheta's fingerprints:

- Mandatory attendance at the monthly managers' meetings presided by the Chancellor
- Mandatory attendance at the bi-weekly Board meetings

The Board meetings would rob her of her Wednesday evenings every other week, but hopefully she would get to spend them with Jim, and hopefully, Myrtle would pass up on them. As to the managers' meetings, Roger assured her that five out of six ended up being cancelled due to the Chancellor's absence.

Other duties were imposed by union and board rules devised as a check on the powers of external consultants:

- First level of approval on all purchasing requests
- First level of approval on all personnel actions: leave requests, performance evaluations, hirings and firings

Purchasing and personnel paperwork being computerized at Pequeno, Grace had to gain access to the respective applications. Here she ran into her first problem: Tiffany, who was normally in charge of granting logon privileges, dragged her feet for so long in this particular instance that Grace ended up asking Jim to intervene. Jim, who had departmental level approval on both purchasing and personnel actions, had permission to add users to both systems, but did not know how, and was reluctant at that point to give Tiffany an ultimatum. So Jim and Grace spent half an hour figuring out the user maintenance screen, which was far from intuitive, and documented in a questionable English. At one point, they found that they had deleted an entire approval route. Fortunately, as it had only four people on it, they didn't have much trouble re-creating it once they understood the process. Finally, the data entry task was complete.

"Way to go!" Grace exclaimed, putting out her hand for a high-five.

"We kick butt, don't we?" Jim replied, slapping her hand with the gusto of a high schooler. "Maybe Miz Prissy will get the hint that she's not indispensable."

"Yeah, maybe I could do her job too," Grace suggested sarcastically.

"I'll tell you one thing," Jim said, sounding dead serious. "If it was up to me, I would clear this place of all the dead wood."

Grace was shocked that her normally good-natured boss should express such a cold-blooded wish to fire some of her colleagues, though she herself occasionally dreamed of being rid of them. And it was unsettling to hear him refer to Tiffany by a derogatory nickname, after all the restraint he had shown a few weeks earlier by declining to even name her attackers. On the other hand, in the privacy of her own mind, Grace called Tiffany "the Queen of the Data Center", which was on a par with "Miz Prissy". She guessed that Jim felt a little freer to express his exasperation with the staff now that Grace herself was a manager. She was glad that he trusted her enough to make some unguarded remarks, but also a little worried about his level of frustration. Was the inertia of the Pequeno IT department getting to him? Did he have other problems she knew nothing about?

Underneath her concern for him, some doubts about his character must have sprouted: it is at this point that words like "hard-hearted" and "ruthless" appear in her journal, unfortunately without any factual context. Other than the episode around Josh's evaluation, which did not occur until weeks later, and the question mark over Stanley's retirement, which only lay on her subconscious at the time, she can't recall any incident that would have justified those terms. Was she intuiting the truth, or only trying to scare herself out of her attraction to him? In any case, one thing is clear to her now: a manager's emotions get magnified in the eyes of his subordinates, hence the advantage of an even temper. "Don't let them see you sweat" indeed. Chalk one up for Jim's management philosophy.

The rest of her new duties were implied in her title of Applications Manager:

- Supervise all programmers
- Prioritize incoming service requests
- Monitor Operations

OK, maybe that last item was not exactly implied by her title, but it certainly fit with Jim's instructions on the paper consumption issue. In practice, Grace saw that she would have to act as Operations Manager as well as Applications Manager. She did not anticipate any problem there. She knew that Mina could be counted on to be a good partner.

As for the Network Services Director's position, which was also vacant, she did not intend to get anywhere near it. Let Myrtle deal with Ruby.

Again, she searches through her memory. Is it really true that she never discussed her list of duties with Jim? If, as she claims, he never brought the subject up, why didn't she? Was she afraid to show what a greenhorn she was as a manager? Or was she dimly conscious of a need on his part to keep things vague?

Having gained access to the personnel and purchasing systems, Grace now undertook to delve into their respective databases. What she found horrified her.

" . . . . greener . . ."

"Sorry, what did you say?"

"I said, did you notice how ever since we crossed the Mississippi, everything is much greener?"

"I hadn't noticed, but it's definitely very green around here . . ."

"Look, even the embankments along the road look like lawns. Isn't that great? I bet people here don't feel that their life depends on irrigation. It must be nice . . ."

"You feel your life depends on irrigation?"

"Sure, don't you? I mean, I look at the canal in El Pequeno, and it makes me think of an IV drip, you know? Put a kink in it, and the whole place dies. It's scary."

"Did you start feeling this way when you lived in the house on Oakdale, by any chance?"

"Hmmm. Now that you mention it, it may have occurred to me after raccoons or some other animal chewed through the drip irrigation tubes, and all the azaleas in the front yard shriveled up. Like a dummy, I thought it had something to do with the sulfur smell around the house. Took me two weeks to figure it out. By then it was too late. Around here, you probably would have some leeway, not feel like you have to fight all the time to stay on top of nature."

"Do you feel that you have to fight against nature where you live now?"

"Not so much. My whole garden is in pots! But we have some plan to dig up the concrete along the back fence and put in some fruit trees."

"But won't you have to fight nature again then?"

"A little at first, while the trees take root. Anyway, we won't have any irrigation system. We'll do our own watering. After all, isn't it a pleasure to walk around the yard with a hose, to see how your plants are growing, to feel the cool mist on your arms? It beats air conditioning and watching TV, if you ask me."

"Sounds like you guys are going the slow life route . . ."

"Slow life, I like that. That's exactly what we are trying to do."

XIII

STALWART

What horrified Grace when she started looking into the Personnel Action database was the gaps in its data. At a glance, it was easy to see that the overall number of days off submitted by the IT staff since Stanley's retirement was much lower than in the same period the previous year. This did not correspond to Grace's perception of her colleagues' attendance. Sorting the query results by team, she found that the bulk of the difference appeared to be in the Network Coordinators team.

To start with, there was no documented leave for Erin or Josh since April. Yet Grace distinctly recalled that both of them had been absent from the staff meeting that was interrupted by Hurricane Katrina. As to Ruby, she regularly took time off to deal with her kids' various problems, the latest instance only a week before, but none of it was reflected in the database. The one entry under her name was for two days of jury duty in May, a type of leave that happened not to be charged against an employee's allowance.

One thing that Grace had learned by chatting with Harriet Jellineck during coffee breaks at the managers' retreat was that accrued sick and vacation leave were a liability for the District, since, upon separation, employees had to be paid for unused vacation leave, and unused sick leave had to be added to their service credits. Harriet had in fact asked Grace whether it would be possible to create a report summarizing these liabilities, and highlighting employees who had reached certain accrued leave thresholds. Grace had promised to look into it, inwardly finding it hard to believe that no such report existed.

Because of her conversation with Harriet, Grace understood that by failing to report days taken off, Ruby, Erin and Josh (and probably others, but she would have to stick to what she knew) were in fact stealing from the District. She couldn't let it happen under her watch—or Jim's.

Alex's and Ray's too perfect attendance posed a different kind of problem. According to their records, neither had taken any vacation in the last two years—and here, Grace was quite sure the records were accurate. However, the result was that they had both reached the maximum accrued vacation leave, and if they didn't take any time off during the next month, they would lose it. As it happened, a memo signed by the Chancellor himself had reached Grace the previous day, reminding managers that it was their responsibility to make sure their subordinate took their earned vacations.

When the cat's away, the mice will play. It occurred to Grace that one reason for Stanley's lack of initiative may have been that since all the managers under him had retired, he had had to assume their administrative chores, including keeping track of staff attendance. The difference between a "manager" and a "leader", according to one of the bright consultant's handouts (and the Berkeley textbooks), was that a manager organized and controlled, whereas a leader created and anticipated—the latter being clearly much more valued than the former. Stanley, finding that "keeping the wheels turning" had become a full-time job, had given up on being a leader. On the other hand, Jim, a leader if there ever was one, had focused on new projects. As a result, the IT department was not being properly managed. It was now up to Grace to pick up the slack.

The first thing she did was to look for evidence of Erin and Josh's absences around the time of Hurricane Katrina by checking their Outlook calendars for that period. Thankfully, Josh had blocked off the entire week of August 29 as vacation in his calendar. Erin for her part had meetings scheduled each day of that week, so she had probably been sick on Monday. Armed with this information, she paid a visit to Josh in his cubicle.

"Hello, Josh," she said brightly. "Do you have a minute?"

"What about?" he asked noncommittally.

"As you may know, I have been tasked with keeping track of staff leave," she continued as brightly. "I have been looking at the recent records, and found that somehow, the vacation you took in the week of August 29 never made it into the system."

"Well, that's weird, I remember submitting it."

"Must have been a hiccup in the application. Anyway, would you mind re-submitting it ASAP? We have to produce a report for Risk Management in the next few days, and I would like it to be accurate."

"All right," he grumbled. "But I wish someone would fix the bugs in that program."

"I'll mention it to Sandip. Thank you so much."

She then went over to Erin's cubicle.

"Hi, Erin. Can I talk to you for a sec?"

"Sure."

"As you may know, I have been made responsible for keeping track of staff leave. I have been looking at the recent records, and found that somehow, the sick day you took on August 29 never made it into the system."

"Did I take a sick day on August 29?"

"Yeah," Sandra's voice shot over the partition. "Don't you remember? That was the day Katrina made landfall. You had a cold, and you told me you watched TV all day long."

"Oh! That . . . I was so busy catching up when I came back to work, I guess I forgot to submit a leave request."

"Would you mind doing it ASAP? We have to produce a report for Risk Management in the next few days, and I would like it to be accurate."

"Would tomorrow be OK? This afternoon, I've got to drive over to Regent Valenzuela's home to fix his printer."

"Tomorrow will be fine. Thank you so much."

Empowered by her success so far, Grace was ready to tackle Ruby. Ruby was not in her office. Grace noticed that after the few weeks of clean living brought about by the change of furniture, garbage was accumulating again on her desk and shelves: a Tupperware with three shriveled lettuce leaves at the bottom, a blender jar coated with a green residue, a mug containing a moldy tea bag, a banana turning black, several desiccated apple cores, a flaccid cucumber with a bite mark, and scattered silverware covered with crud. What she couldn't find was the eternal bowl of congealed oatmeal. Ruby must be on a new vegetable diet. Was this Myrtle's influence?

It took Grace five tries to catch up with Ruby. By then, her brightness quotient had dimmed a little.

"Hi, Ruby. Do you have a minute?"

"Not really."

"When can I come back?"

"Go ahead. We might as well get it over now."

"All right. As you know, I am now responsible for keeping track of staff leave."

"Excuse me, but I don't know that."

"OK, then, I am telling you."

"You're not my manager. I need to hear it from my manager."

"Fair enough. I'll ask Jim to tell you."

Grace had already turned around, when Ruby called after her.

"To be honest, I don't appreciate your talking to Josh and Erin behind my back."

To be honest. Another Myrtle trademark. Grace paused, took a deep breath.

"I am afraid I don't understand."

"If you need something from the Network Coordinators, you should go through me. They have enough work on their hands without getting bombarded by requests from people outside the team."

"Are you saying that you are responsible for funneling all requests to the Network team?"

"That's not what I meant."

"I didn't think so."

"It's just a question of courtesy. I am the Senior Coordinator after all."

"I get it. So, here are the action items as I see them. First, I'll have Jim confirm that I am in charge of verifying staff leave. And then, you'll make sure that all the recent sick and vacation days taken by the Network Coordinators, including yours, are entered into the system. Does that sound right?"

"I don't see why I should be made responsible for verifying other people's leave time. Didn't you say that's your job?"

Grace bit her lip. Don't let them see you sweat, she reminded herself.

"OK, then. Here are the revised action items. First, Jim assures you that verifying staff leave is my job. And then, I do it. Better?"

"I guess."

"Thank you so much, Ruby."

When she got back to her office, Grace did something very unusual: she closed her door and pulled down the shade on the interior glass panel. Having thus secured visual privacy, she spent the next five minutes quietly pacing back and forth, rolling her eyes back in her head and tearing her hair out.

Jim, who was attending some executive committee at the District office, was due back imminently. But the next hour on his schedule was blocked off for a "Private Meeting". There had been more and more of those lately. The visitors, as far as Grace had been able to ascertain, were always complete strangers, always dressed to the nines, and always deferential looking. What was that about?

She was in the lunch room heating some tea in the microwave when she felt the floor vibrate under her feet, the unmistakable sign that Jim was on the move. A second later, he was right behind her.

"What's cooking?" he asked cheerily.

She turned around. He was rubbing his hands together, and looked sunnier than he had in weeks. She was sorry about the prospect of spoiling his mood.

"Tea and headaches," she answered. "But you look happy. Is that because your meeting ended early?"

"That, and the fact that it was productive. I think I found a good recruit for Hartbridge."

"Is that what those "private meetings" are about?"

"Sometimes. I know what you're thinking. And I don't like doing Hartbridge business during the day either. But sometimes candidates are not available in the evening."

"You mean that after you leave the office, you keep working?"

"Yep. That's how I make the big bucks."

"That's how you ruin your health, if you ask me."

"Do I look sick to you?" he asked, squaring his shoulders and raising his chin. He was flirting, though there was no other male around to incite him to such macho showmanship.

"Not yet," she muttered, unable to contradict the evidence of his robust fitness. If she had only known . . . but she wouldn't have been able to do anything, he was so stubborn. Besides, it was probably too late already.

"Anyway, about those headaches . . . you sure you want to talk about them? Wouldn't you rather go for a walk?" he mused.

"How about a talk, and then a walk?"

"Deal. But first let me have some of your tea. I am too wired for coffee."

Grace went back to her office to fetch another tea bag. When she returned to the lunch room, Jim was on his cell phone. He was apparently advising his daughter Cindy on some classes she might take. Grace took Jim's mug from his hand, put the tea bag in, poured hot water over, stuck it into the microwave for a minute, took it out, added two teaspoons of sugar the way he liked, and put the mug back into his hand, feeling a little like a maid, but not disliking the feeling. "Thank you" he mouthed. He told Cindy he would call her back later in the evening, and folded his cell phone.

"My place or yours?" she flirted back.

"Yours, so they can't find me."

By "they", he must mean Myrtle, who usually invaded his office about that time of day. Things were looking up.

They walked back to Grace's office. Jim noticed that the shade was down.

"Oh, that. I had a private meeting of my own."

He scrunched up his face in disbelief. Was she such an open book? She shut the door, sat down. He followed suit, uncharacteristically sitting on the edge of the chair with both feet on the ground and both hands in his lap.

"It's no big deal, really," she said, trying to reassure him. "It just looks like some people haven't been reporting their time off consistently."

He scrunched up his face again, this time sheepishly. She went on to tell him about the discrepancies she had found, and her conversations with Josh, Erin and Ruby. He brightened up.

"Well, now I understand why they were so dead set against your being appointed manager!"

"So, Josh and Erin were the other two people who spoke against me!"

"Sorry," he said, shifting in his chair uneasily. "I shouldn't have let it slip."

"I am glad I know. I hope you trust me not to let it color my attitude toward them?"

She looked at him earnestly. He held her gaze for a few seconds. Something flickered in his eyes, something that wasn't the usual gleam of amusement. At last he answered.

"Yep," he said firmly. "So, what do you want me to do?"

Grace declared that from now on, she would take it upon herself to keep track of everyone's attendance. And to avoid her authority being further questioned, she thought Jim should outline her responsibilities at the next staff meeting. For some reason she couldn't fathom, he was reluctant to do so, preferring to talk to Ruby—or anyone else—one on one. She was pressing him for an explanation of his preference when he interrupted her.

"Look. You want me to trust you. But I need you to trust me too, once in a while."

Grace was about to tell him he had a point, when there was a knock on the door, immediately followed by Myrtle's head sticking in. It was a relief to see that the Stonehenge matron could actually bend her spine.

"Sorry," Myrtle said, not looking it. "I thought Grace was gone, the door being closed and the shade down." (And what was she looking for in Grace's office, then?) "But I am glad I found you, Jim. It's time for our five o'clock."

"Anything urgent?" Jim asked, leaning back in his chair at last.

"Not really urgent, no," Myrtle admitted.

"Then, it can wait till tomorrow. Go home, Myrtle, you've had a long day."

Without another word, Myrtle retracted her head and closed the door softly behind her. It occurred to Grace that leaving the shade pulled down had been a mistake. She got up and pulled it up. Jim wrapped one arm on the back of the chair next to his, and put one foot on the other knee, reverting to his normal relaxed pose. He had been worried about setting the tongues wagging, poor guy. Grace resumed the conversation.

"I was going to say, before we were rudely interrupted, that I see your point about trust. I'll keep it in mind."

Somehow, she couldn't bring herself to tell him that she trusted him completely, even though she would have liked nothing better in the world, and even though that was what he wanted to hear. He seemed to sense her reticence, but forbore to remark on it, thankfully.

"Any other headache?"

"No, that's it for today."

"OK, then, let's go for that walk before it's completely dark out there."

Jim had stood up, and Grace was grabbing her jacket, when there was another knock on the door. Jim opened it. Mina was on the threshold. There was a problem with a job she was running, and she needed Grace's help.

"Oh well, no walk today," Grace sighed.

"Rain check?"

"Totally."

The next day, Grace went to Alex's cubicle to talk him into taking some time off. He was the person Grace found the most difficult to engage in the IT department. Not that he showed any hostility toward her, but he was so uncomfortable simply being addressed by anyone that people pretty much left him alone. A rail-thin guy in his late twenties, always in checked shirts and ill-fitting jeans, with thin hair plastered to his skull in unnatural directions, who kept his head bent and turned to the side in such a way that you never saw both of his red-rimmed eyes at once, he reminded Grace of a frightened rabbit. On top of it, his English was far from fluent. Still, he did not rebuff her, and even offered her a pale smile. Grace explained that he had reached the maximum amount of accrued vacation time, and that he needed to take at least a week off by the end of November, or he would lose it.

"It's OK I lose it," he said.

Stunned by his nonchalance, Grace changed tack. She explained that the District did not want to steal his vacation time, and therefore he had to make use of it. His answer broke her heart.

"I don't know where I go," he said matter-of-factly.

So, she quizzed him about his hobbies. It turned out, not surprisingly, that he was a fan of computer games, that in fact he was developing one in his spare time. By chance, Grace knew of a game conference scheduled the very next week in Austin, Texas. Some of her Berkeley friends were in fact going. They would be happy to send him the conference information, to share tips on flights and hotels. He could even arrange to meet them there if he liked. And Austin was a great city to visit, full of bright people and fun activities, she improvised, never having set foot in Austin. To her great relief, Alex took the bait. Back in her office, Grace immediately emailed her friend Kyle, begging for his help. Kyle emailed Alex within an hour, copying Grace. His email was so enthusiastic and friendly that Grace wanted to kiss him. The next day Alex found his way to Grace's office to tell her that he had bought his plane ticket, registered to the conference, and reserved a hotel room. She could have kissed him too. She asked him to submit his vacation request right away, and to make sure to inform Ruby that he would be gone the next week. He nodded his assent.

Ray Gomes' case presented another type of difficulty. For one thing, as he worked the graveyard shift, she had never met him. For another, there was no one to substitute for him, which turned out to be the reason he had not taken a vacation in two years, as she learned when she got hold of him on the phone. But he had wanted to take his kids to Disneyland for a long time, and so welcomed the idea of taking a week off in November. They decided to conference Mina in. Within an hour, the three of them had worked out a plan to cover for him for a week.

Grace next turned her attention to Harriet's report request. From her own investigation, it appeared that all the data Harriet needed was in the database. It was just a matter of extracting and formatting it according to the user's specifications. She went to see Sandip, who, in Michelle Williams' continued absence, was responsible for the Personnel applications. Sandip was not in his cubicle. It took Grace four tries to get a hold of him. When she finally found him at his desk, he was busy composing an email in some Indian script—not work related, she assumed.

"Hi, Sandip. Can I talk to you for a minute?"

"Sure. Is this about the three days I took off in June? I was just about to verify that they have been properly recorded."

Oh, boy . . . There was more to this leave scam than Grace had imagined. But one good thing about cubicles was that they allowed a free flow of information. Jim didn't need to make a public announcement after all. Everyone had been put on notice by her conversations with Josh and Erin.

"No, no," she reassured him. "Although, now that you mention it, I don't think I saw those three days in June reflected in the database. But you'll check that, anyway. What I want to talk about is the leave report Harriet Jellineck has requested. Don't we have anything like that already?"

"Not really. I know Harriet had talked to Michelle about it, but then Michelle left before the specs were written."

"And you haven't written any specs yourself?"

"No!" Sandip answered emphatically, as if scandalized at the thought. "Nobody asked me to, and besides, I have been too busy with regular maintenance."

"Keeping the wheels turning, as Stanley used to say. So, what are you working on right now?"

"Well, the new tax tables should arrive in a week or two. And then, if the teachers' contract is ratified, there will be some new health benefits to program."

"But in the meantime . . ."

"I am just waiting on the tax tables and the new teacher's contract."

"So, you might be able to carve some time to create Harriet's report? I don't think it will take more than a week of programming, once we have specs. I'd like to schedule a meeting with you and Harriet so we can go over her requirements. I'll help her write up the specs, and you can do the programming. How does that sound?"

"Fine," he conceded. "But programming may take more than a week, and the tax tables have priority."

"I agree. But let's see what we can achieve in a week. We'll cross the priority bridge when we get to it."

At that point, Sandip's cell phone meowed. He jumped out of his seat in a fluster of excitement.

"Please excuse me," he stammered. "This is an urgent message." And he rushed out of his cubicle toward the front door.

Grace was flabbergasted. It had never occurred to her that a programmer could sit on his hands for weeks waiting for future projects, when he knew of a small scale but important user request that he could tackle right now. She guessed that Michelle had accustomed Sandip to being narrowly supervised, specking all projects herself and only assigning him bite-size pieces. Since she had left, he had been content to prevent the Personnel system from failing. What a waste. She was going to have to take the programming team in hand to a greater degree than she had expected.

Grace's investigation of the purchasing request approval database uncovered another red flag. It seemed that Tiffany had created an approval route in which she was the only approver, bypassing Jim's electronic signature. Three purchase requests had been submitted in that route: one for a PC printer, the two others for reimbursement of travel expenses incurred by Myrtle and by the Purchasing Director, Neil Petersen. All three requests had gone through during the first week of September, while Jim was on vacation, so Tiffany could argue that she had created the route out of expediency, except there was no reason Grace could see why these particular requests couldn't have waited a week for Jim's approval. The sums involved were modest, but it was still a dangerous precedent. And then there was the issue of why travel expenses incurred by Myrtle or the Purchasing Director should be charged to the IT budget. According to Grace's understanding, all Hartbridge expenses were supposed to be charged against Measure G funds. As to the Purchasing Director, he had his own budget.

Budget and purchasing information being thankfully accessible to all District managers by role, Grace was spared having to request access from Tiffany. She looked at the IT expenditures for September, and found that the three suspicious requests had been duly paid. She then drilled into the two travel requests, and discovered that they were for the same trip to Reno to attend a demo of some fixed asset software. Grace was livid. Myrtle had no business organizing application demos without consulting with the programming team. If she had, she would have learned that Pequeno already owned a fixed asset module, which only needed to be installed.

Instinctively, Grace shrank from confronting Tiffany on the issue of the spurious route. And she wasn't about to tangle with Myrtle either. So she was going to have to disturb Jim's peace again. As she didn't want to have him worry ahead of time, she did not make a formal appointment to talk to him, deciding instead to wait till he had a free moment—and till she had herself cooled off a bit.

She spent the next two days in a state of hyper-vigilance: her eyes scrutinizing his Outlook calendar, her ears tuned to the sound of his door opening and closing, her nose alert to the wafting of his aftershave, her feet sensitive to the floor vibrations that punctuated his stride. The suspense did nothing to improve her mood or dilute her concerns. Here she was, basically stalking the man like a teenager in the thrall of an unrequited love, when all she wanted was to alert him to some work issues that might reflect badly on him. His unaccountable busy-ness was becoming a real obstacle to good management.

At last, on Friday afternoon, all the signals aligned: she heard his door open, she smelled his aftershave, she felt the drumming of his steps, she saw him in her doorway, his jacket slung over his shoulder, his eyes twinkling.

"How about that walk?" he said. "Mina is gone for the day. Myrtle is on a plane to Cleveland as we speak. My calendar is clear. Let's play hooky."

"Let's" she said, suddenly much happier.

Although he assumed a careless air, Grace noticed that Jim was discreetly checking offices and cubicles as they made their way out. Luckily, the entire staff had left for the weekend. There would be no tongue wagging.

Feeling horribly strategic, Grace waited till they had reached the trail along the irrigation canal before bringing up the purchasing issue. She was glad to find that Jim was as furious about it as she was. He promised that he would talk to both Tiffany and Myrtle. She thanked him profusely. After that they switched to more personal chat. He asked her what her plans were for the weekend. She explained that she was leaving for the Bay Area later in the evening to go spend the weekend at her friend Everett's. Boyfriend? he asked. Ex-colleague and girl friend, she explained. He mused about the tendency of modern parents to pick boy names for girls, as if to give them a leg up in the competition with males, when in fact women now had the advantage, because they were better in school, and in spite of this well-known fact they still benefited from affirmative action. Grace reminded him that affirmative action had been outlawed in California, but agreed that women were often better in school than men, perhaps because they were more disciplined. Sure, but they didn't always know what they wanted, Jim countered. Was he thinking about his daughter Cindy? Yes, he was. And what were Jim's plans for the weekend? He joked about sailing on the San Francisco Bay, climbing El Capitan, and painting El Pequeno red, then confessed that all he had on his entertainment calendar was a golf date with Bob Johnson—weather permitting. Grace felt sorry for him, promised to take him to a concert at Davies Hall some day. He said he would like that very much.

As they walked, Grace became aware that an army of clouds was advancing from the west. A gust of wind shook the sycamore branches overhead, hurtling fat leaves in their faces. The surface of the canal shivered, then darkened. Suddenly it was pouring rain, the first storm of the year, Alleluia! though it meant a more dangerous drive to the Bay Area. Jim and Grace had to turn back and start running. It was exhilarating, in fact, to feel him at her side, keeping pace with her, breathing deeply but easily, his wet face gleaming, his body radiating heat. By the time they reached the shelter of the data center awning, it was fully dark outside. In the dim glow of the security light, she saw that the shoulders of his jacket were drenched, and hoped the stains would be amenable to dry-cleaning.

"Hot dawg!," Jim exclaimed, shaking himself. "We got our exercise for today."

"It was awesome, running in the rain, wasn't it?"

"Totally," he replied, imitating her slang. She laughed.

"I need to go in and grab my laptop," he continued. "Shall I give you a ride back home afterwards?"

Grace looked up at him. His dripping hair was appealingly mussed on his forehead. Rain drops sparkled in his beard and moustache, his lower lip glistened, looking particularly fleshy. But she couldn't see his eyes behind the fogged-up glasses.

"No, thanks, I brought my car in today. I am leaving straight from here to drive to Berkeley. But first, I also need to get my stuff."

He opened the door for her, and they each went to their office to gather their belongings. When Grace stopped by his office to wish him a good weekend a few minutes later, he was on his cell phone. She waved goodbye and left.

Did he have some sexual thought at the back of his mind that night? Would she herself have entertained the idea of a fling if she had not promised to return the management textbooks Everett had borrowed for her from the Berkeley library? Theoretically, there was no reason why she shouldn't have. At that point in her life, Grace still professed the casual attitude toward sex that was the norm in her milieu. Desire was a natural—and therefore good—thing. Yielding to it in the moment did not require being in love or having any expectation for the future—"anything between consenting adults" pretty much summed up the rules she thought she lived by. She has since come to acknowledge that things are not quite so simple, and in particular that sex has a way of unleashing storms of definitely non-casual feelings.

The fact that Jim was (technically) married would not have qualified as a deterrent either. Her parents, divorced when she was five years old, having each subsequently gone through a couple more spouses, a personal experience duly confirmed by well-known statistics, she understandably did not hold the institution of marriage in high reverence. In this respect too she has changed, thanks to her work in the Obama campaign: she is more willing now to honor other people's symbols even if they mean nothing to her.

As for Jim's status as her boss, that was the least of her concerns. There were no taboos against staff fraternization at Pequeno. And in the modern world, since people spend most of their time at work, the office is the most natural place for them to get to know each other, as opposed to Internet dating sites with their misleading profiles. She made this very point to Jim a couple of times when the topic came up in conversation. Wait! How did the topic come up? Who brought it up? When? She can't remember the context, only that his arguments seemed hopelessly old-fashioned to her. As a matter of fact, she has just started a relationship with a man who was basically her boss in the Obama campaign's San Francisco office. And it's going just fine, thank you very much.

Upon reflection, she realizes that with a little ingenuity, she could have got around the problem of her date with Everett. She could have used the rain as an excuse to delay her trip till the next morning. She could have spent the night with Jim. She was so aroused, those few seconds under the awning, that she could have thrown herself in his arms and kissed his wet mouth, resolving all the ambiguity of their beloved hugs. She suspects that he wouldn't have resisted her, his anti-fraternization arguments notwithstanding. The fact is that she didn't seize on the opportunity. Obscurely, she must have sensed that neither of them was ready for such a step. Just as obscurely, she now feels somehow guilty for her reticence. Perhaps if she had been more spontaneous then, everything would have turned out differently later. At the very least, she might now have some definite memories of gratified intimacy to balance against her sense of betrayal. On the other hand . . .

Jim must have made good on his promise to talk to Ruby and Tiffany. Until he left, Ruby never again questioned Grace's authority in the area of leave reporting. To be sure, she had to be reminded several times to record her sick time, but she eventually did it. Until he left, Tiffany also abstained from approving purchase requests—Grace regularly combed the database to make sure of it.

And Jim definitely clued Myrtle in on who was boss. Through his closed door, Grace heard him raise his voice to her a few days after their walk. Her voice remained inaudible. When she emerged, she was her stiff matronly self, but she never again interfered in Grace's domain—not at least until Jim left. He was after all a manager as well as a leader.

XIV

MIRACULOUS

"You never told me how you worked things out with Tarik. How did that come about?" Grace inquires in an effort to reboot the conversation, suddenly aware that she hasn't exchanged a word with Mina since they passed Nashville half an hour ago. For someone as chatty as Mina, this must seem rude. And Grace is really curious about the seemingly miraculous recovery of her friend's marriage.

"Funny you should mention it, I was just thinking about it, and I came to the conclusion that things started to turn around the day we met at Santa Magdalena. Do you remember? By the way, you never told me what you were doing there. You're not Catholic, are you?"

"No, but my grandparents are. They used to take me to mass in Pasadena when I spent vacations with them as a little girl. I have been fond of churches ever since. When I was in France on my semester abroad, I visited a whole bunch of cathedrals, many of them nearly a thousand-year old. Imagine that. And those medieval people didn't skimp on the architecture, let me tell you, even though they didn't have any power equipment. All for the glory of God. Makes you wonder how our own priorities will look a few centuries from now."

"It does, doesn't it? I'm sure Santa Magdalena must have been a letdown, after all those French cathedrals."

"Is Santa Magdalena your church?"

"Now it is, yes."

"It's a pretty nice church, actually. I like Hispanic architecture. Yellow stucco, round arches along the nave, exposed beams, right? And a working organ. It's the sound that attracted me. Then the door opened and the parishioners streamed out, so I went in for a peek, and there you were."

"We came out together, and we were chatting on the steps when it started raining, so we ran to the taqueria across the street. And then I spilled my guts."

"More like you dripped them out. But what was it about that day that turned things around?"

"Several things. For one, it was the first time I set foot in a church since I met Tarik. I had gone in frantic, but I found that the service calmed me down a little."

"The peace of Christ . . ."

"Exactly. And then, seeing you was such a strange coincidence that I felt like there was a message there."

"Me in the role of Archangel? I'd love that, but I doubt it."

"Just your name, Grace, if nothing else."

"Oh, I see. You can thank my grandparents for that one too. And what else?"

"You said you had noticed that the danger of googling questions was that Google gave you too many answers, so you ended up zeroing in on the answers that confirmed your prejudices. It made sense to me, because it was a thought I'd had for a second, before my paranoia got the better of me. But what impressed me most was when you said that if you were me, you would not wait for the other shoe to drop, you would devise some pro-active strategy."

"Did I say that?"

"Yeah, something like that."

"So, what was your strategy?"

"I'll tell you if you promise not to laugh."

"Why would I laugh?"

"Because it wasn't rational at all. You see, I couldn't talk to Tarik. If I was wrong about my suspicions, he was so mad at me already that it would finish destroying our marriage. And if I was right, and he really was a kidnapper or a terrorist, he wasn't going to tell me. As far as I could see I had no way of getting to the truth with words. So I figured I needed to do something that would force him to react one way or the other, but without letting him know what I was afraid of. I was also thinking about how I could get Steven out of harm's way. But for a while I couldn't come up with any plan of action. And in the meantime, the work situation at Pequeno was starting to get to me."

"When was that?"

"Late October 2005, something like that."

"I wasn't aware that things were difficult for you then. What was the problem?"

"That was when Myrtle first arrived."

"Couldn't have been. Myrtle arrived on August 29, the day of Hurricane Katrina, don't you remember the staff meeting where Jim introduced her, and then Sandip screamed that new Orleans was under water? Which by the way wasn't really true yet, I guess he couldn't resist a dramatic opportunity to bring the meeting to an end."

"Yes, you're right. I remember. I guess I didn't pay any attention to her until she started sticking her nose into my business. I mean, she was a nice lady and all . . ."

"Nice? That's not what I would call her," Grace objects.

"No? What did she do to you?" Mina asks, taking her eyes off the road for a second to look at Grace, her eyebrows knitted above her glasses in endearing contrast to her smooth baby face. Not for the first time, it occurs to Grace that for all the enforced promiscuity of office life, people who work together often pass each other like ships in the night.

"That's another story. But what did she do to you?"

"Well, for one thing, she had got it into her head that we should put the Operations documentation on the Web. I told her I couldn't see the point of it. Nobody but the Operations team had any need to look at it, and we all knew where to find it in the binders on my shelf. I couldn't get through to her. She kept throwing big words and weird acronyms at me to the point of making me feel stupid."

"Ah, yes, the acronym game. Typical smoke screen used by people who don't know what they're talking about."

"You think Myrtle didn't know what she was talking about? She had a Ph.D."

"I think that's why Fritz sent her. To compensate for Jim's lack of a college degree in Akecheta's eyes. I don't mean she was dumb. She knew a lot of things superficially. And she talked a good game. But if you scratched the surface, she was no expert at anything. I had an opportunity to work with her on a database query once, and even though she claimed years of experience with SQL, she kept making the most boneheaded mistakes. But the worst was that she didn't think logically, which is quite a handicap for an IT professional, you have to admit. Anyway, you were saying that she bugged you about the Operations documentation."

So Grace also knew that Jim didn't have a degree, Mina realizes. It's not surprising, given how close those two were. Still, she feels a little let down not to have been the only recipient of this secret.

"Yeah, so to get her off my back, I spent hours moving the documentation that was still on the mainframe to the documentation folder on my PC, and then copying the entire folder onto the Web server. Then I told her that if she wanted to create a Web page out of it, she was welcome, but I didn't have time. I thought that would be the end of it, but I was wrong. She kept coming back to me to ask for information, and to tell me how the data should be organized differently here, and how the wording wasn't right there. After a while all I could hear was: To be honest . . . blablabla . . . knowledge base . . . blablabla . . . don't take it personally . . . blablabla . . . kiss . . . blablabla . . . I kept wondering what the kissing was doing in there. I ended up looking it up on Google and found out that it was an acronym for Keep It Simple Stupid, which is supposed to be a documentation standard. Beats me how you could keep mainframe documentation simple. And why would you want to make it stupid? So you can put any high school dropout off the street in charge of Operations, and pay them even less than they pay me?"

Grace laughs. "To be honest and don't take it personally! You pinned Myrtle down to a tee. I had forgotten the 'don't take it personally' bit."

"Anyway, on top of my problems at home, the last thing I needed was for Myrtle to bend my ear day in day out with her criticisms, even if they were well meant. One day, I got so distracted by her standing at my desk that I submitted a job instead of scheduling it for the night."

"I remember that. The job started closing files left and right, and within a minute I had three phone calls from irate users. When I got to your desk you were frantically opening files. I remember noticing that you looked angry. But I didn't see Myrtle."

"Sure, she faded into the background as soon as she saw I was having a problem. I thought, if she knows the system well enough to rewrite the documentation, why doesn't she help me re-open files?"

"That's because she wouldn't have known how to do it."

"You may be right. Anyway, that was the straw that broke the camel's back. That same day I made an appointment to talk to Jim."

"You did? Good for you. What did you say?"

"I gave him one of my own proverbs: if it ain't broke, don't fix it. I told him I was busy enough scheduling jobs and training the work study students, plus coordinating with you on the paper reduction project, without having to babysit Myrtle on a documentation effort I couldn't see the need for. I said that I was starting to feel like I had too many bosses."

Grace winces. "Ouch! I suppose I was one of them?"

"A little bit. But at least, the paper reduction thing was something Jim had assigned. And it was always clear you knew your stuff. You even taught me things I didn't know about my own job. So I didn't mind so much being bossed around by you."

"Not so much . . . I guess I am a little fanatic. Something to remember in my new job."

"A good manager should be fanatic, I think. But sometimes, you could have been just a little more . . . relaxed?" Mina suggests, shooting another glance in Grace's direction, unsure that she's picked the right word. Grace doesn't look offended.

"And what was Jim's response?"

"He laughed. Talk about relaxed. He was such an unflappable guy, wasn't he, you felt he had a solution ready for any problem. I loved working for him, if only for that reason."

"Me too," Grace concurs, although *she* can think of a few times when his famous calm deserted him. "So what was his solution?"

"He told me he would get Myrtle out of my hair, and he did. He only asked me to make sure that all the documentation was kept updated on the Web server, so it would be properly backed up and accessible when I wasn't around. Made sense to me. It's still there, and I think of Jim every time I make a change to it."

"Very nice," Grace says, lingering on her words. Inwardly, she adds a point to her tally of Jim's proven management skills. She never knew that the Pequeno Operations documentation used to be scattered between the mainframe and Mina's own PC. And although she understands Mina's reluctance to share information whose exclusive knowledge insured her job security, her own management experience tells her that information sharing is essential to a well-run organization. It was like Jim, rather than making big pronouncements about change, to quietly seize the moment when change was possible. She did not always understand this. But she is glad now for the opportunity to think well of him.

"But we went off at a tangent. You were going to tell me how you figured out that Tarik was no child-kidnapping terrorist."

"It wasn't really a tangent, because it was my conversation with Jim that gave me the confidence to tackle my home situation."

"So, let's hear it."

"Shouldn't we first find some place to stay for tonight? I would prefer a motel, if you don't mind. I could use a hot bath, and I would like not to wonder if the next person coming into the bathroom will be a serial killer. I'll pay, this time."

"OK. I'll get right on it."

A few minutes later, Grace has made reservations at a Super 8 motel just on the other side of Knoxville, so she will be able to email Jim tonight that they have reached their target for the day. Reassured, Mina resumes her tale.

"I was visiting my parents the weekend after Thanksgiving. I had brought Steven with me. In those days, I took Steven everywhere I went, I was so afraid of coming home and finding him gone. I even brought him to work with me for a couple of days, do you remember?"

"Yes, he toddled all the way to my office one time. He was entranced by my bicycle helmet and my night light. A very quiet little boy, except when he got a nosebleed."

"That's why I couldn't keep bringing him to the office, he cried so much when it happened. He was getting nosebleeds all the time then, and that just added to my panic. The pediatrician said not to worry, it was probably caused by the dry air in the new house. Told me to get a humidifier, but it made no difference."

"God! That must have been such a trying period for you. I wish I could have been there for you a little more. But after that time at Santa Magdalena, you didn't seem to want to pursue the friendship."

"I guess that's true. I've never been good at mixing work and friendship. I feel more comfortable being mysterious. The less your coworkers know about you, I figure, the less they can get their hooks into you."

"I wouldn't know a hook if you served it to me on a platter."

"No, I know. I'm not talking about you."

"Don't take it personally, as Myrtle would say . . . But we digress again. You were visiting your parents' house."

"So, I went into my old bedroom. To tell you the truth, I was contemplating moving back with my parents if things with Tarik didn't improve. So I was kind of measuring the room in my mind, wondering where I would put a bed for Steven. My mom was standing in the doorway, chatting. I hadn't told her anything about my worries. All of a sudden, my eyes fall on a statue of our Lady of Guadalupe that had been on my dresser my whole childhood. It was one of those objects you look at as a kid before going to sleep or when you're sick, completely familiar and reassuring, but still full of secrets: why are there horns on each side of the Virgin's feet? What are those spikes radiating around her, like the quills of a porcupine? How strange the black collar and black belt look on a pink dress! You can't help telling yourself some stories about it, and before you know it you are asleep. I mean, I was aware that the statue represented the Virgin Mary, but it was my own private Virgin Mary, my own friend, doll, charm, guardian angel, what have you. I wouldn't for the world have asked an adult to explain any of the symbols. And as I am looking at it, I see my arm reaching out and my hand closing around it, and then, I swear to God, something unknots inside me, I breathe easier, I feel more solid on my feet. So I put the statue in my purse, and my mom, who is in the middle of a sentence, says in a low voice, without missing a beat: 'Por fin!'. And then she finishes her sentence."

"What does 'por fin' mean?"

"It means 'at last' in Spanish."

"But what did she mean by it?"

"I don't know," Mina exclaims, laughing. "I never asked her. Somehow, it just seemed the right thing for her to say. It made me feel that she knew more about me than I gave her credit for, and I was grateful."

"So, what did you do with the statue?"

"I brought it home, and I plunked it down on the mantelpiece in the living room, right in front of Samir, who was just then crouched in prayer on the floor. I had a moment of hesitation when I realized that the Lady of Guadalupe clashed horribly with the Kandinsky print on the wall above. I mean, the colors on the statue are a bit loud, and the style, well, you could call it kitsch. But then I thought, to heck with taste, this is a matter of freedom of religion. And when Samir stood up, I saw that I had done the right thing. He blinked, he looked like he has seen a ghost. After that day, he confined his prayers to his bedroom. I had won my first victory."

"But how did Tarik react?"

"This is where it gets interesting. I was afraid, or hoping, I am not sure which, that when he saw the statue he would make a scene. Ever since we got together, we had put our religions aside. It was like a silent pact. Even when we got married, we only had a civil ceremony. My parents never complained, but I am sure they were disappointed. I didn't mind. I hadn't been particularly impressed by the old-time Catholicism that was rampant at my parents' church, all about sin and repentance and blind obedience to the Church hierarchy, if you know what I mean. And Tarik, like a typical engineer, had always seemed totally secular. Now that he was playing the Islamic card, though, I felt I had a right to assert my Christian identity. But if he had a fanatic streak, the sight of the statue might push him over the edge. I imagined him striding over to the fireplace, grabbing the statue and smashing it on the hearth. I told myself that it would be my cue to get a hold of Steven and make my exit. I had already packed a bag with a few clothes for both of us, and stored it in the laundry room, next to the garage door. My parents would be surprised, but I knew they would take me in no matter what. Now I just had to wait for Tarik to see the statue. I wasn't going to point it out to him, that would have been too obvious. But I wanted to be around when he saw it. Otherwise, *he* might take it as a cue to make his exit with Steven in my absence."

"And how did you make him see the status without telling him about it ?"

"He had gone out to see some clients that day. So I turned the lights out in the living room, like he always wanted me to do to save energy. When he came home, I called him straight to the kitchen to have dinner. After dinner, we moved to the living room, and I asked him to start a fire. The box of matches was on the mantelpiece, right next to the statue. He couldn't miss it. Sure enough, I see him do a double take, and then he takes the matches and lights the fire, cool as a cucumber. I couldn't believe my eyes. A little later, I went up to put Steven to bed, and when I came down, I could hear Samir talk in Urdu. He sounded upset. I peeked around the corner, and Samir was pointing at the statue. And then Tarik answered in that reasonable sing-song voice that teachers use with first-graders, and even though I don't understand Urdu, I could tell he was telling Samir to back off, that this was my house too. I was flabbergasted. His attitude opened a whole new line of thinking for me. So I waited till their conversation was over, and then I came in, all cheerful and innocent, and I put my arms around Tarik's neck and kissed him on the mouth, just like that. Now it was Tarik's turn to be flabbergasted, but not for long. He returned my kiss as if it was something we did all the time in front of guests."

"Awesome. Samir must have turned green with envy."

"He turned green alright, I don't know if it was envy, but fifteen minutes later he went up to his room, and we had the fire to ourselves."

"So, you must have had a good conversation with Tarik that night."

"No," Mina answers very decisively, and then giggles. "We had better things to do."

"And that was the end of the whole problem?"

"Oh, no. It took us several more months to sort things out."

"Your patience astounds me."

"Everyone gets patient if they have too."

"Maybe. Anyway, go on."

"So the next Sunday, it was right after Thanksgiving, I think, I announced that I was going to mass, and I was taking Steven with me. I said I felt I needed to square myself with my faith, and I wanted Steven to know that the Catholic Church was his home too. And you know what Tarik said? He said: 'Fair enough. But if you're going to make this a regular thing, we should coordinate about Steven's attending Mosque and Church. We don't want him to get tired of religion before he can pronounce the word.' I said that made sense.

So we decided we would alternate: one week Steven would attend Muslim service, one week he would go to mass. I kept my side of the bargain religiously—that's just the right word, here—better than Tarik, in fact, because he often had business meetings on Friday. And what I found was that I loved to go to mass, that it wasn't a chore at all, but a joy in so many ways. There's something about the liturgy that's spellbinding: all the standing up, and singing, and sitting down, and kneeling, praying, in communion with your fellow human beings for a moment with no other agenda, it's like being part of an ancient and glorious play, but at the same time it's real, and you can feel the spirit soar. Plus, the pastor at Santa Magdalena is no old-time priest. His homilies are just as likely to mention the evil of the war in Iraq or the greed of Wall Street as Lazarus or the Pharisees. Every week, I went to mass, and every week, I came home calmer, more confident, more "grounded" as they say. And then, one Sunday, some time in February, I saw an announcement in the Church Bulletin about an upcoming interfaith dinner sponsored by Santa Magdalena, the local Methodist church, and, I couldn't believe it, El Pequeno's mosque, the very mosque that Tarik and Samir attended. I signed up as a volunteer on the spot. And then I went home, and I proposed that we all attend. By the way, do you know that Jim is a Methodist?"

"No, I didn't know that. How do *you* know?"

"Because I *asked* him," Mina answers in a judicious tone. She is the sole recipient of one of Jim's secrets, after all.

"So did Tarik agree to attend the interfaith dinner?" Grace asks, cutting short her own reflections about Jim's religion.

"He did, isn't that amazing? And somehow, he managed to convince Samir, who had barely got out of the house for the last few months, except to go to the Mosque. It took a lot of work to set up the dinner, but we did a great job, if I say so myself. The venue was the basement hall at the Methodist church, a pretty depressing, bare-bone room. So we decorated the walls with carpets and shawls and tapestries lent by all the different communities, all handmade stuff, mostly from the old countries, nothing store bought. It was pretty gaudy, but really welcoming. We borrowed a small stage from the school at Santa Magdalena. We found a band, with an accordion, that played everything from Irish to Middle Eastern music. We had kids from the various denominations prepare short speeches on how they understood their faiths. The food was potluck. That part, I must say, was a little disappointing. I had made my mother's tamale casserole, and Tarik cooked a Pakistani lamb stew, but a lot of people brought take-out stuff: lumpia, chow-mein, and tons of pizza. You would have thought three-quarters of the diners were Italian. I guess people don't cook any more. As Tarik says, instead of spending all their Sundays on bleachers admiring their kids' athletic feats, parents could carve a little time to actually teach them something useful, like how to prepare a meal."

"Even the boys?"

"Of course even the boys."

"So, you're going to teach Steven how to cook?"

"We've already started. We prop him up on a bar stool and let him watch, and then we give him easy tasks to do like stirring and mashing. He loves breaking eggs. He can even separate the yolks."

"How old is he now?"

"He will be five in a month."

"Clever boy! But we were talking about the interfaith dinner."

"Where was I? Ah, yes. The tables were round and had eight place settings on them. And we had made a rule that there must be one representative of at least three different denominations at each table. It was a great idea because it forced people to talk to strangers as they tried to find somebody of a different denomination to sit with. The funniest part was that you couldn't always guess. In the crowd, there were Arab Christians, Anglo Muslims, an Ethiopian Jewish family, and even members of the Baha'i faith, which I had never heard about before. And those guys are pretty international."

"Reminds me a little of the team building exercises we went through at the Pequeno management retreat . . . But for a much better cause, I dare say."

"Now of course, Tarik and I had it easy. Between the two of us, we already had two different faiths covered. Anyway, the Methodist pastor made a welcoming speech, and then there were prayers by our pastor, an imam and a rabbi, and then somebody at each table said Grace in their own way. It was really touching to realize that in every religion, people feel a need to thank God for the food in front of them. And then I thought about how Christian liturgy is built around the symbolic sharing of a meal, and I didn't want to detract from the ecumenical spirit so I didn't say anything, but still I was pretty proud to be a Christian. After dessert, the kids made their speeches, and then there was a brainstorming session for some community project we could undertake together, and we came up with an idea for a World Religions course, which is scheduled to start this fall in all El Pequeno's primary schools. Finally, the band played, and the little kids danced and played around on the floor. And this is when I noticed something else that I found illuminating. Samir was sitting in the kids' corner, teaching them some version of pattycakes. He was the happiest I had ever seen him. Obviously, he wasn't thinking of kidnapping them all. Suddenly I realized that he was just a big kid himself, lazy, spoiled and ignorant maybe, but also homesick and desperate for connection. He had tried to monopolize Tarik and Steven's attention because he was more comfortable with them, being male and Pakistani—and I hadn't been all that friendly toward him, I admit. There was no need to read anything more sinister in his behavior."

"Although many young terrorists no doubt fit the lazy, spoiled, ignorant and homesick profile, don't you think?"

"And not always ignorant, as a matter of fact. The 9/11 attackers were pretty well educated. What I meant was that there was a simpler explanation to his attitude. I decided to try it on and see what happened."

"And what difference did that make?"

"I was more relaxed with him after that, and as a result Tarik didn't feel the need to protect him so much. So I started insisting that he should pull his weight around the house, and Tarik supported me. I showed him how to operate the washer and drier, I sent him shopping. Tarik made him mow the front lawn and bring in firewood. The Virgin of Guadalupe watched it all, smiling her secret smile. And little by little, Tarik and I got to talk. Like me, he had come to a point in his life where he missed the comfort of ritual and the support of faith. He had welcomed the opportunity that Samir gave him to reconnect with his Muslim roots. But in the end, Islam did not fulfill his aspirations. The thing that bugs him the most is that women are separated from men during services, even though there's nothing in the Qur'an that requires it. As long as this doesn't change, he can't see himself attending regularly. You can say what you want about the misogyny in the Catholic Church, but at least you can sit with your husband at mass."

"A feminist Muslim, how lovely."

"I know, I am pretty lucky."

"What about his hatred of America?"

"The same objections you might have. The war on terror, rampant consumerism, the way kids are raised to feel entitled to everything while children go hungry in many other parts of the world, the lack of respect for elders, sexual exhibitionism, ignorance about other countries, arrogance toward them . . . the usual list. I have to say he's really opened my eyes to the flaws of my own country. I can't even watch a supposedly harmless Disney cartoon like Aladdin without cringing anymore."

"What about his secret savings account?"

"Oh, that's the most embarrassing part. It was money Tarik was putting aside for Steven's education. He hadn't told me about it because he was afraid I would pressure him to spend it now. You see, after we bought the house, which wiped out our savings, we kept having to buy more things to furnish it. And it's true that often, I was the one pushing for purchases that I thought necessary. So Tarik came to think of me as an irresponsible spender. I think he was a little unfair there. After all, he wanted the new house as much as I did. And perhaps we should both have considered the additional expenses we would run into. Anyway, that's water under the bridge."

"Indeed. And what happened to Samir? He no longer lives with you, does he?"

"No, thank God. I mean, he may not have been a terrorist, and I ended up feeling a certain amount of Christian compassion toward him, but he was never going to become my favorite cousin. To tell you the truth, I never learned what the deal was with his supposed sponsor. All I know is that a month before his visitor's visa was due to expire, Tarik managed to ship him back to Pakistan. All the chores we kept piling on him may have helped him decide where his true home was. When we came back from the airport, Tarik put his arms around me and he said: "Well, I am glad that's over." That was the first clue I had that he had not enjoyed Samir's visit any more than I had. He had been so intent of honoring the rules of hospitality that he had never breathed a word of his irritation before. Can you imagine that?"

"Very honorable of him. But the stiff upper lip has its downside."

"I know. Anyway, getting rid of Samir was all well and good, but it left two problems on our hands. One, we had to pay for his plane ticket, which put us even more in debt. And two, the sulfur smell in the house did not leave with him."

XV

DISTRACTED

What Jim remembers most about the fall of 2005 is a feeling of distraction. He was being distracted by Fritz's demands and by Myrtle's schemes. By cat fights among the IT staff, by Pequeno politics, by technical glitches and organizational snafus. By his home situation. By Grace. And all these distractions overlapped in such a bedeviling way that he found it difficult to deal effectively with any of them. The worst of it was that he could no longer tell what he was being distracted from. Doubtful about the nature of his mission, disinclined toward some of its tactical requirements, bored with the day-to-day, he felt in danger of losing his inner poise—not a inborn gift, but a hard-won knowledge of his capacity to juggle careful planning and inspired improvisation in order to bring all the random happenstance around him in line with his goals. He was too disciplined to show his disarray, but more and more often, he sensed the abyss under his feet, wondering how long he would manage to keep running.

He couldn't blame Fritz, who was clear and steadfast in *his* goals: to expand his company to the point where it would compete with McKinsey. From a theoretical business perspective, it was an eminently reasonable plan: grow or die is capitalism's imperative. But in practice, growth meant the constant hiring of new employees and the constant acquisition of new clients, two tasks that Fritz knew Jim to excel at. So, at Fritz's request, Jim was spending a good deal of time evaluating potential Hartbridge recruits and wooing community college executives all over the western region. Some of these interviews could be conducted over the phone or through teleconferencing, but some required in-person interaction. Jim also served as floating FTE for two of Hartbridge existing contracts, one in the San Diego area, the other in Tulare county, so he had to show his face there from time to time.

To top it all, he was having to work on a Request For Proposal for the three-year contract Fritz was still determined to obtain from Pequeno. Under regulations that apply to all State government institutions, any purchase above a certain amount must be submitted to public bid, but "Sole Source" exceptions may be granted for products and services that are offered by only one vendor. Given the shroud of mystery that envelops all things technical in the mind of the lay public, IT purchases are the easiest to claim as deserving the Sole Source treatment. This was the loophole that had allowed the current one-year Hartbridge contract to be enacted without an RFP. But the political climate at Pequeno had since made the enactment of a multi-million-dollar no-bid contract unlikely. So Jim was now tasked with writing the RFP for the new contract in such language that only Hartbridge's bid would be considered. A lay person might question the legal and ethical propriety of allowing a vendor to manipulate a supposedly competitive process to insure its own selection. The lay person might argue that this is equivalent to letting students write their own test questions. The lay person would have a point, but, truth be told, it did not cross Jim's mind, used as he was to navigate by hook or crook around bureaucratic obstacles, and conscious that Stanley Gruff's forced retirement had deprived the Pequeno district of its only staff member qualified to write the RFP. What did give Jim trouble was the document's content. After eight months at the District, he still had not settled on a plausible set of projects that would guarantee Hartbridge's presence for three more years.

The net result of all these extra-curricular activities was that he was neglecting his managerial duties around the IT department. This was another problem he might not have noticed, were it not for the reproach he often read in Grace's eyes. He had worked long enough to know that his productivity was second to none, and therefore to feel confident that his clients got their money's worth, no matter the number of hours he had to steal away from them. But Grace didn't see it that way. To a certain extent, this was Jim's fault. He had got her so used to interacting with him on a daily basis that she was now acutely aware of his decreased availability, busy as he often was behind closed doors or away from the office. And to be fair, she may have needed more help with her new duties than he could make time for. Now and then, he was reminded of his guilty sense, when he decided to promote her, that he was in effect throwing his pet lamb to the wolves. But as far as he could tell, it hadn't turned out as bad as that. The wolves were after all pretty toothless, and the lamb was toughening up, as it should.

In fact, Grace never complained directly of his retrenchment, contenting herself with tossing occasional barbs about "private meetings" and "serving two masters", or expressing concerns over the likely effect of overwork on his health. And she was looking out for him, keeping him in the loop on developments within the department and quietly picking up the balls he had dropped. All the same, he knew her well enough to see that she disapproved of the time he spent on Hartbridge business, and that it wasn't just personal resentment but a moral stance. He put it down to her inexperience and literal-mindedness, but part of him withered under the sense of her diminished regard.

He couldn't blame Myrtle for working at cross-purposes with him. She had been parachuted into Pequeno without a clear assignment or defined place in the chain of command. And she desperately needed the job: as Jim learned during their big blow-out, her husband having been disabled in a car accident, she was the sole breadwinner for a family of five, two of them enrolled in fancy private colleges. The peevishness that Jim had at first attributed to her self-importance was in fact only the product of financial insecurity. As to her qualifications, other than the three letters on her business card meant to impress Dr. Akecheta, they looked so dithyrambically diffuse on her resume that for the longest time Jim had not known what to do with her—assuming that he was in a position to give her something to do, which was far from evident, given their equal rank in the Hartbridge hierarchy.

In the absence of an assigned project, Myrtle had looked for other ways to make herself indispensable. Perhaps to compensate for an academic past tainted with the very un-businesslike traits of liberalism and collegiality, she was a big proponent of Machiavellian leadership, especially its best known tenet of Divide and Conquer. Hence her stealth campaign to incite the staff against Grace's promotion, a bit of intrigue meant as much to increase her own popularity among the malcontents as to sap the other woman's chances of grabbing power away from Hartbridge, Jim surmised.

Out of the same Machiavelllian principles, she had courted various Pequeno executives with lavish lunches, questionable excursions and cockamamie promises. Finally, she had tried to insert herself into the day-to-day affairs of the IT department. None of her efforts had met with much success. Grace had not only survived the cabal against her, but she was day by day assuming more authority. The Pequeno executives had soon forgotten Myrtle's favors, either from a general mistrust of women, or because of a lack of follow-through on Myrtle's part, or out of a sense that Jim was the one in charge. And both Grace and Mina had made clear that they would brook no interference in their domains.

It was Mina in fact, diminutive, unobtrusive Mina, who had at last forced Jim to grapple with Myrtle, though Grace had previously sounded the alarm on several occasions. It was partly a matter of repetition, but Mina's very reserve gave her interventions a special force: if even *she* felt a need to put her foot down, there was definitely a problem.

At his next five o'clock with Myrtle, Jim wasted no time laying out what he thought of her performance so far: how her initial coddling of the staff's petty resentments against Grace had created an environment where everyone felt entitled to waste his time with their most minute interpersonal disputes; how her solo flights of client management were tarnishing Hartbridge's cohesive image; how her recourse to unorthodox procedures for approving expenses was encouraging staff to cheat; and how her meddling in Operations and Applications resulted in errors and unreasonable expectations. Having decided against consulting Fritz prior to the meeting, Jim was conscious that he was going out on a limb by playing the reprimand card. Myrtle could easily have walked out on him, then complained to Fritz about his unprofessional behavior. Instead, against all his expectations, she broke down in tears, completely disarming him, as crying women always did. It was then that she revealed her personal situation, which was not so different from his, in the end: they were both shackled to their jobs by money problems. So what else could Jim do but try to find some way to make her useful?

After she composed herself, they discussed her strengths and interests. As you could expect, she claimed that her forte was dealing with academic managers, but she also felt that since her arrival at Pequeno, she had established positive relationships with Ruby, Tiffany, and even Elmore. She had strong Microsoft Project, Visio and Power Point skills, and enjoyed all kinds of writing. She was familiar with the TTIP and CENIC State programs, and had a decent high-level understanding of network architecture.

As Myrtle listed her qualifications, it became clear to Jim that she belonged in the Network Services and Distance Education department, both because of her area of expertise and because that unit was headed by a former dean, a certain Peter Santelli. Shortly after his arrival at Pequeno, Jim had been advised by Bob Johnson that Santelli and his department were off-limit as far as Hartbridge was concerned. Perhaps it was time to revisit that notion. Jim encouraged Myrtle to befriend the guy, dazzle him with her credentials, see if he could use some help with any of his projects, such as setting up a wireless network at the Piedmont campus, which Jim had heard was pretty far flung, therefore probably hard to wire. In the meantime, given her good relationship with Ruby, Myrtle might look into discreetly overseeing the PC technician unit. But what would be most helpful to Jim would be her taking responsibility for the creation of an IT disaster recovery plan, the request for which had landed on his desk that very morning. Thankfully, Myrtle agreed to everything. Once more, Jim had snatched victory out of the jaws of defeat. At the back of his mind, he was looking forward to Myrtle spending time at the District Office with Santelli, perhaps making extended visits to the Piedmont campus, in other words, getting out of his hair.

Jim didn't blame the staff for wasting his time with their trivial complaints about each other. Though he had told Myrtle that this development was her fault, inwardly he acknowledged that the ultimate responsibility was his. It was his willingness to lend an ear to the gang of five's mean-spirited attacks on Grace that had set him up as shrink and umpire for the entire group. Now, not a day went by without one of the staff making an appointment with him to air their grievances: Erin resented Sandra's busybody tattling, Sandra was tired of doing Ruby's work, Ruby was disgusted by the fishy smell of Sandip's lunches, Sandip couldn't stand the way Josh slurped his coffee, Josh thought Tiffany was a bitch, Tiffany was offended by Elmore's patronizing, Elmore was shocked by Rajiv's poor grammar, and everybody wanted something done about Ruby's garbage before rats moved in. A regular round-robin of whining. (Grace and Mina's complaints about Myrtle, although they too ate into Jim's time, he instinctively put in a separate category.)

It had to stop. Without showing contempt for their infantile behavior or rescinding his stated open-door policy, Jim had to convince the staff to deal with their differences among themselves. He finally hit upon the device of proposing that all interpersonal problems should be discussed during staff meetings so that the entire team could contribute to a solution. It worked. After one problem-solving session, during which Sandip was encouraged to bring blander lunches to work, and Ruby promised to clean her office, interpersonal problems seemed to disappear. But Jim later got a call from Classified Union Rep Charlie Weissman, who complained that the shop steward was threatening to resign over the IT staff's constant bickering. Jim sympathized, and Charlie confessed that the IT department had long been known for its toxic atmosphere. The thing was, SEIU was currently conducting several major organizing drives and couldn't afford to spend its resources on psychological counseling for members who had excellent union contracts. Jim explained that he was himself pretty much tapped out between running the department and gearing up for new technology projects. Charlie sympathized. They ended up setting up a bowling date for the next weekend.

Jim didn't blame the teachers for trying to get the best possible deal in the new union contract under negotiation that fall. The Pequeno Federation of Teachers, PFT for short, turned out to be completely independent of the classified union, and affiliated with AFL-CIO instead of SEIU. In fact, by Jim's reckoning, there were at least four different unions battling management and each other for their share of the District's dollars, and their contract periods were staggered in such a way as to keep the Labor/ Management and Legal Counsel teams busy year round while providing a regular supply of adversarial theatrics at Board meetings.

As interim CIO, Jim had been forced to attend Board meetings fairly regularly for eight months, and the spectacle had grown old, for all its educational value regarding Pequeno politics. Now that she was a manager, Grace insisted on attending also, although Jim had excused her from that particular duty. Somehow, they got into the habit of sitting next to each other at the Board meetings. Jim wasn't sure what he thought about the arrangement. On the one hand, her presence relieved the boredom. She was sometimes able to give him some background on one of the speakers or translate some arcane terminology. And he was conscious of the way her youth, her professional reputation, her shapely physique and obvious fondness for him pleasantly reflected on his own image. On the other hand, he wished she was a little more poker-faced, instead of broadcasting her frequent feelings of disbelief, irritation or outright contempt at the proceedings with sighs, rolls of her eyes, pokes into his ribs, and taps of her foot against his. It wasn't just that she lacked a professional mask, but that she didn't see the need for it. Let it all hang out seemed to be her motto. She was never going to make a career in politics, that was for sure. (But didn't Mina mention in her latest email that Grace is going to work on that Obama guy's campaign? Yes, she did. Has Grace changed so much? He can't imagine it.) To be honest, Jim was sometimes afraid that her irreverence would reflect on him too. Mostly though, his concern was that she relieved his boredom a little too much. It wasn't just the pokes and the taps, but more to the point, the steady touch of her thigh, which, the seats being narrow and linked together, there was no way to avoid other than jamming into the person on the other side. After the first time, Jim resorted to laying a memo pad across his lap at every Board meeting. He would occasionally scribble notes on it, meanwhile he was able to relax and enjoy the moment.

According to the laws of adversarial politics, the party that wants a bigger piece of the pie must not only establish its right to it, but dispute the claims and demolish the reputation of all other competing parties. In the fall of 2005, it was the PFT's turn at this edifying exercise. At every Board meeting, one teacher after another would take the podium, arguing that Pequeno instructors' pay was among the lowest in the state while the area's housing prices had risen the most, that the ratio of administrative to instructional employees was violating the 50% rule, that managerial hiring in particular was out of control (a Director of International Education? Didn't we have enough of a job educating the local community? Associate Vice-Chancellor of Admissions and Records? Why this change of title for the Director position? And four new Assistant Vice-Chancellor titles? And new Deputy Directors, Executive Directors, Assistant Director positions? What was the corporate-style multi-tier hierarchy doing at a community college district?) At a time when enrollment was down—up interjected newly promoted Associate Vice-Chancellor of Admissions and Records Roger Wilkins, overall enrollment may be up, but credit FTE was down, countered the teacher representative—at a time when credit FTE was down, we were hiring a record number of people at the District office, the one place that did not generate revenues, while vacant faculty positions remained unfilled.

As Grace remarked in one of her whispered asides, the teachers seemed to fancy themselves as so many Socrates, throwing pearls of wisdom to eager disciples spontaneously flocking to them on the Agora. They did not see the need for classroom equipment, janitorial services, registration systems, payroll clerks, financial aid offices, or the management structure to oversee all these administrative functions. From their point of view, all the student fees should have gone into their pockets. Jim, imagining that the teachers' implied lack of respect for their classified colleagues would not go over well with them, was surprised to see the purple-clad SEIU members clap heartily at the end of the speeches, but Grace explained to him that the classified contract included a me-too clause, so that any pay increase wrestled by the faculty would immediately be applied to administrative salaries.

The teachers' most venomous ire, however, was directed at the Chancellor himself. Only hinted at during boardroom orations, which the speakers—they came in two models: the prim self-important female and the slick self-important male—seemed intent on keeping decorous (and/or safe for their own heads), it rang loud and clear in the pamphlets deposited on boardroom seats before each meeting by an anonymous group that called itself the Save Pequeno Committee. There, accusations of secrecy, tyranny and greed were leveled at Dr. Akecheta in bulleted details. The self-interested nature of these rants notwithstanding, Jim had to admit that they may have a point. His few dealings with the man had failed to enlist his own sympathy. And Grace made no secret that she thought him a pompous ass. (Why didn't he ever caution her against voicing her opinions of the higher-ups so freely? Because she gave vent to feelings he had to keep bottled up? Because her fearless innocence delighted him, and he was loath to spoil it? Or because he did not really have her welfare at heart? A little bit of all three, he is afraid.)

Whatever the merits—or lack thereof—of the teachers' gripes, what was of concern to Jim was that they were busily digging for dirt about the Chancellor. Through a Web search, they had found some damaging stories about a botched administrative system conversion at his previous post. And thanks to the wide accessibility and user-friendliness of the budget query system recently implemented by Rajiv, they had been able to add up his salary and perks (the relocation fee, the housing fee, the company car, the bodyguard, the unlimited travel allowance . . .), compare the total with the previous chancellor's compensation package, and come up with an increase figure that made the 9% raise they were demanding appear like chicken feed.

At some point, they were going to discover Dr. Akecheta's membership on the Hartbridge advisory board, which would throw a suspicious light on the firm's no-bid contract. They might also get wind of the opinion recently delivered by Legal Counsel to the effect that Measure G funds could not be expended on day-to-day operations, which had resulted in Jim's portion of the contract expenses being quietly switched to the general fund. Publicly embarrassed, the Board members, even those who had been promised lucrative sub-contracts for their friends and family, would have no choice but to nix the contract renewal. A mess.

Fritz, who did not attend Board meetings, was overly sanguine about Akecheta's ability to ram his pet projects through in the teeth of universal opposition. But at last, Jim convinced him of the danger of the situation. Together, they came up with a three-pronged attack on the teachers' resistance:

1. Akecheta must be made to resign his seat on the Hartbridge board, and any reference to him removed from the firm's Web site. As it was, the only reason the teachers' investigative team had not found out about the connection was probably that his name had been misspelled on the page.
2. The new contract must be put out to bid.
3. The teachers must find something of particular benefit to them in the contract.

Fritz took care of item #1. The Chancellor was peeved about losing his place on the Hartbridge's Web site, but comforted to hear that he would still get his complimentary trips to Orlando as "honored guest".

Jim got saddled with writing the RFP made necessary by item #2.

Myrtle accepted responsibility for item #3. Eventually, in concert with Peter Santelli, she came up with the idea of using TTIP funds to replace all faculty computers, some of which were nearly five years old, with state-of-the-art, WiFi, Bluetooth and Webcam equipped laptops. The project would be managed by Hartbridge as part of the upcoming three-year contract. Peter Santelli would "coordinate" with faculty. A winner all around.

He couldn't blame Joleen for distracting him from his job. In fact, since the disastrous Labor weekend, she had not called him once. He finally broke down and called her. To his utter surprise, not only she picked up the phone, but she was in one of her most civil moods. Neither of them brought up the credit card cutting incident or her subsequent escapade. He told her that he had arranged for all the regular house bills to be paid automatically from their joint account. She thought it was a good idea. She asked him how his job was going and when he was coming home. He said the job was fine and that he was flying back to North Carolina in three weeks. They talked about the children. Joleen had visited Robby at Leavenworth. She had brought him some chocolate chip cookies she had baked herself. It was a new mix she had found at the Trader Joe's in Chapel Hill, rated best in the newspaper, she thought she'd give them a whirl, and they had come out great. Robby had been real happy. He was hanging in there, poor lamb, but it was tough. There were some real hoodlums in that prison. Not much new on the Cindy front. Her current boyfriend seemed like a real loser. When was the girl going to get wise about men? Yes, she was looking at the junior college course catalog. A complete waste of time, if you asked Joleen. The girl just didn't have it up there. It was a mystery, considering Jim's brain power. No, Cindy wasn't home right then, but anyway Joleen thought Jim should let her be for the time being. She had been real upset after their last phone conversation, she said he was putting too much pressure on her, got her all confused. But she had started going to Church again. Maybe she'd meet a decent guy there. Other than that, Joleen's rock garden was coming along. She had bought a whole bunch of bulbs: tulips, freesias, daffodils, narcissus, hyacinths real cheap at a wholesale nursery, she was going to plant them before the cold weather set in, come spring her front yard would be the envy of the whole neighborhood.

He should have known better than to think the crisis was over. When he came home, it must have been at the beginning of November, he found that all his clothes were missing from the bedroom closet. His first thought was that she had slashed them or just thrown them away. They were a collection of suits and shirts he had had made to order during his years abroad. Most of them were too tight for him now, but they were very costly items, and Robert might find a use for them when he got out of prison. Plus, they had a sentimental value for Jim. He was all the more perplexed that Joleen had for once gone to the trouble of picking him up at the airport. Her greeting may have been a little desultory, but she had been perfectly cordial on the way back. He was standing stock still in front of the closet, unsure of how to handle the mixed message, when Joleen walked in.

"Oh, I forgot to tell you," she said over his shoulder, "I moved your stuff to Robby's bedroom. I thought it would be better if you slept there from now on. To tell you the truth, I can't get a good night's rest with your snoring, and you're getting too fat for the other bedroom stuff. Not to hurt your feelings, but a roll in the hay with you nowadays is about as much fun as getting run over by a Mack truck."

Jim was struck speechless. Joleen was breathing hard in his back. He was afraid to turn around, afraid to see the look in her eyes. He knew from experience that it would be useless to reason or to plead.

She took either as signs of weakness. It occurred to him to force himself on her right then and there. It had worked a few times in the past. But he felt frozen in place, completely emptied out. The truth was, his feelings *were* hurt, deeply, perhaps irremediably. All he could manage to say in the end was: "OK, if that's how you feel . . ." as he dragged his luggage to Robert's bedroom, where he did find all his clothes intact and neatly put away. It was something.

Nothing more happened that weekend. Cindy came home from her job, dutifully welcomed her father, didn't ask any question, and after that made herself scarce. On Saturday Jim and Joleen went out to dinner at some friends' house, and Joleen was the life of the party, as usual. She didn't make any derogatory remark about her husband, was even affectionate toward him in public, but when they came home she walked straight to their bedroom, locking the door behind her. On Sunday they went to Church, and even played a round of golf with another couple of friends. On Monday she offered to take him to the airport, and when he declined, insisted that it was no trouble at all, so he relented. She dropped him off at the curb, and as he was opening the car door, she put an arm around his neck, kissed him on the cheek, wished him a safe flight, and immediately proceeded to turn the radio on. By the time he had shouldered his luggage, her car was out of sight. It had been the most peaceful, convivial visit they had had in years. This was what drove into Jim's mind the realization that sex between them was over.

He spent the flight back to California trying to wrap his head around this new development. Given her mood swings, there was a possibility that she would change her mind. Somehow, the thought failed to cheer him up. Then he tried to picture a relationship with Joleen that would not involve sex. It was impossible. He suddenly understood what a big part sex had played in their marriage. This was what had hooked him, what had kept him coming back. How their conflicts had always ended, compensation for all their other incompatibilities. In sex Joleen was present, dedicated, brilliant, tireless, even tender. Dubai's most expensive whores couldn't compete with her. Jim knew enough about other people's marriages to realize what a rare thing they had had, year after year, through all his absences—perhaps because of his absences? But now she thought him too fat. And yet, there were other women who found him attractive, young women too. It was a balm on his heart, though he was determined not to think about it. Instead, he twisted the knife in the wound by trying to reconstruct the history of his marriage. It seemed such a maddening jumble of ecstasy, agony, and tedium that he couldn't make any sense of it. Less than three years later, it offers itself to his mind's eye with the clarity and breadth of a diorama.

Their first dates. He, gangly, overly serious, shy with women, still working at his uncle's hardware store, but already taking computer courses at the junior college, and discovering that he had a knack for logic. She, a waitress at the coffee shop across the road from the hardware store, a flash of lightning in that dark, dowdy place, her movements efficient and graceful, but as if executed on automatic pilot, her sharp little face, her laughing eyes, her bold mouth telling a different story. How she had proposed they go out, one day over lunch. And when he asked "When?", she answered "Now." She said it was high time he learned to play hooky. Turned out she knew all the swimming holes, lovers' lanes, blues bars, fairs, movie theaters, dope dealers within a fifty miles radius. Right away they had sex, and it blew his world apart. She was much more experienced at it than he was, but he was a fast learner. She also taught him to dance, to dive, to play poker. He helped her pick courses at the junior college. He talked about his career ambitions, and encouraged her to have some too. They saw each other constantly, although after a few weeks, Jim's unshakable work ethic prompted him to curtail the weekday outings. He was so hungry for her that he could think of nothing else. She seemed to be crazy about him too. Was it love? He was too green to even ask himself that question. But soon she got pregnant, and he didn't have to.

Early parenthood. It was just as well he hadn't been told how bearing a child puts a crimp in a woman's libido, because he would have worried for nothing. They had sex all the way to the delivery, and were at it again three weeks later. He never felt he had to compete with the children for her attention, but there may have been a downside to his happy supremacy: the fact was, Joleen didn't have much of a maternal instinct. He remembers the first time they vacationed at the beach, her excitement at seeing the sea, her surrender to the waves, how they ran into the dunes to make love, the baby carrier bumping between them, and how, by the time their lust was satiated, they found that Cindy had got a horrible sunburn.

It was through watching Joleen interact with Cindy that Jim first became aware of some of her more problematic character traits: her impatience, her inconsistency, her lack of sympathy. One minute she would be laughing at some boo-boo the girl had committed, oblivious to her tears. The next moment she would shake her in exasperation. She would rail at Jim because he wasn't involved enough in the baby's care, then snatch her from his arms when he tried. What Joleen excelled at was having fun. Give her a chance for any game that involved noise and physical exertion, and she would become the Pied Piper for a whole group of children. She was a godsend on the playground and at kids' birthday parties. Too bad that, right from the beginning, Cindy had been a quiet, easily scared child.

Robert had more affinities with his mother, but even he couldn't keep her interested in the long run. Joleen had quit her job after Cindy's birth, and now, with two young kids at home, she gave up studying for the real estate license that had been their agreed-upon goal. She complained that her life was going nowhere. She started spending more money than he made. By then, he had found a job as computer operator for a grocery chain, a well-paying job by North Carolina standards at the time. He was also moonlighting as a programmer, developing an inventory system for his uncle's hardware stores. He discovered that work felt restful by contrast with the constant explosions at home, that the esteem in which his bosses held him served as a welcome counterweight to his wife's bitter criticisms. When he heard of the amounts of money that could be made working in the Gulf States, he decided to try for it. Joleen encouraged him. Absence makes the heart grow fonder, they both reasoned. As to the kids, well, they would not be worse off than the countless children in military families whose parents were deployed overseas, as Joleen's father had been. In fact, they would be better off, because at least they would be well provided for financially. All the same, when the offer finally came, Jim hesitated. He was terrified about the prospect of living in a foreign country, worried about leaving the children alone with their mother, and depressed about the perspective of sleeping alone for long stretches of time. What decided him, in the end, was probably one of their fights, at the height of which Joleen threw a pair of scissors that missed his neck by an inch, though it ended in the usual sexual delirium. They bought the house right before he left.

The years abroad went by in a blur as far as Jim's family life was concerned. Those were the days before email, Webcams and Skype. When you were far geographically, you were far psychologically. Meanwhile, Jim was changing. His mental world was widening, his confidence grew, his heart opened to friendship. Joleen kept him informed about what was happening with the children: illnesses, lost teeth, Christmas pageants, athletic feats, accidents, report cards—those, always disappointing. What got lost was any sense of emotional closeness. When he came home every three months or so, the kids had grown, the furniture had changed, Joleen was starting yet a new business with some friends he had never heard of before, ventures that would never be mentioned again. She was incurious about Saudi Arabia (those backward, women-hating ragheads), uninterested in his adventures (she was glad she hadn't been there), bored by his attempts to share his new cultural interests (highfalutin mumbo-jumbo).

By the time Robert started first grade, she seemed to have pretty much given up on parenting. She didn't even keep the clocks running. It was part of Jim's homecoming ritual to plug in the alarm clock in the bedroom, reset all the appliance timekeepers left to blinking eights since the last power outage, and rewind the grandfather clock in the foyer. How the kids got to school on time in his absence was anyone's guess. It was left to him to be the disciplinarian. Not surprisingly, perhaps, the kids came to regard him as an unwelcome intruder. At night, Joleen continued to offer herself willingly, but little by little, a suspicion started creeping into Jim's mind that her sexual favors had a certain element of bargaining to them. Meanwhile, she was turning into a shopoholic.

He can't fathom how the marriage survived Robert's arrest, a perfect storm of anguish, shame, powerlessness, expenses and mutual recriminations. A testament to the power of sexual attraction, or to the force of habit? Thankfully, soon enough, he was on the road again, first as an independent contractor, and then as a Hartbridge employee. And Jim has to give Joleen credit for standing by him when he was first diagnosed with Hodgkin's. His illness turned their sexless arrangement into a necessity. It is only when he relapsed that she called it quits. This kind of thing has been known to happen in the best families.

Still, her eventual desertion has given him a much more cynical view of his marriage than the one he entertained during that miserable flight back to California. He is now inclined to think that it rested on calculation on her part, and misunderstanding on his: he had fallen for her because she taught him to play hooky, while she had zeroed in on a steady provider who could bankroll her lazy habits. From some remarks Robert has floated, he gathers that Joleen now portrays him as a sex-fiend and a miser, to whom she had to sell her body to keep the kids fed. She also accuses him of having consorted with prostitutes while in Saudi Arabia, which, although it is factually true, is still an invention on her part, since he never told her about it, any more than he ever asked her how she got her sexual needs met while they were apart, though there was plenty of evidence that she did.

It was raining when he landed in San Francisco. During the drive back to El Pequeno, his cell phone rang, shaking him out of his misery. It was Roger Wilkins. The registration Web site was out of commission. It looked like a denial of service attack. Roger had tried to contact Grace, but she had gone home. They were in the middle of priority registration, so fixing the system was a matter of urgency. Otherwise the chancellor would have their balls for breakfast. Jim told Roger that he would take care of it and hung up. This is when he realized that he didn't have a clue about the IT department's protocol for dealing with system problems outside of business hours, didn't even have any of the staff's phone numbers. Grace had been right all along. He hadn't been giving Pequeno their money's worth.

He looked at his watch. Six fifteen. Even Mina would had left the office by now. Traffic was crawling even slower than usual because of the rain. He was still an hour away from El Pequeno—barring the likelihood of a storm-related accident, California drivers being notoriously incapable of handling any kind of weather. He took the first off-ramp and pulled over on the side of the road. His headlights barely made a dent in the moisture-drenched darkness, while the windshield wipers echoed the beating of his heart in a sickening fashion. He turned them off. The drumming of rain on the roof filled his brain. He rolled his head around, trying to relieve the tension in his neck. For a dreadful minute, he didn't know what to do.

In desperation, he punched in Myrtle's cell number. Thankfully, she picked up. She was driving back from the Piedmont campus with Peter Santelli. She was unaware of the problem with Web registration. In the two weeks since she had agreed to oversee the PC coordinator unit, she hadn't had time to inquire about its emergency procedures either. At that point, it occurred to Jim to ask her to put Santelli on the line. If, as Roger claimed, the problem was a denial of service attack, it would fall under the Network Services department's responsibility. Santelli pooh-poohed the idea. His staff monitored the network 24/7, and if it had been hacked into, he would know it by now. Jim asked him to check anyway and call him back at the number he gave him.

Thirty minutes later, as Jim, who in the meantime had got back on the road, was approaching the Highway 99 turnoff, his cell phone rang again. It was Santelli. His staff had checked the network, and there was no sign of unusual activity. All the routers and switches were operating normally, so the problem must be with the server itself. The ball was back in Jim's court. He asked Santelli to pass the phone to Myrtle for a second, but she had already dropped him off. He didn't know where she had gone.

He called Myrtle again, who explained that she was on her way to Livermore. She was sorry to leave Jim in a lurch, but she had a family emergency to deal with. At least, she gave Jim Ruby's home and cell numbers.

Ruby's cell phone did not answer, so he tried her home number. It was picked up by a boy with a lisp so thick that Jim thought he was speaking a foreign language. Assuming he had dialed a wrong number, he hung up and tried again. The same boy picked up and this time, Jim was able to communicate that he needed to speak to his mother. "Mom!", the boy shouted, banging the phone down. Jim was left hanging for what seemed like an eternity. In the background he could hear kids screaming, dogs barking, loud rock music. Finally, Ruby came to the phone.

"Who is this?" she asked. Her voice sounded slurred. Was she drunk, on a school night, with her kids around? He flashed on the evening when the team went out for drinks, how familiar she had seemed with the atmosphere of the bar, how uninhibitedly she had taken the mike to sing Karaoke. And then there were her successive diets, all abandoned after a few weeks. That also jived with an addictive personality. Her being an alcoholic would explain a lot about her performance.

"This is Jim."

"Jim who?"

"Jim Wright, your boss."

"How did you get my home phone number?"

"Myrtle gave it to me. I . . ."

"Well, she shouldn't have. I don't appreciate getting work calls on my home phone. That's why we were given cell phones."

"I'm sorry, but your cell phone did not answer, and this is an emergency. I need you to . . ."

"I'm not on call tonight. I mean, I'd like to feel that my time off is my own."

"I understand. Can you just tell me who *is* on call right now? It seems the registration server is . . ."

"I have no idea. I just know it's not me."

"Can you tell me who would know?"

"Why don't you call the Network Help Desk? They have the list."

"Can you give me the number for the Network Help Desk?"

"It's on the Web page."

"Can you give it to me in case I can't find it, or the Web server is inaccessible?"

"I don't have it memorized, if that's what you're asking. I always look it up on the Web."

"OK, then. Thank you and have a good evening."

"And please tell Grace that you called me, so I can charge one hour of overtime."

"Will do."

There was no way around it. Jim was going to have to call Santelli again, at the risk of revealing his ignorance about his own department's procedures. Fortunately, he was able to plead his inability to access phone lists while driving in the rain. All the same, there was a certain relish in Santelli's tone as he gave Jim the help desk number, assuring him that his team was always there to help.

Jim called the help desk. Sure enough, the phone was picked up after one ring. The help desk person, a certain Mike, told Jim that Alex was the PC coordinator on call that day. The problem was, Alex was on vacation. Who was the backup? There was no backup listed, but Mike offered to give Jim the other coordinators' cell numbers. Would that do? That would do fine. Jim asked Mike to hang tight for a sec while he pulled off the road again. He turned on the ceiling light, grabbed a pen and a gas receipt from the glove compartment, and told Mike to shoot. He wrote down Erin's, Josh's and Sandra's cell numbers. As Mike was about to give him Ruby's number, Jim told him not to bother. He heard the guy snort at the other end of the line. Obviously, Jim wasn't the only person she gave a hard time to.

While he was still parked, he called Erin. Her phone did not answer. He called Josh. Josh was there. Jim had barely started explaining the situation when Josh told him to wait for a sec while he pinged the server. He came back on the line to say that the server answered, so it must be an application issue. He suggested that Jim call Grace, then claimed someone was at the door, and hung up before Jim could ask him for Grace's number.

He was down to his last resource. Miraculously, Sandra not only answered her phone and took the time to listen to Jim's tale, but she thought she knew how to fix the problem. By the time he pulled into the IT parking lot, Sandra, bless her heart, was waiting for him under the awning. They hurried in together, made their way to the server in the computer room (at least, he knew which one it was) and without further ado, Sandra proceeded to restart the registration application, explaining that it seemed the server had a memory problem, that the application needed to be restarted every couple of weeks, and that somebody (Ruby, of course) must have forgotten to do it the last time it was scheduled. The whole procedure took thirty seconds. Afterwards, they went to Sandra's desktop to try the Web page. It worked. Jim called Roger and asked him to verify the fix from his home computer. Roger, much relieved, confirmed that the application was accessible again. There were three hours left for registration that night before the whole system was taken down for regular maintenance. Sandra had saved the day. As they were leaving the Data Center, Jim was moved to give her a hug, promising to look into promoting her to a Senior Coordinator position. She was tickled pink, obviously pleased to see her work ethic vindicated at last, and Ruby's sloth exposed. He couldn't begrudge her either satisfaction.

The registration server outage had at least one positive effect: it made Jim forget his personal troubles. That night, in his anonymous condo, instead of feeling sorry for himself, he spent hours on his laptop in a state of manic concentration, working out solutions to his various office problems. Around three AM, having at last regained a sense of control, he poured himself a glass of whiskey and sat back on the anonymous couch. He fell asleep like a stone, still holding the glass.

The next morning, as Roger Wilkins had feared, they were both called into Akecheta's office for a "debriefing". As usual, they were made to cool their heels for forty minutes in the reception area while the Chancellor's three solemn-faced, age-graded secretaries typed purposefully on their computers, their busy fingers seeming to tip-toe on the keyboards, as if the slightest noise might disrupt the thought patterns of their eminent boss on the other side of the door, causing tragic world-wide repercussions. Jim would have given much to see what they were typing. Their resumes, perhaps? At last, the oldest of the secretaries, having answered a curt phone summons, informed them that Dr. Akecheta would see them now, got up, smoothed her skirt discreetly, and led them to the Chancellor's door with a gravity suggesting that without her guidance the journey would have required the use of a GPS.

Dr. Akecheta was sitting at his desk, his plump little hands laid flat on its immaculate cherry-wood expanse, the supercilious glint in his glasses the only expressive feature on his jowly face. As he did not ask them to sit, they remained standing. Fortunately, the meeting didn't last long. Dr. Akecheta wanted to know what had caused the unaccountable system failure of the previous night that had prevented students from enrolling for a full four hours, and what steps were being taken to prevent a reoccurrence of any such problem. Roger wisely yielding the floor to the CIO, Jim smoothly launched into a "thirty-thousand-foot view" of the various tiers of hardware and software implicated in Web applications, laying the emphasis on the cooperation between the IT and Network Services teams that had allowed the problem to be promptly pinpointed and solved in spite of this architectural complexity. He was glad that in his ignorance, Akecheta had not seen fit to include Santelli in the drubbing session, as the Network Services Director might have poked holes in Jim's rosy tale. He concluded by promising Dr. Akecheta a copy of the revised emergency protocol being documented as he spoke by his Hartbridge partner.

All that remained to do was to actually assign the project to Myrtle, which Jim did as their next five o'clock. Sheepish about her desertion the previous night, Myrtle complied. In collaboration with the PC team, she eventually set up functional server maintenance and on-call protocols, though she could never get Ruby to agree to have her home phone number listed on any District document, however securely kept. In any case, there were no more server snafus for the duration of Jim's Pequeno gig. But he knows from Grace's frantic emails that all the protocols fell by the wayside as soon as he left.

He shouldn't have blamed Grace for the—major—part she played in distracting him. But he did, he now realizes. He resented her for his attraction to her, and this, more than anything else, accounted for his periodic fits of aloofness or annoyance toward her. And yet, she didn't do anything specific to fan the flames of his lust. It wasn't her fault if she was well put together, or if the currently hip fashions—the short skirts, the form-fitting tops, the bare legs—were designed to draw attention to the fact. Within those parameters, you could even say that she was modest. Unlike Tiffany, she didn't go for plunging necklines. Since her promotion to management, it even looked to Jim as if the hems of her skirts had been lowered. In fact, her whole appearance seemed to have undergone a subtle change. He would have put it down to the tricks played by his imagination, if he hadn't been able to point to one objective detail: she had let her hair grow so that it hid the question mark tattoo on her neck—though he never stopped remembering that it was there. But he would have also sworn that her hair, her lipstick, her nail polish were less dark, that her eye makeup was more artfully applied. In short, she was turning into a woman, and that made her all the more dangerous.

As to her physicality, the hugs, the pokes, the taps, even the thigh contact, it was all pretty guileless, of a piece with her general gawky trustfulness and lack of inhibition. She behaved in the same way with Roger Wilkins and Bob Johnson, straight-laced, closeted gay as the latter was—but perhaps not including the thigh contact? If he had been enjoined to tell the truth under penalty of death, he would have had to admit that he had come to believe she was attracted to him too, and that it pleased him. But he had no intention of putting his belief to the test.

His reasons were written in red bullets in his mind:

- Womanly or not, Grace was the same age as his daughter.
- Office romances were a disaster waiting to happen.
  Sooner or later, one of the people involved broke it up, and the other one had to live with the daily sight of the jilter. It was a kind of heartbreak Jim wished on no one, having once experienced it himself. The fact that the woman who jilted him had been forced to do so by the suspicions of her Arab family had made no difference to his deep feeling of abandonment. He had been in love with Aisha, the only time in his life when he knew for sure.
- By now, Grace had made pretty clear that she wasn't, would never be on Hartbridge's team.
  For reasons that Jim didn't quite comprehend, her loyalty was entirely committed to the Pequeno District. She wasn't a native of that hole of a town, she had never attended a community college (whereas Jim had), she wasn't that well paid, and even her promotion had been dictated by politics, not a recognition of her merits. Plus, she was of a generation not known for their loyalty to their employer. In any case, Hartbridge's anti-fraternization rule still applied. It wasn't even that Jim was afraid for his job. To protect Grace as much as his pride, Jim had let Fritz believe that he had her under control. But he knew how sexual congress had a way of leading to babbling, and there were many things about Hartbridge that he couldn't afford to let Grace know. For better or for worse, *he* was of a generation still imbued with company loyalty.

A phrase is floating like a balloon over the train of his reflections. Playing hooky. This is how Joleen enticed him on their first date. Ever since, the expression has had a sexual meaning for him. Suddenly, he remembers that he used those very words to entice Grace on their second walk. He wriggles uncomfortably on the couch, struck with shame at his dishonesty with himself.

Yes, consciously, he was determined not to get entangled in a dalliance with Grace. But another part of him—Sigmund Freud's descendants would call it the Id, but Satan is just as apt a metaphor—was stealthily working toward that very end. He can see himself walking side by side with her along the canal, jaunty, relaxed, unthreatening, discussing business, admiring the color of the leaves, commenting on the advancing clouds, all the while trying to ascertain whether she had a boyfriend (she didn't), to elicit her pity for his loneliness (it worked), to find an excuse for driving her home (the weather) and getting invited in (wet through and through). The weather had cooperated, but not her weekend plans, although there was a second there, under the Data Center awning, her dripping face raised to his, her pupils so dilated that her eyes seemed black instead of blue, the twin peaks on her upper lip quivering, when his satanic alter ego sensed that it wouldn't have taken much to convince her to change them. However that would have required getting physical right then and there, and just as his alter ego was taking over, he heard a car slow down on the road as if it was about to turn into the parking lot. His alter ego made himself scarce.

It would not be the last time in his relationship with Grace that Jim was saved from temptation by serendipity as opposed to his own virtue. A Christian, not a Freudian (though he did find the Interpretation of Dreams interesting), he does not see sex as a compulsion. He believes in free will, and therefore in sin. He admits now that he sinned in his heart against Grace by plotting to seduce her, and repents. Is that all there is to his guilty feelings toward her? He guesses there is more, but his conscience seems exhausted at this point.

In any case, he was soon punished for his lustful thoughts. A week or two after the infamous walk, in fact on the very morning following the registration server outage, right after his "debriefing" with the Chancellor, he found that Grace had still not shown up at work. She wasn't scheduled for a vacation. Tiffany knew nothing of her whereabouts. This was not like Grace. He went into his office and saw that the message light on his phone was blinking. Somehow, in its red urgency, it seemed to be flashing Grace's name in Morse code. Sure enough, there was a message from her. Her voice was wobbly with distress.

"Hi, Jim. This is Grace. My grandmother is in the hospital. The doctors think she may have caught the avian flu. She is very sick. I was abroad when my father died. I never got a chance to say goodbye. I am not . . . going . . . to let that happen again . . . I am flying down to LA this morning. I'll probably be out the rest of the week. I'll be in touch as soon as I know more. Sorry to leave you in a lurch. Take care."

Jim slumped down in his chair, utterly desolate. He felt for Grace. He was sorry he had not been there when she called. He would have liked to comfort her. For the first time, he let himself experience real tenderness toward her. It scared him.

She was gone. What was he going to do without her? He wasn't thinking about the management of the office, but about the management of his own heart. Truth was, he was depressed about his marriage, and he had counted on her to cheer him up.

For the next couple of days, he dragged himself through the routine of flattery, appeasement, arm twisting and entropy battling that was his job. None of it seemed to matter. All the stuffing had been taken out of him.

On Tuesday night he went bowling with Charlie Weissman, and on Wednesday night he had dinner at Peter Santelli's house. He was only too glad to be able to stay away from his condo.

On Thursday afternoon, he ambled over to Mina's desk, ostensibly to inquire about the progress of the paper reduction project. Mina brought up her project spreadsheet, listing in blue the reports that were now put on the Web in PDF format, in green those that were now sent to remote printers—which had the advantage of shifting the printing costs to other cost centers—and in red those whose requestors still insisted on their reports being printed in IT. Mina was going to need Jim's help with those. He told her she could count on it. She had even created a couple of pie charts illustrating the before and after, and one showing the savings realized. Jim was impressed.

They went on chatting of this and that: her big new house, her boy's learning to speak in both English and Urdu, their respective plans for Thanksgiving. (Mina and her husband were going to spend it at her parents. Jim was going to go home, of course. He was always in charge of the turkey. Fancy that, her husband cooked too.) They even touched on religion. To his amazement, Mina told him she was Catholic. It turned out she was of Mexican, not Pakistani, origin, as he had been led to believe by the salwar kameez she had worn the day of his arrival. Mina, letting out a pearly laugh, told him to keep this a secret. He promised.

And then, out of the blue, she looked up at him, her dark eyes quizzical over the gold rim of her glasses.

"You miss Grace, don't you?" she said, and smiled. Her smooth round face was the face of a Madonna—with glasses.

Jim was so caught off guard that he nearly choked.

"You bet," he managed to stammer out. Then, clearing his throat, he added: "You guys are the only two people I can count on around here."

She went on looking at him with that absolutely pure, maternal expression. He was humbled, and strangely grateful. They never exchanged another word on the subject. But they understood each other.

On Thursday night he stayed at the office, working on the Hartbridge RFP, until Ray Gomes came in for his night shift. It had occurred to Jim that it was high time he met the guy. They had a pleasant conversation about basketball, Jim even offered to change the paper form in the printer, gaining the operator's respect.

On Friday morning, he got a call from Grace. She was still in Pasadena but her grandmother was out of danger, and she planned to be back at the office on Monday. He told her to do what she had to do, they could manage without her a few more days. But he missed her. She said she missed him too. That statement carried him through the day.

In the evening, however, he found himself in his condo with the desert of a weekend in front of him. For the first time since he had started at Pequeno, he made his way to the gym that was part of the apartment complex. It was high time he got back into shape, he reasoned. He swam for half an hour, though his heart wasn't in it. He thought of the open-air swimming pools in the expat compounds in Riyadh, palm fronds singing over his head, the intricate tile designs at the bottom of the pool reflected in kaleidoscopic patterns on the rippling water surface, white tables under umbrella where you could sip lemonade afterwards. He had been spoiled by luxury.

After dinner—a reheated carton of Chinese food instead of a restaurant meal to cut down on his caloric intake—the thought occurred to him to purchase some company. He knew he only had to flip through the condo's phone directory until it opened by itself, and if the page he landed on wasn't dedicated to take-out food or dry cleaning, it would list "personal escort" services. Prostitution was one of the main types of business, along with airlines and hotel chains, that consulting firms kept going. But then, suddenly, Mina's face floated in front of his eyes, and he put the directory down.

He grabbed his car keys and went for a drive. Twenty minutes later, he found himself in a neighborhood that looked familiar, and realized that he had unconsciously navigated toward Grace's street, though he had been there only once before when he rescued her from the bad-news ex-boyfriend. He slowed down, scanning the shadows for a sight of her cottage. At last, he got a peek of it, at the end of a tunnel of trees and bushes. Her porch light was on, but the windows were dark. A cat was scratching at her front door, its mournful meows audible all the way to the street through the car's rolled-down window. Jim felt like joining the cat. At least, it was clear that Grace was away. Until then some part of him had not completely bought her story.

Meandering through El Pequeno's slumbering streets, he came to a stop light. The cross street attracted his attention for some reason. He turned into it. The street was narrower than usual in that town of pointless boulevards, and it was lacking a tree canopy. But it had several small store fronts interspersed among the run-down stucco houses, their doors still open, squares of light creating welcome mats on the sidewalk. In front of one of these, a man was sitting at ease on his heels, smoking a cigarette and watching life pass. His posture reminded Jim of the Middle East. He pulled over, got out the car, walked over to the store. "As-Salamu Alaikum", he said to the man on a chance. "Wa Alaykum-us-Salam" the man answered, standing up, without showing any sign of surprise.

The shop was a combination of liquor store, drugstore and deli. It even had a halal butchery counter. Jim bought some Peptobismol, engaged the shopkeeper in conversation. Before he knew it, he had been invited for tea in the little restaurant next door, which communicated with the shop through an arch hung with a beaded curtain. They sat on carpeted ottomans and drank mint tea out of a brass pot. In a corner of the restaurant, a musician picked tunes on the oud, and a little girl with grave eyes danced to his rhythm with complete absorption while her parents ate and chatted, occasionally casting a bemused glance in her direction. Jim relaxed, all his cares draining away. He felt more at home in that shabby, unfamiliar place than he had in years of living in the US. Before he left, he asked the restaurant owner whether he could have one of the restaurant's menus, promising himself that he would bring Grace here one day.

XVI

DOUBTFUL

"Goody! A whole evening to vege out!" Mina squeals, throwing herself backwards on one of the twin beds after concluding her obligatory room inspection. No lint under the beds, no pubic hair on the bathroom floor, no spider webs behind the drapes, and a heater that works quietly and efficiently. She can relax at last. She lies back against the pillows for a second, then rolls over on her side and leans on her elbow, watching Grace, who, her back turned, is busy digging through her backpack. Grace smiles to herself, charmed by the girlishness this trip seems to be bringing out in her friend.

"I hope all the relentless driving isn't too much for you?"

"You're kidding? I love it. But it's nice to make a pause. We have a big day ahead of us tomorrow."

"Yes, we do," Grace agrees, and then wonders what exactly Mina means by "a big day". She casts a glance over her shoulder and for a second, she sees her own gnawing anxiety reflected on her friend's face. She is both glad and sad to find this evidence that faith is not a bulletproof vest, and admires Mina's courage all the more. It is true, of course, that Mina's loving concern for Jim does not have to contend with contrary feelings of anger and mistrust, as Grace's does. On the other hand, it is possible that the negative feelings are Grace's own armor.

"I'll shoot a quick text to Jim to let him know where we are. And then, shall we watch some TV?" Mina suggests. Before Grace can answer, her BlackBerry rings. It's the first time this has happened since the beginning of the trip, Mina realizes. Grace walks around the bed to grab the phone out of her handbag which lies on the nightstand. Mina catches a flicker of surprise and pleasure on her face as she reads the screen. But then she puts the phone to her ear, says coolly: "Hey there," and walks to the bathroom, closing the door after her. Left alone, Mina grabs her own cell phone and starts moving her thumbs across the keyboard.

When Grace comes back into the room fifteen minutes later, Mina is watching TV. She darts a quick glance in Grace's direction, and notices that her eyes are shiny, her cheeks slightly flushed.

"Was that Jason?" she asks nonchalantly.

"Yes. How did you know?" Grace gasps. She doesn't remember having so much as pronounced his name.

"Just a wild guess. So, is it serious between the two of you?"

Grace laughs. The word "serious", as it applies to relationships, has not quite yet entered her vocabulary.

"I have no idea."

"Well, he called. Did he say he misses you?"

"Kinda."

"Do *you* miss him?"

"Is missing somebody the test of seriousness?"

"Pretty much. So, do you miss him?"

"I don't know. I know I'll be glad to see him when he comes to Raleigh in a couple of weeks. Does that count?"

Mina looks at Grace above the rim of her glasses, her eyebrows raised in half-mocking interrogation.

"Yes," her verdict finally comes. Then, sensing that no more confidences are forthcoming, she smoothly turns her attention back to the TV set.

Grace follows her eyes, and is immediately able to identify the show as one of those movies made especially for the women channels: a pajama-clad beauty is standing in her kitchen with her back to the camera, humming a tune while she prepares an innocuous sandwich, ominous cello trills in the background clueing the viewer (but unfortunately not the beauty) to the presence of the intruder who is about to attack her. Grace can't fathom why women enjoy scaring themselves with this hackneyed representation of their vulnerability. In any case, she is not going to watch. She pulls out *The Shock Doctrine* and discreetly settles down to read. But though Mina has turned the TV sound down to a murmur, and though Naomi Klein's arguments against free-market capitalism are compelling, Grace's attention wanders.

Is missing someone truly the test of your feelings for them? Easy as a pregnancy kit, the plus sign appears, boom, you're in love? Nah, it can't be. She remembers how Jim once told her he missed her, when she called him from Pasadena the week she spent watching her grandmother fight the flu. It was Veteran's day, but he was at work, all alone in the office. She could see how that would make him nostalgic. She told him that she missed him too, but it was mere polite automatism on her part. She had no sooner uttered the cliché that she realized it was untrue. Not only she had not missed her boss, but she had not thought about him, or about any of her Pequeno colleagues and problems. In fact, her entire work life had vanished from her brain's landscape, like a spiritual Atlantis. She saw this as a very healthy sign.

It is true that her family worries would have been a sufficient cause to forget everything else. She had spent the first couple of days mostly holding her unconscious grandmother's hand, trying to breathe for her, to blanket her with love, to tether her to the living, all the while, atheist as she was, sending up inchoate prayers to the great non-Being in case It might listen. But on the third day she woke up from a doze to find that it was Grandma who held her hand, as she had many times in the past, that gentle pressure, more than the accompanying words of homely wisdom, always managing to take the edge off her youthful despairs. Don't you worry, the hand now said, I have no intention of letting go just yet, I still have a bit of mothering to do. Grace hardly dared to trust its message, but the doctors soon confirmed it. The great non-Being had listened after all.

The rest of the week was devoted to taking care of Grandpa, getting to know the nurses and doctors, checking up the validity of the treatment on the Web, finding ways to entertain the recovering patient, keeping family and friends informed of her progress, and helping the housekeeper spruce up the house for her return, in particular arranging bouquets from the flowers in the garden. Grandma came home on Sunday, still a little weak but pretty much her old sprightly self. They spent the afternoon looking at old photo albums. In the evening, Grandpa drove Grace back to the Burbank airport. It was only as she took the El Pequeno off ramp that she remembered the office. The memory wasn't all that pleasant.

Barely two months into her new position, Grace was disenchanted about it. She was spending entirely too much time on red tape, and entirely too little on software development. As to managing people, she was discovering that it was next to impossible, at least for her, at least in her current environment. Even as she worked longer and longer hours, she identified less and less with her job. For all her desire to rise to Jim's expectations, she still couldn't not see herself building a career in IT management, particularly at Pequeno. She felt as if she was plodding through a long tunnel, the light at the end of which remained out of sight. So it had been exhilarating to be lifted out of it for a week, to rediscover that she had a life of her own, even it that came with its own heartaches.

But it was her forgetting Jim that pleased her the most, attesting as it did to her psychological equilibrium. The truth was that lately she had found herself thinking about him a little too much. The blissful camaraderie and mutual admiration of the first few months had somehow morphed into an abortive love affair, marked by mixed messages, mood swings, inexplicable advances and retreats, and constant sexual pining. There was something faintly ridiculous about it.

Grace was not unused to being found attractive by older men, despite her lack of effort to conform to their feminine ideal. Although out of principle she herself did not flirt, she did not mind bathing in the flirtatious vapors generated by middle-aged guys too savvy to do anything else with their horniness. But until now, she had never reciprocated the feeling.

It was all the more humbling that Jim, all in all, had done rather less than the other middle-aged guys to cause this response. So, why him? He was overweight, his face was nothing special, he wore thick glasses, he stomped around like a bear. Was his flowery aftershave his secret weapon? Was Grace being literally led by the nose? No, there was more to it than that: a submerged physicality, an aura of steadfastness, of dominance—in short, a manly persona, the oldest, most stereotypical of all aphrodisiacs. How embarrassing for a woman who had been taught to despise romance novels. (Now that she thinks about it, Grace realizes that Jason has some of the very same traits, as did Zach. Is this a red flag? Ah, but Jason is a much better match than Jim culturally, not to mention age-wise. And she has known him long enough to be assured that he is no lunatic, as Zach was.)

Herein lay the main rub: Jim was not a good match for Grace culturally. As much as she subscribed to her generation's belief in sex as an autonomous realm in human relationships, she in fact objected to being sexually attracted to a man who did not share her values or references. Her admiration for his managerial abilities notwithstanding—tarnished at that by her growing suspicion that while he worked at Pequeno, he was *not* working for Pequeno—she felt a certain amount of condescension toward his mental furniture. Talking to him reminded her in fact of entering her room after it had been cleaned by a new maid—a fairly frequent occurrence at her mother's. At first glance, everything seemed fine, but when you looked more closely, you found some things out of place, some unaccountably missing, and some imported from other rooms where they belonged. It was very disorienting.

But not surprising, given his Southern red-neck background and his lack of a college degree. Grace gave him points for being an autodidact. She knew many college graduates with less intellectual curiosity or factual knowledge. Still, in conversations on any other topic than work, she found herself having to rein in her own fluency for fear of making him ill at ease—or less attracted to her?

From one retrospective note in her journal, it seems that they managed to have some "good arguments". What did they argue about, other than Hartbridge's intentions or the viability of various software solutions?

He was a typical Republican: anti-government (while his company was making all its money out of government contracts), anti-unions (though he was friends with the Pequeno SEIU union rep), pro-business (but heaping scorn on the likes of Kenneth Lay). Unexpectedly, he was against the war on Iraq, which he thought was the brainchild of the Israel lobby. Then again, his best friend was Palestinian. Anyway, he was a Republican, whereas Grace's entire family tree was colored blue. It was as deep a divide as the one between the Capulets and the Montagues. You couldn't talk your way across it. The only political argument Grace remembers concerned Bill Clinton, who, five years out of office, still seemed to raise Jim's dander to the nth degree. He was a liar, he was a cheat, he was a hypocrite, he was a womanizer. What's that got to do with politics? asked Grace, who had campaigned for Clinton in 1996 alongside her father, although she was too young at the time to vote. Jim could not give a rational explanation for his hatred of the man. If politics was that visceral, democracy was in trouble.

He was a proud Christian. To Grace faith was the purview of old people, like her grandparents, an excuse to socialize on Sundays, a crutch to lean on in the face of death. But intellectually, let's face it, it was bankrupt, particularly the Protestant versions, with their insistence on a six-day creation and their eye-for-an-eye morality. Plus, Grace was well aware that it was proud Christians who had violently tried to deny African-Americans the right to vote, to attend white schools, even to sit at lunch counters. She had never detected in Jim the slightest trace of racial prejudice—his best friend was Palestinian after all. Still, his Southern Christianity carried a sort of stigma. Loath to let it mar her feelings, Grace carefully avoided the topic of religion.

Other than that, even though Jim was twice her age, he wasn't half as well read. He had never set foot in a theater, had only attended a few concerts, did not think of visiting museums. His idea of entertainment was golfing, bowling, fishing, sailing (but he didn't seem to avail himself of the opportunities for the latter offered by the San Francisco Bay), watching shoot-them-up movies, perhaps even partying with call-girls, if there was anything behind the jokes he occasionally made on the subject.

In view of all these incompatibilities, was it any wonder that Grace chafed under her attraction to Jim, or that she rejoiced in having been able to put him out of her mind completely for a week? Alas, when she returned to work, it was to find that her happy indifference did not survive the sight of him.

He on the other hand seemed to have changed—again. He did not check on her until mid-morning, and then only as an afterthought, on his way to some place else. Seeing her door open, he stopped, smiled his most general-purpose smile, and accosted her in a booming voice:

"Ms. Kirchner. How are you? Grandma all recovered? Glad to have you back."

"Mr. Wright. I am very well. Grandma is fine. I could have used a longer vacation."

"Couldn't we all?"

He was about to move on. Instinctively, Grace stood up and opened her arms to give him a hug. He caught her movement and stepped forward, but just enough for an arms-length embrace, adding insult to injury by concluding it with a little pat on the back.

"We'll talk later," he promised as he walked away. Grace was left standing in the doorway with her arms still open in the shape of his body. A second later, she was mortified to realize that "Mr. Wright" was a double entendre. She was mad at him for having provoked it.

This greeting inaugurated a period of exquisite professional courtesy—and nothing else—on Jim's part, to which Grace responded with strict professional deference—and a brand new timidity. It lasted until Thanksgiving. If Grace had had nothing else to worry about than Jim's moods, that week and a half would have seemed an eternity. Fortunately, she did have other things to worry about, the first one being how to manage the programming staff, as her title demanded.

She had started scheduling regular staff meetings. She had hoped that they would make the team more efficient: knowledge would be shared, standards strengthened, concepts explored, and the laggards shamed into greater productivity by sheer exposure to the output of their more disciplined colleagues. What she experienced instead was the tendency for the members of a work group to adjust their performance to the group's lowest common denominator. It didn't help of course that the hardest-working programmers, namely Wei and Rajiv, were also the least proficient in English. It was a cinch for Elmore and Sandip to drown their timid attempts at relating their progress and ideas with pontifications on customer relations and test protocols, snide District gossip and literate asides. The same verbosity served to hide how little they themselves got done from one week to the next. By the third meeting, not only Wei and Rajiv had retreated into their shells, but Grace noticed that Rajiv was less eager to take on new projects, and Wei more determined than ever to be guided by his own lights. Elmore and Sandip's performance was unaffected.

To have a better idea of the team's workload, assign tasks equitably, make sure deadlines were respected, and provide some metrics for Jim, Grace wanted all the known ongoing and future programming projects to be entered into a database that she could query along various dimensions. At Jim's suggestion, she had thought to use the help desk ticketing system for this purpose. But according to the documentation she had been able to scrounge, and with the permissions that Tiffany had reluctantly granted her, she couldn't make the ticketing system do what she needed done. So, in her spare time, she designed a Microsoft Access database to hold the information. She felt nearly guilty at the joy that this bit of programming gave her. According to the management science textbooks, a manager did not waste her time on such grunt work.

She asked the programmers to enter all their projects into the new database. Wei promptly obeyed. Rajiv justifiably deferred to Elmore, who as the senior analyst received all the service requests in the financial area. Sandip tried to plead the same excuse, though the senior analyst in his area had been absent for the last nine months. Grace countered by suggesting that he start with the projects he had mentioned to her, and hinting that if his plate looked empty, she would make sure to fill it. A week later he had entered a dozen projects into the database, all but one tagged with a status of "pending requirements", none with any indication of deadline or time estimate. As to Elmore, week after week, he entered nothing at all, frankly admitting that he was procrastinating, the apologetic tenor of his words somewhat undercut by his tone of self-satisfaction. Eventually, Grace would resort to doing the data entry herself from Elmore's verbal account.

Grace pondered the mystery of Elmore and Sandip's low productivity. Both men were highly intelligent, technically adept, skillful at interacting with users. What prevented them from putting their talents to good use?

In Sandip's case, what was visible was an addiction to cell phone and email chat. Meanwhile, though the teachers' contract was still pending, he had barely started working on the leave report for Harriet Jellineck. But unlike Elmore, he was seemingly unaware that his performance left anything to be desired. He didn't even try to minimize his email window when Grace walked by, though the Hindi script of his messages left no doubt as to their personal nature. He was like those kids for whom school is just another venue for goofing off, the kind who will do their homework only when a parent is standing at their elbow. Was his problem a lack of maturity, did he suffer from some deeper psychological issue, or had he simply adapted to the lack of demand of his current job? Grace felt out of her depth in trying to assess his motivation. She was contemplating asking him to cut down on the social distractions, but as he worked in a cubicle, she would have to call him into her office to talk, a step which seemed too scarily formal at this point. For the moment, she made a point of stopping by his desk frequently to review his progress on the leave report. This might spur him into action, or it might make him hate her. Either way, it would have been quicker for her to create the stupid report herself.

Elmore was another story. She had been able to delegate to him some minor modifications to the registration system, and he had done an excellent job of them (she knew because she had quietly checked his code, which contained some elegant bits she could in fact learn from). And she credited him for keeping the financial systems running smoothly year after year. It was the larger development jobs that seemed to stymie him. He could perform the analysis, map the technical requirements, code and test. What he could not bring himself to do was to call a project complete. Without Rajiv's enthusiasm and Jim's support, the new online financial query system would never have been put into production.

Another project in Elmore's area that Grace was aware of, something to do with fixed assets, had been languishing in the planning stage for the last two years. Now that the Purchasing Director was making a show of scouting for a fixed asset software package, it was imperative to revive the concept of an in-house solution. But Elmore was visibly reluctant to tackle it, arguing that the initial analysis was by now obsolete, that he had too much on his plate to focus on such a big job, that the user didn't know what he wanted anyway. And then, out of the blue, he was confiding that his reluctance was due to a mental block, that what paralyzed him about large projects was a fear of failure instilled in him by a perfectionist father. Grace was taken aback. She had not expected such a pathetic confession on the part of Elmore, whose trade image was one of sanctimonious superiority. Yet something about it bothered her.

For one thing, it had been made in the privacy of his office, and could be assumed to be strictly for Grace's consumption. But it had also sounded a little too smooth, as if it had been rehearsed many times, or as if Elmore thought his handicap rather charming. Grace suspected that she was being played. In any case, she saw that if she wanted the fixed asset project to go anywhere, she would have to get seriously involved in it, which meant learning a lot of things about financial systems, an area she had no interest in. She wasn't even sure she understood what fixed assets were.

Jim's solution to the IT department's productivity problem would have been to "clear the place of the dead wood". The threat of being fired might perhaps have caused Elmore and Sandip to modify their behavior. But as Jim himself acknowledged, it was a moot point. The Pequeno District had strict policies regarding the firing of employees. A manager could not send an employee packing at the drop of a hat. Poor performance must be carefully documented, opportunity for correction must be provided, the union must be allowed to act as the employee's advocate. These were all good rules as far as Grace was concerned. After all, someone's livelihood was at stake. In practice, though, employees who had passed probation could relax in the knowledge that their managers were unlikely to go to the trouble of attempting to get them fired. Senior employees with a consistent record of positive evaluations, like Elmore, were basically guaranteed to be kept on the payroll until they decided to retire or felt a sudden urge to go on a shooting rampage.

In any case, none of the programming staff was due for a performance evaluation for the next three months. On the other hand, rummaging through the personnel database, Grace discovered that the deadlines for Mina and Erin's evaluations were approaching, and that Josh had never been evaluated, though he had been hired nine months ago. Pequeno's hiring policies required that new employees be evaluated after three months, then again after six months. The first evaluation was supposed to detail the employee's deficiencies to give him/her time to remedy them by the second evaluation, which would determine whether the employee was made permanent or let go.

Having made this discovery during a strictly professional phase of her relationship with Jim, Grace scheduled an appointment to inform him of it. At issue was the question of who would perform the evaluations. Grace knew enough about Mina's job to trust that she could evaluate her fairly (and besides, Mina was such a model employee that her evaluation was a cinch). But she did not feel qualified to write Erin and Josh's evaluations, though as the only internal manager in the department, she would have to sign them. What did Jim propose to do? He said he would think about it and let her know. She reminded him that the Thanksgiving break was coming right up. He knew, and in fact, he had meant to tell her that he would be away the week after that. On vacation? On vacation from Pequeno, yes. (In other words, none of your business, Ms. Kirchner.) Could he give her an answer before the break? She was especially concerned about the delay on Josh's evaluation. Well, it had waited three months, it could wait another couple of weeks. All right, then. The ball was in his court. Understood. Anything else? Not a thing.

On the Wednesday morning before Thanksgiving, Grace was happily adding a few touches to her project database, attaching color charts to a couple of reports she had created, and feeling pretty pleased with herself, when she sensed a presence at her back. She glanced over her shoulder and recognized Jim's red suspenders. She had been so focused on her programming that she had not been aware of his approach. In a blur, she saw one of his well-turned hands hovering near her neck. She rotated her seat, stood up and faced him. His face looked unfamiliar, as if distorted by some kind of pain.

"What is it?" she whispered, her heart going out to him.

She lay her hands on his forearms. He grabbed them, held them. His touch was wonderfully soft and warm. He pulled her to him, squeezed her so tightly that it took her breath away, released her, and gazed down on her with an unmistakable expression of longing. Suddenly he pulled her towards him again, and this time his eyes focused on her lips. He was about to kiss her. She felt her mouth moving toward his. It was irresistible. But no, it was crazy. Her door was open, her shades were up, anyone passing by would see them. He must have seen the fright in her eyes, because he stopped himself in mid-motion. His face came undone, then put itself back together with a rueful air. They had to content themselves and each other with a regular hug.

"I'm out of here," he said, grabbing the handle of his attaché case. "You're in charge. Be good."

"Of course," she answered. "Have a restful vacation."

He made an equivocal grimace, and was gone.

For the first time, Grace apprehended that there may be more to his changes of attitude toward her than office politics or random moods. His feelings for her were stronger than she had supposed, but they obviously were a source of conflict for him. Was he more attached to his wife than the evidence suggested? Was he afraid of committing what his Christian morality would call the sin of adultery? Or was there some other, bigger problem? Something to do with his company, his boss, his health? He had seemed less upbeat lately. You couldn't spend half an hour in his presence without his cracking his neck vertebrae at least once. He also had acquired two new tics: inserting his fingers inside his shirt collar as if he felt strangled, and scratching his back against door jambs. What was that about? (Oh, she knows now what it was about. If she could have figured it out then, would it have made a difference? Probably not. Anyway, feeling guilty won't help.)

Jim had left Grace "in charge" of the whole department. She was promptly to discover that the term had a one-sided application in her case. Basically, anyone with a need was perfectly willing to trust her to fill it in Jim's absence. When, on the other hand, *she* needed anything, it became necessary to wait for Jim's return.

Tiffany was transferring to her all the phone calls that would normally have gone to Jim: hardware and software vendors trawling for new clients, Board members complaining about their Internet connection, teachers wanting to know when their new laptops would be issued, the Purchasing director questioning a requisition, the marketing director unhappy about outage hours. But she declined to make a single photocopy for Grace, arguing that, per her job description, her administrative assistant functions were reserved for the CIO. (Later, Grace would find out that Tiffany routinely photocopied stacks of pages for Myrtle.)

Ruby came to complain about Sandip leaving a puddle of shrimp curry in the microwave. She wanted Grace to remind him of his promise to spare his colleagues' sense of smell. But when Grace asked her to expedite the addition of a memory card to one of the enterprise printer servers, Ruby claimed that only Jim could reorder her priorities.

"Should I talk to Myrtle?" asked Grace. "I understand she has been acting as PC Coordinator Manager."

"Not to my knowledge," Ruby answered.

Grace had been bluffing. She had no intention of asking Myrtle to intervene in this or any other situation, because that would have made her feel important. To be fair, in adopting this dismissive attitude, Grace was merely returning Myrtle's favor: since the travel reimbursement incident, the sneaky matron had basically ignored her, declining to acknowledge her managerial role. Fortunately, Myrtle had been spending most of her time at the Piedmont campus. But Grace has to admit she was slyly gratified to see that even Ruby did not recognize Myrtle's authority. That was the price Jim paid for not making his organizational decisions official. He had not even dared assign Erin and Josh's evaluations to his Hartbridge colleague, though it was the obvious thing to do. Grace could not understand his reluctance.

One morning, a Computer Science instructor showed up in her office. He had come to talk to Jim about the possibility of setting up a large number of Linux virtual machines on the mainframe for use by his students. IBM apparently offered a rebate on licensing fees to educational institutions willing to go that route. Until that moment, Grace had not even been aware that the mainframe could run the Linux operating system. She was intrigued, and pleased to find one person outside the department without prejudices against mainframes. She asked him to sit down. He enlarged on his idea. Grace expressed an interest, took his coordinates, promised to talk to Jim. They ended up making plans for a lunch date before the Christmas break. Grace accompanied him back out, proud of her small role in encouraging innovation.

When she got back to her desk, there were a dozen messages with a subject line of "Invoice Question" in her inbox. She sorted the messages by time stamp, and opened the most recent, hoping that it would contain the entire conversation, and that its parts would be in chronological order, instead of some answers being added at the top, and some at the bottom, according to the writer's predilections. Both hopes proved to be unfounded. She had to read every last message before she could reconstitute the thread, which went something like:

Mina to Tiffany:	Have we paid all our mainframe licensing fees this year?
Tiffany to Mina:	Why do you ask?
Mina to Tiffany:	Because I am getting a message on the console that says we haven't.
Tiffany to Mina:	What message are you getting?
Mina to Tiffany:	

CAXXXXXX LICENSE WARNINGS/ VIOLATIONS ON CPU @@@@@@
CAXXXXXX PRODUCT SORT ABOUT TO EXPIRE OR IS EXPIRED AND IS IN USE

Tiffany to Mina:	It's Greek to me. What company are we talking about?
Mina to Tiffany:	I don't know. I guess it's the sort software. Do you know what company that is?
Tiffany to Mina:	No.
Mina to Tiffany:	OK, I found it. It's Computer Associates.
Tiffany to Mina:	When was the fee due?
Mina to Tiffany:	I don't know. Somehow I don't have this piece of software in my spreadsheet. Can't you look up the payments to Computer Associates?
Tiffany to Mina:	No, invoices are filed in order by payment date and by invoice number. Do you have the invoice number?
Mina to Tiffany:	No, I don't have any information on this software license.
Tiffany to Mina:	Then I can't help you.

The email exchange, cced to Grace in its entirety, had lasted for over an hour, at the end of which nothing had been accomplished other than Tiffany demonstrating once again the futility of asking for her help. The most aggravating thing about it was that Mina and Tiffany worked within a few feet of each other.

Having composed herself by tearing her hair out and making faces at her computer, Grace walked over to the front office. Tiffany was on the phone.

"No, I couldn't watch it," she was saying. "We were staging a house. Real prime property. We're asking for $700,000. With the bidding, it'll probably go up to $800,000. Not bad for a $500,000 investment, don't you think?"

Grace approached the reception desk, stood in front of it in an expectant attitude. Tiffany pretended no to see her.

"So, what was it about? . . . A haunted house? Seems a little hokey to me . . . No, I mean, it's a gimmick . . . Yeah, I remember, but that was different . . ."

Grace cleared her throat. Tiffany turned her head slightly, gave Grace a once-over, and mouthed "one minute", her ear still glued to the phone.

"All I'm saying is it's not realistic . . . Like I tell Eduardo, *we* could be on that show. I'm like, for one thing, we'd be way sexier than the Richard Davis gang . . . Ain't that the truth . . . No, I'd go more for the nitty-gritty . . . Show them what house flipping is really about . . . Anyway, the Central Valley is where it's at, not Charleston bleeping South Carolina . . ."

Make them work for what they want—until they give up on wanting it. Tiffany was an expert at the tactic. Feeling her temper climb, Grace walked out of Tiffany's airlock and went to see Mina instead. It was a mistake, as Mina ended up paying for her irritation at the other woman.

"I just read your email exchange with Tiffany," Grace started, a little out of breath. "Why didn't you talk to her directly? Don't you think that would be more efficient?"

Mina looked up at her. She seemed scared, and hurt.

"As if . . ." she muttered.

Grace laughed, realizing that she had just seen for herself how impossible it was to talk to Tiffany directly. She put a soft hand on Mina's arm.

"Sorry," she said. "That was a ridiculous idea."

Mina smiled timidly.

"OK, how about looking for the invoice information online?"

"I don't have access."

"But of course! I should have known. Tell you what. Let's look it up together. And then I'll make sure that you *do* get access."

Mina seemed to revive. She grabbed a pen and yellow pad, and followed Grace into her office. It took them five minutes to find out that the license for the Sort utility was due for renewal that very day, and that the invoice for the new year had not been recorded. Practically every batch job used a sort, so it was urgent to fix the problem. Grace called the number listed on the vendor record, and after a few transfers, was connected to someone who explained to her that there was a three day grace period, during which a temporary license key could be activated, but this required system level permissions. She asked that a copy of the lost invoice be faxed to her right away and hung up. Using the number Mina gave her, she then called the contractor who did the systems programming on the mainframe. He was a little sheepish about his failure to notice the warning message on the console, and agreed to take care of the temporary key right away. A few minutes later, he called back to say it was done. While she had him on the phone, Grace submitted a test job containing a sort, and was able to confirm the fix.

This bought her some time to figure out how to pay for the license renewal, a task she could not postpone until Jim's return the next Monday, because by then the temporary key would have expired as well. The problem was, Jim's electronic signature was required on the payment request. The obvious solution was to create a special authorization route with only her name on it, which, the irony did not escape Grace, was exactly what Tiffany had done during Jim's previous vacation. Grace called the Purchasing Director to get his agreement on the workaround. He would not hear of it.

Grace ended up asking Bob Johnson to intervene. Thankfully, the Vice-Chancellor for Business Services was one of the few Pequeno employees who was nearly always reachable by phone, and when not, returned his messages promptly. He was also quick to grasp the consequences on his daily reports of an expired sort utility. He took care of instructing the Purchasing Director to process the payment request as soon as he received it that day.

Grace created the route, entered the replacement invoice into the system, submitted it for payment. She got a processing error. This is when she found out that her software maintenance budget had no money left in it. A further query revealed that Constanza had emptied the account the day before.

She had to call Bob Johnson again, who talked to Constanza, who restored the funds. The license was finally renewed and the new license key installed late Friday afternoon, with not a minute to spare. Grace wrote Jim a long message explaining what had happened, and asking him to instruct Tiffany to give Mina access to the purchasing database. He answered right away.

Good job!

I don't know what I would do without you over there. Come to think of it I could use your help here too.

I'll be back Monday morning. In the meantime, don't let Tiffany push your buttons. No point getting into a pissing contest with a skunk. I'll deal with her soon enough.

It was five fifteen on a Friday afternoon. What were the chances of Tiffany still being around to push Grace's buttons? And of course, not a word about the near-kiss incident. Grace was obviously supposed to pretend it hadn't happened. At least, Jim was indirectly letting her know that he had spent his vacation working at another Hartbridge site. What a miserable life the poor guy led! And how unfair to the District his divided attention! In any case, if he passed up on the opportunity to spend a week at home, it must mean that his marriage was a negligible factor in his sexual scruples.

Jim's rental car was parked in front of the Data Center when Grace came around the building pushing her bicycle on Monday morning. Against all reason, her heart did a little dance. She firmly ordered it to chill before going in. She need not have bothered reining in her feelings, since she practically saw nothing of Jim for the next couple of days. At last, on Tuesday evening, he called her into his office. He seemed tired, but not in a bad mood.

"Shall I close the door?" she asked, guessing that they were going to talk about evaluations.

"Naw," he answered. "Everybody's gone. It's just us chickens."

They talked about the license renewal issue. Jim had duly instructed Tiffany to give Mina read access to the purchasing database (it would take her a month to execute this command).

They talked about the Linux virtual machine idea. Jim was receptive. He would follow up with the Computer Science instructor.

They talked about the Marketing Director's complaint regarding the nightly maintenance system outage. Jim took it more seriously than Grace. These days, he argued, people expected 24/7 Internet service. The problem was that the mainframe was set up in such a way that online access could not co-exist with batch operations. It was an issue that was going to have to be addressed.

They talked about Constanza's raid on their budget. Jim laughed at the absurdity. He would make sure it did not happen again.

They talked about the registration server outage that had taken place during the week she was in Pasadena.

Finally, he brought up the subject of the evaluations. He agreed to let Grace take care of Mina's evaluation. As to Josh's and Erin's, Myrtle would write them, but Grace would get to approve them. Jim and Grace would both participate in the evaluation meetings with the employees. Myrtle would not. Sounded fair enough.

The meeting was interrupted by a phone call. No personal topics had been broached, but Grace didn't mind. She recalled how Jim had not long ago yielded to an uncontrollable hunger for her, and felt a sense of power over him.

As expected, Grace had no trouble writing Mina's evaluation, which she was planning to use as leverage to get her colleague a pay raise. The evaluation meeting with Mina went well, though Grace noticed that Jim was very nervous during most of it. After the evaluation was signed, there was a general round of hugs, and Jim finally relaxed. One down, two to go.

It took another week for Myrtle to turn in her evaluations. Grace scanned Erin's first. Myrtle had checked the "satisfactory" box without comment for every performance measure. But as, per the instructions on the form, a satisfactory rating did not require any elaboration, Grace decided not to make an issue of Myrtle's nonchalance.

She then took out Josh's evaluation, and was so shocked by what she saw that she coughed up a mouthful of tea on her keyboard. There, on the summary front page, under the "RECOMMENDATION (for probationary employees)" header, Myrtle had checked "Non-retention". Grace looked at the evaluation details. Every performance measure was marked "Unsatisfactory" or "Fair—Improvement needed", which was basically the same thing for probationary employees. Again, there was no comment. Myrtle's incredible unfairness made Grace's blood boil. As far as Grace could tell, though Josh was not a model employee (none of the PC coordinators were), he was rather more knowledgeable and diligent than Erin. Every time he had had occasion to work on her PC, he had done a good job. He even had acquired a little fan club among District users. What did Myrtle mean by this hatchet job? Had Josh failed to butter her up? Did she have a replacement in mind? A friend, family member, client?

Grace was so upset that neither tearing her hair out or making faces at her computer succeeded in cooling her temper. Jim was away for the rest of the day at some executive meeting. She couldn't wait for his return. She was going to have to confront Myrtle, who coincidentally was in her office that day, keeping herself busy as usual by typing endless documents that would never surface anywhere, as far as Grace could tell.

Grace strode into the sneaky matron's office, and without apologizing for the interruption, closed the door resolutely behind her. Myrtle raised her eyes from her keyboard, looking annoyed. Grace was waiting for her to remark on the rudeness of her entrance so she could counter that as Myrtle herself was prone to barge in, Grace had assumed she could do the same. However, the sneaky matron didn't say a word.

"I just read your evaluation of Josh," Grace started. "I am afraid I can't sign it."

Myrtle remained mute, the look of irritation on her face fading into an expression of brute passivity.

"As indicated on the form," Grace continued, a little discomfited by the other woman's silence, "any rating other than satisfactory must be supported by written comments."

Myrtle sighed discreetly.

"My understanding," she said in her marshmallow voice, "is that probationary employees may be let go without justification. To be honest, I assumed that the evaluation was just a formality."

"To be honest, I find your attitude extremely cavalier. We're talking about somebody's livelihood here."

"I am aware of that. But it is a manager's role to make some tough decisions."

"And so I will, but not without justification."

"Please, don't take it personally, but don't you think I am better qualified than you are to determine whether Josh has the necessary skills for his position?"

"That may be. But I won't sign the evaluation unless you manage to convince me of his unfitness. Don't take it personally, but so far you haven't," Grace concluded, putting the evaluation form on Myrtle's desk.

Myrtle took it, slipped it into her attaché case. Grace had to give her credit for not letting any confidential document lie around. In fact, there wasn't a piece of paper on her desk.

"I'll see what I can do," Myrtle said with another sigh.

Two days later, Grace found on her carpet a sealed envelope that had been slipped under her door during the night. It was the second draft of Josh's evaluation. This time, it contained comments. The non-retention recommendation was unchanged.

JOB KNOWLEDGE: Josh has a very limited understanding of network architecture. *(No more limited than the other PC coordinators, network maintenance being the province of another department.)*

QUALITY OF WORK: On at least one occasion, Josh failed to perform a routine restart on the registration server, causing a system outage that lasted several hours. *(This was in fact Ruby's flake-out, according to Jim.)*

JOB EFFORT: When called by the CIO himself, Josh did not contribute to the resolution of the registration server outage. *(He had at least pinged the server, which was more than Ruby had done.)*

COOPERATION: Josh is not always sensitive to his cubicle neighbors' need for a quiet working environment. *(Could she possibly be referring to Josh's habit of slurping his coffee?)*

ATTENDANCE: Josh does not always submit his leave requests on time. *(He had failed to do so once to Grace's knowledge. And he wasn't the only one.)*

JUDGMENT: Josh completes assignments in the order received, without regard to their level of priority. *(Grace recalled one argument he had with Tiffany, who had tried to dispatch him to a Board member's house while he was showing an instructor how to connect his BlackBerry to his laptop.)*

Once again, Grace had the feeling that she was trapped in a Kafka novel. What perturbed her the most was the realization that to come up with this preposterous list of outright lies and insignificant peccadillos, Myrtle must have pumped the staff for information: Ruby, Tiffany, some cubicle workers—and Jim. This time she would have to talk to him directly. For once, she wasn't looking forward to the opportunity.

That night, she found Jim in his office. He looked tired again, and his brow was cloudy, but Grace didn't care. She closed the door and sat down.

"Can't this wait till tomorrow?" he pleaded. "I have a headache."

"Tomorrow I may not have a chance. You're hard to catch these days, in case you haven't noticed. But I'll get you some Ibuprofen if you'd like. Gimme your cup."

"Yes. That would be nice," he said, resigned, handing her his cup. His fingers were burning. Was he getting the flu?

She went back to her office, got the pain killer, stopped by the lunch room to make him a cup of tea, came back, waited till he had swallowed the pills. Maid and nurse, she was thinking. But the interlude had calmed her down.

"Tell me why you want to fire Josh," she said, surprising herself with her words. She had no idea how or why the knowledge had sparked across her synapses, but she suddenly was convinced that Jim, not Myrtle, was responsible for the non-retention recommendation. Amazingly, he did not deny the charge.

"Look," he said. "You saw how hard it was to get something as basic as server backup procedures implemented here. The fact is that none of the PC coordinators are up to snuff. We are stuck with the others, but if we get rid of Josh, we can make room for more qualified personnel."

"But that's unfair. Josh is not the worst by far."

"Life's unfair."

"All the more reason to be fair ourselves. Have you thought about what being fired from this job will do to Josh's chances of getting another one?"

"You're looking at it from a personal point of view. We need to look at the needs of the organization."

"From the point of view of the needs of the organization, we should get Rick to come back. He could finish implementing the server failover stuff, spend some time training the staff. He would be much more useful to us than Myrtle."

"You're talking out of turn. You don't know what Myrtle is working on."

"Well, that's another problem. Why don't I know?"

"Because you're not the CIO," he said angrily.

He was pulling rank. Grace couldn't believe it. Her pal, partner, repressed lover was pulling rank on her. And also implying that he and Myrtle, both of them outside consultants, were keeping some IT affairs a secret from the department's internal manager. It was a gross violation not only of personal trust but also of business ethics. However, Jim seemed so near to blowing his top that she had to back down. He cracked his neck vertebrae a couple of times and resumed in a softer voice.

"Anyway, I did try to get Rick back, but he is working at another site. We'll have to do with Myrtle for now." He made a open palm gesture of fatalism that Grace imagined he had learned in Saudi Arabia. She laughed, happy to see him confess indirectly that Myrtle wasn't his choice of a partner.

"So, will you sign the evaluation?" he asked.

Grace felt torn between contrary feelings. But she did not hesitate before answering.

"No, I'm sorry. Aside from its unfairness, it does not conform to our policies. Josh was not evaluated after three months as he was entitled. So this has to serve as his three-month evaluation. Which means that we can't fire him now. If he is deemed insufficiently qualified, we have to provide him with a detailed list of the things he needs to do to qualify himself. I'll let Myrtle come up with it. Then in three months, we can evaluate him again. But I don't think the union would look kindly on our demanding skills from him that we don't demand from the others."

"Will you at least sleep on it?"

"Sure, but I don't think it will make any difference."

"OK, we'll talk tomorrow."

Grace did not in fact sleep that night, so she didn't have a chance to experience the mind-changing powers Jim attributed to this unconscious state.

The next day, he appeared in her doorway, Myrtle's hapless face poking in the crook of his arm like a tumor.

"Have you reconsidered?" he asked, sounding defeated already.

"No," she said, and turned back to her computer.

A day after that Myrtle handed in her third draft of Josh's evaluation. The recommendation had been changed to "Retention in this position" and all the performance measures had been set to "satisfactory". There were no comments. Josh became a permanent employee. Grace and Jim barely exchanged a word for days. But one afternoon, a snippet of phone conversation wafted in from the parking lot through a crack in Grace's office window. It was Myrtle's voice, and she was saying: " . . . understand, but without hiring and firing prerogatives, I cannot assume a supervisory . . ." A car engine overlaid the rest of her sentence.

A week or two later, a new contractor showed up. He was going to work on the failover project, which had been expanded to include the virtualization of all the enterprise servers. He was not a Hartbridge employee, but would report to Myrtle. It would be months before Grace learned that the company that employed him was headed by the nephew of one of the Board members, and that Hartbridge got a percentage of the fees charged to the District by the subcontracting company. Thankfully, the new contractor turned out to be competent.

The second estrangement between Grace and Jim ended with a postscript he tacked on to an email on another subject:

"Even if we don't always see eye to eye, I appreciate your candor. Don't give it up."

Bound up to him by an ineradicable affection as much as by professional circumstances, Grace buried her doubts and forgave him.

XVII

ENLIGHTENING

Jim and Grace did end up discussing religion at length, one December evening in the lunchroom. Except for this one sharp memory, the whole period between Josh's evaluation and the Christmas break is a little hazy in Grace's mind. There were no major technical crises, no overt staff conflicts, no ethical disagreements or erotic emergencies with Jim. Her relationship with her boss seemed to have settled to one of melancholy friendship, as becalmed as the leaden sky that pressed down on the Central Valley day after day. He was busier than ever, the strain showing in frequent headaches and sporadic listlessness, but he no longer took his moods out on Grace. Without ever referring to the complaint of secrecy she had leveled against him during their big argument about Josh, he made an effort to keep her abreast of Myrtle's activities: the sneaky matron was working on a disaster recovery plan, on a new issue of laptops for faculty, and on the wireless networking of the Piedmont campus. Nothing objectionable there. Jim didn't say what *he* was working on, aside from the routine management tasks that would arguably have filled a less gifted CIO's schedule. Grace, eager to prolong the truce, forbore quizzing him about his own projects.

That day, a little after five o'clock, they met, as if by chance, in the lunchroom where they were both in search of refreshment. Jim was about to fill his cup with coffee, but seeing Grace, asked if he could have one of her tea bags instead. Grace made two cups of tea. When she turned away from the microwave, she found that he had sat down at the table. She sat down across from him and handed him his cup. He sighed with satisfaction.

"I'm too tired to work," he declared by way of explaining his dilatoriness.

"Me too," she answered agreeably, inwardly enumerating her roles: maid, nurse, Geisha.

They sipped their tea in companionable silence, while his gaze wandered idly around the room, lingering on the relics of long-ago parties on a set of metal shelves: bristling strings of Christmas lights, faded paper leis, the dangling leg of a cardboard Halloween skeleton, complete with frolicking maggots, a dented foil roasting pan; on the yellowing, curling layers of OSHA and Worker's Comp postings, Whistle Blowing instructions, Girl Scout cookie order forms, Dilbert cartoons and diagrams of ergonomic exercises that made the bulletin board look like a found-object sculpture; on Ruby's dirty dishes in the sink thumbing their nose at the sign above that admonished the staff against such inconsiderate behavior; on a couple of vigorous plants on the window sill, cared for by an unknown green thumb; on the blank night beyond. It was the first time Grace saw Jim take notice of the objects around him, and she realized how unobservant she herself had been of the physical environment in which she spent so much of her life. Yet, objectively, the Pequeno IT lunchroom was as worthy of interest as the American-Indian room in the Oakland Museum, both settings being replete with clues about an alien culture. Yes, alien: one thing she and Jim had in common, it suddenly occurred to her, was that they were both strangers to these parts. Then again, he may have looked around the room to avoid looking at her.

"You're surveying the scene," she remarked in a tone of surprise. "What do you see?"

"I see a bunch of crap that's weighing us down," he answered. "I have a good mind to organize a weekend clean-up party. And I do in general pay attention to my surroundings. It's part of my curious nature."

"You—curious?" She meant, but did not say, you, who never ask me any personal question.

"You bet. If you don't believe me, look under that roasting pan on the shelves. You should find a photo album with a brown cover."

"A photo album?"

"Yep."

Her own curiosity stirred, Grace walked to the shelves and lifted the foil pan. Sure enough, there was a brown photo album underneath. She pulled it out, releasing a cloud of dust. She brought the album to Jim's side of the table, but did not sit, subliminally conscious that too much physical closeness might pop the bubble of intimacy precariously forming around them. She opened the album and started flipping through it. There were no captions, no dates anywhere. Many of the pages were blank, stacks of loose pictures inserted between them. The person who had started this labor of love had never finished it.

The first few pages were dedicated to a sixties-era Christmas lunch: women in a-line mini-dresses and plastic boots, little bows perched atop their beehive hairdos, men with sideburns and wide ties, a huge tree wrapped in old-fashioned tinsel, a serving table covered with potato-chip-sprinkled casseroles and phosphorescent jello molds. Grace did not recognize the building where the party took place, let alone any of the partiers.

Then there was a barbecue in a parking lot, which Grace was able to identify as the Data Center's thanks to the metal awning visible in the background. From the preponderance of bell bottoms and platform shoes, she guessed the period to have been the seventies. The casseroles and jello molds seemed to have been recycled from the previous party.

"See anyone you know?" Jim asked.

Grace scrutinized the pictures.

"No. Do you?"

He pointed to a slim, cocky-looking young man with long unkempt hair, big square glasses, and a paisley vest over an open-collared shirt.

"My God, it's Elmore!" Grace cried out.

"What do you think of that?"

"I don't know . . . It makes me . . . sad? I'm sure he never imagined he would still be here in 2005, his friends long gone, and his bosses way younger than he is."

"See why it's good to be curious?"

"I guess," she half-agreed, flittingly intuiting that curiosity may lead to empathy, and that too much empathy may in fact be detrimental to a manager's effectiveness. "Did you recognize anybody else in the rest of the album?"

"No, that's it."

Grace continued to flip album pages desultorily, merely to prolong the moment. Suddenly she stopped, recognizing a face on her own.

"Look," she said. "This is Michelle Williams. But of course, you've never met her."

Jim bent over the album. Michelle was one of a row of people seated in the very IT lunchroom where Jim and Grace were now conversing. Grace had identified her from the large enameled crucifix on her chest, her dark features being made indistinct by the poor quality of the picture. On her left sat an unknown man in a pirate costume, on her right a witch. The wormy skeleton hung on the wall behind them. In the foreground, a blond woman all dressed in pink with a large red L taped to her sweater seemed to be acting out some kind of charade. Grace couldn't figure out what she meant to represent.

"What's the story with Michelle Williams?" Jim asked.

"To tell you the truth, I have no idea," Grace answered ruefully, recalling that in the nearly two years they had worked in the same office, they had exchanged no more than a dozen words.

Having reached the end of the photo album, Grace closed it and replaced it under the roasting pan on the shelf. Then, as Jim gave no sign of getting up, she walked back to her side of the table and sat down again. Somehow the conversation segued into books, and from there into his listing the three books that had influenced him the most. Grace can't imagine that the idea came from her, as she would have been hard put to limit to three her own list of influential books. In any case, the next thing she remembers, he was writing down his list on a paper napkin he had grabbed from the table, his pen tearing through the flimsy tissue on every downward stroke. There was something touchingly adolescent about it. The list, still etched in Grace's brain, went as follows:

1. *The Bible*
2. *The Crack in the Cosmic Egg*
3. *Guns, Germs and Steel*

Grace was a little put off by the prominence he gave to the Bible, though to be fair its place at the top of the list may have only reflected the chronological order of his readings. Considering her more extensive literacy, she was also embarrassed to admit that the second book was one she had never heard of. With the third book, thankfully, she was on more familiar ground.

"I have been meaning to read *Guns, Germs and Steel*," she exclaimed. "What did you like about it?"

To her utter astonishment, Jim launched into a very cogent summary of the book's argument, which had solidified some thoughts he had had for a long time about the amount of sheer luck, as opposed to natural superiority, that had gone into the triumph of European civilizations in the last five hundred years. He had been particularly impressed by the comparison of the number of genetic mutations involved in the domestication of wheat and corn, which he had never seen mentioned anywhere before. The thing was, Grace hadn't either. Jim had just taught her something outside of the realm of IT management. Elated by this evidence of intellectual reciprocity, she found herself more willing to listen to what he had to say about the other books.

"How about the Bible? Why was it important to you?"

"Before we get to that, let's make an experiment. I'll give you a common English phrase, and you tell me where you think it comes from."

"My, we're in the mood for guessing games today, aren't we? Go ahead. This should be fun."

"You shall know the truth, and the truth shall set you free."

"That's engraved on the façade of Berkeley high school. So it must be a quote by some educator. I'd guess John Dewey."

"A house divided cannot stand."

"Wait a minute. Aren't you going to tell me if my answer to the first quote was correct?"

"No, I'll give you all the answers at the end."

"I'm not going to remember your phrases that long."

"I'll remember."

"All right, all right. Did you say 'A house divided cannot stand?' Must be Abraham Lincoln."

"The love of money is the root of all evil."

"Right on. Some socialist, obviously. I vote for Eugene Debs."

"To everything there's a season."

"That one is easy. It's a folk song my father played for me when I was a kid. By Pete Seeger, I think."

"Eat, drink and be merry."

"Shakespeare."

"Love is patient, love is kind."

"Hallmark card. You have many more of these?"

"No, that's it."

"So, how did I do?"

"Zero out of six. All these phrases are from the Bible."

"You're kidding!"

"I never kid about the Bible. I'll email you the exact references so you can check."

"You are so sneaky! But I can see what you're driving at. The Bible as foundation of the English language. On a par with Shakespeare, and like that."

"You got it. So don't you think it would be a good idea to teach the Bible in school? If only to give kids a sense of where their culture comes from?"

"But what about the kids who don't come from a Judeo-Christian culture?"

"Doesn't matter. Anyone who speaks English is steeped in biblical tradition, whether they know it or not. So why shouldn't they know? Why do we make them read Homer and Shakespeare, but not the Bible? Makes no sense to me."

"You may have a point there. But I suspect the Bible is important to you for reasons other than its literary value, right?"

"Sure. When I was a young man, reading the Bible made me look serious in the eyes of the girls."

"I wouldn't recommend this seduction tactic to any guy nowadays."

"At least not in Berkeley."

"Definitely not in Berkeley. But aside from its literary value, and other than as an aid in picking up girls, what did you find so compelling about the Bible?"

"Simple. Everything there is to know about human beings is in the Bible."

"Everything? How about the subconscious? Child development? Brain specialization? Addiction? Gay studies? All the contributions of modern psychology?"

"All academic fads that get their fifteen minutes of fame, and then are retired on the sly because they don't make a difference in practice. Except Al Anon, by the way, and that relies on a spiritual approach. The problem with modern psychology is that it's based on a shallow secular humanism: people are basically good, so if they turn out rotten it must be their mommy or daddy's fault. Or human beings are a mass of compulsions, so they can't help themselves. Or the compulsions are what makes people free, so they should yield to them. Just a bunch of excuses for spoiled kids who don't want to grow up. But the Bible has it right: there's both good and evil in human nature, and each person is endowed with free will to turn toward good and away from evil."

"What's evil? Isn't that culturally relative? Didn't the very definition of evil evolve in the Bible from the ten commandments to the teachings of Jesus?"

"I see you know more about the Bible than you let on. Yes, morality is always in the process of evolving, though all in all, I don't think you can much improve on Jesus' most important moral teaching: Love one another, just as I have loved you."

"That's very nice, but a little vague, in my opinion. In practice, we're confronted with more precise ethical dilemmas."

"Give me a for instance."

Grace hesitated. She had a "for instance" alright, but feared that her bringing it up might shatter the moment's delightful spirit of give and take. Reflexively, she grabbed a paper napkin from the center of the table and started folding it into origami shapes, trying to buy some time before answering. It was ironic, wasn't it, that after making light of Jim's use of a napkin to help his thought process, she found herself resorting to the same device.

"Let's say one course of action would be beneficial to a group, but unfair to an individual. What should I do?"

"That's a tricky one," Jim said, without giving any indication that he recognized the dilemma. "But let me ask you something. What would eventually guide your decision?"

"I would probably pick the course that goes against my self-interest!" she cried out, surprised to discover that such had in fact been the clinching criterion in her refusal to let Josh go, in spite of his role in the uproar around her promotion.

"And where do you think this guiding principle comes from?"

"From my parents, grandparents?"

"And where did they get it from?"

"You tell me."

"From their religion. From God."

"Which one?"

"All of them and the only One dwelling in every heart."

"So why would someone else not make the same decision as I made?"

"Didn't I say there was evil as well as good in human nature?"

A heavy footstep was heard in the corridor. Jim and Grace simultaneously glanced at the clock on the wall. It was seven ten. Who could be entering the Data Center at this hour? Had one of the staff been there all along? Had anyone been a witness to their long discussion? They remained frozen on their chairs, a look of alarm on both of their faces, until a thick man with a mustache appeared in the doorway.

"Howdy, Mr. Wright!" the man said, his hands at ease on the door jamb. "I had some business in town. I figured I might as well start my shift early."

"Glad to see you, Ray!" Jim answered while in one smooth movement, he grabbed the napkin on which he had written his book list, crumpled it up into a ball, and lobbed it into the trash can twelve feet away. The gesture struck Grace as symbolic: he was dismissing the philosophical ramblings elicited by his interaction with her, and switching to male-bonding mode. More intimidated than she knew by his age, status and mood changes, she did not consider the simpler explanation that occurs to her now: that he may have wanted to impress her with his physical prowess, in case the force of his intellect had failed to do the trick. It was a mark of his genius that, whichever goal he had pursued, he achieved both of them: bonding with Ray, and dazzling Grace.

"Good shot," Ray coolly commented. "I see you ain't lost your touch."

"That's cause I practice every day. But where are my manners? Grace this is Ray Gomes. Ray this is Grace Kirchner, who you've only talked to on the phone, I believe."

"Nice to meet you, Miss Kirchner," Ray said, extending his hand. "Shall I make a pot of coffee?"

"Not for me," Grace answered, standing up. "I should head home. It's later than I thought."

"Not for me either," Jim said, standing up in his turn. "I'm coffeed out for today. But I'd better get back to work. No rest for the wicked."

"Another Bible quote?" Grace asked.

"Isaiah, 48:22."

Having lobbed this parting shot, which netted him a couple more grudging points on the scoreboard of Grace's regard, Jim made his exit.

As she drove home, the weather in those days being too cold and gray for bike riding, Grace realized that they had not had time to discuss his second influential book, *The Crack in the Cosmic Egg*. While her dinner cooked, she looked it up online. It seemed to be some kind of New-Age self-help book about breaking out of a logical way of thinking to attain spiritual truth. A book against logic, beloved by this eminently logical man. More amazingly, the reviews on Amazon.com claimed that the book had been informed by the insights of a number of respectable thinkers, the child psychologist Jean Piaget among them. And they implied that it belittled religion as a cop-out.

The book had first been published in 1983. Jim must have been, what, twenty-eight? What had made him turn from the Bible to New-Age spirituality, and back again to the Bible? Unless he didn't see any contradiction between the two, unless he had made his own synthesis. She recalled the mysterious and poetic phrase that had concluded his religious argument: "All of them (the gods, she assumed) and the only one (also God?) dwelling in every heart." Had he meant that how we portrayed God(s) was unimportant, and that the divinity was actually located in human minds? That would certainly make religion more palatable intellectually, though apparently no better than secular humanism at fostering ethical behavior. For he had as much as admitted that his attempt to fire Josh had been evil, and he seemed as complacent about his sinfulness as the people who hold their parents responsible for all their faults.

She tried to imagine Jim as a bible-reading adolescent, reeling girls in with his serious demeanor. Tall, probably beardless, probably skinny, probably ill-dressed (no college degree, therefore poor family), shy (but athletic), sexually repressed?, technically gifted, lost in spiritual speculations. She wouldn't have given him the time of day.

She tried to imagine him as a young father, working far from his family in Saudi Arabia, having substantial discussions with his friend Waheed under the palm trees, reading New-Age books at night in the solitude of his compound. The image was more appealing, except for the far-away family. Her own father had traveled quite a bit, but never for more than a week at a time. It was inconceivable to her that a man might allow his children to grow up in his absence. It seemed to bespeak a callous heart.

At last, at fifty, his children grown, his career crowned by an executive title, his physical appearance made over by middle-age heft, good clothes, and sexual confidence—the athletic deftness being unimpaired—his mind sharpened by random readings and wide-ranging experiences, his will (more or less) unopposed, he was an object of desire to a twenty-six-year old.

"O how the mighty have fallen" is the biblical phrase that now springs into Grace's mind.

XVIII

ENTREPRENEURIAL

Coming back to the topic of blessings in disguise: it was Josh's firing fiasco that opened Jim's eyes to the inadequacy of the Hartbridge business model, eventually unleashing his own entrepreneurship.

Though, out of a sense of managerial decorum, he had let Grace believe that the idea of terminating Josh had come from him, it had in fact been the brainchild of his fellow consultant. The thing was, Myrtle had discovered that her policy of coddling the staff's foibles got her less than expected traction among the PC technicians she had agreed to supervise. Ruby, who at first had seemed thrilled to make a friend, soon became disenchanted—as her type invariably did—when she realized she would have to share the friendship with others, consequently retreating into her comfort zone of unproductive antagonism. And where Ruby went, Josh and Erin followed, albeit less obtrusively. As for Sandra, her sights trained on the promotion that Jim had dangled in front of her eyes, she did not waste any time ingratiating herself to someone who did not fit in the official hierarchy. It would have been a lie for Jim to claim that he had not in any way anticipated these developments.

Obviously, this was not the way Myrtle explained her loss of influence, nor did she give any indication that she took it as a personal blow—in general, except when she cried, Myrtle made of point of not taking things personally. Instead, she argued that managerial power rested on the ability to reward or punish (for good reasons, she did not mention charisma or technical expertise as alternative sources of authority, but Jim himself had experienced their limits). She saw Josh's evaluation as an opportunity for the Hartbridge team to show that they were in charge by exerting their disciplinary prerogatives—at little risk, since Josh was a probationary employee lacking union protection or essential knowledge. The action would in fact kill three birds with one stone: it would make the rest of the staff more pliable, it would justify the hiring of a contractor or two, an objective Fritz had been pressing on them rather relentlessly of late, and it would help conciliate the most troublesome of the Board members, whose nephew would be asked to provide the contractor(s).

Myrtle's logic was flawless. What she didn't count on, could not have predicted, given her dismissal of Grace as Jim's mere puppet (it is true he had never tried to disabuse her of the notion), was the young woman's veto. But Jim, by then quite familiar with his dear girl's independent spirit, had predicted it, would in fact have betted on it, if there had been anyone around with whom to share his insights. He flattered himself that he would have beaten some impressive odds, since, on the surface, she had at least a couple of incentives to go along with the termination: for one thing, it gave her the opportunity to repay Josh for speaking out against her promotion; and for another, Jim was now physically certain of her attraction to him.

Again and again he replayed in his mind that delicious, dizzying moment when her mouth had readied itself for a kiss, not puckering up, but on the contrary relaxing, the willful little peaks on her upper lip smoothed out, her lower lip as plump as a pillow on a newly-made bed, and her eyes, their blueness simply limpid, washed of all challenge under the invitingly lowered lids. For a second, he had summoned the sensuality that smoldered under her gawky demeanor, and felt his power over her.

He told himself that was all his convulsive embrace had meant to achieve: the knowledge, in his bones, his muscles, his blood, not just his brain, that she wanted him as much as he wanted her. That even if her eyes had not suddenly rounded and darkened in fright at the thought of their being found locked in a kiss, he would have soon released her, affectionately, regretfully. That it would have had no consequence, as in fact proved to be the case. But he could not quite forget how he had felt himself losing control, how for a second he had been overpowered by his evil twin, the lurking side of him that wanted it all and wanted it now, and for whom the only knowledge that counted was knowledge in the biblical sense. To keep that dangerous creature at bay, Jim made a new deal with himself: he would not give up the pleasures of Grace's friendship, but would conduct it entirely in public places, where his evil twin didn't dare act out. The deal worked. Without a word being said about it, Grace somehow grasped its terms, and fully cooperated in its implementation—though, at times, Jim wished she was a little less obliging. But at night, he dreamt of lions roaming the streets, and naïve, sentimental citizens, reluctant to shoot the beasts, seeking to protect themselves by surrounding their homes with waist-high picket fences, which the lions had no trouble leaping over.

In contrast to Myrtle, Jim had not only predicted that Grace would balk at terminating a not clearly incompetent colleague, he had more or less counted on it. Not that *he* felt any particular compunction against firing Josh, a young man unburdened with kids, who would soon find another job, and perhaps apply himself a little harder in the future. Not that he relished the prospect of Myrtle's stratagems being foiled, although, to be honest—in Myrtle's own wording—he derived a certain enjoyment from the thought. No, what he welcomed, in his heart of hearts, was the opportunity to wrestle with Grace.

He is aware that this may sound perverse, but it wasn't, not really. First, there was the intimacy of their fights. Because, before telling him off, she would of course have to close the door. For a short moment, they would be on their own, insulated from the humdrum atmosphere of the office, and still they would be safe: she might tear up, but she wouldn't sob, or shout, or get personal in any way, the passion of her anger dissipating in righteous words and irrepressible humor across the surface of his desk. And then it was so stimulating to watch that rare little soul burst out of its shell, proud, uncompromising, impractical as it may be. (This much he can say in his defense, he didn't like her only for her body.)

What their clashes remind him of, now that he thinks of it, is the one time in high school when he, the wallflower, had been called upon to play the part of Shylock in the famous "Hath not a Jew eyes" scene, and how he had temporarily been transformed by it. How the play's elevated language had made him grasp that radically different points of view might coexist, each with its own validity, each with its own serious stakes. How he had felt inhabited by the humanity of the villain. Yes, his collisions with Grace were like scenes from a Shakespeare play: comic and profound, and more real to him in some way than all the business meetings that filled his days.

Not proud himself, he didn't feel threatened by her reproaches (and anyway she liked him, she *wanted* him, she wanted *him*), even when she forced him to assert his authority. It was all in the spirit of the contest, and she knew it: she never backed down, in the end, from what she thought was right, friendship and lust notwithstanding. And he let her have her well-earned victories, sensing that he was learning from her as much as she learned from him, that she was in fact leading him, willy-nilly, in a new direction.

In the end, Myrtle's stratagem was only half-defeated: she was not able to gain control of the PC unit by demonstrating her firing powers, but she managed to pry the funds for one Windows contractor out of the newly elevated Admissions budget by scaring Roger Wilkins with the vision of another registration system failure. And she touted the wireless network project she had got Santelli to approve as a treasure trove of contracting opportunities. If Jim did not exert himself, he was going to be outdone by his less talented colleague.

Jim was not sanguine about the likelihood that a contractor hired for purely nepotistic reasons would do a good job of the server virtualization project. He would have preferred to bring back Rick, who had already proved his technical chops, and was appreciated in the department. But Fritz had nixed the idea. The current contract only called for two FTEs, and it was out of the question to remove Myrtle, who was making herself politically useful at Pequeno—not to detract from Jim's own achievements in that area. Besides, per the contract's own language, the Hartbridge consultants were there to "assess", "recommend", "plan", "monitor" and "oversee", not to stick their hands down in the engine—that was the province of subcontractors, and a necessary revenue stream at this stage in the company's growth. Fritz acknowledged that he had made a mistake in sending Rick in the first place, or at least in not making clear to him where his responsibilities ended. But it was all water under the bridge. He knew better now.

Even if the Windows contractor turned out to be a technical wiz, the bottom line was this: as suitable as it might be for filling Fritz's pockets, the Hartbridge business model was not well adapted to getting things done. Management consultants, without any real authority over the client's staff, could not manage them in the long run. And handing out technical subcontracts as political favors was no way to insure competence in those who would do the actual work recommended, planned, monitored and overseen by the management consulting firm.

Meanwhile, Jim was still struggling with the RFP for the new contract. The wireless network and server virtualization projects were already initiated, so presenting them in a light that would make Hartbridge the only reasonable contender for their completion was fairly easy. But the RFP's piece de resistance, the Administrative System Migration on which the chancellor relied to make his technological mark on the District, and which alone guaranteed Hartbridge's continued presence in the foreseeable future, seeing as this kind of project, typically advertised as a three-year effort, never took less than eight, the Administrative System Migration was the item Jim kept stalling on.

His indecision was partly the result of his friendly arguments with Grace. The usual migration strategy consisted of replacing the old applications, typically written in-house, with ready-made software packages—oddly acronymed as ERPs—the two best-known ones being Peoplesoft and Banner. For the last few years, Peoplesoft and Banner migrations had been Hartbridge's bread and butter. A dozen of those were trumpeted on the firm's Web site—what was not indicated was that none of them had so far been completed.

The arguments for these multi-million dollar projects were normally easy to sell:

1. Both Peoplesoft and Banner were integrated, in other words, the student, financial, and HR components all talked to the same database and to each other.
2. Both ERPs had a Web-based user interface, in contrast with "legacy systems" that often presented information on a character-based, unwieldy green-screen format.
3. Both ERPs sat on modern hardware and operating system platforms, as opposed to clunky, no-longer-supported machines.

4. Both ERPs had built-in "workflows", AKA the ability to define approval routes for sensitive paperwork such as purchase requests and personnel actions.
5. The Web-based user interface allowed data entry into the database to be distributed to a wide variety of end users: enrollment to students, grade reporting to faculty, etc.
6. A modern database platform enabled the use of sophisticated data analysis tools, empowering decision makers to create their own spreadsheets and performance charts.
7. A modern database obviated the need for the nightly batch window, during which the data could not be accessed by online applications.
8. Peoplesoft and Banner made use of the latest development tools (though in fact, under the covers, a good deal of the business logic in Peoplesoft was still written in COBOL, but no one had to know). As the baby boomers retired, their old skills were dying with them, leaving many institutions without the means to maintain their legacy software.

The problem with these well-honed arguments was that, as Grace had taken care to demonstrate to Jim over the ten months he had been there, none of them applied to Pequeno, except number 7, and even then, Grace claimed there was a remedy to the problem, short of throwing out the entire system.

And while Grace made her case with Jim about the functionality of the in-house system, she did not miss any opportunity to alert her users about the drawbacks of packaged software:

- Their inflexibility of features, and in particular the little attention they paid to the specific needs of community colleges.
- The loss of control over maintenance costs and upgrades. When an ERP's new release came out, you had no choice but to install it, and then to reapply whatever modification you had made to the system. Needless to say, this put a damper on programmers' willingness to indulge their users' love of customization.

- The uncertainties of the hi-tech industry. Software firms constantly folded, merged, were bought out, and each time, their clients had to wonder whether their products would continue to be supported. Only the previous year, after a long and dirty fight, Peoplesoft had been acquired by Oracle, to the scandal of many in the IT world, who had no love for Larry Ellison.
- The length, difficulty and frequent failure of software migration projects. It wasn't hard to find examples of preposterous delays and spectacular snafus with which to scare departmental heads, and Grace had quite a repertoire of those, some of them new to Jim.

It was a treat to listen to this Millennial, skilled in several of the most up-to-date technologies, defend the virtues of software written a generation ago on an out-of-fashion platform. You would have thought she would jump at the chance to expand her skillset that a migration project offered. When Jim brought this oddity to her attention, she retorted that she didn't care about the tools, only about the end product. Deep down, he approved of her common sense, however impolitic it might be, and of the respect it showed for old-timers like himself.

He remembers something she said once about having a gut-level bias against any decision that would further her self-interest. He now sees how her defense of the in-house system was all of a piece with her declining to attend the Hartbridge retreat or her refusal to terminate Josh, the result of an active conscience. Love thy enemies, guard against all covetousness, turn away from evil and do good. He knew the verses, but she practiced them, atheist as she was. To be fair, who would think of applying Christian ethics to the work place, that supremely Darwinian environment? In any case, he believes that without knowing it, she shamed him into looking for an alternative to the standard package migration, one that would serve Pequeno's interests while it secured Hartbridge's profits.

Besides, he was bored with package migrations. Bored with the proprietary templates, the gap analysis charades, the fruitless requirement gathering, the users' inflated expectations and subsequent disappointments, the impossible data conversions. He wanted to work on something different, something outside the box, a project of his own.

All through December, he ruminated on the issue. One thing he had learned from Grace was to take full advantage of the Internet to pursue his research. He had observed how, when she was faced with any question or problem, her first instinct was to turn to Google. Like all techies of her generation, she downloaded free software, copy-pasted bits of code, found definitions for new jargon, took part in technical forums, searched vendors' knowledge bases. When Jim set about to follow her example, he made several discoveries:

- The Internet was the ideal medium for acquiring the kind of superficial overview of new technological trends that was essential to an IT executive, quicker, broader, more critical, more detailed than the trade magazines he had relied on for most of his career.

- One of the much talked-about new trends was "cloud computing". The concept was still ill-defined, but basically promised a future where organizations would be able to plug into a Web connected grid for all their IT needs instead of having to maintain their own computer facilities.

- The Internet was a community. There were all kinds of people out there willing to share their knowledge for free, and in a language that made it understandable, as opposed to merely boosting their aura of abstruse expertise. He was particularly impressed with Wikipedia, which was progressing by leaps and bounds only four years after its creation.

- One aspect of this communal spirit was the open source movement, which allowed developers to piggy-back on each other's work.

- Another aspect was the increasing availability of analytical documents, such as RFP templates, software package comparisons, implementation plans, all the "proprietary methodologies" on which Hartbridge based its competitiveness.

- Finally, the Kuali project, officially launched the previous year, proposed to pool the resources of a number of universities and colleges in order to build a complete, open-source suite of administrative applications tailored to higher ed specifications.

All fascinating stuff. Now, if Jim could only connect the dots, the shape that would emerge, he hoped, would be nothing less than a new paradigm.

Sensing the imminence of a breakthrough, Jim welcomed the approaching Christmas break, which would allow him to devote some quality time to his thought process—and perhaps to rest a little. The fact was that he had never been so tired in his life. Plus, his neck was bothering him, one side tender and swollen, probably from stress, he thought. At least, since he started watching his diet and swimming whenever he got a chance (which wasn't that often, unfortunately), he had lost seven pounds. Whether she noticed or not, it was at that time that Grace started expressing concerns for his health. He sternly warned her not to take on his well-being, a piece of advice she totally disregarded, and he had to admit he was glad she did. It was nice, it was comforting, if he couldn't have her sexual heat, to feel the warmth of her care for him.

Per the unspoken dictates of their new deal, their—very proper—parting hug was performed in front of the entire staff assembled around the Data Center entrance, just one of the many displays of affection and good cheer that marked the period. It was a beautiful day, he noticed, with a few brush-strokes of clouds smeared on the innocent sky, and red leaves from who knows where threaded through the chain link fence around the parking lot. He felt his chest tighten as she left his arms. She didn't look back when she heard his car start, but he hoped she knew he cared for her too.

Of course, the Christmas break ended up being less restful than he had hoped. The first couple of days had been earmarked for the usual festivities: Church, the exchange of presents, the Christmas dinner at a Chinese restaurant (Joleen was too depressed by Robby's absence to entertain at home). It had all felt remarkably normal, considering. Perhaps that hollowed-out normalcy was the best Jim could hope for in his personal life.

The day after Christmas, Joleen left to spend a few days in Florida with her sister. Jim and Cindy flew to Kansas to see Robert in prison. They might as well not have bothered. Robert hardly said a word to his father during the whole visit, and treated his sister with amused contempt. But in the plane, and in the Kansas City hotel where they spent a night, he became aware of a timid current of affection emanating from Cindy, wholly unmerited, as far as he could tell. Perhaps, it now occurs to him, it was the memory of Grace's fondness for him that opened a path in his heart for the recognition of his daughter's love.

Setting aside Joleen's advice, he got up the courage to ask her about her educational plans, and she turned out to welcome his interest, to actually want his help. Had Joleen been mistaken when she claimed that Cindy resented his interference, or had she deliberately tried to keep them apart? It was a scary train of thought that Jim put out of his mind at the time. And now, it doesn't matter.

He didn't get to see Waheed, who had been prevented from coming to the US, his name having inexplicably appeared on a no-fly list. On the other hand, back in Greensboro, he ran into an old high-school friend at the post office, and in Joleen's absence, felt free to spend some time renewing the friendship. And then, of course, he was in frequent phone contact with Fritz, who never took a vacation. Still, he managed to think, and to write, and by the time he was back in El Pequeno, he had a plan.

Grace was the first person he tried it on. He waited till five o'clock, when she typically made herself a cup of tea before ticking off the rest of her to-do list for that day. When he heard the tink of the microwave, he ambled toward the lunchroom. She was there as expected, in a long gray tube skirt over soft boots, a matching sweater with complicated seams, a sparkly scarf carelessly knotted around her throat, and new pearl earrings that seemed to have been lifted from that Vermeer painting, instead of the bits of hardware she normally favored. There was a definite part in her hair, and her lipstick was a rosy red. He was at a loss to explain how he could ever have nicknamed her Geek Goth.

She broke out in a smile while wordlessly holding out her hand for his cup. There was such a tender familiarity to her gesture that it made him woozy. He was home, there with her, in that melancholy bazaar.

"So, how are you?" she asked cheerily, turning away to fill his cup, but not fast enough for him to miss the cloud of worry that passed over her face as she did so. Was this why she turned away? Had he aged in a mere ten days?

"Did you follow my advice and spend every morning in bed with a good book?" she continued.

"As much as you did, I'll bet."

"Oh, I did, I did, except when I was skiing."

"I guess I'm not much one to lounge around."

"But you didn't do any work, while you celebrated the birth of Jesus Christ, right? You wouldn't dare."

"It took only one day for Jesus to be born, like the rest of us."

"That's blasphemous talk, I'm sure, Mr. Wright. *I*, on the other hand, did not give one thought to this place. It was wonderful. I could barely remember my password this morning."

She handed him his cup. Their fingers touched.

"Well, that's too bad, because I was just about to tell you of an idea I came up with during the vacation. But it's about work, so you may not be interested."

"Really? Of course I'm interested," she declared, sitting down at the table. Her pearl earrings swung energetically, as if to underline her curiosity. Jim wondered if they were a Christmas gift, and if so from whom.

He grabbed a chair, turned it around and sat with his elbows on the chair back. The gesture reminded him of a lion tamer's defensive stance. In truth, this was a little bit how he felt.

"What would you think, if instead of replacing our in-house administrative system, we used it as a model for other community colleges and universities?"

"I'm listening."

"Have you heard of the Kuali project?"

"Vaguely. It's a group of universities trying to develop a community source ERP for higher ed institutions, right? But last I heard, they had barely started working on the financial component."

"What if we joined them? What if we leveraged Pequeno's considerable software assets—old hand as I am, you've convinced me of their value, and that's saying something—into a leadership role in the Kuali group? We have the institutional knowledge, we have the analytical and programming skills, we have most of the database design and business logic required, at least for the student component. And we can be advocates for the specific needs of community colleges, like MIS reporting, which tend to be short-changed in ERPs. We can be pioneers in the community source movement, take part in the design of something elegant, highly functional, and sustainable, and then share it for free with less fortunate institutions. I'm thinking we could even go the cloud-computing route, make the applications available on the Web from a central server farm that we would provide. A lot of smaller colleges would be relieved not to have to maintain their own hardware and software platforms. How does that sound?"

At the beginning of his pitch, Grace had been merely attentive, but he saw how her eyes lit up more and more at each of the bait words he threw at her: leadership, value, community, elegant, and most of all sustainable. He could do this. He could convince her, he could convince anybody. Still, she wasn't going to let him win the argument without a fight.

"And what would be in it for Hartbridge?" she slyly asked. But he was ready for that question too.

"Don't you worry about Hartbridge. There's always a need for the middleman."

"Is that what Hartbridge is, a middleman?"

"Sure. We bring together people and resources, executives and technology experts, institutions and vendors . . ."

"You know, I sometimes worry that the American workforce is soon going to consist entirely of middlemen."

"Good. Let other countries take care of the nitty-gritty."

"But *that* does not seem sustainable, does it? Besides, you don't strike me as the middleman type."

"How do I strike you?"

"As someone who likes to take care of the nitty-gritty. Like me."

"Makes me a better middleman. Same with you, you'll see."

"But what would Hartbridge's role be, in the Kuali scenario you just outlined?"

"Hartbridge would be a partner in the foundation, on a level with Pequeno. We would help recruit institutions, coordinate development efforts, provide implementation support, that sort of thing. And I would still be located here. So, what do you say?"

"I like it, I really like it."

The next person that needed convincing was Fritz—a less receptive audience, as Jim knew, since, on top of suffering from a short attention span, (and, of course, not being attracted to Jim), the Hartbridge CEO had spent too many years focused on the balance sheet to still be interested in new technologies. With Fritz, Jim emphasized the need for Hartbridge to switch to a more sustainable business model in these days of Internet document sharing and open source software development. (A good new buzzword, sustainable, as apt to trigger the buying reflex in the lazily virtuous as a dirty-beige-and-grass-green packaging scheme for toilet paper.)

In its broad line, Fritz was amenable to Jim's plan, giving him the green light to sell it to the Pequeno constituency. Yet when it came to the RFP, he insisted on the tried-and-true package-migration template being used, even though it did not help differentiate Hartbridge from any number of other consulting firms. In Fritz's experience, educational executives in general, and Akecheta in particular, were a pretty risk averse bunch, underneath their pretense to "innovation" and "outside-the-box thinking". The Pequeno chancellor would not gladly sign on to any technological enterprise that had never been attempted before. But, Jim countered, Akecheta was intimately acquainted with the risks of package migrations, seeing as he had presided over the failure of one at his previous post. Better the devil you know, Fritz quipped, infringing on Jim's copyright. It was one thing to fail like everybody else, another to fail at something new, because the failure would then be entirely attributed to your decision to try a different approach. No, let the usual wording stand in the RFP. Once the contract was signed, it would be time to bring the chancellor around to Jim's idea. But, if Jim started campaigning for it among the lower ranks, wouldn't Akecheta hear of it and be peeved? Fritz snorted. The chancellor never heard any idea that came from the lower ranks, according to him.

If Jim's conversation with Fritz depressed him, it also made his job easier: he was able to pretty much copy-paste the Administrative Systems Migration section of the RFP from another document in the Hartbridge library, only making a few global name changes. By the end of January, he had submitted the RFP to his boss, who would submit it to Akecheta, who would have it reviewed by his underlings, approved by the Board, and then opened for bids so quietly and shortly that only three or four firms would respond, out of which Hartbridge would naturally be selected, if only because that was the path of least resistance. By May, when the current contract expired, Hartbridge would have a new one, and for three years this time. What they actually did with it would be up to Jim—hopefully.

For the next two months, Jim and Grace did their homework on the Kuali project. They pored over the foundation's Web page, followed all its links, made contact with the membership liaison officer, downloaded business case documents, worked on financing numbers. Grace rustled up enough staff development funds to send several of her staff to a Java course for Kuali developers. Jim interviewed executives at several firms that had become or were planning to become commercial affiliates of the project.

They talked up the Kuali solution to various Pequeno managers. Both Bob Johnson and Roger Wilkins rallied to their cause, feeling vindicated in their appreciation of the in-house system, and proud to imagine Pequeno as an font of innovation.

They brought it up at the one IT staff meeting they had during that period. Wei, Rajiv and Sandip, taken by the community sourcing aspect of the project, immediately signed up for the developer course, as did Grace. Elmore himself reacted positively. He was too close to retirement to learn Java, but was confident he could contribute his institutional knowledge and analytical skills to the design of the new system. For their part, Sandra, Erin and Josh loved the idea of cloud computing. Mina asked how the project would affect her, and was relieved to hear that she would be involved in porting the data over to the new system. Tiffany saw herself handling the business aspects of the project. Only Ruby abstained from the conversation, but she took many notes. Jim came out of the meeting mentally energized, if physically as tired and achy as ever.

And they went on field trips, just the two of them. They attended a meeting of California Community College CIOs, where Jim was pleased to discover that the Pequeno IT department had long been viewed as a model for its early adoption of Web registration and the accuracy of its MIS reporting. It was true that these achievements dated from before Jim and Grace's time, but the District's enduring reputation would help garner support for the new project.

They visited a Kuali development site in Berkeley, and another one in Stockton. Jim was aware that they made an attractive pair: experience and youth, business savvy and technical clout, Southern charm and urban chic. He saw their combined image as a definite business asset.

They drove everywhere together, in Jim's car, at his insistence. There were a few male prerogatives he wasn't prepared to give up. She teased him, but submitted, as was proper.

It was a fulfilling period for both of them, if devoid of sexual thrills. They were too absorbed in their common project to think about anything else. In fact, their professional partnership got so comfortable that Jim relaxed his vigilance a little. They resumed their walks along the canal, and once they even saw a movie together. Nothing untoward happened.

But while they were on the road, exposed to a wider world than the constrained office turf, he did get to know her better, and in particular to see her faults, which, as far as he could tell, all stemmed from her being a child of privilege. She made fun of Akecheta's obsession with college degrees, but her disdain for popular culture smacked of a similar elitism. She didn't watch TV other than PBS, she didn't read newspapers other than the New York Times, she subtly tuned out speakers who mangled their grammar. She was full of abstract compassion for the poor, but avoided direct contact with them. She wouldn't be caught dead walking into a Walmart or a McDonald's, and she could articulate political reasons for her distaste, but underneath Jim sensed her horror of the fat, the slovenly, the ill-mannered, the wrecked. She railed at the anti-immigrant sentiments they occasionally witnessed, on a sign, in a traffic confrontation or the looks passers-by directed at groups of laborers waiting to be picked up at street corners. It did not occur to her to put herself in the shoes of native working-class people, whose jobs were being taken away from them by cheaper illegal aliens, and whose neighborhoods, one of their only sources of comfort, were being turned upside down by the massive influx of foreigners. How could it have occurred to her? She lived in a 100% Anglo part of town, and if she ever found herself in danger of losing the competition for jobs to foreigners, she had the wherewithal to raise herself above them again by going to graduate school, a plan she once floated as Jim extolled their Kuali future.

In a way, her upper-middleclass background made her spunk a little less exceptional. She had been raised to believe in her right to express herself, the unseen wealth of her family poised, like a sort of psychological airbag, to cushion the blow of any disaster that might result from self-expression. Not that Jim was unaware of all the children of privilege who were nevertheless wimps and toadies. Still, the realization that it was easier for her to maintain her integrity than for most people (himself included) made her seem more . . . human, and in the end more lovable.

To him, but probably not to her coworkers. Jim suspected that the subtle aura of money around Grace, about which she probably didn't have a clue, was one of the reasons they had been so intent on forestalling her promotion.

Another way Grace was not exceptional at all was her typically female faith in personal questions. "Don't you want to know how my grandmother is doing?" "Aren't you going to ask me how I liked the presentation?" "Aren't you interested in how *I* spent my weekend?" All these hints offered in a teasing tone, but deadly serious underneath. As if she needed any proof of his attention, as if she was afraid not to be understood, as if she was not doing a perfectly good job of revealing herself to him without any prompting. Sometimes he teased her back, sometimes he humored her. He was convinced that he knew her better than she knew him.

Now it occurs to him that "knowing" may not have been the point of the exercise. That perhaps she wanted him to care for her in a way he didn't. Not as a colleague. Not as a pal. Not even as a suitor. What was it that she needed from him, and how come, if he can't figure out what it was, he is certain he did not give it to her, and feels guilty about it?

Pretty ironic, that while she complained of his detachment, he was entertaining dreams of a closer partnership: a company of their own, sexual benefits, on the road together, his hand in her lap, torrid nights in hotel rooms . . .

The chimes of his laptop inform him of an incoming message. Not wanting to appear too eager in his own eyes, he waits for a few seconds before turning away from the TV, where pundits are debating the respective chances of Hillary Clinton and Barack Obama, as if it was at all likely that a novice black man might win the Democratic nomination, smart and personable as he seems. It would be political suicide. It ain't gonna happen. Which is why his attention had drifted away from the show.

Yes, it is a message from them, from Mina more precisely:

> Taking advantage that Grace is talking on the phone to her boyfriend to let you know that we made it to Knoxville without any problem. We'll see you tomorrow, God willing, after two long years. Isn't it amazing? We'll have so much to catch up on.
>
> In the meantime I am looking forward to driving through the Smoky Mountains. I hear they're really beautiful.
>
> Love and blessings.

Ah, Grace has a boyfriend now. Well, what did he expect? Surely not that while stationed in Raleigh, she would want to take up where they left off, with him, aged by sickness as he is, with no entrepreneurial future. That her love would miraculously bring him back to life. He would despise himself for nurturing such childish hopes. And yet, for a second, his heart contracts, he feels more abandoned than ever. He snaps out of his despondency. He knows that if he pulls through, it will be from his own effort, and with God's grace, not Grace the person. But friendship will help, a kind of love after all, she has pledged that much in her latest email.

And now that the expectations have been clarified, thanks to Mina's tactful hint, he can let them know that his wife won't be attending the party without it being taken as a hint of his own.

So glad you're both safe and getting close. My daughter Cindy and I are looking forward to welcome you in our home. I want to hear everything about the goings-on at Pequeno and about the Obama campaign (Don't worry. We won't argue. I'm barely a Republican these days).

Now you girls get to sleep early, you hear? I'm going to do the same.

But before he goes to bed, he checks their route on Google Maps. This does not enlighten him as to the real distance between them. He will have to wait till tomorrow to know more, and in one way it's too long, and in another way it's not long enough.

XIX

GOSSIPY

"Do you realize we're in North Carolina?" Mina exclaims, trying to convey unmitigated cheer.

"Yes, I do," Grace answers in a subdued tone.

Right now, Mina is concentrating on three things at once: handling the gearshift on the mountain road, drinking in the scenery, and assessing her passenger's mood. Amazingly, she finds it's no trouble at all. Somehow, all her preoccupations flow together in one stream of clear, buoyant consciousness, a sense of spiritual power. She will get them to Greensboro, she will shore up Grace's courage, she will engineer a glowing reunion with Jim, come what may.

It was Grace's idea, bless her heart, to make a slight detour, switching from I-40 to US-441 through the Great Smoky Mountain National Park, the most visited national park in America, according to its Web site. They even had time to take a short hike on the Appalachian Trail at the very top, their feet tracing the exact dotted line of the border between Tennessee and North Carolina. The view from up there lived up to its hype. Never in her whole life has Mina been so awed by nature. Until that moment, to tell the truth, she had found the land through which they drove rather less inspiring than the maps that charted their course.

Though she has traveled very little, Mina has always loved maps. You learn so much from them: elevation, temperature, precipitation, population, crops, minerals, forests, deserts, oceans, all neatly color-coded for your instruction. You can see how Africa once fitted into the crook of the American continent, you sense the power of government in a straight state line, you feel the pulse of a metropolis from the starburst pattern of roads converging toward it. The best maps of course are the raised ones. Once, in fourth grade, Mina made her own raised relief map of California out of paper maché for a school project. But after the San Joaquin river had been painted in blue, and the mountains in green, and the valley in pink (orchards) and red (tomatoes), there was still something missing. So Mina made little people out of quilting pins, copper wire and bits of yarn, and she stuck them in at strategic points. Her map looked so perfect to her that she imagined it coming to life at night: the river flowed, the pin people worked the orchards and tomato fields, fished and had picnics in the mountains, shopped in El Pequeno. But the teacher couldn't see it. She said the pin people were out of scale, and made Mina take them out. It felt like tearing the wings off a butterfly.

Driving on the interstate is exhilarating in its own way, but it's an abstract kind of ecstasy, born of speed for speed's sake, and best expressed in numbers: miles covered, miles remaining, miles per hour. You feel like you're shooting off into a blank future, the past a mere point of the map. And the landscape is flattened out on the other side of the guardrail: mountains like walls or paper cutouts, depending on the distance, the rest an empty waste lined with endlessly-repeated, all-too-familiar landmarks: yellow twin arches, red targets, blue and red chevrons, so that you end up wondering whether you're driving in circles.

But on the two-lane road that winds through the Smoky Mountains, you hug every contour of the relief, the lacy canopy kindly parts at intervals to offer tantalizing glimpses of rushing water and serene vistas, until you get to the top, when you think you've died and gone to heaven, a whole sea at your feet of finely delineated, infinitely varied, softly bobbing, lamb-coat-textured ridges in marbled shades of mauve and green, all the way to the horizon where the mauve-green melts into the blue of the sky, also dotted with lamb-shaped clouds. A scene both majestic and human-scaled that opens you wide to the present. This is the day the Lord has made. Let us rejoice and be glad in it. Mina sang the psalm in her head and felt strengthened against any contingency.

"Wasn't the walk along the Appalachian Trail the best?" she tries again, at the risk of sounding like a broken record, as she has already much enthused on the subject.

"You mean better than camping out among the serial killers of Memphis?"

"Seriously now. Didn't you think it was awesome?"

"It was seriously awesome. I agree. I want to come back and hike the back country. Maybe after the primary. Before the summer crowds."

"With Jason?"

"Maybe with Jason, there's an idea."

"Talking about hikes. Do you remember the time we went for a walk along the canal with Jim?"

"Sure, I remember. It was sometime in February, I think, shortly before . . . he left. I was always trying to get him to exercise for his health. That day, the weather was on my side. We had a good hour of sunshine ahead of us. He was tired and itchy. I managed to convince him."

"I saw you guys pass by my desk, so I asked if you'd be back or if I could close up shop. And Jim said: 'We'll be back. We're just going to play hooky for a bit.' He winked at me and started walking again. I thought you were out of there. But then he turned back and added: 'Want to come with us?' I had wrapped up the scheduling for that day, and Tarik was watching Steven, so I thought, what the heck. Besides, I figured you guys could use a . . . whatchamacallit . . . a chaperone."

"A chaperone!"

"Yeah, you may not have been aware of it, but Erin was still in her cubicle, probably hanging on our every word. There was enough gossip going on about you two in the office without somebody being in a position to report that you had gone out to play hooky together."

"There was gossip about us?"

"Of course. Everybody could see you were sweet on each other . . ."

"Sweet on each other!"

"You know what I mean. You liked each other a lot. And when a man and a woman like each other, other people like to think that they're sleeping together."

"Sleeping together!"

"Didn't it occur to you that they might think that? Especially as it seemed to explain why you had been promoted. Much easier on their self-esteem than acknowledging you were smarter and worked harder."

"I'm afraid it did not occur to me that people would think I slept with someone unless I did sleep with him. I guess I thought it was written on my face that I didn't. Call me naïve. But who thought that, anyway?"

"Everybody."

"Everybody! Including you?"

"No. Give me more credit than that."

"You mean you could see it on my face?"

"Kinda. Anyway, like I told anyone who would listen, if you had been sleeping together, you wouldn't have been so keen on palling around at the office. But mostly, I felt that it would have been out of character for you to sleep with a married man. You were so straight and serious. I couldn't see you doing it."

"Me, straight? Anyway, it's really nice of you to have defended me. I had no idea. But what about Jim's character? Would you have thought him capable of having sex with someone other than his wife?"

"You can't rely on any man's character when it comes to sex."

Grace bursts out laughing, so unexpected is this bit of matter-of-fact cynicism on the part of her demure, sheltered, innocent friend. Coming on top of the revelations about the office gossip that surrounded her relationship with Jim, it sets her mind reeling. Not for the first time in the last few years, she senses that she has much to learn about the incredible complexity of human beings, their strengths, their apparent contradictions, and especially their treacherousness. She is still a nerd after all, in spite of the months developing people skills in the Obama campaign. It's a bit discouraging. But it makes her effort to figure out Jim even more crucial.

"So you came on the walk merely as a chaperone? I hope you weren't bored out of your skull."

"Not at all. We made a good team, the three of us, don't you think? It was great to be out and about, away from the petty squabbles in the office, to see you relax for a change. And Jim was so cool. Do you remember how he tried to teach us how to skip stones on the surface of the canal? You got the hang of it, but I was hopeless. I couldn't even find the right kind of stone. My stones just plopped into the water and were never seen again. I was afraid they'd make a dam and stop the water from flowing. It was hilarious. And then we got to the playground, and we decided to get on the swings, so he pushed us, back and forth in opposite directions, it was like a ballet, and we went so high I thought I would fly right over the top bar. I said he must have had a lot of practice with his kids, and he said: 'not enough', which made me feel kinda sad. And on the way back, he noticed how the Japanese plum trees were coming out in bloom. He was surprised because it was only February, so we started talking about gardening, and he explained how to prune fruit trees. I filed the whole conversation in my head. To this day, I could follow his advice. And in fact I intend to as soon as we get our trees planted."

"I don't remember Jim's pruning instructions, but then again I don't have a garden. What I do remember is how lovely it was to see *him* blossoming out of his business persona to show his handy, physical, silly side. I think it was thanks to your presence. It was the last time I saw him that carefree."

"We finished the walk with a hundred yard dash, and Jim won, and you said it was no fair, because we were not wearing the right kind of shoes."

"But didn't you notice how winded he seemed when we got back? I thought he was about to have a heart attack. Little did I know . . ."

"There was no way we could have known. And I don't think that walk hurt in any way. I bet Jim remembers it as fondly as we do. And we'll have good times together again, you'll see."

"I hope you're right," Grace concludes, lapsing into her internal ruminations.

It *is* really nice of Mina to have defended Grace's reputation, but in fact, she is mistaken. In February 2006, Grace was not above wanting to sleep with a married man, with that barely married man, at least.

A few days after their third walk, the one in which Mina played chaperone, on a Friday evening—it was always on Friday evenings that things happened—Grace popped into Jim's office to announce the completion of Harriet Jellineck's report. She was feeling triumphant: she had not succumbed to the urge of creating the report herself, but had hounded Sandip to the point where he figured it would be easier to do the work than to endure her continued visits. She was hoping against hope that the lesson would stick in the future.

Jim on the other hand had complained of feeling "bushed" when they ran into each other at the water cooler earlier in the afternoon. They had gone on one of their Kuali field trips the day before, and he had insisted on driving, as usual, even though driving aggravated the tension in his shoulders. When she came around his doorway, a little before five o-clock, he was cracking his neck vertebrae, his hair ruffled, his tie loosened, his suspenders unhooked, his shirt wrinkled where the suspenders had pressed against it. He had removed his glasses, and his eyes looked naked without them. There was something so private about the sight that Grace's instinct was to retreat. But he saw her, and putting his glasses back on, smiled at her in welcome. She felt like coming around his desk and smoothing out his hair for him, but remained standing where she was.

They had a short business conversation, at the end of which Grace politely asked him what his plans were for the weekend.

"Oh, nothing much. It's supposed to rain, so golf is out. I'm not looking forward to rattling around in my skivvies in that big empty apartment, I'll tell you that."

"Why don't you invite some friends over for a party?" Grace proposed helpfully.

"The trouble is I don't have any," he said in a forlorn tone that pretended to be facetious but was meant to be taken seriously.

"Well, that's sad," Grace replied, going along with his act.

"I was thinking about going to see a movie on Saturday night . . ."

Where was this conversation going? Could he possibly be fishing for a date? It would have seemed the obvious conclusion to draw, except for the fact that they had spent quite a bit of time alone together in the past few weeks, and he had never made a move toward her. In the end, Grace had more or less decided that she had imagined the whole near kiss incident, that of the two she was the only one with a sexual fixation. Unsure how to respond to his overture, she let him hang himself if he would. There was a pause, during which Grace gazed out the window as if to confirm the weather forecast, but saw absolutely nothing.

"Would you like to go see a movie on Saturday night," he resumed coolly, as if he just had come up with the idea, and a very innocent one at that. But the way his eyes hunted for hers as he spoke contradicted this message. Grace was mortified to feel herself blush.

"I'd love to," she blurted out, choking on her words. She shook herself and repeated breezily: "Sure, I'd love to. What do you want to see?"

They had trouble finding a film they both might like. That should have been a clue, she realizes. She proposed Brokeback Mountain. He nixed it. No queer love story for him. He proposed Munich. Too bloody for her taste. They finally agreed on Match Point, which was supposed to have both characters and mayhem in moderate quantities. They looked up show times on Google. Jim said he would pick her up at her house at six forty five. She gave him her cell phone number. He punched it in his own cell phone, recording her personal coordinates for all times.

Grace went home in a trance. It had happened. After eleven months, he had asked her out. Her boss, twice her age, managerial wiz, paragon of manliness if not of business ethics, had asked her out. She can see now the part that vanity played in her excitement, but it was far from being the main ingredient, she is still convinced. What did *he* feel, what was he hoping for, that is the question.

Her mouth was dry, she couldn't swallow her dinner, her brain was fizzing, her limbs seemed about to wrench themselves out of their sockets. Fearing a sleepless night that would leave her debilitated for the crucial date, she went over to her landlord and landlady's next door to beg for a glass of wine. The three of them ended up watching the Winter Olympic Games on TV for over an hour, a welcome distraction, even if by the end of the evening, Grace couldn't have said what events they watched, much less who won. She walked back in the dark to her cottage, a half-full glass of wine sloshing in her hand. The air was sultry, the dense bushes that lined the path soaked up the noise in her head. Furtive creatures skittered in the undergrowth, going about their mysterious business. Above the roof of the cottage, in between the bare branches of a tall sycamore, a single star peered out of the cloud cover, beaming an undecipherable message. Grace stopped, looked, listened, breathed in the smell of damp earth. For a second, she felt at one with the universe. Then the universe folded back on itself, and she went in.

She finished the glass of wine before going to bed. As soon as she was tucked under the covers, she was overcome with desire for Jim. The foam pillow under her head had the dense texture of his chest, the flannel sheet caressed her neck like soft warm hands, the blanket wound itself around her as powerfully as his legs ought to do. She could hear his heart beat, strong and fast, feel the scratch of his beard against her breasts, smell the musk of his sweat mingling with the musk of his aftershave. She imagined his glasses on her night stand, his eyes movingly naked, his whole self inside her. The next thing she knew, the rain was beating down on her windows, and it was morning.

Enough! If the mountain won't come to Mahomet, Mahomet must go to the mountain, she said to herself as she jumped out of bed, quoting from her own authoritative sources. She was no longer going to play along his now-you-see-it-now-you-don't game. She was not going to let him shepherd her around like a benevolent uncle on some falsely chaste date. If he was too chickenshit—or too . . . whatever—to get down to brass tacks, she would. She was going to seduce him, that very night, that's what she was going to do.

She spent a considerable amount of time pondering what to wear. Something not too unfamiliar, or he might get uncomfortable, but not too businesslike, or he might treat her as a mere colleague. She ended up deciding on the flippy skirt she had worn at the Pequeno retreat, a V-neck silk top, but without the usual decolletage-erasing camisole underneath, and an expensive pair of black and white cowboy boots she never wore, a long-ago gift from her mother, who went for such things. With her black leather jacket to complete the outfit, she would look on her way to a country-western shindig. That should appeal to Jim's aesthetic sensibilities. Unseen until the right moment, if all went well, would be her best lacy black thong and matching demi-bra.

She took a bath, she tweezed and shaved and ex-foliated, she blew-dry most of the curls out of her hair. She did her finger and toe nails, taking great care to file or snip any sharp bit that could scratch another person's skin. She dabbed perfume behind her ears, under her arms, between her breasts, on the inside of her thighs, creating an olfactory approach guide for the untried lover. She applied mascara sparingly so as to prevent any physical exertion from translating into raccoon eyes. But she didn't stint on the lipstick. Let it bleed on his mouth, his neck, his shirt. He would have the rest of the weekend to wash it off.

She went out to buy a bottle of whiskey, letting herself be guided by the price, as she never drank the stuff. She fashioned a bouquet out of the camellias that drooped in the rain against her porch. She made sure she had a supply of condoms on hand. By the end of her preparations, she felt slightly nauseated, like a fat Odalisque groomed at length for the Sultan's pleasure. She should have done something for herself that day, gone for a run, cut out a pattern, but she had been too wound up to think of it. She even forgot to have dinner.

Around six-thirty she was ready, and bouncing off the walls. The rain had stopped. She picked the landlord's cat from the couch where he liked to take refuge from his masters' screaming toddlers, carried him out with her, locked the door and ambled down the alley. The landlord was smoking a cigarette on his porch. They started chatting, which thankfully took her out of herself. By the time Jim showed up, punctual as always, she had recovered her equilibrium, and was simply looking forward to being with him.

He on the other hand seemed tense, she noticed as soon as she opened the car door. For the first time in her experience, he had really dressed down, wearing jeans, a windbreaker and work boots, comb tracks visible in his damp hair. But that wasn't what made him look uncomfortable. His attire was nicely weathered and fitted him to a tee, the jeans hugging his quadriceps, the windbreaker loose but not bulky, the work boots slightly scuffed. These were his normal weekend clothes. He had not gone out of his way to make himself presentable, and Grace appreciated his casualness, although it made her worry for a second whether she had overdressed. But then she told herself he would put it down to the different sartorial customs of her generation, and decided to flaunt her own sense of style.

In her landlord's presence, they only exchanged verbal greetings before peeling out of her driveway. Jim was monosyllabic on the way to the theater. Breathing in his aftershave, Grace made herself relax so he could too.

Downtown El Pequeno was fairly hopping that night. They had to park several blocks away, along the old Mission-style post-office, on an insufficiently lighted street that Grace would not have chosen on her own. With six foot four of pure muscle at her side, however, she felt quite safe. It was lovely in fact to walk in the dark under the dripping trees, steam from their breaths commingling in the chilly air, the puddles at their feet iridescent from oil stains. Jim, his hands in his pockets, seemed to have recovered his normal jauntiness.

Grace did not much frequent downtown El Pequeno, preferring to drive to Berkeley or San Francisco for her shopping and entertainment needs. But in the three years she had been in residence in the Valley, she had noticed how the housing boom was bringing new life to this sleepy town. Along the main drag, there were now several trendy cafes with outdoor seating parsed among the chain restaurants, nail salons, tuxedo rental shops and bail bonds, and the crowd milling around seemed to have its fair share of Bay Area transplants, taller, leaner, whiter, and more entitled-looking than the locals. What were they doing there? Probably staffing the real estate agencies, mortgage companies, legal offices, art galleries, home decorating outfits, high-end electronics vendors, gardening centers, storage facilities and counseling services that had sprouted all over town in the wake of the formidable increase in residential units. What would happen to them when the housing bubble burst, as it must sooner of later? Grace hoped she would not be around to see the carnage.

The theater was a modern multiplex with a chrome marquee, slabs of marble in the bathrooms, and reclining seats spaced widely enough to accommodate Jim's legs. So far so good. They had barely sat down when the preview of coming attractions started. Jim settled in comfortably, elbows on the armrests, legs crossed ankle over knee, and immediately proceeded to forget all about Grace's presence. Somehow, she could not bring herself to remind him of it until the end of the movie, when she leaned against the armrest, touching his upper arm. He did not remove his arm, but did not increase the pressure either. She was baffled.

When they came out, Grace was famished. Jim, however, had already had dinner. She managed to convince him to look for some place where she could eat and he could have a drink while they discussed the movie. He sounded less than enthusiastic at the idea.

It took a while to find a restaurant that would combine fresh food with a minimal waiting list. By the time they settled on an un-gentrified sushi bar, the movie no longer seemed worth discussing. They tried several other topics, but none of them clicked. Jim was antsy, distracted, his eyes roaming the outer reaches of the restaurant as if he was expecting someone. At last, after a couple of glasses of sake, he relaxed enough to launch into some Saudi Arabian tales of sand storms, date plantations, the stores closed at prayer time, making bootleg alcohol out of palm juice, but it felt like he was talking to himself. For once, they were together strictly for pleasure and without a time limit, and the electric arc between them was completely flat. In an attempt to rekindle the spark, Grace resorted to quizzing him about the meaning of his Middle East experience, which was far from obvious to her. He complained that she was "too deep" for him.

On the drive back to her place, Grace discovered she had a splitting headache, which mooted the question of whether to invite Jim in. As she was about to get out of the car, her hand already on the door latch, she turned toward him. And though his face was barely distinct in the dim illumination provided by street lights, she saw, clearly, amazingly, that he was as disheartened as she was. For a second, they were united again in longing, but it was too late.

"Alright," she said "see you on Monday!"

"See you on Monday," he said.

And she got out. They had not even hugged.

Her head ached too much that night to permit introspection. But over the next few days, Grace wondered why she had chickened out of her seduction plan. It was true that Jim's aloofness and self-absorption had not made things easy for her, but it was the first time in her life that her decision to have sex with a man was not followed by consummation.

She did not for a second buy the headache excuse. She knew it must have been a psychosomatic ploy cooked up by her subconscious. So what was her subconscious trying to tell her? It seemed to hint that with Jim she had bitten more than she could chew, that older guys were too fraught with problems: the incomprehensible weight of their past lives, their bizarre dating mores, their uncertain health (she vividly recalled the scene in *Dave* where the President collapses from a stroke on his secretary's naked chest), not to mention the possible sexual dysfunctions daily publicized in the Viagra ads on TV, one of which featured a near dead-ringer for Jim. Guiltily, Grace acknowledged that she was probably not equipped to deal with any of these issues. Ever since her father's death, she had shied away from any situation that could remind her of other people's mortality. And though she now sees that it's no way to live, she knows she hasn't changed, that this is partly why she so dreads seeing Jim again.

A dream she had last night seems to reflect her fears. In the dream, she was looking from afar at a medieval island fortress, its pink brick towers shimmering in the southern light above a smooth turquoise sea. But on the horizon, a monstrous wave was approaching, lit by the same sun and colored in the same turquoise hue as the sea from which it rose, yet deadly. She woke up screaming. Fortunately, Mina slept undisturbed.

For all her skittishness when it came to taking action, Grace knew that she did love Jim. Not as being in love, and not just as an object of desire, but with a more rooted, tolerant, generous feeling. And he loved her too, in a way she understood no better than the way she loved him, but tangibly enough to make her certain of the fact in the days following the date fiasco. It showed in his continuing to seek her out, to welcome her feedback, to yield to her ministrations, to protect her from Myrtle's oily venom. So, brushing off the introspection, she told herself that the failed date was a mere comedy of errors. Jim's contract would be renewed, there would be plenty of other opportunities to get together if they both felt like it. Three weeks later he was gone for ever.

Coming out of her reverie, Grace realizes they are now driving through a valley.

"OK," she proclaims, trying to sound as if she has been concentrating the whole time on her navigational duties, "we should start looking for the US-74 turnoff. We want to go east on 74, toward Asheville."

"Actually, we are on 74, we've been on it for the last fifteen minutes," says Mina, covering her mouth with her hand in her usual glasses-adjusting gesture to hide the beginning of a grin.

"Oh my God! Sorry I'm such a space cadet. If you had relied on me for directions, we'd be in Georgia by now."

"It's no problem. I memorized the whole route from Google Maps. I guess you have a lot on your mind."

"And/or I didn't sleep enough last night. Tell me, since it was so obvious to you that Jim and I liked each other a lot, did you ever wonder why?"

"Why you liked each other? It's not that complicated. You're both really logical, you both love to argue, and you're both workaholics."

"Is that it?"

"I mean apart from the fact that he's a handsome man, and you're a handsome woman."

"You're handsome too, and logical, and a pretty hard worker."

"So Jim and I liked each other a lot too. But it's not the same when the woman has a family. It limits the friendship, but it makes it easier to handle. I didn't have time to cater to him the way you did. And on the other hand, he couldn't feel paternal toward me as he did with you. There was less risk of mixed-up feelings."

"You think I catered to him?" (But when could Mina have observed all this? She walked in on Grace's private conversations with Jim no more than four or five times.)

"Sure."

"And he was paternal to me?"

"Yes. I always thought you were both trying to work out some father-daughter issues."

"Dang! I can't believe what an astute psychologist you are. I think you've hit the nail on the head. You should go back to school and get a degree in counseling instead of wasting your talents in IT."

"Hey, I like IT. Besides, because you're good at something doesn't mean you should try to make money out of it."

"Ouch! Caught red-handed indulging in capitalist thinking. You're right again."

"Thank you for all the compliments. And now, can I ask you a question?"

"Go ahead."

"Why are you angry with Jim?"

There's no denying it, Mina's powers of divination are on the order of the uncanny. How does she know what's been gnawing at

Grace ever since she agreed to make a detour through Greensboro on her way to Raleigh? Grace herself has never breathed a word to anyone about the hard feelings she developed toward Jim after he left and she discovered what Hartbridge was really about. You can't speak ill of a dying man. But can you face him with the necessary warmth and equanimity when you no longer respect him?

Yes, that's it. It is not just a fear of sickness and death that makes her so ambivalent about the imminent reunion with her former boss, but the suspicion that she bestowed her affection on a man who was not worthy of it, a shady character, a patsy.

How can she explain her feelings to Mina without shocking her? Jagged phrases are jockeying for position in her brain. At last, in her frustration, she grabs the first one she can get a hold of and releases it into the confined space of the car, where it seems to explode with the rudeness of a firecracker.

"Because he never told me the truth."

"About what?" asks Mina, letting go of the steering wheel to rewind her hair, a gesture with millennia of womanly patience and self-denial behind it. With a pang of regret, Grace recognizes that womanly patience and self-denial are virtues she has no hope of ever emulating, her year of dilettantish catering to Jim notwithstanding. For better and for worse, she is a product of a self-actualizing age: she wants what she wants and she wants it now. Love, beauty, but especially the truth.

"He never told me the truth about anything: what he was trying to do, the role he meant me to play, who he was really working for, his feelings for me."

"Don't you think he did his best under the circumstances?"

"That's no good to me. Everybody does their best under their circumstances."

"Not everybody does. But I'm sure he did. Deep down, he was an honorable man. But he was swimming with sharks, I'll grant you that."

"Maybe he shouldn't have. As Jim himself would say, lie down with dogs, get up with fleas, if you'll excuse the shift in metaphor."

"It's easy to say when you don't have a family to feed."

"Ah, the family to feed . . . The perfect excuse for unethical behavior. Are you saying that it's OK to hurt others if it is to provide for your loved ones? That the entire burden of morality falls on single people?"

Grace is pleased with the way she has just elevated the debate, but stung underneath by the reminder that Jim did have a family, an aspect of the situation she willfully disregarded during her whole relationship with him.

She tries to remember what she knew at the time. The wife did not seem to work, but was a big spender. The daughter, Cindy, the same age as Grace, was living at home, trying to decide on a career. There was also a son, whom Jim never talked about. Could he have been in some trouble? Was Jim buried in debt? What was the story with the wife, who now seems to be out of the picture? Was she sick, disabled, or mad? Did they love each other, against all evidence?

"I am not saying that," Mina answers quietly, flustered by the sweeping scope of Grace's arguments as much as by the anger in her voice, but determined to stay on a conciliatory track. "All I am saying is that Jim may not have been in a position to simply walk away from a well-paying job as soon as he realized it was a scam. So, he tried to turn the scam into something useful, like taking part in the Kuali project. I am sure that he would have succeeded, that *we* would have succeeded, if he hadn't got sick."

"All the same, he was lying when he said that as long as he worked at Pequeno, he worked for Pequeno. The whole time, he was taking orders from Fritz and Fritz only. And you saw for yourself that Fritz had zero interest in the Kuali project. So, I don't think we would have succeeded, even if Jim had not got sick."

"Maybe you're right. Maybe he would have lost that battle too. But don't you give him any point for trying?"

Mina turns her face toward Grace, her dark eyes overflowing with all the sadness in the world. Chastened, Grace puts her arms around her friend's neck.

"For your sake, and in the name of Christian love, I do."

"That's more like it," Mina says with a hitch of her chin, and adjusts her glasses to focus on the road again.

XX

DETECTIVE

"I-40 turnoff coming right up. See what a good navigator I am when I put my mind to it?"

"Outstanding! How far to Greensboro now?" asks Mina as she switches on the turn signal.

"A little over three hours. We're ahead of schedule. Shall we stop in Asheville to grab some lunch?"

"Don't we have some cheese crackers and a couple of oranges left? Remember that we have a Southern dinner waiting for us. If we keep making detours, we're going to end up *behind* schedule, I am afraid."

"But we don't want to get there early either, find Jim in the shower or something."

"God forbid! But if we have to cool our heels, I'd rather do it in Greensboro. We can drive around town, buy some wine, find a park, sit on the swings. It'll give us an opportunity to see where Jim comes from."

"You think that will give us some insight into his character?"

Mina completes the merge onto I-40 before answering.

"Don't worry so much about his character—or yours. Concentrate on the friendship. That's plenty real, or we wouldn't be here, would we?"

"But we haven't seen him in two years. And he's been really sick. What if we can't recognize him? What if we have nothing to talk about?"

"Of course we will recognize him. And didn't you read his last email? He's already lined up two topics of conversation: Pequeno and the Obama campaign. Trust him. He may be sick, but he is still his old sociable self. And his daughter Cindy will be there. She'll help us keep things in perspective. It's going to be fine, I promise you. So relax already, for my sake and in the name of Christian love."

"I'll try," says Grace doubtfully. That Christian love business she's rashly committed herself to is a little bit beyond her capabilities, she fears. But she is, indeed, willing to give it a try, with Mina's help. In the meantime, she could use some distraction.

"By the way, did you ever figure out where the sulfur smell came from in the new house? Is that why you no longer live there?"

"To answer your questions, yes, we did figure it out, and yes, it has something to do with the fact that we don't live there any more. But it's a long story, you sure you want to hear it?"

"The longer the better."

"I think I left things at the point when Samir went back to Pakistan in April 2006."

"And you thought the smell would disappear with him, but it didn't."

"That's right, it didn't. And it took a lot of detective work to find the real source. But first, I had to let go of my superstitions about it."

"Superstitions?"

"Yes, you know, the smell of sulfur is associated with the devil. That was one of the reasons I thought it came from Samir. I saw him as some kind of diabolical figure, so the smell fit him to a tee."

"Or maybe it was the smell that made you see him as a diabolical figure?"

"Could be. Either way, the two were linked in my mind. And then, because of the role that the statue of our Lady of Guadalupe had seemed to play in straightening my relationship with Tarik, I started feeling superstitious, like everything that happened to me was a sign from God. So, when Samir moved out and the smell continued, I started wondering if I was the one causing it, especially as I was the only one to smell it. I wracked my brain trying to find what sin I had committed to deserve this. And I found plenty to choose from, let me tell you."

"You, a sinner? Please do tell."

"Oh, you know, like buying the house had been motivated by pride and greed, like I had abandoned my parents and disowned my heritage, like I wasn't spending enough time with Steven, like I found other men than my husband attractive . . ."

"Jim, for instance?"

"Jim, TV actors, a guy at the swimming pool, nothing I would have acted on, but technically, it's still coveting."

"Don't you think your moral standards are a tad high? I mean, blaming yourself for merely finding some men attractive? What's wrong with that?"

"If nothing else, it's an escape."

"So, we escape in books, movies, nature. Life would be unbearable if we couldn't."

"Sure, but some escapes end up making your life look worse. Anyway, I know I wasn't thinking rationally. It was the smell that drove me crazy, making me feel like I must have done something dreadful, that I must figure it out and repent."

"You know, I experienced something similar when my Dad died, even though I am not religious."

"Yes, human beings are naturally superstitious, but superstition is quite a separate thing from religion. It was the pastor at Santa Magdalena who explained the difference to me, when I finally broke down and went to see him for the sacrament of reconciliation."

"What's that?"

"That's what they used to call confession. But you do it face to face, not through a grille like in the old days. What Fr. Gabriel explained to me is that superstition stems from fear, but faith stems from love."

"Wow! That sounds deep!" exclaims Grace, realizing that until this moment, she has blithely equated religion with superstition. But there is something in the distinction that immediately strikes her as true, even though she thinks she is much more familiar with the fear side of the equation. For what is love, other than an ephemeral, unreliable feeling, or the name we give to our obligations? How could it be transformed into faith? She thinks about Barack Obama, supremely intelligent, highly educated, self-assured, liberal, progressive, who claims that he has found faith. Assuming there is more to his claim than political posturing, how has he achieved this feat of alchemy? She will reflect at length on this conundrum in the months to come.

"I know, Fr. Gabriel is really deep. He listened to all my concerns, he told me he could see I had a lively conscience, to continue exercising to it, but that he thought my problem was chemical, not spiritual. The funny thing is that when I came out, I felt totally absolved."

"So, what did you do?"

"I switched to investigative mode. My first clue was that the air conditioner broke down just over a year after we moved in. Since we knew nothing about air conditioning systems, it did not occur to us to find this suspicious. We figured we couldn't afford the repairs, so we just decided to do without air conditioning. But a couple of weeks later, the fridge stopped working too. Now, a fridge, you can't live without. We called a repairman, who noticed that the coils on the back of the fridge were corroded right through. He said the fridge would have to be replaced. That didn't make any sense to me. The fridge was brand new. How could the coils have corroded so quickly? The fridge in our old house was thirty-year old if a day—it was painted that avocado green they didn't use after the seventies—and we had never replaced the coils that I knew of. I thought of asking him to take a look at the A/C unit, even though we were not planning to get it fixed. He found it had the same problem: the evaporator coils were covered with a black dust that was caused by corrosion. Suddenly I remembered how I had been puzzled by the way the light fixture in the upstairs bathroom seemed to have tarnished since we moved in. I showed it to him. He scratched his head, then he asked me if we had noticed lights flickering in the house, or if we often had to reset the circuit breakers for no apparent reason. I said we had. He scratched his head again, and said it was the third house in our development he was called to that had all these problems. I asked him if he had any idea what could be the cause. He didn't. I asked him if he could give me a list of the houses where he had been. He hemmed and hawed, and finally claimed he couldn't because of confidentiality. It was ridiculous. He wasn't a doctor or a lawyer, for Pete's sake. But I could see he wasn't going to budge, so I let it go. When Tarik came home, I told him about the repairman's visit. We started unscrewing electric plates in various rooms, and in every one of them, the ground wire was discolored. Same with the circuit breaker panel."

"So, there was some sulfuric compound in the air that corroded all the copper in the house and also caused the smell?"

"Exactly. It was Tarik who made the connection, because of his work in the oil refining business. He remembered that copper pipes can get corroded by a type of crude oil that contains sulfur and water. So we went online to look for articles on sulfur corrosion of copper. We did find a bunch of references on engineering sites, but nothing about copper corrosion in a residential context."

"That must have been frustrating. If you can't find something on Google, it's hard to believe it exists."

"But because of the physical evidence, I knew that I hadn't been imagining things. Like Fr. Gabriel said, it was a chemical, not a spiritual problem. And I knew that our house wasn't the only one affected."

"So did you go around the neighborhood trying to find which ones did?"

"Well, that would have taken a lot of time. There were about two hundred houses in the development. But also, I didn't feel comfortable knocking on doors around there. In a year of living in that house, we hadn't made any friend among our neighbors. Everybody worked hard, and many people had long commutes. You started hearing cars start at four o'clock in the morning, and you heard them dock back into their driveways as late at ten PM, sometimes with a load of kids who would start crying when their parents woke them up to get them into the house. During the day, the streets were completely deserted, all the alarm systems armed. Once, when I had taken the day off, I saw a coyote walk down the street in the middle of the afternoon. He was trotting along, his head high, looking idly around like he was in familiar territory, completely unfazed by my presence. I got the feeling that he owned the place much more than all the humans did."

"Doesn't sound like much of a community."

"No, it wasn't. It wasn't just that people didn't have time to be neighborly. I think they were all a little intimidated by their big new houses, vaguely suspecting that they did not deserve them, and leery of other people who had made the same choices. At least, that's how *I* felt."

"But couldn't you talk to the people at your church, or at your Interfaith committee?"

"I did, but none of them lived in my development, and none of them had a similar problem."

"So you were stymied."

"Yes, for months, we were stymied. During that time, we had to replace the TV, the DVD player, the microwave, and Tarik's computer. Needless to say, that didn't help our finances. I started hating that house. It was as if it was intent on destroying itself, and us. I needed to remind myself daily of Fr. Gabriel's words to avoid taking it personally. Tarik and I made bets about what piece of equipment would fail next. We nicknamed the house Hannibal, to rhyme with cannibal. So, what's Hannibal been up to today? I would ask when I came home. I was overjoyed when it hadn't done anything.

But then, during the Christmas vacation, we got another break. We were spending a few days at my parents, partly to get away from Hannibal. I went over to our old house across the street to collect the rent from the current tenants. The guy who opened the door was holding a bloody handkerchief to his nose. It made me think of Steven, who continued to have nosebleeds that the doctor told me not to worry about, but I did. I asked the man what was the matter with him. He explained that he was allergic to the drywall he had been installing. He was completely matter-of-fact about it. There was another guy in the house who had the same symptoms. I asked to talk to him too. The man with the nosebleed invited me in. Turned out there were six men living in the house I had thought too small for the three of us. They offered me coffee in my old kitchen. I noticed that it was neat as a pin. There was even an apron hanging from a hook next to the stove. Imagine that. Six guys and an apron. Working at the dirtiest, most back-breaking jobs, fifteen hundred miles from home, and they cooked with an apron on. It made me feel like crying.

None of the guys spoke any English, so I got to practice my rusty Spanish. It was hard going, I am ashamed to say, but I didn't think of calling my parents in. I was on a mission: I was going to get to the bottom of the mystery.

The six guys all came from the same village in Mexico, and they were all drywall installers. They had been lured to the Valley by the housing boom. Illegals, paid under the table, no health insurance of course, and a big fee on every money order they sent back to their families. Entire villages had been decimated of their men. And the reason Mexican workers were particularly in high demand was that the native, unionized drywall installers had started refusing to install drywall made in China, which was the most common type at the time, because they had figured out that it made them sick: headaches, asthma, nosebleeds, all kinds of respiratory problems. The Mexican workers couldn't afford to be that fussy. They choked, they bled, and went on working. They thought themselves lucky.

Later, I got a chance to talk to someone at the local branch of the Carpenter's union, and to a couple of contractors—one of them employed by Tiffany's husband, by the way. They had all heard about the Chinese drywall problem, but none of them wanted to be quoted on it. They pooh-poohed it as an urban legend with no scientific backing. When I asked them if they had done anything to establish that, they admitted they hadn't. They were all too busy making money to worry about anybody's health. And I guess homeowners were too concerned about property values to squawk either. That's probably why the problem did not surface on the Internet as long as the housing boom continued.

But we didn't wait that long. If the house was making Steven sick, we needed to do something about it right away. That very day, we went over to the big house with my dad and one of his tenants, and we ripped a wall apart to expose the back of the drywall. Sure enough it was made in China. So, we packed some clothes, loaded all the electronics we could on to my dad's truck, turned the alarm on, hoping it would hold out, and left like we had the devil at our heels."

"To return to the diabolical motif . . . which seems highly appropriate under the circumstances. So, that was, what, January 2007? I had already left Pequeno then, but Twiddledum and Twiddledee were still having the run of the place, right?"

"Right."

"God! Your whole life must have felt like a disaster zone. How come I never heard about any of this?"

"Well, it's not the kind of thing you write about in your Christmas letter, is it?"

"Why not? It would make for a much more gripping read than the wonderful trip to Fiji and how little Amelia is on the honor roll at her nursery school. Anyway, where did you go after you left Hannibal to fend for itself?"

"We moved in with my parents. We were lucky in our misfortune to have family to stay with. Some people in our development lived in motels for months, even while they were trying to keep up with their mortgage payments."

"So you managed to contact some of them?"

"Yes. I typed up a flier explaining what I had found out and asking anyone with the same issue to contact me. I made two hundred copies of the fliers on the office copier—with my own paper, mind you, but I still got a scolding from Tiffany, who, as it turned out later, had done much worse—and I dropped them off on every door step in the development. I tell you, I got to know my neighborhood much better after I left it. Not that it really improved my opinion of it. I mean, the houses looked pretty nice, architecturally. They weren't the type of cookie-cutter boxes with tar roofs and aluminum windows that you found in older developments. Lots of red tiles, gables, shutters, moldings, those squiggly things that support bay windows? . . . brackets, swimming pools, ceramic friezes, every house with its own decorative touches, like our own version of the OC."

"The osea?"

"You know, the TV series set in ritzy Newport Beach."

"I missed that one."

"Anyway, what I came to see is that the development had been made possible by exploited immigrant labor and knock-off materials made in China without any manufacturing controls. It was a sham, starting with the shutters that didn't shut, and the plastic brackets that didn't support anything, and we all bought it because we wanted to be like the Cohens."

"Who are the Cohens?"

"The family in the OC. Except we were not the Cohens, and we were going to pay dearly for our mistake."

"So you did find other people with the same drywall problem in your development."

"Yes, I heard from thirteen other families, all in the same area, the newest. Apparently, there was so much construction going on that American drywall manufacturers couldn't keep up. So, around 2004, suppliers started importing second-rate drywall from China that was contaminated with sulfur, they still don't know how. And that's what we got."

"But given that it was a construction defect, and that a whole bunch of you had the same problem, couldn't you force the developer to replace the bad drywall?"

"It wasn't just the drywall that needed replacing. The electrical circuitry also had to be redone. You're talking tens of thousands of dollars for each house. Add to that the replacement cost for the destroyed appliances, and rental expenses for the people who had moved out. We figured it was going to be an uphill battle to get compensated. So we got all the affected people together at my church to devise a strategy. We decided to put pressure on the developers. The developers referred us to the builders. We tackled the builders. They passed the buck to the subcontractors. The subcontractors pointed the finger at the suppliers, and the suppliers accused the manufacturers, who were conveniently located at the other end of the world, so that was the end of this particular line of attack. Then we tried to get our homeowners' insurances to kick in. The insurance companies must have had their own little powwows, because they all found various exclusion clauses in our policies that meant we weren't covered."

"It's like a Kafka story."

"Who is Kafka?"

"A Czech novelist. He wrote about absurd situations."

"Yeah, well, I could give Mr. Kafka a few pointers. Anyway, there we were. We couldn't live in our house, and we couldn't afford to get it fixed. And that's when the interest rate on our mortgage reset, at the very same moment that the housing boom went bust."

"Sorry, I know nothing about real estate. What does it mean that your interest rate reset?"

"It meant that our mortgage payments went up a huge amount all of a sudden. You see, we had got a type of mortgage—it's called ARM, for Adjustable Rate Mortgage—where you pay a low fixed interest rate for the first two years, and then the interest rate is adjusted to the current conditions, usually up. It's not that we didn't know about this, but when we bought the house, everyone assured us that by the time the interest rate reset, our house would have appreciated, and we would be able to refinance at a lower rate. What happened instead was that by May 2007, all the houses in the development had lost 30% of their value, even those without any drywall problem. *Our* house was basically worth nothing. So, we couldn't refinance, and we couldn't afford the increased payments. My parents were willing to sacrifice all their savings for us, but Tarik and I said no, we felt it would be throwing good money after bad. In the end, against the advice of all the professionals we talked to, we decided to simply walk away. The nice thing is that Tarik and I were in complete agreement about it. Still, it was a pretty scary decision to make. The professionals had all tried to make us feel like it would be immoral to renege on our debt, and then, in case that didn't do the trick, they appealed to our self-interest by warning us about the effect on our credit rating. So, when we finally told them we gave up on the house, it felt as if we were being excommunicated."

"Excommunicated from the Church of Consumerism. A fate worse than death . . ."

"It was the hardest on my parents. They're kind of old-world about money. But personally, I couldn't feel that obligated to the mortgage company or the bank. It turns out that they had steered us to this kind of risky and in the end very expensive ARM loan when in fact we qualified for a regular, fixed-interest-rate mortgage, because they all made more money that way. And apparently, there was a racial aspect to the scam, because every person of color I know who bought a house during the boom was given an ARM loan, but white people with the same income and credit rating often got regular loans."

"Why am I not surprised? But didn't you try to fight back?"

"Like how?"

"Sue the bank for discrimination. Sue the developers, builders, contractors, suppliers for malpractice, or whatever the term is for shoddy work and hazardous conditions."

"As a matter of fact, several class action suits have been filed about the toxic Chinese drywall problem, but we can't join them, since we no longer own the property. Anyway, it's going to take years of litigation, and in the end the lawyers will get most of the money. It's not worth the aggravation for us. We'd rather move on."

"If everybody thought like you, the big bastards would get away with murder."

"The big bastards always get away with murder. Whenever they lose a lawsuit, they just pass the cost on to the consumer, and get busy thinking up a new scam."

"So how can we improve the system? Do we have to start a revolution?"

"A moral revolution, maybe. Get everyone to live by the Golden rule, you know, to treat all others as they would want to be treated themselves, to stop being slaves to money . . ."

"The love of money if the root of all evil, Timothy 6:10."

Mina turns to Grace, astounded.

"How do you know that quote? Chapter and verse too!"

"Courtesy of Jim's catechism."

"Jim taught you about the Bible? And you doubt his character?"

"I wouldn't dare. But how did you end up moving back to your old house? Did your parents have to evict the drywall installers?"

"They wouldn't do that, and we wouldn't have let them do it either. It's a Golden Rule thing. What happened is that when the housing bubble burst, construction ground to a halt, and a lot of Mexican construction workers had to go home, including our drywallers. But they left me their apron as a parting gift because I had commented on it. They must have figured I found it pretty, which wasn't why it had attracted my attention. I guess my Spanish was even worse than I thought. Anyway, I didn't have the heart to throw it away after they left. It's still hanging in the kitchen, even though it clashes with the other colors in the room.

So, we moved back in, and after nearly a year of living at my parents, the old house looked spacious by comparison. We've decided to stay there. It's good to live close to my parents, for them and for us. And I feel more comfortable in the old neighborhood, even if it's crowded and a little seedy. Every day I count my blessings."

"You are indeed a dangerous renegade, my dear friend, as harmless as you may look. And what about Steven's nosebleeds, by the way?"

"Gone as soon as we left the big house. The pediatrician swears there won't be any long-term effects. As I said, I count my blessings."

XXI

PIVOTAL

Squatting on his heels on the narrow footpath that winds from the front porch to the driveway, Jim is attempting the long-admired stance of a Middle Eastern shopkeeper on his doorstep: an attentiveness free of expectations, an unselfconscious presence to the bustle of the outside world, an inner composure. Or to put it in the language of his stoner days (and precious few those were), he is trying to be here now.

Except that the street in front of him is far from bustling, the possibility of any foot traffic (runners, dog walkers, kids on skateboards, recycling poachers) deliberately foreclosed in this strictly residential neighborhood by the absence of sidewalks. Except that after two minutes, his leg muscles ache so much from the no longer familiar position that he has to compromise by sitting on the porch stairs instead. Except that he is conscious of offering a strange sight to any neighbor tempted to peek out of their shrubbery-concealed windows. And except that his brain is abuzz with so many expectations and counter-expectations that he can barely take notice of his surroundings. Yet he persists, feeling a little bit like the man in the old Sufi story who is looking under the street light for the key he lost in his house, because it's too dark inside to find anything. But what kind of key has he lost?

The morning has gone relatively well. The pulled pork is simmering in the crockpot, the coleslaw is macerating in the fridge, the sweet potatoes are peeled and cubed and covered in water on the stove top. By the time he got to the hush puppies, however, Jim had a wicked attack of nausea. Luckily he remembered that Grace can't abide fried foods anyway. Cindy will buy some biscuits or a loaf of bread along with the key lime pie. She is gone now on an outing with some girlfriends. She offered to change her plans, but Jim told her to go. She doesn't have many opportunities for fun these days, and he can use the time alone to reflect. She has promised to be back by three-thirty to help set the table, but he has gone ahead and unearthed a tablecloth and four napkins, which he has washed and ironed and laid out in place on the kitchen dinette—good thing the table is built-in, or they would have had to eat on their knees. And then, while he was in a rummaging frame of mind, he retrieved the Fed Ex box in which, at his request, Grace packed the personal effects left in his office once it became obvious to everyone he would never return to El Pequeno. There, among the business cards and memo pads, he found the pile of CDs she burned for his entertainment and instruction while he was undergoing his first round of chemo. They were still folded in the piece of gauzy black and gray cloth that had merely seemed a fanciful alternative to bubble wrap at the time he received the package, but in which he now recognized the fabric of the skirt she wore when they went to see a movie together.

He never told her how lovely she looked that night, or how wonderful she smelled, because that would have confirmed her belief that they were on a date. But as he stroked the swishy fabric, remembering how intensely he had felt like pawing it then, in the car, in the movie theater, in the restaurant, and congratulating himself again on his unfailing restraint, he remembered something else: how he was the one who had asked her out, and this in a shifty, loaded manner that could leave little doubt, in her mind or his own, about his amorous intentions, and how it was in fact the fear of being seen with her in public by some blabbermouth of a District employee that had caused him to keep his distance. Even so, on the way back, he recalled desperately wishing her to make a move toward him that would absolve him of any responsibility in the ensuing sexual interlude. Fortunately—unfortunately—she was too smart to fall into that trap. During the few weeks they had left together, she didn't seem to resent him for stringing her along in such an ungentlemanly manner. But her personal disappointment in him, soon augmented by her frustration with his less talented successors, might explain why she eventually stopped writing to him.

The CDs were an eclectic mix: Handel, Rameau (he had to look that one up), Miles Davis, and some Gen Y pop group that Grace would not expect him to know about. Why, in two years, had he never listened to them? Now that he wanted to make up for lost time, he no longer had any stereo equipment. That's when he remembered that Cindy listened to music on her desktop. Pretty emblematic of how far down he has fallen that he should get any hi-tech tip from his technophobic daughter. He set his laptop on the windowsill, plugged Cindy's speakers into it, inserted one of the CDs into the drive, and lo and behold, without having to install any driver, his laptop became a record player. The CD he had picked randomly turned out to be the one by the Gen Y pop group. It was electronic music, but surprisingly inoffensive, with layered contrasting beats and inventive melodic riffs on a sort of upbeat minimalist foundation. No hint of a generation conflict there. As he listened, he caught a definite Middle Eastern motif, and recognized the care Grace had taken in putting together her musical care package. It made him feel even more of a cad.

But it may have been the Middle Eastern theme that prompted him to open the window and step outside, to see if aided by that soundtrack, he might find a way to re-enter his life. It occurs to him that this is the key he has lost, the key to his own existence, and he knows exactly when it happened: Tuesday, March 7, 2006.

He had gone home the previous weekend, and had fallen asleep so deeply on the plane that the stewardess had to wake him up when they landed. He looked up at her uncomprehendingly, her smile seeming to float several inches away from her face. Her fingers on his arm felt cold and wet. He realized his shirt was drenched in sweat. While he waited for a cab, he did something he hadn't done in years: he made an appointment with his family doctor.

By the time he shook the old guy's hand the next day, he had come up with his own diagnosis: mono, a teenager's affliction—but fitting the circumstances to a tee. It was just what he deserved, after all, falling in love with a girl his daughter's age, even if they had not exchanged any bodily fluids. The doc, no doubt unwilling to be shown up, proceeded to ask him to undress, and then to poke at every inch of his body, all the while eliciting details about his tiredness, night sweats and weight loss. The doc found two additional swollen lymph nodes, aside from the one on his neck, one under his arm, one in his groin. He asked if they hurt. Jim said no, thinking that would about wrap up the case, but the doc sent him over to the hospital next door to get a biopsy, just in case—just in case the hospital wasn't making enough of a profit, Jim thought.

It was a waste of time, but he went anyway. He had his laptop with him, he could work just as well in a waiting room as at home, maybe better. He paid no attention to what he was being told or what was being done to him. The procedure didn't even hurt that much. He didn't tell Joleen about any of it when he got home.

He flew back to California on Monday, feeling a little better. On Tuesday evening, his cell phone rang while he was in the shower. Harold Steinberg, said the message screen. For a second, he had no idea who that was. When he realized it was the family doctor, his first reaction was to be irritated. In his El Pequeno refuge, he had imagined himself safely out of range of North Carolina medical shenanigans.

Dr. Steinberg had received the biopsy results and urged Jim to call him back at this earliest convenience. There was something creepy in the very warmth that zigzagged through the old guy's tremulous voice. It was already ten o'clock in Greensboro, why wasn't the good doctor in bed instead of harassing his patients? Anyway, Jim figured he might as well get the return call over with. Within the space of a sentence, he found himself blown out of the world he knew and dumped into the limbo where he has vegetated for the last two years. The name of the explosive: Hodgkin's lymphoma, in other words CANCER. Further tests would be needed to determine its extent, but the long and short of it was that Jim was going to have to take a leave of absence from his job, starting the very next week, for how long, the good doctor couldn't say.

He was sitting on his anonymous couch, already experiencing the relief that comes with the dawning sense of absurd discontinuity you get just before waking from a dream. The next thing he knew, he was tapping the knocker on Grace's door, only aware that there was light and music inside. The door opened as if by magic. She was standing a foot from him, in floppy pants and a bulky sweater, her head wrapped in a towel, her face backlit, which did not prevent him from registering the quick succession of feelings: surprise (she was expecting someone else), joy (thank God, she was happy to see him anyway), and dismay (she had already guessed that he brought bad news) that played on her features. It was only then that he asked himself what he was doing.

"Hi there," she said nonchalantly, proving that she was perfectly capable of exquisite tact when necessary. "Come in! Come in!"

He walked into a tropical climate that felt as if it emanated from her.

"I have to dry my hair. Make yourself comfortable," she cried out as she disappeared around a wall.

He found himself in the kind of situation he relished the most: free to assess at length the environment in which he was to make his next strategic move. The first thing he noticed, he has to admit, was the couch, a Victorian sofa with a carved wooden frame, plushly upholstered in red velvet, and big enough to hold two entwined bodies, but covered with pieces of fabric pinned to their paper patterns, on top of which, oblivious to the risk of injury, a gray Persian cat slept with his paws over its eyes. It was the cat Jim had seen scratching at the door the night he had driven by Grace's while she was away in Pasadena.

She sewed. How come he didn't know about it? The sewing machine was on a long table in front of the window, on which also stood a laptop, a cell phone, a flower arrangement in a vase, and various sewing implements. The shades, made of fabric, perhaps by her, were down, insuring privacy. The room had a fireplace, empty now, but with logs stacked on the side. On the mantelpiece, Jim noticed a framed color photograph of a man and a girl. The man wore a European-style evening jacket and a black bow-tie, an attire he seemed to have been born in. He had a handsome, entitled-looking face, a high forehead partially covered by a shock of thick dark hair, and the kind of lines around the eyes you don't get from worrying about your mortgage. He was turned toward the girl, and the look of adoration on his face made clear that she was his daughter. The girl herself was looking at something off-camera. She was twelve or thirteen years old, in a shiny dark-blue dress with some kind of ruffle around the neck, long dark hair of the same sleek, bouncy texture as her father's held on one side by a barrette, her upper lip touchingly distended by a retainer. It was in the humorous fearlessness of the goggling blue eyes that Jim recognized Grace.

The rest of the décor was what you would expect from a Millennial haunt: posters with foreign lettering, collages of well-known and more obscure pictures probably meant to be taken ironically (Arnold Schwarzenegger with a milk mustache?), a little shrine of ladies' hats from the forties and fifties in a corner, a fridge door plastered with snapshots of friends in adventurous settings, a bicycle and a pair of skis propped against the back wall like furnishings in their own right. What surprised Jim was that the music, none other than Bob Dylan's John Wesley Harding, came from an old-fashioned LP, a whole collection of which was crammed on one of the shelves around the fireplace.

The music stopped just as the sound of the hair-dryer died down in the faraway bathroom. It occurred to Jim to look for another album to play, which would give him a countenance when Grace returned, but he couldn't face the effort of figuring out what would fit the mood. The truth was, if his powers of observation were as keen as ever, and the information they collected as apt to orient his strategy, it was as if this purposeful curiosity of his was now a mere running banner at the bottom of his mental screen. The top part was completely blank, a massive blizzard of pain and incomprehension.

"Sorry to keep you waiting," Grace said in an unfamiliar gracious-hostess lilt as she reappeared in the room, her hair sticking out electrically in every direction. She had changed into jeans and a less bulky sweater. Her feet were bare, their daintiness accentuated by the half moons of pink varnish over her toe nails.

"You sew," he managed to say.

"Yep. Measure twice, cut once, that's my motto."

"You must have laughed every time you heard me say it. Why didn't you tell me?"

"Because you never asked."

"Fair enough."

"And now can *I* ask you a question?"

"Depends," he growled, feeling himself rounding his shoulders against the approaching storm.

She came closer, looked up at him searchingly. Her childish toes wiggled as if they were themselves brimming with questions.

"I am getting worried," she said, still sounding half-playful, half-coaxing. "What's wrong?"

"I can't tell you," he replied with stupid stubbornness.

Her face turned pale, then reddened. When she spoke again, it was in anger.

"Yes, you can, and you are going to. You can't come over here to dangle some horrid news in front of me, and then not tell me what it is."

"If I tell you, you have to promise two things."

"What?"

"That you won't tell anyone else, and that you won't cry."

He had no sooner dictated this last condition that her eyes filled with tears.

"See why I don't want to tell you?" he grumbled, well aware of his cruelty, but unable to act any other way. He felt weak enough as it was, he couldn't bear the additional burden of her sadness.

He saw her bravely strangle her anger. She pressed her fingers against her eyes and replied in a softer voice.

"Never mind if I cry. Just tell me."

And so he told her. At the first mention of cancer, she grabbed his wrists. "Oh my God!" she whispered, all the color draining from her face, as if she was retreating into herself to confront some awful memory. Jim was suddenly reminded that her elegant daddy was in fact dead, may have died from cancer for all he knew. For the first time in their relationship, he felt truly remorseful over the harm he may have caused her, strangely enough—or perhaps not so strangely—in the one instance where the harm was not the result of his actions.

By the time he finished his tale, they had both regained a semblance of composure. After all, many people beat cancer, the doctor himself had said that the survival rate for Hodgkin's was 80%, a statistic that had not registered in his mind until that moment. He would go home to complete his treatment, but he would remain in charge of the IT department. Grace would be his eyes and ears, they would correspond regularly, they would continue to plan the Kuali migration. He would come back. What neither of them mentioned, though it weighed heavily on their hearts, was that they were going to be physically apart for many months, if not forever.

But they were physically close right now, Jim standing with his back to the empty fireplace, Grace in front of him, her hands still clutching his wrists. The running banner at the bottom of his brain was flashing arguments for the repeal of the fraternization interdict:

sick man deserves all the comfort he can get . . . one-night stand unlikely to lead to the divulgation of trade secrets . . . Grace officially enlisted in CIO's personal team . . . Minimal risk of professional repercussions . . . I want her, I want her, I want her . . .

"Would you like some tea?" she asked, as if she too felt the need for a change of pace.

"Don't you have anything stronger than that?"

"You're in luck. I have some whiskey," she said brightly, walking toward the kitchen area.

"Just what the doctor ordered. Can I move some of the fabric off the couch so we can sit?"

"Go ahead. The cat too. Her name is Sugar. She belongs to the landlords, in fact, not that you'd know it from the way she takes her ease here."

By the time she came back, holding two jelly glasses half-filled with alcohol, he had cleared the whole couch. She still looked a little pale from their harrowing talk, but her eyes were big with a more promising kind of apprehension. She was going to give herself to him, in sorrow and in joy, and he was going to forget his troubles by cherishing her to the best of his ability.

"I forgot. Do you want ice in your drink?"

"Naw. It's fine," he said, holding out his hand for the glass, unwilling to let her out of his sight one minute longer.

He sat down at one end of the couch. She sat down at the other end, tucking her bare feet under her. The ball was in his court, and this time he wasn't going to fumble it.

"Come over here," he stammered, his voice hoarse from the emotional roller-coaster of the last hour.

She understood his body language if not his words, and was already nudging herself closer, when there was a knock at the door. She rolled her eyes, but went to answer it.

"I came to collect my cat," he heard a male voice say. "It's time for her pill."

The landlord. He hadn't even said hello. Just to confirm his proprietary rudeness, he now strode into the room without permission, his heavy footsteps rattling the window panes. He looked like the proverbial bull in the china shop: a shaved head with a pugnacious low brow, a thick neck, an oversized torso and foreshortened legs, a hard paunch that could double as a battering ram. Very friendly for all that, the friendliness of the guy who has no clue he is not wanted.

He came straight at Jim with his hand extended. Grace had no choice but to make the introductions.

"Gordon, my landlord. Jim, my boss."

Damn the girl's honesty. Why did she have to introduce him as her boss? Now he was going to have to behave like one. But it was worse than that, because the landlord turned out to be a computer groupie. Before long, he had involved Jim in a discussion of the future of cloud computing and hand-held devices, while Grace fetched another glass of whiskey and pulled the desk chair out for him. In the meantime, the cat had hopped back on the couch, stretching itself luxuriously between Jim and Grace.

As the conversation went on, filling the narrow band of his consciousness lately occupied by the rationalizations of lust, the rest of Jim's brain went from snowy to a murky black. Not a blizzard but a wooden box at the bottom of a hole in the ground, every word thudding on its lid like a shovelful of dirt. He was going to die, and it was just as well. Without work his life had no meaning, and the only other thing he wanted he wasn't going to get, he could see now. It wasn't just that the landlord's total lack of flirtatiousness toward Grace reminded him of the shocking age difference between them. He thought of her dead father, and realized he couldn't in conscience involve her any deeper in a relationship that she was shortly going to be bereft of. Sure, he had heard of the ease with which her generation "hooked up", as if sex was no more consequential than a game of checkers, but he was old enough to know better. So, in the end, it was his moral conscience, not any business consideration, that prompted him to get up from the couch. This much he can be proud of, even if it took the landlord's untimely visit to bring him around.

"But I should probably let you guys get back to work," the landlord said, suddenly considerate.

"It's alright. We're done. I need to get myself to bed. I am a little under the weather," Jim answered magnanimously.

"I'd better get home too," the landlord said. "Or my wife is going to think the cat has run away."

He scooped the cat up from the couch while Grace gave Jim a full-body hug.

"See you tomorrow."

"Sleep tight."

"Hope you feel better."

"Say hello to Linda and the kids for me."

The door closed on the two men. They shook hands and went their separate ways.

Strangely enough, once Jim and Grace had given up on sex, their relationship took on a quality of pure sweetness such as he had never known. It is literally what propped him up during the next few days, when an overwhelming sense of futility constantly sapped his efforts to put his business affairs in order before he went away. Mindful of the need to keep his illness under wraps, Grace forbore to fuss about him at the office, but a mere hello from her felt like a shot of pain killer. From the empty shell of his office, the door to which he kept open the whole time, he listened to her tapping determinedly on her keyboard, helping Mina set up new scheduler variables, acknowledging Elmore for the niftiness of his code, sorting out some billing problem with the accounting staff, and felt reassured that the world was not coming to an end.

On Wednesday night they attended a Board meeting together. The teachers had finally ratified their new contract, but it was clear they had not buried the hatchet. During the break, one of them came over to chat Grace up while Jim was talking to Bob Johnson. It was the guy who had proposed the Linux deal. Jim had since learned that he was one of the main conspirators behind the Save Pequeno campaign. Even from a distance, the forced geniality of his manner toward Grace was so obvious that Jim figured he must be fishing for some information he could use against Hartbridge and hence against the Chancellor. Jim thought of warning her to watch her mouth around the guy, then decided not to. She would follow her conscience, as *she* always did, and wherever that led her would be fine with him, Hartbridge be damned. All he wanted at this point was to sit next to her, to abandon himself to the loving warmth of her body against his.

On Thursday they went to lunch. It was a cold and rainy day. She said she wanted soup. He proposed a Vietnamese restaurant half a block ahead, its garish marquee dissolving between each pass of the windshield wipers. And though the place looked like the kind of dive that serves imitation crab and seasons every dish with MSG, she agreed. Miraculously, they found a parking spot right in front of the restaurant. They ran across the eight feet of sidewalk, and came in breathless and laughing as if they had just won a marathon. There was a free table in a corner, far from the door and close to a heater. Grace made a show of smoothing out the paper napkin wrapped around the chopsticks, then placing its ten square-inches demurely in her lap. The dimple on her left cheek was like a star. The busboy brought a pot of hot tea and she poured it out for him, recapitulating their entire relationship with this simple gesture of filial devotion. They both ordered chicken soup, and he wasn't far from believing in its curative powers as he drank it, so whole he felt at that moment. They talked about food. He bragged about his cooking skills.

"You're really a Jack of all trades," she said admiringly.

"And a master of none," he sighed in reply.

She smirked at him, calling his self-deprecating bluff. She wasn't going to let him chip at his own pedestal.

"One day, I'll fix a real Southern meal for you and Mina," he promised, so wrapped up for the moment in their little dream world that no wish seemed too absurd. When he looked back at her, she was crying. He let her sadness be.

On the way back, she took his hand, and held it until they reached the District parking lot. It was the closest they ever got to a declaration of love. And it was to be their real goodbye. He spent the afternoon in meetings, and the next morning, when he went into her office for a last embrace, he found Myrtle biting as his heels, hell bent on not letting go. As he was officially only leaving for a long weekend, he could not even justify a public hug.

"I'm out of here. You're in charge," he said lamely, resorting in his mute distress to their ritual parting phrase.

As Myrtle was standing behind him, he couldn't tell how she greeted his passing of the baton to Grace, but he was rather pleased that she was there after all. It occurred to him that his dear girl was going to need this blessing of her authority.

"Take care," she answered in the same standard way, and pivoted her chair back toward her monitor, probably to hide her tears. As his eyes glided away from the slope of her neck, where he had unconsciously searched for the question mark tattoo though it had been hidden under her hair for months, he noticed her one monitor, and remembered ordering Ruby many months ago to provide her with a second one. His order had never been executed, and he had let it slide. So much for his Good Samaritan pretensions.

But Myrtle must have got his message, because by the time he turned to face her she was gone.

He ambled down the corridor, carrying his laptop and garment bag. Elmore was in his office, drawing a flowchart for some unknown customer on his white board, but seeing Jim pass by, insisted on conducting a formal round of introductions. Jim complied, his misery slightly allayed for a second by Elmore's obvious pride in his boss.

Next door, Ruby was sitting on her medicine ball, looking very much like Mother Goose brooding a gigantic egg. Both her hands wrapped in carpal tunnel splints, her head wedged between her monitors, she was abstractedly twirling a strand of limp hair. Jim noticed several new yoga posters on her walls. Her latest fad, probably—and no more likely to do her any good than the previous ones. She didn't seem to be aware of Jim's presence, and he decided not to call it to her attention.

He ran into Sandra, who was on her way to the bathroom or lunchroom. She asked him if he had heard anything about her promotion. "Not yet," he answered, the truth being that he had done nothing about it. It was one of the chores he would have to ask Grace to take over.

Rajiv poked his head over the top of his cubicle, and Wei, on his way out to smoke a cigarette, shook his hand.

He stopped by Mina's desk. She was engrossed in a phone conversation that didn't seem to be going well. But she shot him a glance over her glasses, broke out into her best smile, and waved him goodbye. She had not guessed that he was sick, and it made him feel less so.

He also got a perfunctory wave from Tiffany, and an histrionic salute from Sandip, who was pacing the parking lot while talking on his cell phone. His departure felt like the tape of his arrival playing in reverse. The question was, what had he achieved in between, other than a change of furniture? But this was no time for assessments. He got in his rental car and drove away.

The night before, he had finally bethought himself to prepare Joleen for his return. She surprised the heck out of him by taking the news in stride. Perhaps her very lack of empathy prevented her from perceiving the gravity of the situation. In any case, beyond some I-told-you-so remarks to the effect that his constant traveling was bound to make him sick at some point, she did not complain about a turn of event that was sure to cramp her style for the foreseeable future. In fact, she not only came to fetch him at the airport that night, but over the many months of his first treatment, she diligently drove him to all his medical appointments, made countless trips to the pharmacy, bought a flat screen TV for his bedroom, fended Fritz off when necessary, arranged a steady stream of visits from all their friends, wrote thank-you cards for the flowers and casseroles and prayer meetings they were showered with, all the while treating him with the distracted indulgence of a mother toward a malingering kid. She gave no indication that she had a lover waiting in the wings. And Jim has to admit that if anything could have helped him out of the black pit of despair into which he had fallen, her perky obliviousness might have been more effective than Grace's sorrowful concern, which continued to ooze through her emails and phone calls. As to Cindy, as long as her mother occupied center stage in the drama of his illness, she retreated into her unwelcome-guest shell.

He himself was of no help, snarling at his wife, surly with friends, suspicious of doctors, disgusted with his body, uninterested in anything else. The reason Joleen gave for her eventual desertion was that he had sabotaged his own healing, and whatever her real motives may have been, he can't deny that she had a point. He thinks back on the optimistic, driven, pragmatic man who walked into the Pequeno data center a mere three years ago, and can't figure out what happened to him. Was he killed by cancer—or the drugs he had to take against it—or was he always a precarious façade?

He had always been confident in his inner resources, nurtured by youthful spiritual explorations and later strengthened through years of exile. He had never succumbed to the lure of self-importance. He did not presume that he was favored by God, that he was entitled to a long healthy life. He did not really care about the trappings of success. He didn't think the purpose of life was to have fun. Yet when health, success and pleasure were taken away from him, he found his inner resources forsaking him too. He could not muster hope, or faith, or stoicism. And so, in wretched bitterness, he let himself be carried along the torrent of things beyond his control, from treatment to remission to relapse to his wife's abandonment. If it hadn't been for his gradual realization that Cindy needed him, he would have wished for nothing but a speedy death.

The Gen Y group having shot its wad, Jim has replaced it with the Rameau CD, a harpsichord suite whose title suggests it has something to do with bird calls. It is a charming piece, both stately and sprightly, the tinkling tone of the harpsichord in perfect harmony with the nippy spring air. Another good choice on Grace's part—no trace in it of human angst. At the top of a still leafless locust tree across the street, a mockingbird is working on its own composition. Jim wonders what it thinks of Rameau, whether it might be inspired by his tunes, themselves apparently plagiarized from some French birds. But no, this bird is completely impervious to classical music. Its song continues to sound like a succession of unimaginative ring tones, interrupted by bouts of aerial dancing, when the bird lifts itself straight up in the air and then swoops crazily around, flashing the white on its wings, until it drops back on its branch and starts singing again. Trying to please a female, no doubt.

There are also squirrels abroad. A couple of them are chasing each other up the trunk of an oak tree, the one that's being pursued turning back every so often to taunt its pursuer, its body upside down, its ears pinned back, its claws firmly planted in the bark, its fluffy tail wagging in squirrelly trash talk. And then they're off again, swinging so fast from branch to twig that they seem to escape gravity, shrieking all the while like a couple of kids on a merry-go-round. At ground level, a more sedate member of the family is sniffing around in the grass, trying to locate the acorns it buried last fall. Finding one, it digs it out, clamps it in its mouth, and scrambles up the stump of the ancient pecan tree that Joleen ordered cut down to make room for her rock garden. From the safety of this perch, it surveys the surrounding landscape of dirt clods, looking as if its opinion of it is no higher than Jim's. At last, its appraisal completed, its takes the acorn in its hands, peels off a section of skin with its teeth, and proceeds to enjoy a meditative snack.

A whirring sound is approaching along the street. Jim looks across the lawn, and in a gap between the trees and bushes, sees a flash of bicycles speeding by. There were four or five of them, all mounted by kids who looked Vietnamese, the leader no more than fourteen years old, improbably dressed in a black trench coat and porkpie hat, the coat's tails flying behind him like a banner, the expression on his face, in the fraction of a second that it was visible, one of unalloyed freedom. The vision, brief as it was, unlocks something in Jim's heart. Not a memory exactly, but a memory-like identification with the youth, a sense of the wonder of the world he rides through. Jim feels as if he is inside the adventurous boy, inside the practical squirrel, inside the showboating bird. The trees bend their branches toward him, the grass slope rolls up to his feet. The sun shines on his face. Just like that, life has re-entered him.

He notices that the forsythia is in bloom. He goes to the garage, finds a pair of rusty shears, cuts a few branches of the yellow blossoms. They will make a fine flower arrangement on the coffee table.

XXII

REPENTANT

From the /My Documents/Pequeno/Grace/ folder on Jim's laptop:

From: Grace.Kirchner@Pequeno.edu
Date:Wednesday, March 15, 2006
To:Myrtle.Gatewick@hartbridge.com
Cc: Jim.Wright@Pequeno.edu
Subject: Areas of Responsibility

To summarize our agreement of today:

- As prescribed by my job title, I assume full responsibility for the development, maintenance and operations/scheduling of all Pequeno business applications, whether on the mainframe or Windows servers, batch or online.

- Given our respective areas of expertise, I also assume primary responsibility for the resolution of mainframe system problems. But I will consult with you in cases where the integrity of the system may be at stake, or when problem resolution will entail additional expenses.

- You assume full responsibility for faculty and staff PC hardware/software installation and maintenance.

- We will both immediately refer to each other any problem in the other's area of responsibility, except in case of absence. We will assist the other only when asked for help.

We are currently very short-staffed. We need to avoid duplications of effort, as well as the appearance that lines of authority are unclear. Please let me know of any correction that should be made to the above agreement.

There is no evidence in the folder, Jim notices with a pang, that he ever ratified Grace's proposed pact with Myrtle. But he can easily read between her message's lines. He had no sooner turned his back that Myrtle must have tried to assume control of the IT department, in spite of the official chain of command which gave that role to Grace, and in disregard of Jim's—admittedly off-hand—reminder. Jim can see the situation from Myrtle's point of view. She was only answerable to Fritz, and Fritz needed to preserve the impression that Hartbridge consultants were fully in charge. The problem was that Myrtle was not quite up to the job. Jim imagines her sticking her nose in some programming or operational issue in her flat-footed imitation of helpfulness, and Grace, in the midst of her sorrow, getting her dander up and laying down the law. Grace won that round. Two days later, Myrtle resigned from Hartbridge, supposedly to attend to her husband's health problems.

By then, Jim's Hodgkin's had been "staged" as IVb. At best, his treatment was going to take many months, but as his popularity was essential to the upcoming renewal of the Hartbridge contract, the nature of his illness was not communicated to anyone at Pequeno aside from Grace, who dutifully kept it a secret. With Myrtle gone too, Fritz had to scramble to find two substitute consultants for the Pequeno site. From Grace's later emails, Jim got the impression that she liked them even less than Myrtle. Granting that the new guys may have been less than ideal choices, picked in an emergency as they had been, Jim always assumed that Grace's unhappiness with them was mostly a function of her attachment to him. Now he wonders whether he missed some deeper problem, whether his very inattention to it was what caused her to drop the friendship.

From: Grace.Kirchner@Pequeno.edu
Date:Monday, March 27, 2006
To:melvin.grossbach@hartbridge.com;   jonas.tosser@
hartbridge.com
Cc: Jim.Wright@Pequeno.edu
Subject: Areas of Responsibility

On behalf of the team, I wish to welcome you both to the
Pequeno IT department. We appreciate your willingness
to fill in for Jim and Myrtle at a moment's notice, and will
do our best to help you come up to speed on the work left
unfinished by your predecessors.

In lieu of the orientation meeting you have been unable
to fit into your schedules so far, let me state in writing my
own areas of responsibility.

As Assistant Director/Applications Manager, I:

- Oversee all applications development and
  maintenance
- Supervise operations staff
- Communicate with systems programming personnel
  (outsourced)
- Approve all personnel actions and purchasing
  requests
- Keep track of the IT budget
- Act as CIO in Jim's absence

I assume that you have been briefed on Hartbridge's
projects. To my knowledge, they consist of the following:

- Disaster Recovery Plan: this was Myrtle's project.
  The due date was March 15.
- New faculty laptops. Myrtle was helping the Director
  of Network Services and Distance Education, Peter
  Santelli, manage this project. Peter will have a copy
  of the project plan.

- Wireless network at the Piedmont campus. Also co-managed by Myrtle and Peter Santelli. Refer to Peter for more information.
- Kuali application systems migration. This was Jim's and my project. I have a copy of Jim's proposal. There is no project plan yet, pending the Chancellor's approval of the concept.

Please do not hesitate to contact me if you have any question on the above or any other IT topic.

Funny how time changes your perspective. When Jim first received this message, he took it at face value as a courteous gesture of welcome toward his colleagues on Grace's part. He remembers experiencing a mixture of relief and sadness at the smoothness of the transition, and wishing all of them well. But now, underneath the polite verbiage, he perceives the intent that should have been obvious to him then: her frantic effort to assert her authority in the face of the new consultants' apparent disregard. In truth, he has no trouble believing that the two rookies may have behaved from the start like a conquering army: disdainful of the local power structure, oblivious to the natives' sensibilities, happy to insulate themselves within a fortified green zone—a fairly common attitude on the part of management consultants in those days of triumphant empire, and one that Jim himself might have been tempted to adopt were it not for his long friendship with one of the conquered in the person of Waheed.

What he can't imagine, never having met the two men, is the feeling of utter desolation that overcame Grace at the first sight of them. It wasn't just that their arrival marked another stage in her mourning. Right away, she perceived that the only thing they had in common with Jim was the tailored suits. They were both short and portly, Melvin on the flabby side and Jonas more like a swollen wrestler. They were both balding, Melvin still resorting to the comb-over ruse, Jonas satisfied with an eighth-of-an-inch buzz cut that exposed all sections of his scalp equally. They both wore expressions of thwarted dominance: irascible, suspicious, mulish, with an additional note of perfidy on Melvin's face. Neither of them looked very bright, although it was possible to detect a glimmer of commonsense in Jonas' round eyes. Needless to say, neither of them was gifted with the least amount of charisma.

Still, Grace would have reserved judgment if Melvin and Jonas had not immediately proceeded to prove her first impressions right.

First they did not bother to introduce themselves to anyone except Tiffany, whom they obviously expected to act as their secretary. Grace assumed they were in for a surprise, but the surprise was Grace's when by and by, Tiffany started complying with their expectations. Given the role the Data Center Queen later played at the time of the contract renewal, and remembering the Hartbridge retreat episode, Grace eventually concluded that she must have been offered some kind of bribe for her cooperation.

Next, even though neither of them had been conferred a managerial title by the District authorities, they had the gall to requisition Stanley's old office, thereupon engaging in a shouting match about which one of the two would get it—a scene reported with horror by Mina, who heard the whole thing thanks to a trick of the air conditioning vents. In the end, probably following Fritz's arbitration, they contented themselves with Myrtle's old office and the empty room next to it. To maintain the fiction of Jim's imminent return until the signature of the new contract, his office was left alone. It was at that time, or shortly thereafter, that Grace and Mina nicknamed them Twiddledum and Twiddledee. Their respective places in the hierarchy were never clarified.

Undeterred by Twiddledum and Twiddledee's flagrant snub, Grace had taken the initiative to introduce herself to them at the end of the first day, had handed each one a business card with her title prominently displayed on it, had proposed an orientation meeting. Their eyes had glazed over. Even after her subsequent clarifying email, which they left unanswered, they continued to ignore her to the same degree they ignored the rest of the staff, which had the (probably designed) effect of sapping the small amount of authority she had acquired under Jim's tenure. Later, in one of his more congenial moments, Jonas would confess that it had taken him two months to realize she was a manager. What had apparently opened his eyes was to find her in attendance at the only one of the supposedly monthly

Managers Meetings that actually took place during Grace's entire managerial stint. Jonas' confession seems so incredible to Grace now that if she were to write a memoir of her Pequeno times, she would not include it for fear of being denounced as a fabricator.

Under Twiddledum and Twiddledee's reign, the aspect of Jim's management style that had made Grace most uncomfortable, the mysterious bits of business he frequently conducted behind closed doors or away from the office altogether, became generalized. Both of them kept their office doors locked and their shades down at all times, absented themselves for days or weeks without any explanation, talked exclusively on their own cell phones, never printed any document on the public printers, did not publish their schedules in Outlook, were not even connected to the District network. Their hallway conversations were carried in an often angry whisper. They avoided the lunch room altogether. After a while, the staff started imitating their secretive habits. It got to the point where walking down the corridor, you couldn't tell if anyone was in, except Mina, whose desk was completely exposed to view, and Tiffany, who, heedless of the receptionist functions listed in her job description, started petitioning for an office of her own. Grace herself kept her door resolutely open, mostly out of defiance, as there was no team spirit left to nurture in an environment that made her appreciate what East Germany must have been like under the Stasi.

Unlike Jim—at least in the first part of his tenure, the new management consultants did not convene staff meetings or participate in any way in the department's daily affairs, and yet they seemed to be making no progress on the development projects initiated by their predecessors. Thanks to her conversations with one of the instructors who had been behind the Save Pequeno campaign, Grace would eventually understand that for the first three months of their assignment, Melvin and Jonas had worked exclusively on the renewal of the Hartbridge contract. In other words, they had been paid hundreds of thousands of dollars by the Pequeno District to single-mindedly further the interests of their own company. The worst aspect of her realization was the new light it threw back on Jim's intermittent unavailability: he too had spent a good amount of Pequeno's funds serving another master. In her naïve affection for the man, Grace had made up for his professional lapses. But she felt no such obligation toward Twiddledum and Twiddledee.

Sadly, Jim can't find any evidence that he responded to Grace's overtures to Melvin and Jonas one way or another. The next message he finds is dated two weeks later and is not part of the same thread. It seems to be a response to another email from her, which is also missing.

> From: Jim.Wright@Pequeno.edu
> Date:Monday, April 10, 2006
> To:Grace.Kirchner@Pequeno.edu
> Subject: A little story
>
> Your positive words and thoughts are foremost in my mind. Thank you.
>
> I am much more optimistic today than a few days ago. I will keep your thoughts in mind, and you're right, I'm not going to give in easily. We have a system to migrate to Kuali!!!!!!
>
> Please support Melvin and Jonas, they're there to help, they'll just need to find their way around first.
>
> Talk to you soon!

Aside from its grammatical awkwardness ("thoughts"and "mind" repeated on consecutive lines), which is excusable considering the state he was in at the time, several things about his message strike him now. For one, its formality. Is this the kind of tone you adopt with a young woman you've recently held hands with, who has shed passionate tears over your misfortune? He knows he has never mastered the language of affection, particularly in writing, but here his stiltedness seems an outright denial of intimacy—intimacy being a notion that his two years of exposure to women's talk shows have taught him to respect. From the title of her original message, (*A little story*. What little story was that? The very fact that he does not remember is a mark against him) he can tell that *her* tone must have been one of innocent familiarity, in keeping with their acknowledged friendship, if not with its underlying sexual currents.

Another thing that surprises him is his reference to being optimistic. He does not recollect feeling anything but an unmitigated gloom in those days. Perhaps Grace did manage to cheer him up for a couple of days, or perhaps he was just keeping up a good front.

But what bothers him the most is the one-sidedness of the exchange. The message reminds him that in those early days of his illness, she spent a lot of energy trying to comfort him. Yet in return it looks as if he did nothing to ease her professional trials, though, as official CIO, he was still in a position to do so. Even from his sick bed, he could have made her position clear to his two substitutes, he could have insisted that they consult her, worked with her, deferred to her. And if that didn't work, he could have enlisted Bob Johnson in her defense. But he didn't, instead putting the onus on her to "support" the new guys. She must have felt completely betrayed.

He could argue that he was too overwhelmed by his medical problems at the time to attend to anything else, but his conscience won't let him off that easily. Or he could put his inaction down to male selfishness, another concept he has become acquainted with from watching daytime TV. But that does not quite cover it either. The truth is that he kept mum out of company loyalty. Present a united front, don't air the firm's dirty laundry in public, maintain the illusion if not the reality of control, do what's good for the firm, not what's good for the clients (but convince the clients that what's good for the firm is good for them too). These were the dictums he had unquestioningly lived by for many years as a management consultant, no matter the up-front, just-one-of-the guys image he had projected for his own benefit as much as to rope the clients in. Against this corporate ethos, his sympathy for Grace never stood a chance.

From: Grace.Kirchner@Pequeno.edu
Date:Tuesday, May 2, 2006
To:melvin.grossbach@hartbridge.com;
        jonas.tosser@hartbridge.com
Cc: Jim.Wright@Pequeno.edu
Subject: Disaster Recovery Plan

Bob Johnson was kind enough to lend me a copy of the Disaster Recovery Plan due to be presented by the Hartbridge team to the Board of Trustees at tomorrow's meeting. As it is an 81 page document, I only had time to scan it briefly. In particular, I skipped the 22 pages devoted to descriptions of various types of disasters, assuming that they were copied from a general template and therefore require no editing. In the sections that I did read, I noticed the following problems:

- Our mainframe is referred throughout as Hal, which I believe was the name of a rogue computer in the 70's sci-fi movie 2001. A global change should be made to the document, replacing every occurrence of "Hal" with "IBM z/890".
- Appendix A, which, according to the table of contents, is supposed to list the address and phone coordinates of the staff assigned to various recovery tasks, is missing.
- My name appears as the person responsible for restoring the backup tapes onto an alternate computer. I am not qualified for such a task, which needs to be supervised by a systems programmer.
- On page 5 of the overview, a note warns that THERE IS AN INHERENT WEAK LINK TO THIS PLAN AS THERE IS NOT AN IDENTIFIED BACKUP SITE FROM WHICH TO OPERATE IF THE PRIMARY FACILITY WAS LOST.

The expression "backup site" is ambiguous, and should be replaced with the expression "remote DR site" currently in usage.

More importantly, contracting with a remote DR site provider to insure business continuity in case the whole data center becomes unavailable is an ESSENTIAL step in disaster preparedness and should be executed BEFORE the disaster recovery plan is submitted to the Board. I believe this task falls to the Hartbridge team.

Jim has to admit that he has no idea whether Melvin and Jonas ever arranged for a remote disaster recovery site. If it had been up to him, he would certainly have taken care of it. But he can see why his successors may have let things slide. As far as they were concerned, they had performed their due diligence by inserting the capitalized disclaimer in the document. If a bomb ever destroyed the Data Center and the Pequeno District found itself without a registration system for weeks on end for lack of replacement hardware, Hartbridge would not be legally liable.

From: Grace.Kirchner@Pequeno.edu
Date:Friday, May 12, 2006
To:Robert.Johnson@Pequeno.edu
Cc: Jim.Wright@Pequeno.edu
Subject: IT Maintenance Contracts

As you requested, I am attaching a list of all the hardware/ software service contracts the IT department must maintain to safeguard our mission critical systems. The contracts are mostly for the mainframe operating systems software, mostly long-standing, and mostly sole-source.

Re-approving these contracts every year would be a waste of your time or the Chancellor's. Your blanket on-going approval will help us expedite the payment process and avoid interruptions of service.

Jim is starting to understand Grace's frustration with Melvin and Jonas. This message should have been sent under their names, not Grace's, if only to prevent Bob Johnson from suspecting that the Hartbridge consultants were asleep on the job. The fact that Grace did not even copy them on it says a lot about their disengagement.

From: Grace.Kirchner@Pequeno.edu
Date:Wednesday, May 24, 2006
To:melvin.grossbach@hartbridge.com
Cc: Jim.Wright@Pequeno.edu;
Robert.Johnson@Pequeno.edu
Subject: Chain of Command

I wish to document a problem with the IT Department's chain of command.

Before leaving last Friday, you stated that during your absence of the next ten days, you had assigned Jonas to serve as CIO.

Jonas was absent on Monday. On Tuesday morning he was still absent when Jerry Valenzuela, or the Physical Plant Department, asked for a management decision as to whether the team installing the UPS should be allowed to perform a task that might cause a power outage. I asked to defer the decision to Jonas, but the UPS team needed an immediate answer. We called Jonas on his cell phone but could not get a hold of him.

As the only IT manager on hand, I felt at that point that I had no choice but take responsibility for the decision. I conferred with Jerry and the contractor, who came up with a safer way to complete the task. I gave the OK. The task was completed without incident.

Because of the high likelihood of such situations, given your and Jonas' schedules, I believe that my job description should continue to state, as it has in the past, that the Applications Manager "serves as acting CIO in the CIO's absence" as opposed to your proposed wording "serves as acting CIO when assigned by CIO". I don't believe that the old wording interferes with Hartbridge's contractual obligations to the District, considering that for the moment, the position of CIO is filled by a company as opposed to an individual. In the absence of a Hartbridge representative, I (or my successor) must be empowered to act without a specific assignment.

Hot damn! Here is an episode Jim has no recollection of. Can the two bozos have seriously plotted to demote Grace while *they* failed to assume their most elementary managerial responsibility, which was for one of them to be present at all times? What kind of a position did that put his girl in? No wonder she threatened to resign. And no wonder the Hartbridge contract was only renewed for one year.

All of a sudden, Fritz's decision to keep Jim on the payroll after he got sick looks a lot less altruistic. If Melvin and Jonas represent the competition, then, as Fritz himself claimed, Jim is truly one of Hartbridge's irreplaceable assets. Still, he owes Fritz a huge debt, because without the health insurance that came with the position he has retained, he would have been bankrupted long ago.

Again, Jim regrets his failure to answer Grace's calls for help. By the end of May 2006, truth be told, though he was still Pequeno's official CIO, he had been relieved by Fritz of all responsibilities at that site. He hardly even read his Pequeno email before filing it away because it depressed him too much. But of course, until the contract was renewed, he could not let Grace know of the real state of affairs. And so the poor girl dutifully continued to copy him on key email communications documenting her struggles, though she must have sensed his actual lack of power, since she never brought up business when they interacted on the phone.

From: Grace.Kirchner@Pequeno.edu
Date:Friday, June 16, 2006
To:Fritz.Applefield@hartbridge.com
Cc: Jim.Wright@Pequeno.edu
Subject: Contract Renewal

After much deliberation, I must decline to speak to the
Board of Trustees in favor of the renewal of the Hartbridge
contract. It is for me a matter of conscience.

Jim is not surprised by Grace's refusal to prop up the two bozos. But there is much behind her pithy message that no one has ever cared to tell him.

How the Hartbridge CEO swooped into the Data Center a week before the fateful Board meeting, glad-handing every member of the staff as if they were long-lost friends, greeting Tiffany in Spanish and Mina in Arabic on the strength of their respective last names (which both of them in fact owed to their husbands), boasting that he had come to "kick butt", clamoring for decent coffee, joking about the backwardness of the town, and generally creating such a stir in the by now funereal hush of the department that Grace thought a group of demonstrating students must have managed to get past the security airlock.

How Fritz commandeered Stanley's old office, put his feet on the desk, and had Tiffany drag Grace out of her office to meet with him. How he turned out to be a tiny man with the hardened tan of a Florida retiree, big black nostrils that looked like an extra pair of eyes, and gelled hair receding in tight waves from a pockmarked forehead—the "marcelled" hairstyle P.G. Wodehouse reserved for his most sinister characters.

How he called Grace "girlie" (another unbelievable detail she would have to omit from her memoir) and asked her to take dictation on a letter of support for Hartbridge which he had determined she must write. How Grace replied that unfortunately her IT training had not included shorthand, which caused Fritz to chuckle, claiming he had been warned (by Jim?) that she was "a handful". How he offered to let her write the letter, provided it was given to him for final editing. How Grace demurred, arguing that she was uncomfortable with the whole idea of a letter, and how Fritz, unfazed by her reluctance, proposed that she spoke to the Board instead. To get rid of him, Grace had to take shelter behind Jim's old saw about "sleeping on it".

How the very next day, David Byrd, the instructor who had proposed the Linux deal, reiterated his offer to take Grace out to lunch, and how Grace, desperate for intelligent company, accepted on the spot. It was then, over a basket of French bread, that Grace learned about Fritz Applefield's criminal past, about Chancellor Akecheta's membership on the Hartbridge's Executive Advisory Board (from which, in a typical act of corporate whitewashing, he had recently resigned), and about the fraudulent RFP process that had resulted in an easy win for Hartbridge (not only the RFP had been written by Hartbridge—which meant Jim, but of the twenty companies that had supposedly been invited to bid, only four had actually received the invitation, and of those, only one besides Hartbridge had responded, the others having detected conspicuous signs of bid rigging in the document).

David Byrd also explained how it was to Hartbridge's advantage to hire as many outside contractors as possible, since they got a cut on every such contract. This was why Jim had tried to get rid of Josh, and why under Melvin and Jonas's tenure, no fewer than five contractors had been hired at different times for jobs that never seemed to yield any work product. But what outraged Grace the most was to discover that on the District budget, a copy of which David had managed to obtain, the positions of Operations Manager and Technical Services Manager had been marked as "outsourced to Hartbridge Consulting". Even while Jim was present, Grace and Mina had performed most of the duties attached to these two positions. Since Jim's departure, they had been completely in charge. And Grace couldn't get a measly 5% pay raise approved for Mina, while Twiddledum and Twiddledee lived it up! By the time her broiled mahi-mahi showed up, she was no longer hungry. On the other hand, her mind was made up as to how she would respond to Fritz's request.

But of course, as P.G. Wodehouse himself would have remarked, Fritz had not got where he was by easily accepting defeat. The night of the Board meeting, Grace was surprised to find Tiffany among the audience. When the time came for public comments on the contract renewal, the Queen of the Data Center stood up, her blond curls newly set into a helmet of innocence, her plunging neckline revealing a vast expanse of blushing bosom, and read a skillfully clumsy letter in support of the Hartbridge consultants. The letter had been signed by most of the IT staff, including Mina. Tiffany had no sooner finished speaking that David Byrd jumped out of his seat to accuse Hartbridge of having coerced the staff into this demonstration of allegiance. Tiffany coolly asserted that the idea had been hers and hers alone. David Byrd expressed his skepticism with a roar of laughter, other members of the audience booed, and in the ensuing pandemonium, the issue was tabled. A week later, the contract was quietly renewed for a year under the existing terms.

Grace was so disappointed in Mina that she nearly gave up on their friendship. But the next day, she got up the courage to ask her why she had signed that horrid letter. Mina was flabbergasted. Tiffany had caught her at a busy time, and desperate to get back to her scheduling, Mina had signed without reading what she believed to be a birthday card for Jonas. Tiffany herself came by Grace's office later that day to apologize for failing to give her the opportunity to sign the letter. "You see," she explained, "Fritz had told me that you would speak at the meeting, so I assumed you were covered." So much for Tiffany instigating the show of support.

The day the contract was renewed, Fritz took the whole staff out for drinks, selecting the very bar where Jim had taken them many months before. Out of curiosity, as well as a desire to downplay her enmity while she pondered her next move, Grace went along. Right after the first toast, Fritz got down to business.

"The next step," he beamingly proclaimed, pounding the rickety table with a diminutive fist, "is migrating the administrative systems to a vendor package."

The staff exchanged furtive glances of astonishment and dismay. The Kuali project, in which many had invested a lot of hope and pride, the Kuali project was dead, which also meant that Jim was never coming back. No one spoke as the news sunk in, but Grace became aware of a subtle shift in her colleagues' focus of attention, away from Fritz and toward her. They were counting on her to voice their objections to the change of plan. But she was too sick at heart to take the bait.

"So, we're gonna start by doing a functional analysis of the legacy system," Fritz blithely continued.

In an instant, despair gave way to anger, and Grace found her voice.

"Are you aware that one of your consultants already led such an analysis, and that many Pequeno managers spent quite a bit of time filling his questionnaire?"

"Ah! But this is a new contract," Fritz rejoined without missing a beat. "We are starting from scratch."

It was pointless to argue against such cynicism. Even Elmore gave up hoping that Grace would make a scene, and tactfully turned the conversation to some historical facts about the neighborhood in which the bar was located. Mina discreetly squeezed Grace's hand under the table, Wei went out to smoke a cigarette, Sandip answered a call on his cell phone. Tiffany sat erect and aloof at one end of the table like a constitutional monarch bored by parliamentary proceedings. Twiddledum and Twiddledee squirmed in their seats. Ruby scribbled a few words in a little notebook she had lately started to tote around, ordered a second drink. There was no Karaoke singing that night.

From: Grace.Kirchner@Pequeno.edu
Date:Monday, July 10, 2006
To:jonas.tosser@hartbridge.com
Cc: Jim.Wright@Pequeno.edu;
Robert.Johnson@Pequeno.edu
Subject: Budget Oversight

Puzzled that no purchase requisition had come my way since I left for my vacation, today I discovered that my name has been removed from the approval route.

I recall hearing you mention that you wished to lighten my administrative load so I could devote more time to the administrative system migration project. I assume this is the reason you asked Tiffany to change the route. Thank you for your concern. Indeed, approving purchases is time-consuming.

However, I would like to state a few concerns for the record:

1. I believe that as you and I are a team, we need to discuss issues involving our respective responsibilities before changes are implemented. It is very awkward for me to find out that staff members know more than me about my own duties—or lack thereof.

2. My understanding is that it is inappropriate for an external consultant to make final purchasing decisions against the District's budget. I believe that I, as the only internal IT manager, or Bob Johnson, as Vice-Chancellor, must be included in the approval route for auditing purposes. In the last few months, there have been several instances when those checks and balances have been needed.

3. Budget tracking is one of the duties included in my job description. If I am relieved of this responsibility, the Vice-Chancellor must be informed so that I won't be held accountable for things I have no control over.

From: Grace.Kirchner@Pequeno.edu
Date:Friday, July 14, 2006
To:jonas.tosser@hartbridge.com
Cc: Jim.Wright@Pequeno.edu;
Melvin.Grossbach@hartbridge.com
Subject: Mainframe authorization functions

I am requesting your help in getting mainframe authorization functions handled appropriately.

One of the tasks that I took on after our CIO's retirement is the granting of access to various mainframe software tools. As I have no training in this area, I have frequently had to get help from Heller Inc., the company that is contracted to do our systems programming.

On more than one occasion, I have found that:
- I didn't have the security needed to grant access, but Ruby does.
- I could not find the system documentation, which turned out to be in Ruby's office.

Looking at Ruby's job description, I noticed that it includes "mainframe system administration" functions, which explains her high level of security. Last week, I asked her to see if she could figure out one authorization problem after she saw me take care of another. She declined, arguing that systems programming was above her pay grade.

I showed her the relevant paragraph in her job description. She seemed greatly surprised, and wondered what system administration functions she could possibly be asked to perform. When I suggested that she should perform the functions for which she had the necessary security, she replied that I wasn't her boss and couldn't tell her what to do.

She also expressed a belief that she should get special compensation for "working very hard". You may be able to judge this better than I am, as I am not supervising her directly. However, looking toward her performance evaluation, which is overdue, I would like to point out a few things:
- Since we are short-staffed, we have all been working very hard. But over 50% of this year's overtime funds have been spent on Ruby.
- I am aware of only one project that Ruby completed satisfactorily this fiscal year: the Faculty PC training. On the other hand, I had to take over the installation of the check server, which had been languishing for

months, and the equipment promised in May to Roger Wilkins is still sitting in boxes. Performance must be judged on achievement, not a subjective perception of effort.

- Ruby's belligerent attitude is inappropriate and creates tension within the department. I request that as her acting supervisor, you impress on her the need to be cooperative with all IT staff and management.

From: Grace.Kirchner@Pequeno.edu
Date:Friday, July 21, 2006
To:Jabari.Akecheta@Pequeno.edu
Cc: Jim.Wright@Pequeno.edu;
Subject: Improving Staff Morale

At the last Managers' Meeting, you asked for input on how to improve staff morale. I believe that appropriate monetary rewards for outstanding contributions would go a long way toward that goal.

Mina Hussein has worked in the IT department for seven years. Originally hired as an operator, she was promoted four years ago to the position of scheduler. After the retirement of the Operations manager, she took on many of his functions. When Jim Wright obtained permission to hire two work study students as operational interns, Mina became their trainer and supervisor.
She has blossomed, taking the initiative in streamlining many of our processes, revealing leadership and communication skills, providing great customer support, and maintaining her cool under the most trying circumstances. She has been my best support since Jim left.

Mina's salary has not kept pace with her responsibilities and accomplishments. Before Jim left, he tasked me with trying to get a desk audit for her. We both felt that she should be reclassified as Operations Supervisor, an

existing, non-managerial classified position. However, the Personnel Classification Analyst I consulted on the issue denied my request, arguing that union rules prohibited any promotion not based on seniority.
I talked to Charlie Weissman, the SEIU Union Representative, who disagreed with this interpretation.

I also talked to the Assistant Vice-Chancellor for Human resources, who could see some merit in our request, but was afraid of creating a precedent. According to him, "many classified employees think that they should be paid more".

In the last few years of economic boom in the Central Valley, we have lost a number of very talented staff because of self-defeating personnel policies and procedures. Any help you can provide in effecting change in this area, as you have in so many others, will be much appreciated.

There are several more messages from Grace in the folder, but Jim decides to skip them, going straight to the last one.

From: Grace.Kirchner@Pequeno.edu
Date: Monday, August 21, 2006
To: Robert.Johnson@Pequeno.edu
Cc: jim.wright@hartbridge.com; jonas.tosser@hartbridge.com; melvin.grossbach@hartbridge.com
Subject: Letter of Resignation

Dear Bob,

Please consider this email as my official letter of resignation from the Pequeno Community College District, effective August 31, 2006.

As you already know my reasons for taking this step, I won't enlarge upon them. But I want to thank you for your unfailing friendship and support in the last few months.

Take care.

Jim was in the hospital when this message was sent. By the time he tried to answer it, her email address had been deleted from the Pequeno directory. A few weeks later, he obtained Grace's personal email address from Mina. He sent her a short message congratulating her on her decision to leave an institution that was never going to reward her talents, and hoping they would stay in touch. She never answered. He can see why now.

The "Dear Bob" has done it. In the affectionate salutation, more than in her thanks for Bob's "unfailing friendship and support", which could after all be taken ironically, since his support doesn't seem to have made a bit of difference, Jim reads all that he failed to provide for his supposed protégé: call it caring, a steady, disinterested, proactive desire to be of help. Of Bob's purity of motive, Jim has no doubt, given that Bob is gay.

So, in the end, the issue his conscience has been trying to bring to his attention is not how close he came to fucking her, or what degree of virtue he can claim for the fact that he didn't.

It is not even how much guilt he should feel for the series of hardships she endured as a result of his promoting her to a management position that no one but her would ever take seriously. After all she has survived, and more. There is a maturity of judgment, a consciousness of strength emanating from her caustic emails that she did not possess when he first met her. He did help her grow, whether or not it was his intent. He is confident that her resignation from Pequeno was a good move, that her talents were indeed wasted at that place. She has now embarked on a political career. He doubts that she will stick with it, but she is young, her life is ahead of her. All in all he can't feel bad about the ultimate effects of their encounter.

The issue is precisely one of intent. For all the feelings that Grace awoke in him, attraction, fascination, infatuation, partnership, amusement, respect, solace, he never truly had her best interest at heart. He kept himself closed to her, he did not act out of love. He is tempted to argue that it was his very attraction to her that forced him to be reticent, that the professional setting of their relationship led him to do what men do best: compartmentalize—another useful word gleaned from daytime TV. But he rejects the argument, recognizing in it the perversity of modern secular thinking. As Christians we are called to love every person selflessly, to seek their well-being at all times. Eros is meant to be Agape's servant, not its enemy. We may not always answer love's difficult call, but we should at least be honest about our failings.

It occurs to Jim that he is in fact perfectly capable of Agape, that it is at the core of his relationship with his daughter. For however un-spontaneous his love for Cindy may be, he has never had any other motive in his dealings with her but a sincere wish to foster her. It even seems that little by little, his caring is making a difference, not only for her, but in his own feelings.

But here is the basic dilemma: Christian love is incompatible with the corporate ethos. In the corporate world, it is tacitly if not overtly understood that people are not ends in themselves, but tools in the pursuit of profit. Even "humanistic" management theorists attempt to justify treating employees well by claiming—unrealistically—that it will result in better productivity. Viewed for that angle, Hartbridge's way of doing business: the (mostly negligible) bribes, the inflated claims of expertise, the make-work projects, the contract-prolonging delays, the taking of credit for work done by the client's staff, the cultivated secrecy, the management by intrigue and ultimate denial of responsibility, all the practices that make management consulting a con job are hardly exceptional or objectionable. Anything to make a buck.

Jim recognizes that he has himself been a tool, the only difference between him and Grace on that score being his level of pay. And now he grasps how much his humanity has been diminished by his acquiescence to that role—another difference between him and Grace.

He promises his conscience that if he ever recovers from his illness, he will resign from Hartbridge. He will compensate Fritz for his loss by offering to consult for him occasionally, but pro bono, and on his own terms. Uncle Will has been talking about retiring. Jim could take over the management of the hardware store, a business with no aspiration to profit that treats its employees as family. He can see himself advising customers on solutions to various plumbing problems, making improvements to the computerized inventory system, motivating the staff to excel. He won't be rich, but he will be content.

In the meantime, he'd better take a nap before Cindy's return. He closes the Pequeno folder on his laptop, repositions the computer on the windowsill and plugs the speakers back in, goes into his bedroom, sets the alarm clock for three-fifteen, and tucks himself into bed. He falls asleep immediately.

XXIII

CONCLUSIVE

It is 3:05 PM in Greensboro. After purchasing a bottle of wine in a shopping center on the edge of town, Grace and Mina have found a deserted children's playground in one of the large parks that dot the city, not far from Jim's neighborhood. They are now sitting on the swings, the chains cold against their thighs, their heads bent to the ground where their boots are tracing hieroglyphs in the dirty sand. On the interlaced branches above them, thousands of tender green buds strain to unfurl their leaves to the widening sun. But the two young women fail to notice that miracle of nature. The problem is, there is no one to push them on the swings, tilting their faces toward the sky.

"So, what do you think of the new Pequeno CIO?" Grace asks, having checked the time on her BlackBerry and realized they have another hour to kill.

"Oh, he means well, but he is no Jim," Mina answers with a sigh.

"Still, he finally got you promoted to Operations Supervisor, didn't he?"

"No, that wasn't his doing. Bob Johnson is the one who pushed it through. I don't know what I would have done without him after you resigned."

"I did leave you in a lurch, didn't I? I am really sorry about this. I should probably have given more notice, but I was on the verge of a nervous breakdown."

"I never blamed you for leaving. Anyway, if you're right about Twiddledum and Twiddledee deliberately trying to force you out, you didn't really have a choice. The funny thing is, guess who was the most upset about your resignation?"

"Who?"

"Elmore."

"Elmore? I was sure he would be happy to be rid of me. For one thing, being supervised by a younger woman must have deeply hurt his macho image, and on top of that I forced him to work harder than he was used to."

"That may be, but all the same he was really outraged. Like you, he thought that all the stuff Twiddledum and Twiddledee had done amounted to what-is-it-called?—'constructive discharge'. He was hoping you would sue the District for breach of contract. He told everybody that from that point on he wasn't going to cooperate with the Hartbridge people. And pretty much everybody followed his example."

"And what did this lack of cooperation entail?"

"Oh, nobody ever refused to obey orders. But they did the strict minimum amount of work required to avoid getting fired."

"That's not so different from the way they behaved under Stanley's leadership—or even under Jim's, come to think of it."

"Here's that cynical streak again," Mina comments half-reprovingly.

"What about you? Did you follow Elmore's example?"

"Believe me, I would have if I knew how. But I could never figure out what part of my job I could leave undone."

"That's the problem with having a work ethic. You end up collaborating with the enemy."

Mina cringes inwardly. Does Grace include Jim among the enemy? She decides not to ask. After all, they have reached their destination. It is too late to back out now. She trusts that the sight of their ex-boss, an hour from now, will be enough to dispel her friend's suspicions.

"Is Elmore still there?" Grace continues.

"Yes. He was planning to retire this year after his son finished college, but then the economy tanked, and his son couldn't find a job, so Elmore has to support him again. Anyway, with the Hartbridge people gone, and the migration project underway, he is much happier."

"How about Ruby?"

"She finally won a worker's comp claim for her carpal tunnel and bad back, and is now on long-term disability. The lady they hired to replace her is very nice. So it all worked out for the best."

It certainly worked out for Ruby, Grace thinks with irritation. But how does it work for the taxpayers, who are stuck subsidizing Ruby's laziness? Then it occurs to her that all of Ruby's dysfunctions, the ones she observed, and the ones she guessed at, did in fact amount to a serious disability. In any case, as much as Ruby contributed to making her life miserable after Jim's departure, Grace finds that she can't hold a grudge against the crazy woman. She suspects that her lack of resentment is nothing as noble as forgiveness, but only a reflection of her innate sense of superiority, which is probably what enraged Ruby in the first place. It worries her that she hasn't quite figured out yet how to be more humble. She fears she never will.

"By the way, did you ever find out what she kept scribbling in that little black notebook of hers the last few months I was there?"

"Not really. Nothing ever came of it that I know of. I suspect it was some exercise her therapist had assigned her."

"Ah, she was in therapy, then. I thought she was building a case against Hartbridge on behalf of the union."

"I don't think so. As Jim would say, the woman was all hat and no cattle."

Grace snickers.

"Who's cynical now?" she asks jokingly. "But I agree with you. And that's why I always assumed Elmore was the chief conspirator in the plot against my promotion, though I have to say that he atoned for it later by being decent to me during Twiddledum and Twiddledee's tenure. Now that I think about it, he did send me a personal email when I resigned to say that he would miss me. I was sure he didn't mean it. But maybe he did, after all. How about the others? I only know that Wei left shortly after I did. I have kept in touch with him. He works in Silicon Valley now."

"Rajiv, Sandra and Josh are also gone. The others are still there."

"Even Tiffany?"

"I didn't tell you the story about Tiffany?"

"No. There's a story about Tiffany? You did say something about her having done something bad, if memory serves."

"Oh yes. Turns out she had not only committed mortgage fraud, but she had also embezzled thousands of dollars from the District."

"Mortgage fraud?"

"Yes. You remember how she had a house flipping business on the side with her husband?"

"How could I forget, when that's all she ever did around the office?"

"Well, they would buy a wreck of a house dirt cheap, the kind of house repossessed after a meth lab bust, they would make a few cosmetic repairs, then they would sell the house for three times the price . . ."

"Isn't that what all the house-flippers were doing?"

"Yes, but Tiffany and her husband added their own touch. You see, they made verbal agreements with the buyers to get the house appraised at an inflated price by one of their friends, so the buyer got a much bigger loan than the house deserved, and Tiffany and her husband split the difference with the buyer in cash. To tell you the truth, Tiffany had tried to talk Tarik and me into this kind of deal. We didn't go along because we didn't trust her, but we didn't realize that it's actually illegal."

"And meanwhile she was embezzling from the district?"

"Apparently it all started when Jim put her in charge of ordering the new office furniture. She got the supplier to kick in some shelves for her home office and have them delivered to her house directly. Of course, the supplier bumped up the invoice, but no one at the District noticed. That gave her some ideas. Then you became a manager and started looking at every purchase with a magnifying glass, so she was stymied for a while."

"Which may explain why she was so dead set against my promotion . . ."

"But after Jonas removed you from it, she had a field day. She was creating bogus purchase orders for office supplies and computer equipment that no one needed. She had an accomplice in Receiving sign for the goods even though nothing was delivered. The invoice was paid to a company headed by a cousin of her husband. They plowed the money right back into their flipping business."

"Reinvesting the profits. A perfect little capitalist scheme. But how did it all come to light?"

"Someone in Receiving blew the whistle on her and her accomplice. After that, several District employees that she had tried to sell houses to reported her mortgage scheme to the FBI. Tiffany was put on paid administrative leave while the charges against her were investigated. Then the housing bubble burst. Turns out there are so many mortgage crooks out there to prosecute that her case will probably never go to trial. And she made restitution on the money she stole from the District before filing for bankruptcy on her flipping business, so the District dropped their complaint against her. I hear she is now working as a receptionist for a law firm that deals with foreclosures."

"Down but not out. I'm sure that with her winner mentality she'll bounce back higher than ever. By the way, do you know if Myrtle ever bought a house from her? She seemed very keen on it."

"No, she didn't. Tiffany was pretty peeved about it. She felt that Myrtle had wasted a lot of her time leading her on."

"Tiffany out-conned. There is justice in the world after all. And talking about justice, did you ever learn why the Board ousted Akecheta? Was it as a consequence of the Hartbridge contract being scrapped?"

"They never quite explained it. But if you think justice was served in Akecheta's case, I am sorry to have to disappoint you. You see, he had managed to wrangle a rolling three-year contract from the Board, which meant that if ever he was fired—but not of course if he resigned, he would have to be paid a full three years of salary from the date of his termination. What we didn't know was that he had got the same deal at his previous job, so that the whole time he was working at Pequeno, he was collecting two fat salaries. But time was running out on his previous contract, so it was actually to his financial advantage to get canned from Pequeno: that way he could get another job and continue to be paid double. And guess what? That's exactly what happened. He got hired as chancellor by some community college district in Texas with an even cushier contract. I hear Hartbridge has been retained to oversee their administrative systems migration."

"Oh my God," exclaims Grace, kicking at the sand in a paroxysm of outrage, and finding herself asway on the swing, "you mean that

Akecheta may in fact have relied on Hartbridge's failure to insure his own exit?"

"I hadn't thought about it that way," Mina muses, pushing off on her own swing, "but it would make sense, wouldn't it?"

"That is so evil it's funny."

Indeed, Grace is laughing as her feet come back in contact with the ground. She propels herself backward again.

"But you don't think Jim knew about this, do you?" Mina can't help asking.

"I don't think even Fred knew, otherwise he wouldn't have sent Jim in the first place. I mean, it couldn't be to *his* advantage for his company to get a record of failure."

"But doesn't that reasoning also apply to the Chancellor?"

"From the evidence, I'd say it does not. After all, this is at least the second time he gets booted out, and each time, he immediately gets another job. It seems that the higher people are in an organization, the less they are held accountable. I remember how right after the dot-com bust, a lot of executives who had run their businesses into the ground were snapped up by other high-tech companies while their ex-employees remained on unemployment, including some of my friends. Those guys belong to a very selective club, and they take care of each other. But Fritz is not in the same league, and besides, he can't jump ship. He owns Hartbridge."

Grace pauses as her swing comes back to the vertical. She pivots around on her feet, twisting the swing's chains, and lets them untwist with a twang. The jerking motion shakes another idea out of her.

"Now that I think about it, there's another set of people Akecheta may have used to further his plans: the teachers. They spent a lot of energy and cunning trying to get rid of him because of his lack of collegiality. I was myself baffled by his extreme arrogance. I wondered how he could be so oblivious to the political realities of an educational institution that he endangered his own job. But he didn't care about keeping his job. So the whole time the teachers were conspiring against him, they were unwittingly doing his bidding."

Grace lets out a peal of sardonic laughter, and pushes herself off again.

"It hurts my head to imagine all these convoluted plots," Mina sighs by way of begging off the topic, as her swing reaches its top forward point and she tucks her legs in again.

"Mine too. Which does not mean that such plots aren't hatched every day."

By now they are both swinging. And as they swing, the squeak of the chains hypnotizes all thoughts of conspiracy right out of them. Soon they get in sync and fly higher and higher. They don't need anyone to push them after all, but the memory of Jim's hands on their backs is an integral part of their current pleasure.

The neighborhood they are driving through is definitely posh. Set far back from the street, beyond profligate lawns ornamented by nothing more than crisscrossing mower patterns, massive houses with elaborate roof lines peek through gaps in a curtain of artistically arranged trees. Most of the architectural details plastered over El Pequeno's boom-time developments are represented here, spelling the American Dream: Mansard gables, Greek porticos, Tudor half-timber, Palladian windows, and especially the dark green shutters that Mina suspects of not shutting. But she can tell these houses are no Mcmansions. For one, they have been around for a long time, as the size of the trees attest. For another, they are made of more solid material: mostly brick, or real stone, with slate on many of the roofs, and their design is more sober. Lastly, the universal lack of any kind of fence is in marked contrast to the cul-de-sacs, perimeter walls, and pillared gates that (symbolically) protect the homes of the well-to-do in California, that in fact protected her own home when she thought she had something to protect. Rich people in Greensboro must feel very confident about their security, the social order so well-established that beggars and thieves wouldn't dream of entering their domain, as open as it looks. But then, Mina notices the absence of another urban feature: sidewalks. There is no way to get here except by driving, as effective a strategy as fences to keep out the riffraff.

For the first time, Mina is seized with doubts about the projected reunion, suddenly aware of the social distance between herself and her ex-boss. Are they imposing on Jim by dropping on him uninvited, and was he too polite to say so? She glances at Grace, whose concentration on her driving betrays no class uneasiness. Fortunately, as they turn a corner, the neighborhood becomes more modest. The lawns are still large, the trees still tall, brick and green shutters still dominate, but the architecture now tends to the one-story ranch house, the few Greek porticos scattered around looking merely wishful.

A couple more turns, and they are on Jim's street, in fact they drive by his house.

"It's here, on the left, you just passed it," Mina cries out nervously.

"I know, I'm just going to go around the block to be on the right side," Grace answers, her voice a little strained too. What has pained her about Jim's house is precisely how modest it is. She thinks about all the hours he put in at Pequeno and elsewhere, all the compromises he must have made, all the secrets he kept, all the isolation he endured. For this? And then she considers the achievement that mere middleclass comfort is for a man whose grandfather died in a coal mine accident, who was the first in his family to graduate from high school, who started his career as a clerk in a hardware store and married too young a girl he probably got pregnant. Swept by a new wave of compassion, she lets go of her project to stand in judgment of his character—a release which has the drawback of leaving her defenseless against his mortality.

Over Keith Jarrett's delicate fingering of Handel's keyboard suites, Jim has heard the rattle of Grace's car, he has recognized her squeaking brakes. He strides toward the front door, aware of the anxious glance Cindy throws at him over her shoulder as she mashes the sweet potatoes in the kitchen. He comes out on the porch, sees nothing. Still, he is sure in his heart that they are here. They must have missed the house number on the first pass. They will be back. He walks along the path to the top of the driveway and waits, shielding his eyes from the sun with one hand, a conspicuous monument of expectation, but he doesn't care.

Sure enough, he hears the car approaching, he sees its white shape break out of the trees. The tires squeak, the car pulls over and stops. The engine dies. There is some agitated movement on the front seat. The passenger door swings out part way, gets stuck in the grass that rises straight from the curb. A form squeezes through the narrow opening. It's Mina. She is dressed in tight jeans, high-heeled boots, and a snazzy purple leather jacket, and still, to Jim, she has the aura of a young South Asian matron, shy and plump and kind and indomitable. If she started wagging her head, she wouldn't surprise him at all. Instead, she winds up her hair, adjusts her glasses, looks up uncertainly at the house, perplexed by the lack of a path from the street to the front door.

"Come this way," Jim shouts, motioning her toward the driveway.

"Jim!" she cries out in dismay or delight, it's impossible to tell, and minces rapidly along the curb in her unsteady heels. At that point the trunk opens. Mina turns back. The top part of her body disappears under the hood, re-emerges holding a pink cake box. The baklava. She resumes her journey along the curb, and turns into the driveway, coming toward Jim with a face simply beaming. So maybe he isn't such a fright after all.

"We made it, can you believe it? We had a wonderful trip. The Smoky Mountains are awesome. We even hiked on the Appalachian trail. It's so nice to see you, and here is the baklava I promised," she babbles as she teeters forward, holding the cake box like some kind of shrine, her eyes radiating blessings.

Jim takes the box from her, snags her big purse from her shoulder while he is at it, deposits both on the ground, and folds her into a hug that makes her disappear.

While they are thus embraced, Jim sees Grace come around the other side of the car. At first, he nearly fails to recognize her. She has let her hair grow and wears it in a pony tail that echoes each one of her movements with a humorous bounce. Even from a distance he can see that she is wearing no makeup. If anything, she looks younger than when he first met her. At least she is wearing the many-zippered Goth jacket he remembers so well. He notices that she is carrying a wine bottle in a brown paper bag.

"Hi, there!" she calls out nonchalantly, seeing that he is looking at her, and gives a little wave. But instead of walking along the curb toward the driveway, she strikes diagonally across the lawn, her heels sinking in the grass, the gait of her long legs more fawn-like than ever, her pony tail seeming to make fun of her shambling progress. In his peripheral vision, he sees her stop by the ex-rock garden, bend over the one tulip that has bloomed on its own this year. He figures she is stalling.

She is stalling. She has taken in the completely white hair and beard, the stooped shoulders, the shrunken torso. Her heart has frozen in her chest. She has glanced at him again to try and get used to his sad appearance. She has noticed that his jeans fit his new leanness, that his untucked polo-shirt gives him a more modern look, that his hands are still beautiful. She has swallowed hard her fear and sorrow. She looks down in wonder at the tree stump and the stray tulip among the dirt clods, keenly aware that there are many things she doesn't know about the man she has come to visit. And still she finds herself drawn to him, as a sailboat tacks around the lighthouse on a cliff, as a hiker seeks the shade of a sprawling oak tree on a summer day, or perhaps as one drives toward a mirage on the road, fully conscious that the shimmering lake will eventually resolve into asphalt.

He is drawn to her. As he releases Mina, he feels his right arm straining against the impulse to pull her in, though she is still ten feet away. His blood suddenly feels fizzy, a dangerous thrill courses through his entire body. Is he going to have another attack of lust?

She reaches the driveway, walks around the pair, and coolly drops her handbag and bottle of wine next to Mina's belongings, demonstrating without a word her grasp of Jim's new hugging protocol.

At last he turns fully toward her. They meet each other's gaze, and are both amazed to reconnect as friends, deeply and simply. Whatever else may be true: the fancies they may have adorned each other with, the personal issues they may have been working out through their relationship, the selfish agendas they may have pursued, clear as day, they do like each other as full persons. The fact that neither of them still has any idea what to do with such a precious feeling does not make it any less of a gift.

And so they do what they know how to do: they throw their arms around each other and hug with abandon. Yes, a gift from God, Jim realizes, in other words, grace. All along her name has been a clue. And Grace, who does not have ready access to a religious vocabulary, still perceives dimly that love in all its forms is our escape from death.

Mission accomplished, Mina thinks, not at all quoting George W. Bush. As much as she wishes Grace well, her main concern here is with Jim, because he is sick, and because in the last two years, she has come to think of him as family. Indeed, given that she has never developed any other framework for close relationships, it is the only place where her affection could have fitted him. Since he stopped being her boss, Jim has been a regular topic of conversation within the Hussein household, an object of prayer, a charitable project. This conspiracy of love has rubbed away any sexual edge there may have been in her feelings for him. As to his professional faults, she has never felt competent to judge them. By hugging her just now, he has affirmed the footing of kinship on which she is determined to stand. And by hugging Grace, as far as she is concerned, he has achieved the reconciliation with loved ones that is essential to spiritual health. Other than that, she doesn't worry about tomorrow, for tomorrow will take care of itself.

Reluctantly loosening his grip on Grace, Jim has a niggling sense that there is something else he must attend to. He turns back toward the house, and sees Cindy standing on the porch on one foot like a cautious wading bird. He motions her over toward the driveway. As she approaches, her face opaque with uncertainty, Grace becomes aware of the music that filters through the open window.

"I know that tune," she muses, looking at Jim with brimming eyes.

"Keith Jarrett, playing Handel," Cindy says as matter-of-factly as if she had first heard the piece in her cradle, though she just looked up the CD's cover info on her father's laptop.

Jim is surprised by her sudden expertise. It then occurs to him that this is something his daughter has inherited from him: an interest in music, and a willingness to educate herself about it.

"You must be Cindy," Grace says brightly as she surges forward without waiting for Jim to conduct the introductions. "I'm Grace." She opens her arms to Cindy, who after some fumbling, willingly submits to a hug.

"And I'm Mina," Mina says, opening her arms in turn. By that time, Cindy has got the hang of the procedure.

"I've talked to both of you on the phone," Cindy reflects, feeling more and more at ease with the visitors.

"And here we are! It's so nice to meet you at last!" Mina enthuses. "We've heard so much about you."

"Yeah. We used to hear your father bug you on the phone about school." Grace adds.

"Oh, he wasn't bugging me. He was helping me figure out my G.E. requirements."

"So, where are you in your studies now?"

"I am in my first year in the nursing program at UNCG."

"That's great!"

"Good for you!"

"And what about your little boy? Does he still have nosebleeds?"

"No, he's all better now. I'm amazed that you remember . . ."

On and on it goes, a feast of female chattiness. Jim smiles upon them, perfectly content not to be the center of attention. All the burners have been turned off on the stove, so he has all the time in the world to watch them get acquainted.

At some point, Mina expresses a wish to have a group photo taken in front of the house, while there is still plenty of sunlight. Jim tries to explain to her that there is nobody around to do them that favor, but Mina is not so easily deterred. As it happens, an old lady in slippers is standing in her driveway on the opposite side of the street, her arms dangling at her sides, looking as if she has no idea why she is there. Before Jim has had time to say anything, Mina has darted across the street, and this little brown person manages to convince the old lady to walk, leaning on her arm, all the way to where they stand. Mina demonstrates how to operate the camera on her cell phone, and the old lady seems to get it. They arrange themselves for the picture, Jim in the center, the girls pressed together in front, their heads resting against his chest.

He finds that there is room in his arms for all three of them.

ACKNOWLEDGMENTS

Many thanks to Christian Marouby, Charlie Drucker, Joan Long, Nick Allen and Arthur Allen for taking the time to read and critique the manuscript for this book, to Kali Armitage for providing the Chinese drywall idea, and to Holly Terndrup for coming to my graphic design rescue in the middle of the holiday season.